things in ditches

things in ditches

by

jimmy olsen

NORTH STAR PRESS OF ST. CLOUD, INC.

Cover art: Tim Dybevik
Cover concept: Naomi Primus
Author photo: Ruth Bushman

Printed in Canada

Published by:
North Star Press of St. Cloud, Inc.
P.O. Box 451
St. Cloud, Minnesota 56302

ISBN: 0-87839-157-6 Cloth
ISBN: 0-87839-158-4 Paper

Dedication

To my mother
Edna Marie Olsen
who first read to me

Acknowledgements

This author owes a debt of gratitude and love to Jon Hassler, who not only wrote the title, *Things in Ditches*, but fed me lunch and wisdom for a decade.

The author also wishes to thank Paulette Pueringer, Deborah Ranney, Susan Lasota, Al Eisele, Brenda Randolph, Mike Hamilburg, Dr. Walter Ellis, and Abigail Jacobo for their considerable efforts professional and personal. Special appreciation is due Richard Martin for a lifetime of encouragement.

things in ditches

Prologue

VICKY JOHNSON'S KILLER ROLLED onto his right side, drew his knees up under the warm covers and cautiously peeked through the darkness at the crisp digits of the clock-radio counting his last moments on earth, death waiting patiently for him to shower and dress. The secret he thought, is not to open your eyes and let the world in.

"Dutch!" Jean's clear voice ascended the stairs. "I know you're awake."

Six forty-five. The radio made a soft, electronic noise and came alive. ". . . barrows and gilts moved steadily higher in South St. Paul with feeder pigs lagging behind earlier gains at yesterday's closing market . . ." He snapped it off. They'd find Vicky's body this morning. Maybe had already. Then a day—two at most—they'd come for him, but he'd already be dead.

His toes curled against the cool varnish of the hardwood floor, and he stood erect. He'd slept soundly. He switched on the lamp with a steady hand feeling quite normal, refreshed if anything, and recalled a television interview he'd seen where a Mafia hitman told what it was like to kill people. Like nothing at all, the man said, sitting in shadow to hide his identity, just a job.

What if it only took one murder to get like that? What if he was already as calloused as a hired killer? He wondered if they really got paid as much as everybody thought. Probably not.

"Dutch? Did you hear me?"

"I'm up."

"Your eggs are getting cold."

"Be right there." He stepped toward the closet, caught sight of himself in the mirror and stopped dead. Aside from the mussed hair and morning stubble, he looked normal. Clear hazel eyes, spaced well above a pinched nose, no more sinister than before. He stared hard into them. They didn't seem to mask any repressed madness, but it was there. Had to be. His mouth drooped with slack morning skin. Poking a finger into the cleft of his chin, he wished it was deeper. He made a face and turned to find his clothes.

Mafia guys love their kids. He knew that had to be true. They may work as hijackers or extortionists, even enforcers, but that wouldn't make them mean to their kids. It might even make them love those close to them more deeply. Make them better fathers or husbands. Why should he be any different? Why shouldn't he feel the same afterward? We just like to think murderers are different from the rest of us. We need to think it, or we'd go nuts. Except for the guilt of course, that horrible weight of remorse laying across his shoulders like heavy bags of fluid, soaking through to the base of his brain until the pressure was fearful. Sometimes it swept him entirely, waves that left a hollow aching in his stomach so acute nothing but sobbing could purge it and bring him back. He'd had enough of that last night before falling asleep. Quite enough.

"Dutch!"

"Coming!" With the palm of his hand he flattened a hair lump, dressed, and clomped down the stairs two at a time.

The kitchen was warm and Jean looked wet-headed and radiant, dolled up in a soft blouse, cream white under a buff vest. A corduroy skirt and leather boots sheathed her athletic legs.

"Nice outfit," he mumbled, choked suddenly by the realization he'd never see her again. "Heavy for this weather."

"Radio says snow." She bent suddenly at the waist, dumping her bark-brown hair inside out and blasting it with hot air. "Running late. Little tardy getting in last night weren't you?"

"Sort of." He helped himself to coffee.

"Dutch." She flipped upright and leveled her black eyes on him. "Where were you?"

He slurped, using the time to think.

"Well?" she said.

Empty-headed, he only shrugged.

"Not going to have to start worrying about you again, am I?" Her slender hand caught his jaw. "No more little revulsions like that Icky Vicky business, right?"

"Naw," he said lightly. "This time it's murder, not adultery." Betrayal, he thought, the gift that keeps on giving. The years slipped by but she hadn't forgotten. "Finally did her in last night," he allowed truth to tumble out, sounding the perfect lie.

"Always a logical explanation for everything." She laughed. "Where's the body?"

"Left it in a ditch."

"Clever."

He changed the subject. "Meeting with Kirby this morning?"

She frowned. "Avoided me all day Friday."

"Go easy."

"Why?" She folded her arms. "Because he's a friend of yours?"

"That," he said, "and because . . ."

"Don't say it. Because I shouldn't make trouble, right?"

"Something like that."

"I hate this town sometimes." She looked down and brushed toast crumbs from her vest. "Think teachers in LA get up early to argue with their principals about rap music?"

"Don't know what they do in LA," he said, hoping to avoid an argument. "Suppose Kirby just wants to know what rap has to do with teaching English."

"It's a form of communication," she said loudly, her face reddening. "Not everything in life is neatly weighed and packaged, like meat. Rap's relevant."

He thought they understood each other about as well as married couples do. Her world of paper ideals marrying his world of warm blood hosed from a slaughterhouse floor.

The week they were to be married she arrived at the slaughterhouse unexpectedly and found him in black rubber boots and apron, sharp knife to a hog's jugular as it hung by its hind legs, squealing. She watched in horror as he waited patiently for blood to collect, bulging in its neck and head, then flicked his wrist to open a small slit and release it, gushing hot over his hands, pulsing with each beat of the hog's frantic heart. She paled and collapsed onto the wet concrete.

How could she marry a man who killed so smoothly?

He'd explained then the reality of eating. The eternal cycle of life and death. How he was a vital link in the food chain. He was death. She never came to the slaughterhouse again and he thought maybe he should've written it up as a rap tune: "Kill the Pigs." If they weren't four-legged it didn't seem to offend her appetite.

They didn't need that discussion today. "Sorry I brought it up," he said, sincerely. "Especially today."

"Why especially today?"

"I don't feel like fighting today." A boyish pout. "Let's kiss and make up."

She bent over and brushed his lips with hers. "You're a pain in the ass."

"Not much of a kiss," he complained.

"Oh! I'm late." She swept her books from the table. "Haven't you heard? Kissing's like rap in Willow River — banned." She swung her hips wide and smiled brazenly over her shoulder. "Looks like you're stuck with that bimbo in the ditch."

The door bounced shut bringing a cool, muggy draft. He waited at the table until he heard the engine rev, then moved to the window and watched the little Jeep fade into an autumn landscape of rolling hills and rich fields and farm windbreaks. Her disappearance brought relief and fear.

No hurry now. He remained at the window trying not to think of the pistol in the basement. Its barrel inside his mouth. He concentrated instead on the marsh below the hill, always rich and green in summer, now a golden-brown quilt of tall grasses hiding small nests and trails. He'd dropped his first pheasant there on an autumn day not much different from this.

Dutch recognized Casey Andersen's pickup parked on the far side. He and another man were edging along, carrying shotguns. Casey wore an orange cap. Dutch couldn't identify the other man and his gaze wandered toward the village two miles away—a four-legged water tower, three church steeples and a silver grain elevator—naked masts above the trees. Behind, low cloud banks scudded south, moving fast and floating the town like an old freighter on a gray sea. A comforting last sight. Home.

Maybe, he thought, butchers are among the few who understand that death is commonplace, common as a haircut, people dying as fast as they're born. He slaughtered on Tuesdays and Thursdays. Live animals became dead animals. A bullet to the brain buckled the knees of a 1,600-pound steer and the curved tip of the knife ticked the jugular of the hog and "Love Me Tender" piped sweetly from the slaughterhouse radio. He received no jolt of joy when he pulled a trigger, any more than he felt regret. Killing was an important job in the scheme of things. To deny the importance of killing animals upset him, and he wondered did critics of such killing ever know any cows? Slaughtering days he went to the pens and stroked their patchy coats and talked softly to them. They responded by coming close and tentatively placing their wet noses against his outstretched hand. "Come boss," he said quietly.

Human beings die quickly in abundant numbers like animals, and even the conditions are similar, penned in nursing homes or hospitals. Thousands more slaughtered on the roads like skunks and in numbers like war dead. He thought these roadkill vastly more gruesome and without heroism— lonely, unnoticed—even the media covering their corpses with cloaks of apathy. But then, he supposed, death close to home doesn't sell.

His familiarity with death lent favor to his own death. He understood the process and knew it could be painless, quick, anticlimatic. And in suicide, the other ingredient is justice. The murderer must not go free. Punishment to fit the crime.

Anyway, he'd eventually be caught, though he didn't care so much about that, not really. It was exposure he feared— the embarrassment, his nakedness before lifelong friends, neighbors, enemies. His image, like everyone's, couldn't stand truth. He didn't think it was fair that it should.

Punishment is a different matter. Like most Americans he accepted capital killing. It was no deterrent, especially to murder since those responsible were often driven by passion or hatred or heartlessness, but death did prove a fair and final solution. The dead commit no murders. He judged himself guilty and determined the fair punishment, leaving nothing to lawyers, judges, and juries. No hand-wringing relatives in some frenzied courtroom. There was a measure of dignity in a nice clean suicide, and it squelched his fear of publicity since suicides go largely unreported. They'd talk in Willow River, of course, once they linked him to Vicky, and heads would nod, townspeople eventually would hug his poor widow. A few years later and Phillip "Dutch" Cleland would be forgotten almost entirely.

Not much of an epitaph, or legacy either. He'd leave no children and a wife so self-sufficient she'd get over him like the mumps.

It was time. He turned away and descended the wooden stairs into the basement. The air was cooler and smelled of paint. A new doghouse, built to resemble a barn, sat on saw-horses near his workbench. It hadn't fit through the door and he planned to take it apart and reassemble it outside. He wondered if he should leave instructions. A suicide note had-n't occurred to him but he rejected the idea as obvious, even profane.

He crossed to the bench and pulled open a drawer, feel-ing inside for the pistol. His hand touched the soft bundle of cloth and drew it out, placing it carefully on the bench. He couldn't remember if the cartridges were inside or stored separately. It didn't seem to matter. Very slowly, he lifted away each corner of the cloth until he exposed the weapon. The cartridges were there in a clip. He snapped them into the handle and jacked a round into the chamber, then out of habit lowered the hammer to half-cock and placed the barrel inside his mouth, angled upward. The .45 was cool and tast-ed oily. There was a sharp metallic click as he brought back the hammer with his thumb, unafraid.

Chapter One

THE BIG WHEEL AND THE TWO small wheels of Walleye's home-made tricycle slowed almost to a stop. The grade up Wilson Hill was too steep for pedaling. Walleye slid forward and stood on the pedals, forcing them down and up again in jerky motion. The big wheel trembled and squeaked loudly in protest, slipping in the gravel, threatening to pitch Walleye over the handlebars. Anyone else would've gotten off and walked.

Walleye bore down with all his strength and swore at the tricycle. "Get up, you sonabitch!" The pedals turned, slipped, turned. Then jammed. Walleye dismounted, kicking the trike onto its side. "Sonabitch!" he swore. "Bearings!" His staccato voice, carried away by the wind, fired the words rapidly but they came out rounded, blurred at the edges. "Bearings," he said more softly. Most mechanical problems could be traced to bad bearings.

There was very little Walleye didn't know about tricycles. People sneered—grown man riding a trike—because they didn't understand front-wheel drive. He arched his back and spit into the ditch. Three miles from Willow River without tools and in a wind and a mist. He'd catch cold. Traffic was light and unlikely to stop for him, a retard. A dummy. He smiled. Not a moron. Not a moron, he knew for sure, because he got tested once. Just slow, mother said, in that stubborn way she had of defying her haughty neighbors.

1

Walleye preferred to think he wasn't slow at all—other people were just too fast. He'd gotten used to them fast people.

Since the newspaper lady talked to him and did a story on how he made his own living he was the most famous person in Pomme de Terre County, though it didn't mean anything to these birds. If they seen him standing here along the road they'd smile, wave like they was in a parade, and drive right by. He'd gotten used to these birds.

He done their dirty jobs. Lugged their old batteries, plastic pails, sooted bits of stovepipe, rolls of shag carpeting someone had puked up on. Dragged it all out of their sheds and loaded it into the two-wheel trailer he made for the trike. Wasn't anyone in Willow River didn't think he was crazier than a pet coon. Still, they let him keep things.

Walleye stepped around the lame tricycle and looked into the woods. He didn't like woods. Trees tangled around in odd shapes, all mixed up and dark, hiding stuff. But ditches weren't so bad. There were things to be found in ditches, especially these, cut wide to keep the trees back from the road and make snow removal easier.

He scanned the ditch carefully. Gold mine. Plenty of cans, even a few glass bottles. Further in, just beyond where the trees began, he spotted something white. Maybe a usable piece of plastic.

If it was plastic and he dared go in there and get it, he'd use it to wrap up the cans and bottles, fix the tricycle somehow and haul the whole works back home. He looked again into the woods. The trees were wet, dripping. The wind slid through their naked branches, and he didn't care much for the noise it made.

He crabbed sideways down the incline, keeping an eye on the plastic until he reached the bottom and lost sight of it. Glancing back, the road seemed far. Dead, soaking grass wetted his filthy trousers, numbing his skinny legs. He responded with big exaggerated steps across the ditch to the trees, then halted. The trees, dark dripping hulks flooded by fog made his nostrils tingle with smells of rotting leaves, mushy wood, and damp earth. He wanted to go back.

Walleye couldn't explain what happened next. It was a feeling and he wasn't good with feelings, like how he felt that time Larry his black lab got run down on the highway and he watched blood bubble from his nose and refused to turn away. Some things were too terrifying to miss.

A feeling like that drew him deeper into the dim woods. Step by step, closer to something waiting like the death of Larry. He had the jitters watching for it and his head jerked side to side. He had to pee.

The land bent, plunging before him, slick with mud and decaying leaves. He'd forgotten to lace his boots and when he tried to edge down sideways his feet rolled inside and sailed out from under him. He came down hard on his rump. Desperately grasping the slick leafless brush, he skidded into a small gully.

There in the leaves a white ghost had arisen from some abandoned grave to eat him. Naked and wide-eyed, she stared right into him. Wet leaves clung in her yellow hair and she smiled at him with a hungry mouth and he thought she shrieked his name.

Walleye's own screams stuck in his throat as he lay panting beside her, fighting for breath, incapable of looking away.

It was a pretty lady. Not perfect pretty, like soap ladies on TV. An oval face long in the chin. Not too feminine nose, and eyebrows—thick, bushy, darker than her golden hair. He wanted to concentrate on these things, and the eyes, because this was the first time he'd seen a naked lady. Though he'd seen his mother's saggy breasts once when he surprised her and she called him naughty.

The blue eyes held him too. They weren't yet dull and flat like doll eyes and it seemed to Walleye they could still see. He stared into them and some of his fright drained away.

3

He tried to avoid looking at her mouth. It gaped in a horrible manner, mid-scream, choked by the hand of death. Inside, it appeared dark and tongueless.

The rest of her was without blemish except the neck, which was purplish, yellow-brown. Her waist went in and flared again forming ample, smooth hips above long legs. Her feet, like her hands, were slender with soft pink nail paint. She had a round belly and a full mound of hair between her legs. She didn't have a little winkus.

It embarrassed him to see her like this. He sought to cover her but all he had was his peacoat. He needed that. When people die they cover the heads. Not the bodies always, but the heads. He'd seen it on TV. They did that so they didn't have to look in the face of death. Anybody knew that. He'd rather cover the naughty parts.

Walleye struggled to his knees, right leg less than a foot from her head. Shifting his weight slightly, his gaze fell again on her mouth. One of the front teeth had snapped and the cavity behind was dark. Inside, he thought something moved. Walleye drew back. Maybe leaves got inside. They were stuck all along her body. Cautiously, he leaned closer, peeking inside the dark cavity. Maybe it was her tongue that moved trying to say something. Tell him what happened to her and who stole her clothes.

Walleye placed one hand on each side of the lady's head, careful not to disturb her hair, and lowered himself so one eye was inches from the open mouth.

Something was there. It seemed wet, slimy, like her tongue cleaning her teeth or feeling around inside her mouth for something.

The tongue had a black head. It came out. It was the head of a black and yellow snake.

Walleye gasped and fell backward, tangled up in his own legs. The snake's dark head wagged from side to side, most of its body yet inside the lady's mouth where it had found

4

warmth. A forked tongue darted in and out. Walleye watched it grow longer and longer as it uncoiled and slithered out between her lips.

The snake kept its head raised, sliding down her cheek and through her hair, right for him.

He knew it was only a garter snake when he saw the yellow spine, but if you've ever sniffed your hands after touching one you don't forget the decaying, reptile smell. Anyway, Walleye hated snakes. He watched a mommy garter give birth once. They do it like pigs, baby snakes coming out alive, no eggs like other snakes. Eggs are cleaner.

Walleye kicked at the snake and didn't wait to see if more snakes were in the lady's mouth.

On all fours, bladder bursting, he scrambled up the bank toward the light.

Chapter Two

CHARLIE BENSON HAD BEEN chief of police in Willow River since Lyndon Johnson's Great Society. An overheated office came with the title but Charlie preferred the outdoors, patrolling on foot or driving his city car, a green, souped-up Chevy Caprice.

He was a big man, a lummox according to Aunt Agnes, who raised him after his mother died. They lived together and she kept house and bossed him. Neither ever married.

Standing uneasily in the woods near Wilson Hill staring at a naked corpse, Charlie Benson thought of Agnes. Shock wouldn't begin to describe her reaction to this. Her lady friends would be paralytic. The whole town would be paralytic. He'd driven her car here because the Chevy was at Bagg's Auto again getting its steering unstuck. He'd parked the Plymouth with its personalized license plate, Agnes-1, on the road just ahead of Sam Lynstrom's hearse. Sam, undertaker and coroner, was standing next to him. He'd draped the body with a plastic boat cover.

"Who found her?" Sam said, noticeable tremor in his voice.

"Ervin Wertz."

"Walleye?" Sam looked at Charlie and rolled his eyes. "What was he doing way out here?"

"Riding his trike. Looking for cans, I guess."

"Must've scared the little bugger half to death."

"Wet his pants," Charlie said. "Came bawling out of the woods and flagged down Loren Peterson's milk truck. Loren couldn't make sense of him. Brought him in town to me."

"Bizzaro," Sam hooted. "Good thing she was dead before Walleye found her. Hate to have him come up on me all of a sudden in the woods. Hey. What about that? Suppose he only pretended to be scared."

"He's harmless."

"Yeah? That's what they said about Jeffry Dahmer. When they finally arrested him, there he was, frying up a human heart in a big cast iron skillet."

"Thought he was using Teflon?"

"What? Oh. Funny." Sam tried to smile. Charlie was known for his dumb sense of humor. "Walleye looks good for it to me. This is serious business. We got us a dead woman here."

"I noticed that." Charlie's gray eyes went from Sam's face to the plastic covering and back again. "Don't start speculating on who before we know what. Doesn't take a whisper to start rumors in this town."

Sam didn't appreciate a lecture. Charlie had a tendency to take his job a little too seriously. Wasn't anything but a small-town constable. "Playing the big investigator now, Charlie?" he said. "Then you better pay attention to the evidence."

"What evidence?" Charlie's face darkened. "Walleye Wertz? A sorry dimwit who wouldn't hurt anybody! That's your idea of a suspect?"

"Just exploring the possibilities." Sam endured enough stern talk from Mrs. Lynstrom. He didn't need this. "Sorry to upset you."

"I didn't ask you out here to speculate." He took a step closer to the body and pointed down. "Just examine the remains and tell me what killed her."

"Right now?"

"Before half the town gets here," Charlie said. "It's your job, remember?"

"Like hell it is! I'm a mortician." Hard to explain some things to Charlie. "They made me coroner to pronounce people dead, not investigate causes of death. That takes a medical examiner. If we had a doctor in this town I wouldn't even be coroner. I'm a mortician."

"Then do the best you can, Mortician, before Sheriff Mattson starts jerking me around." Charlie took Sam's arm and led him closer to the body. "I mean it."

Charlie wasn't surprised at Sam. People in Willow River seldom took him seriously, even treated him with contempt sometimes. Price you pay for living in your hometown. People remember you as a kid and nothing you do later ever counts.

A military policeman on routine night patrol, Charlie smelled smoke and rescued eight soldiers from a burning barrack, gravely scorching his hands and arms. Army gave him a citation but in Willow River people remembered him for the time his cousin bet him a quarter he wouldn't dare pee on an electric fence. Afterwards he tried to collect and his cousin said, "Anyone that stupid doesn't deserve a quarter." Hardly a year went by when somebody didn't say, "Hey, Charlie. Give you a quarter!"

Now he wondered, shoving his badly scarred hands deep into his jacket pockets and watching mist pool on the white boat cover, if maybe this corpse wasn't going to end up his fault. He was the police, after all. Willow River's thin blue line. He inhaled, sucking in his stomach. Not so thin, maybe.

Sam was down on one knee pulling back the plastic. The dead woman lay face up on the soggy ground, left arm resting casually on a rotting log. Against the dark, littered earth, her body glowed. Dear God, he thought, skin like somebody's commode. He wished Sam would brush away the dead leaves sticking to her neck, sagging breasts, belly, and thighs where the forest had sought to cover her shame.

8

This was the second time Charlie viewed the remains and a second time it soured his stomach. Eyes on the back of Sam's head, he fought to keep the bile down.

"Charlie." The head turned. "This isn't my job."

"Do it."

Sam slapped his leather gloves to the ground, replacing them with rubber ones from his pocket. Forcefully, he turned the blonde head away so the blue eyes stared off into the woods. Charlie wished he'd close the lids, but kept quiet, forcing himself to watch the examination.

"Rigor mortis is well established. Muscles are stiff," Sam said. "She's been dead awhile. Some time yesterday, I suppose."

The mortician's thin hands moved in a practiced way, palpating the body almost as a doctor examinating a living patient. Charlie tried to watch the hands, not what they touched.

"Tits sure sag funny on a stiff, eh?" Sam remarked, a breast in each hand. "Quite a good sized mole under the left one here."

Charlie couldn't help but look at it, angered by his own morbid curiosity.

"See this?" Sam forced the head back so Charlie could see her neck and throat. "Bruises." Swollen yellow stains as if something had infected the skin. His fingers sinking into the darker stains at her throat, Sam said, "I'd bet this is what killed her." He placed both hands around her neck. "See? Strangled."

He brought the head back down and bent over it, peering into her mouth. "Why don't you get down here where you can see something?"

Charlie remained standing.

"What'd you think broke this tooth off?" Sam spoke into the corpse's ear. "Maybe it's still in there." Both his thumbs pried at the mouth. "Wish I had a flashlight." Nose flat

9

against her cheek, he edged his left eye between her lips. "Something's in there all right. Half down her throat."

Charlie felt a tickle and coughed.

Sam turned to the noise. "Getting to you, huh?" He grinned. "I don't suppose you got a tweezers?" Charlie shook his head. "Ball point?"

He handed it over.

Sam stuck the pen down the woman's throat. "Gotta be careful not to push this slippery little sucker any further down."

Charlie resumed staring at the back of Sam's head.

"Got it!" Sam sat up, holding a shiny bit of tooth between his fingers. "Give me your hand."

Charlie stepped back.

"Investigating officer looks a little pale," Sam observed, dryly. "Here's your pen."

"Keep it."

"Don't suppose it occurred to you to write any of this down?"

"What? You think I'm going to forget!"

"Okay," Sam said, dropping the tooth into his shirt pocket. "Let's stop here for now. I need your help to roll her face down. Come on. Grab her ankles."

She felt surprisingly heavy, like a mannequin filled with sand. Sam ran his hand down her spine, brushing away dead leaves. "No apparent spinal injury. Rules out a fall, maybe. This is just guess work."

"I know. Keep going."

"Roll her back."

Once again she lay exposed. The plump mortician stood and pressed a fist into his lower back. "That's it," he said. "Hand me the cover."

"Not quite." Charlie remained on the ground near the woman's bare feet. "Check her vagina."

"What?"

"I want to know if she was sexually abused. Raped."

"How many times I got to tell you?" Sam whined. "You need a medical examiner. A lab. All that!"

Beads of perspiration stood out on Charlie's wrinkled forehead. His brows knit. Cool eyes locked on Sam's pudgy face but when he spoke, the words came gently. "Sam, it's important. I won't hold you to any of this. Check for bruises, anything unusual. Just do your best."

Sam stood motionless, knees of his wool trousers stained dark from the wet ground, gloved hands held out away from his body. Charlie thought for a moment the mortician would simply turn and walk away. Instead, he looked at the policeman as if seeing him for the first time.

"What's going on here, Charlie?"

"What do you mean?"

"I mean, where's the sheriff? Ambulance? The county rescue squad?" Sam looked tired. "Where is everybody, Charlie?"

"They'll be here."

"You didn't call them, did you?"

"I will."

"Should've known. Just the two of us out here." Sam flopped onto the soaked ground, oblivious to the damage done the seat of his pants. For a time, neither spoke, then Sam said, "You're going to try and play detective on this, aren't you?"

"Sam . . ."

"Wait." The little mortician held up a hand. "Listen to me. We're just a couple middle-aged, small town geeks. People around here die, I drain 'em and bury 'em. I've got last year's model Cadillac hearse parked up on the road with forty-eight payments due. You haul drunks out of Casey's on Saturday nights." He paused but Charlie made no move to reply. "You're out of your league. So am I. Let's call the cops."

"Not yet." The policeman struggled to his feet, towering over Sam and grinning. "Not going to argue with you. Guess we are a couple middle-aged geeks, but this is my town and they're my drunks." The smile faded. "We're a quarter mile from the scout camp. Less from Wilson's house. Just as easy been one of the Wilson girls lying here. Years ago, you and I hunted arrowheads up this hill, remember? No dead folks in the woods back then, eh, Sam?"

"Things change."

"For the worse if we let 'em. If we don't do anything."

"You can't do anything." Sam spoke more forcefully. "It's outside your jurisdiction. Sheriff Mattson'll have you by the short hairs."

"Probably. But before he does, you and I are going to have a look between this woman's legs."

Slowly, the mortician got up, dug out a handkerchief and blew his nose. What do you do, he thought, with a guy like Charlie? Wasn't always a good idea to cross him. One night in 1966, two Minneapolis punks out cruising for an easy score broke into several Willow River businesses. Charlie caught up with them in the drug store. He didn't attempt an arrest, just sat on the curb across the street, steadied his long-barreled .38 between his knees and opened fire through the display window. One burglar bled to death in the candy aisle before the other one persuaded Charlie to let him surrender.

"What the hell," Sam shrugged. "It's your neck. Spread her legs."

The examination took only a moment. Afterward, Charlie covered the body and caught Sam by the sleeve. "Well?"

"It's a guess. But I couldn't see signs of forced entry, anything like that."

"Thanks, Sam. I had to know."

"Let's get the hell out of here. I'm soaked clear through."

"Just one more thing." Charlie fished a set of keys from his coat pocket. "Ever see these before?"

"They're car keys, Charlie."

He fanned them in his broad hand. "GM. An entrance key and an ignition key. Two others. A house maybe, and something else. The fob is very fine leather. Brass emblem and everything."

"So? Where'd you find 'em?"

"In the ditch."

"Probably been there ten years." He turned to go.

Charlie stared down at the keys. They weren't rusty and the leather was wet but clean. He said nothing more to Sam.

They started up the incline together, moving slowly, striking their feet against the dirt to gain a footing in the slippery terrain. They paused at the crest of the gully, catching their breaths as Charlie fumbled at a tin of Copenhagen. He rolled a pinch of the moist snuff inside his lower lip and gazed up at the slate sky. The wind had freshened, bringing with it a steady rain and the promise of snow. The men strode quickly toward the road.

Behind them, the body's plastic covering rustled and folded away, exposing again the young woman's startled, broken smile and wide blue eyes fixed in disbelief on the last person to see her alive.

*   *   *

Ninety miles away at the National Weather Service office in St. Cloud, anxious men and women hunched over radar sets and sucked the ends of their pencils. The unspoken word was blizzard.

Meterologists don't use the word blizzard to describe a heavy snow as people do sometimes. Blizzard is a specific kind of snowstorm with winds often reaching fifty miles per hour or greater, heavy snow, rapidly falling temperatures, and a likely duration of several days. The storm is followed immediately with extremely low temperatures—twenty or thirty degrees below zero. What a hurricane is to Florida a

13

blizzard is to Minnesota, and professionals aren't about to say blizzard until they mean it.

But they all knew that sometime that afternoon, maybe that evening, they'd have to say it. Across the plains on the eastern slopes of the Rocky Mountains there was a blizzard of gigantic proportions spinning into life like some prehistoric animal against which there was no modern defense, only a warning. It was their job to sound it—not too early and not too late.

Chapter Three

DUTCH RESTED FLAT ON HIS RUMP on the ground, limp hands palms up atop crossed legs. A faded maroon shirt, darkened by the icy rain, clung to his heaving chest and round belly. The morning was a blur. He felt bewildered and wet hair hung in strings across his forehead. He thought maybe he'd been crying for a time.

Nimrod stood in the grass nearby. His master's behavior confused the golden retriever and he approached cautiously, nuzzling the man's arm. After a time, Dutch's hand came to rest on Nimrod's head. The touch of damp fur roused him. "Good old pup," he said, stroking. "You don't care what I've done, do you?"

Better for the dog he'd chickened out on the suicide deal. Jean loved animals in theory; didn't like to touch them. "Old gray-nosed pup," he said, hugging him tight. "They'd ship you to an inhumane society, cut off your balls and give you to some yuppie bitch who'd make you live indoors."

Nimrod uttered a high-pitched whimper and shook free, confused by his master's uncharacteristic affection.

"Trouble with infidelity," Dutch lectured him, "is you fool yourself into believing it's harmless. Can love be wrong?" He stared into the dog's curious brown eyes. "You go slightly mad in the end, of course, kill your girlfriend and try and blow your own head off." He grinned. "All for harmless, little old love." He caught the dog by the collar and drew him close until they were nose to nose. "It's not only me, you know. Remember the schoolteacher out east who hired a hit man to bump off her husband so she could fool around with this eighth grader? And the guy with the neck chains, what was his name? Him and the babysitter tried to murder his wife and it flopped." Hard to explain, he thought, even to a dog.

Who really understands and who knows where love leaves off and lust begins? Mad passion may appear as convincing as any storybook romance. Did Cleopatra and Mark Anthony have true love or were they merely sexually active? Imagine them as eighty-year olds squinting at each other through their cataracts and listening to the dance band at their Fiftieth Wedding Anniversary. And after all, didn't their love end in suicide too?

Maybe love was too complicated to understand. Souls never yield their secrets, and people understand themselves about as well as they understand others. Or maybe it wasn't complicated at all. Maybe people just didn't care. They did what felt good to them at the time and to hell with the consequences, meaning love itself was imaginary.

That seemed most logical.

"That's it," he told the dog. "We just don't give a shit about anything but ourselves."

He was right and it was a comfort. Anyway, sometimes people rose above it, like on Iwo or in Selma. He rose above it too, he remembered some times, though few, and when he did screw up, well, what can you expect? Humans were a miserable race that satisfied every urge even the most base and could excuse anything, even murder. Lately he'd been thinking that murder might actually be society's last line of defense against self-indulgence. Just a matter of time before this too goes the way of gluttony, addiction, and sexual wantonness of every variety. Hell in a handbasket.

"I'm a moralist," he said. "A reformed adulterer turned killer, now lecturing on a variety of moral questions of interest to intellectual society." Smashing. But shouldn't his present circumstance be one of those times when he rose above his base nature? When he confessed his crime and made amends? Accepted his punishment?

How hard could it be really—prison? They didn't starve you or beat you. You didn't even have to work hard from what he'd heard. All the Hollywood stuff about getting raped in the shower most likely happened about as often as most Hollywood stuff.

But of course he didn't fear prison. He feared exposure— the world seeing him for what he really was. The mask of his life removed and him there naked and small as only God knew him. That would be the killer. Could he indeed deal with that?

Willow River was the one place on earth were he fit perfectly. They knew him, and while not everyone loved him, he had here as much love, respect, and place as he would ever get in life. Some people feel at home wherever they are, but not him. This was the only home he'd ever known. He'd heard the same sentiment from a New Yorker once who claimed not to be his real self outside the city.

Hard then to tell the truth, when his unmasking might both convict and vindicate him. People had come to expect the truth from him after all. No one knew him as a liar.

So what should he do, walk into Charlie Benson's office and confess? "Hi Charlie, did this murder last night out by Wilson Lake. Don't know what got into me really. Hell of a week at work. Beef prices up again and this old girlfriend of mine shows up and brings back a lot of old memories so I popped her, you know, I'm sorry as hell but I suppose you got a job to do. Thought I better come in. So, do you lock me up right away now or do I get the phone call? Do you really know that speech about the right to remain silent? I can't imagine you have one those little cards to read it from, I mean holy shit, Charlie, you borrowed my suit coat to take Darlene Erickson to the prom."

17

"No Nimrod. No. I can't."

And that wasn't even the worst of it. Now Vicky had won. She got to ruin his life twice—once when he loved her and once when he killed her.

"After I've told it all to Charlie Benson I bet they give me one of those court-appointed psychologists," he told Nimrod.

"So, Mr. Cleland. Describe your affair with Victoria Johnson. Take your time."

"Hard to say, Doc. Before I met Vicky I was one person. Now I'm another."

"Come now, Mr. Cleland—may I call you Dutch?—married men have had affairs since Moses was a pup. You know, the old libido. Nevertheless, something usually sets it off. Something in your marriage most likely."

"Sex?"

"People love talking about sex." The imaginary psychologist smiled. He looked like Tommy Lee Jones. "Talk it to death, in fact, missing the real power it has over us. Sex is a kind of door to your id, your reservoir of psychic energy. Keep it closed, you wither. Open it too wide, you go nutsy wacko." A quizzical, Tommy Lee Jones expression. "Technically speaking."

"I love my wife."

"Is that why you didn't go through with your suicide?"

"Partly. I mean, it's kind of hard to explain. I was right there in the basement with the barrel in my mouth and everything like you're supposed to, and got to thinking about the mess. Bites of bone, brains and blood. Who cleans all that up? Started thinking of Jean standing on a ladder scrubbing ceiling joists with a sponge and cursing me, what was left of me, so I stuck the pistol in my belt and went out to do it in the pole barn where they could hose everything down easier. Had a pretty good reason to kill myself, you know. Life for a life. Mine for Vicky's, all that, but I got to wonder-

ing if I wasn't just chicken. Dying to escape the consequences you might say."

"I'm getting the picture." Thoughtfully, Tommy Lee Jones
removed his eyeglasses. "Quite frankly, I don't accept your
wife's cleaning problems as the sole reason for aborting the
suicide. Had to be something more."

"Well, I started crying—grieving more like. Made me mad
finally. I blamed myself for Vicky, of course, but it was her
fault too. I decided not to die for her. I gave her my marriage
and everything else I had. Now my life?"

"To understand that I need to know a little about your relationship with Mrs. Johnson. How did you meet?"

"Minneapolis. Computer seminar."

"Really?"

"Vicky was the teacher. Got my attention with that Nordic
princess look—blonde, blue eyes, straight nose, full lips. She
brought it off somehow. Good looks are trashy on a woman
sometimes but she wore her's like some women wear a daring outfit and make it seem discreet."

"So you were attracted physically?"

"Enough to ask her to discuss some banal computer theory over dinner. Impulse, unimportant at the time, but
changed my life. Surprisingly, she accepted and I found this
place called Nightingale's in the Yellow Pages. A period
place—New York City, 1940s. Small lamps on the tables.
Waiters, no waitresses. Tiny dance floor near the piano.
Solitary female singer named Phyllis. (The pianist called her
Phyl.) Club even employed a cigarette girl. Do better selling
bubble gum in Minnesota. Vicky dressed kind of forties too,
the big shoulders and heavy material. Think I'm crazy if you
want to for falling for it all. Maybe it was the martinis or the
goofy intimate way she had of listening to me, like she'd
never heard anything so deep and bright and clever. Most
romantic night of my life. Men are susceptible to that too,
you know?"

"More susceptible, in my experience," the psychologist said.

"So one thing led to the next and pretty soon she's in my arms on the dance floor and I'm smelling her hair and thinking how her hips flare so nice the way women's hips were before diet cola and she's barely touching me. No mashing, just brushing, each contact more intimate then the last and you began to anticipate. Well, this is getting sort of personal."

"Believe me, I've heard it all, Mr. Cleland. You won't shock me. Go on."

"Isn't much more to tell really. Phyl sang an Anne Murray tune popular that year, 'Could I Have This Dance.' Know the one?"

Tommy Lee Jones nodded.

"We danced sort of detached from the people around us, Phyl's sultry voice drifted in and out. '. . . the first time we danced and I knew, as we swayed to the music and held to each other, I fell in love with you.' Vicky sang too, soft lips against my ear. 'Could I have this dance for the rest of my life? Would you be my partner every night? When we're together it feels so right. Could I have this dance for the rest of my life?' She lifted her head, all sleepy-eyed, and confessed she meant every word. There was an innocent wantonness to her that made me wonderfully sick to my stomach. We went to my room."

"You made love?"

"Like two ferrets in heat."

"That doesn't explain why it led to violence afterwards." The psychologist smiled. "You look confused. What I'm asking, if you had a sexual encounter—heat of the moment—why isn't that enough? How did you get from there to killing her and trying to end your own life? The acts you committed are out of proportion to the guilt. You still haven't given me a motive for murder and suicide. Your relationship would have to deepen greatly for that. Much more."

"It did. Listen Doc, I don't know if I can explain this to you. Like I said, I love my wife and I loved her then, but this was something different. I try to tell you and it's just sex, some one night stand in a hotel room and you're wondering why I'm all guilty and off murdering and losing my mind. Well, it wasn't any kind of love I'd known before. Maybe I'm just a hick from a small town, who knows? But I'm telling you she opened up something inside me I didn't know was there and then she sucked it out and I felt deeper and thought deeper and discovered passion, or whatever you call it, and it lit me up day and night. She made me crazy. Not all at once, it just grew in me like some kind of love tumor. So what do you think? Do I have an insanity defense?"

Dutch stared at the dog and listened to the rain clatter on the metal roof of the pole barn. "What if I'm not crazy?" The rain beat down harder and he shivered uncontrollably. What if giving himself up was the wrong thing too?

He struggled to his feet. Nimrod brought him a stick, one end chewed ragged. Dutch gave it a high, spinning toss and laughed as the dog ripped across the yard. When he returned, prancing, head high, stick clenched in his teeth, Dutch said, "Pesky dog. Drop it." Nimrod obeyed, circling first as he'd been taught, then waited impatiently for his reward.

Dutch patted the dog's head. "Big baby." He picked up the stick, wet from the rain and Nimrod's mouth, then snapped it across his knee. "Enough. Let's go in and warm up." They trotted toward the house together.

Nimrod wasn't allowed inside—Jean's rule. They crossed the brick patio to the rear door, Dutch swung it open and called to the dog. Tracks of mud and wet leaves accumulated on the polished kitchen tile as Nimrod followed him to a counter where Jean kept cookbooks and a note pad.

"We'll leave her a note," Dutch said to the dog. "Then pack up and make a run for it."

This was the only clear choice. You gave up—maybe if you really were crazy you killed yourself—or you got away. He wasn't going to fool anybody after all. He was the only person in town who knew Vicky and the police wouldn't be long in discovering the connection. So there it was—confess or run. The more he examined it in those simple terms the more he realized why most criminals run for it. They run from the bank and try to hide in the city or escape into the woods after abandoning their stolen car or they bury the body in some isolated spot until a hunter finds it months or years later. They almost always run away. Suddenly it was all clear to him. Running was the last vital ingredient. Didn't Adam and Eve hide themselves in the garden when they heard God coming and they knew they were naked? They became fugitives—so too, he and the dog—traveling town to town one step ahead of the law, like Dr. Richard Kimbal searching for the one-armed man. In each new place maybe they'd do some good to make up for all the bad they'd done. There were worse ways to live.

He remembered something else too, they almost always got caught. But were they any worse off? In the end didn't it all come out the same? "We got nothing to lose, Boy," he said. "We're on the lam."

Chapter Four

"WHAT'S THE DIFFERENCE BETWEEN a dead dog and a dead attorney lying in the road?" Mavis Faggering baited him, her heavy face flushed with excitement.

"I'm sure you'll tell me, Mavis. But please," Len begged, "more coffee?"

"There's skid marks in front of the dog!" she bellowed, giant breasts trembling. She slopped coffee into his cup, overflowing it, then traipsed away offering refills along the counter.

A country lawyer laughs at that joke every time he hears it, Len reminded himself. The old Minneapolis C. Leonard Davis, of Higgins, Higgins and Bagdonavich, wouldn't have laughed, but Len Davis of Willow River, who rolled dice for slices of pie and had eaten ten years worth of lunches at Berkie's Cafe, laughed at almost anything.

The partners at H. H. & Bags hired Len fresh out of law school, brought him along painstakingly, molding him into one of the best corporate tax attorneys in Minnesota. When he went fishing near Willow River ten years before and never came back they suspected mid-life crisis and advised counseling. When they finally took his desertion seriously, they wrote him a nasty letter subtly revealing what a fool he was, and fired him six months after he quit.

The wooden floor heaved as Mavis, still grinning, bore down on Len.

"Insulting the customers," complained Len. "New marketing technique?"

"Poor little titty baby." She reached out and not too gently caressed his cheek. "Got something more important to talk to you about in a minute." She winked, hurrying to the cash register where four elderly ladies waited to pay their bill.

Mavis Faggering wore eye shadow the color of beet blood and knew more jokes than Buddy Hackett. "Takes some getting used to," Dutch told him on their first fishing trip, quickly adding, "But a good egg." If Len had sympathy for Mavis and other Willow Riverians, it grew from Dutch's lively descriptions of them as the most fascinating people on earth, which in some ways he guessed they were.

Len had schemed to make Dutch his friend. With new contempt of jurisprudence and old friends left behind, he needed solace. He found it in Dutch, and gin. He'd taken to drinking martinis before lunch. Not that gin was so bad really, made from grain and other natural ingredients. One could almost think of it as liquid granola.

A thunder of female laughter rolled out from behind a large, portable screen to his right. "What's that?" he asked when Mavis returned. "The WCTU?" (Willow River still had an active chapter.)

"Second Monday of the month."

He'd forgotten. On Michele Pixley's day off from the Royale School of Hair Design in St. Cloud, about a dozen obese females (nowhere near the town total) assembled at the cafe to have their toenails clipped. Michele got five bucks a head (fifty cents a toe) and sponsoring the event earned Mavis a freebie.

Above the intermittent whir of the malted milk machine and a grill hood with a bad exhaust fan motor, the air thickened with the smell of fried onions and nail polish remover. Len stared at the long row of large glass jars on a shelf behind the counter. Number 4 was his favorite. An overweight cookie, rich with molasses. He glanced down at the three-inch roll sagging over his belt. Not today.

Mavis had a suspicious glint in her eye as she leaned heavily on the counter, massive cleavage dangerously close to his nose. "Daydreaming?"

"Dreaming of you, my melon-breasted soprano." He blew a sultry kiss into her bosom. "What's for lunch?"

"Hear about the murder?"

"Just what's on the radio."

"Who done it?"

"The fiendish serial killer of Willow River."

"Don't be smart aleck." She reached inside her blouse and adjusted something. "You know what I mean Mr. Big Shot Lawyer. You guys all lap outta the same bowl."

"Contracts and wills, that's my gig these days, not murder."

Mavis knew he'd duck the issue, like anyone in authority. "Never had nothin' like this around here before." She lowered her voice. "Scary. Ben, over to Lund's Foods, says it's Vietnamese gangs comin' up from Minneapolis."

"Sounds like Ben."

"I don't believe him either," she whispered. "It's Satan worshippers. They're looking for rural areas."

Len coughed.

"Walleye found her," she continued. "Buck naked. Big old snake coming right up outta her vagina. Satan was a snake, you know. That's why them devil worshipers use 'em in their ceremonies. Way I heard it, he ain't telling about the half-burnt candles and devil hex signs he seen around the body."

"Mavis!"

"Don't Mavis me! Stuff goes on in this country they don't want us to know about." She licked her lips, lowering her voice again. "Over one million people been abducted by aliens already and the Republicans in Congress keep it secret 'cause they're all members of the Religious Right. They think it's the Rapture."

"Don't want to toss any water of reason on your flaming liberalism," Len said, "but murder is usually pretty mundane. Most likely some domestic squabble. No bloodsucking cults, no bubble-eyed aliens."

"People make fun of things they don't understand." Mavis looked a little huffy.

"Sorry." Len put on a humble face. "Not to change the subject, but right now I'm concerned about only two things, which are, in order of their importance: Lunch and the weather. Lunch, because that's why I'm here, and the weather because according to those weather goofballs this rain's supposed to turn to snow and my snowblower is sitting in my garage and the engine to run it has been rusting on a table at the back of Bagg's since March. So how about some food to strengthen me for what's likely to be a strenuous and frustrating afternoon?"

She eyed him closely for several moments then rumpled his hair and nodded. "Whole thing might be weather related. Affects people strange sometimes," she said, jolly manner restored. "Too warm for November anyhow. Like before the Great Armistice Day Blizzard of 1940. Killed hundreds."

"About sixty," Len corrected.

Mavis frowned. "Thousands injured."

"Stranded."

Mavis looked peeved. "What's your order?"

"Ham and cheese."

She wrote it down and went away.

The door opened, scraping its weather-stripping along the floor. A camouflaged stranger slid inside and surveyed the dimly lighted surroundings. A large man and powerful, typical of the booted hunters who descended on Willow River for several weeks each autumn. The man had Bill Clinton's eyes, flat and blue, dodging banefully between rolls of puffy, sore skin. He headed for the empty stool next to Len and straddled it. "Davis?" he inquired.

Len instantly disliked the thin, caustic voice. "Yes?"

"Murdock," said the man. "I'm told you know pretty near everybody in town."

"Really? Who told you that?"

"Motel clerk."

"What can I do for you?" Len drew a low-tar cigarette from his pack on the counter. Murdock lit it with a silver Zippo.

"Got in last night from out west." He slipped the lighter into a vest pocket below a row of high-powered rifle bullets. "Colder than a witch's tit up here."

"Yeah? We think it's too warm." Len saw how Murdock's eyes sparked between the folds. "Here for the hunting?"

"Never shot anything in Minnesota before. Got an old Navy buddy here."

"Oh?" Len blew a cloud of smoke toward the cookie jars and forced a smile. "What's his name?"

"Philip Cleland. Dutch, we called him."

Had Murdock spoken any other name in Willow River Len might've just nodded and offered his help but a lifetime defending liars and bringing lawsuits on behalf of liars, taught him to be wary. "Navy buddies you said?"

"Served on a tin can together. *Turner Joy.*"

"That a fact?" Dutch had served on the *Joy.* Len remembered stories of air raids near Hiaphong and plucking downed pilots from the drink, and he'd heard the names of Dutch's Vietnam shipmates. He didn't recall a Murdock. "Funny they didn't tell you at the motel where to find Dutch? He's well-known here."

"They did." Murdock signaled to Mavis. "Black coffee." Then studied Len, obviously aware the attorney was being evasive. "Couldn't find him at that Meat Market though. Place is closed."

27

Len shrugged to conceal his surprise.

Murdock placed one hand affectionately on Len's shoulder. "I've known lawyers who were hard of hearing." Tightening his grip just enough to create a dull pain, he went on, "I said the place was shades down locked."

"I can't help it." Len tensed his shoulder, wondering if the man had purposely tightened his grip or just didn't know his own strength. "Doesn't sound like Dutch." Usually, if Dutch were ill or away, Harry Peters filled in. The business remained open.

Removing his hand, Murdock slopped coffee into his saucer and slurped it. "I didn't just pick your name out of a hat," he said, enjoying Len's confusion. "Little fella at the motel said you're Cleland's best friend."

"We're acquainted," Len admitted, drawing a business card from his sport coat. "I'll check it out. Call me later."

"I don't call people later. I come and see them."

Even the most veiled threat of violence set Len's heart racing. He told himself he was no coward, just preferred to handle life's troubles intellectually not physically.

"Hope that's not a threat," Len said, trying to sound indignant and unafraid.

Murdock smiled. He had fine teeth. "You college boys catch on quick." He drummed his fingers on the counter close to Len's cup. "Thing is, you're all bloodsuckers. Let me ask you something. You ever been a public defender?"

Len shook his head, keeping his hands on his lap. "I'm a corporate attorney."

"Impressive." He chuckled. "Finding a big corporate attorney like you way out here in Podunk." Murdock hunched, glancing around conspiratorially. "Bet you really rake it in when a couple these pig farmers do a merger, huh?"

Len said nothing and avoided the man's wormy eyes.

"You're going to do some lawyering for me Mr. Corporate Attorney," said Murdock. He seemed almost jovial. "Detective work, like locating the heirs of some stiff's estate, instead, you find your buddy Dutch. Call me. We get together. Don't worry about your fee, I'll do right by you. Say . . . jackshit? How about that? A nice little check for jackshit?"

Mavis arrived with Len's sandwich and stared openly at Murdock. "I'll let you eat," he said, wiping his tongue across his front teeth and slipping a folded bill onto the counter. "Later we'll have a reunion—you, me, and Old Dutch—drink some brewskis and lie about 'Nam."

Len watched him walk out, struck by something familiar in the way he moved. That swagger men feign in prison. On the counter, Len's unsmoked cigarette had turned to ash. He shut his eyes and exhaled. A naked corpse, a scary ex-con tracking down your best friend who's mysteriously disappeared—Monday in Podunk.

Len opened his eyes and stared at the sandwich oozing melted cheese, then brushed it aside, appetite gone.

* * *

Carroll Johnson was extremely fond of his hair, and he had a lot of it. Long, black and wavy. It took time and money to keep it that way, to keep the perm fresh, natural, not let the color fade at the roots. That meant giving up lunch on Mondays, trudging the Minneapolis Skyway System, and using a secret code in his appointment book so his secretary didn't get wise and spread hair rumors.

Indeed, Carroll was fond of his entire body, but unlike his hair, the flat stomach and lean, sinuous legs were genuine. And costly. Two hours each morning in a mirrored workout room he pumped and pedaled himself toward perfection. At forty, Carroll watched sweat glisten from solid pecs and biceps, thighs and calves. He could stand erect, clad only in Speedos, and flex his buttocks. A rewarding sight. His computer firm ran a photograph of him in a white shirt and suspenders on the inside cover of its color brochure. He kept a stack of them on his coffee table.

Today, Carroll was late for his noon appointment at Gasquet's, and as he hurried across the Crystal Court toward a bank of elevators, he hoped Gasquet would not be peevish and give him a rush job. When the bronze doors parted and he stepped out on the thirty-third floor, he produced an urbane smirk, which he wore casually into the salon, so that Linda, the receptionist, should know that he knew he was late but could hardly be expected to care. He'd no doubt that secretly, she was in love with him.

"Gasquet is waiting, Mr. Johnson," she said crisply. "Go right on back."

Gasquet was dressed in tropical attire—colorful Hawaiian shirt and Bermuda shorts—part of his effort to create the proper mood for "Minnesota Migration"—the salon's annual trip to Maui. Carroll had been one of the first to pay his deposit and he was correct in assuming Gasquet would do nothing now to offend such a loyal customer.

"Didn't mean to hold you up," Carroll said reasonably, sliding into the chair. "I should know better by now than to believe that bitch."

"Ah!" Gasquet sighed. "Women."

"My ex."

"Vicky? Isn't she trying to find herself in Oklahoma, or whatever?"

"Was. Flew in Saturday, or so she told me on the phone. Supposed to meet this morning at Rennie's for cappuccino." Carroll watched himself in a mirror opposite the chair. His expression suitably demure. "I sat there an hour, cooling my heels like some teenybopper on his first date."

"How dreadful!"

"No clue what she wanted. Likes to call on the phone every so often to keep me in her life, she says." Carroll unbuttoned his shirt at the neck so Gasquet could fold the collar down. "Married an ex-con from Tulsa. Murdock or something. Thoroughly disgusting individual."

"Oh, my God." said Gasquet, flourishing a mauve sham-
poo cape and fastening it around Carroll's neck. "Wasn't she
with us on the Migration in eighty-eight or eighty-nine?"
    "Eighty-eight. God only knows who she slept with."
    "Well, it wasn't me, dear boy."
    "That much I knew," Carroll said, a bit more unkindly
than he'd intended. "It all started with that butcher from
Willow River, and went downhill from there."
    "But the divorce went well?"
    "Surprisingly. I gave her the Volvo and some cash. Kept
the house and everything else. She married this Murdock last
year. Reformed rapist, of all things. But she 'understands'
him."
    "Naturally!" Gasquet slid his hands lightly through
Carroll's hair. "Where does one meet such a person?"
    "Never asked. She's such a slut." Carroll fixed a forefinger
above his upper lip, perpendicular to his nose. "Think I
should grow a mustache?"
    "Daily coloring if you do."
    "Forget it."
    Gasquet tripped a foot lever and the chair reclined. "We're
going back now." He cradled Carroll's head gently, guiding
it over the shampooing sink.
    "I can't shake the feeling there's something wrong,"
Carroll said. "Two things I give Vicky credit for. In all the
years we were married, she never looked anything but gorgeous—even in the morning—and she never stood me up."
    "New man. New habits."
    "Not Vicky. She has a time fetish. Every day, every minute
is planned. We made love by the numbers."
    Gasquet's response to this was garbled by the sound of
water running in the sink inches from Carroll's ear. He
closed his eyes, enjoying the warm tingle of water and sham-
poo against his scalp. Gasquet was an artist. Gentle, yet
firm, faintly sensuous.

31

"She'll turn up," Gasquet said, more loudly. "Dead, I hope."

Chapter Five

"IT'S THE SHERIFF, CHARLIE!" Marlene's sing-song voice echoed a warning in the police station's high-ceilinged outer office. The granite ashlar building housing Police Head-quarters was shared with the Willow River Volunteer Fire Department, the city maintenance garage, and the City Council Chambers. "Better shag ass! His jowls are all ajiggle."

"Calm down. I'm coming."

Charlie Benson had grown up with Cedric Mattson, sher-iff of Pomme de Terre County. Both sought careers in law enforcement but there any similarity ended. Mattson was a Hubert Humphrey Democrat, a wily campaigner plotting his third re-election fight. Charlie just wanted to be a cop.

Through the glass doors, Charlie watched the sheriff hoist himself from the front seat of his immaculate squad car, assisted by a young deputy who struggled to open the door and a collapsible umbrella at the same time. The umbrella deployed above the sheriff's head just as they reached the sheltered porch. Both were decked out in full uniform and belted rain coats. Charlie wondered if news had reached Mattson yet about the election. Did he know Charlie would run against him again?

"Shake the mothballs out of the red carpet, Marlene." Charlie spoke in a loud, resonant voice. "Prepare the way for His Highness, Pompous Assus."

"Shush! He'll hear you."

33

The sheriff's pouting, bullhead-jowled face appeared just outside the door.

"Fear not," Charlie continued with great pomposity. "To the Great One, the prattle of mere mortals and Republicans is but a cottonwood seed blown in the wind."

The door popped open. "Good afternoon, Sheriff," they said together.

"Can't imagine what the two of you find to grin about on a day like this," Mattson said, slapping a wet campaign hat against his flabby leg. "Lousy rain. Stinking corpses."

"We're hardly to blame for either," Charlie said, suppressing a smile.

"Perhaps." Mattson paused, leaving room for doubt. "No murders here in my day."

Expressionless, Marlene pivoted and marched to her chair behind the dispatch desk. Mattson was even taller than Charlie, but below the neck the Sheriff was a man headed in two directions. The generously cut raincoat failed to hide his obesity. "Coffee, Sheriff?"

"Makes me pee." Mattson jabbed a stubby finger toward Charlie's office. "Let's talk." Turning to his deputy, at parade rest near the door. "Stand by, Scotty. This won't take long."

"Better get around here more often, it seems," the sheriff said once they were safely inside. "Iron out a few chain-of-command wrinkles."

"Meaning?"

"Meaning this murder investigation is county business." Mattson's beady eyes narrowed. "Outside city limits, per se. Put it this way. It don't concern you!"

Charlie's face reddened but his voice held. "No question of your having jurisdiction here, Cedric. None at all. But I was the first officer on the scene, and it's pretty close to home." He chanced a thin smile. "You've got the ball. No argument. I only want to throw a couple blocks. Open a hole."

"And maybe get your name mentioned in dispatches, eh?" He returned Charlie's smile. "Little grist for the ole political mill?" The smile broadened. "You may learn this political game yet. I'll still win a'course, matter-a-fact. Always have."

Charlie remained silent, leaning back against his desk, arms folded across his chest. That solved the political mystery. Mattson knew.

"Let you in on a little secret," the sheriff continued. "I'm pleased you filed again this year. Voters come to expect it. The loyal opposition. All that, per se. Hells bells! Can't have an election with just one candidate, eh?"

Why not, Charlie thought? We always do in Minnesota. DFL goons have controlled everything for decades until they elected Jessie (The Body) Ventura. "This isn't about politics," Charlie said, looking beyond Mattson toward the window, rain pelting against it with renewed intensity. "I want this guy even more than I want your job."

"Don't worry. I'll drill the perp."

"I was hoping you'd say 'we.'" He managed a shallow sigh before asking Mattson what had been accomplished since the murder was reported to the county cops.

"I'll put it this way." The sheriff drew an orator's breath. "The corpus is in the morgue. But since you got no real morgue, we shipped her to Lynstrom's Funeral Home for an interim period. In a like manner, without your basic first responder ambulance service, I was hoping you'd see her transported down to the M.E." Charlie nodded agreement. "Our crisis team, the usual crime lab boys, myself personally—the whole ball of wax. We're on it, like stink on shit. Not to say you can't help in other ways. Why, directing traffic for the news media alone could tie a small force down. Rest assured I'll be keeping you informed every step of the way."

"I've written a preliminary report . . ."

"Great, Charlie, just great," the sheriff cut him off, moving toward the door.

"I'd like you to see it before the autopsy," he continued. "Might help the M.E."

"No doubt," Mattson tugged at the door. "Be sure and send me a copy."

"Damn it, Cedric!" Charlie exploded. "Get your fat ass back here!"

Outside the office, Charlie's outburst lifted Deputy Scott from parade rest to full attention. He started for the door.

"I wouldn't if I were you," Marlene said pleasantly. "They both have guns, you know."

Scotty gave her a pained look and patted his revolver before knocking on the door. "Sheriff? You all right?"

Mattson's face, swollen with anger, pushed out almost nose to nose with Scott. "Did I call you?"

"No sir."

"Then stick your nose in your own business." The door slammed shut and Mattson turned to face Charlie Benson. "You got yourself a bad temper there, Mr. Benson. You rein in on it maybe we can talk this over with some semblance of decorum."

"You were the one walking out the door," Charlie reminded him.

"Never mind that." Mattson fanned the air with both hands. "What's stuck in your craw, anyway?"

"Her face." Again he called up that lovely cold face with its frozen eyes and his shoulders sagged and his anger cooled. "Maybe her fingers and toes."

Mattson looked as if he were about to call for Scotty. "Fingers and toes?"

"They were perfect."

"So?"

"Nails painted a blushing, rose color. Delicate. Neat. Evenly clipped. Very clean." He could still see them. Hands

36

almost like a model's. Creamy, silken feet, without callus or hardened skin—even at the heels. "She must've been somebody."

"Holy Shit!" Mattson beat a fist against his palm. "You got corpus fever, or what? One Minneapolis hooker gets dumped in a ditch and you're mooing like some love-sick calf."

"I want in on this investigation." Charlie stood ramrod straight. "Just once Cedric, forget the bureaucratic mumbo jumbo. Screw jurisdiction." His voice rose. "I know I can do this."

This was Charlie Benson forty years ago, thought Mattson. Charlie "Boomer" Benson, charging eighty-five yards for the Willow River Bearcats and winning the friggin' Homecoming game. Name in the paper every week, then finally forgotten. There were times when guys like Charlie Benson just couldn't help themselves. They had to be heroes.

If Charlie ran in for the touchdown this time, it wouldn't do any harm. The sheriff was coaching now. Right there to take credit, and if things went sour, well, that's to be expected when small town cops stick their noses in. Voters can be made to see it either way.

"All right. You feel strongly," Mattson said, folding his arms. "Far be it from me to spoil the stew. If you got any real evidence let's hear it. Convince me."

Charlie hesitated, collecting his wits. Mattson was a blowhard politician stuck on himself, but a shrewd, sort of rural Sidney Greenstreet. Charlie struggled to present the case clearly and convincingly.

"A great many questions will be answered by the autopsy," Charlie began. "But the condition of the body, especially her lack of clothes, is going to throw things out of whack. Make it seem like a sex killing. I don't think it was. Lynstrom took a good look at her. Found no molestation. Nothing."

37

"Lynstrom's not qualified," the sheriff injected.

"I know. But if the autopsy bears him out, then there's another reason for her being left naked and another motive for killing her."

"Such as?"

"Hatred. I'm convinced the killer knew her. Hated her. Strangled her in a fit of passion, then stripped and dumped her like garbage." He spoke rapidly. "She's too pretty and well-kept to be some tramp. She was a lady."

"Bringing us back to fingers and toes?"

"I know it's more hunch than evidence, but go back down to Lynstrom's and take another look."

"Okay, Charlie. Suppose I buy this theory of yours. What's the bottom line?"

Again he paused, hands shoved deep in his pockets. "You're not going to like this." He drew in a long breath and let it out slowly. "I'm convinced this is a local job."

"Don't be a damn fool!" The sheriff jerked a thumb over his shoulder. "Out in that squad car I've got two rolls of film on that corpse. Looked at her from every angle—so have you. Ever see her before?"

"No."

"That's because she ain't from around here. You think she just came cruising along Highway 11 out there and somebody from Willow River jumped up and wasted her for no reason?" Mattson shook his head in desperation. "Even Walleye Wertz ain't that dumb."

Charlie wandered to the window and nodded at the rain drops. "Right out there someone knew her. She came here to see somebody and they killed her."

"Take another look," Mattson said. "Where's her car? Assuming she didn't fly in here on a broomstick. What happened to her clothes? That's called physical evidence. Where is it?"

"It's our job to find it. And then there's the keys."

"What damned keys?"

Charlie strode to the desk and picked up the car keys. "These." He dangled them before the Sheriff's eyes.

"Where'd they come from?"

"In the ditch near the scene."

Mattson snatched them from Charlie's hand and tossed them carelessly in the air, thinking. Finally he flipped them back onto the desk. "Lot's of things in ditches. Don't mean shit." A moment later he said, "I might've been wrong about you, Charlie. You aren't politically motivated at all. You're goofy in the head. Old keys and toenails." He turned to the door.

"Well?" Charlie called after him.

"Well, what?"

"Am I part of this investigation or not?"

"You bet," said the sheriff. "You're so far out in left field there isn't a chance we'll bump into each other until it's over. Have at it."

"Thanks."

"Don't thank me." Mattson opened the door and Charlie followed him into the outer office. "You're about to make a public jackass of yourself. Incidentally, wouldn't let some nosey reporter wring that story out of me if I were you. Voters get a whack at me every four years. City Council can put you on ice in ten minutes. Take it from me, if people in this town find out you think one of 'em is a killer, you'll be finished, and fast."

Charlie watched the sheriff waddle off, a spring in his step. The outer door slammed. "My idol," he told Marlene in answer to her smirk.

"Don't make fun," she said. "He gave you a break. Hike back to the conference room now and see Walleye. He's waiting."

"What's he want? I already talked to him."

"Maybe he wants to talk about your mystery lady's nice fingers and toes." She lifted her skirt above the knee, placed one hamy white leg daintily onto a chair and batted her eyes. "Wanna see my toes?"

"Quit eavesdropping."

"Don't talk so loud." Grinning, she held the conference room door for him. "Know what you are Charlie? You're the politically incorrect detective."

"In that case," he said, jerking the door from her grasp, "I long for the days when women knew their place."

Walleye sat at the head of a long conference table, dirty hands spread open on the varnished walnut. His pinched face seemed even more birdlike than usual as his head wagged side to side, studying the City Council chairman's gavel in gawkish fascination.

"Hello, Walleye," Charlie said. "Feeling better now?"

"Sure. Come about the lady."

"Okay."

"Been to see her again."

"At the funeral home?"

"Sure. They closed her eyes up."

Charlie pushed aside a chair and sat on the table, enough distance between them to prevent Walleye's odor from choking him in the overheated room. "Why'd you want to look at her again, Walleye?"

"To stop dreams."

"Dreams?"

"I dream stuff, sometimes. Sure. I do it. Like TV. Stuff I see."

"She's dead. Nothing to be afraid of. She can't hurt you." He smiled, guessing Walleye must be at least forty-five or fifty by now, with the mind of an eight-year-old. "We all die someday."

"Sure. I know."

"Try not to think about it."

"I thought about snakes," he said, crossing his arms and stuffing his hands into his armpits. "Snakes have babies."

40

"Eggs, Walleye. They lay eggs."

"No. They have babies."

"Eggs." Charlie said this gently, more to teach than correct.

"I seen it before. The babies come out their butts. Ain't no bigger'n angleworms."

"Was there something else you wanted to talk about?"

"Can dead people see?"

"No."

"Her eyes looked at me." Walleye relived his long walk down the ditch, then added, "Before."

"They looked, but they didn't see you."

"Sure," Walleye said. "They didn't see me."

"No."

"They saw him."

"Him?"

"That man what done it."

When Walleye walked out he still had his hands stuck in his armpits. Charlie followed him to the door before shoving Marlene's wilted jade plant aside and draping himself across the top of her filing cabinet.

After a while he asked, "Ever hear of snakes giving live birth?"

Marlene clicked the save icon and drew back from the blue and gray screen. "Snakes lay eggs, Charlie." She tossed her thick glasses on the desk beside the keyboard. "They lay eggs."

The policeman nodded thoughtfully and examined his large, smooth hands. "Call up the library and see if there are any snakes that give live birth," he said, shoving his hands in his pockets and ambling toward his office.

Marlene stared at the telephone and wondered what went through his head, if anything.

Chapter Six

JOGGLING ALONG THE WASHBOARD gravel toward Willow River, the RAM insignia on the side of Dutch's pickup snapped a pin, causing it to dangle by the R. It caught his eye and he fought an urge to stop and fix it. Just the kind of dumb mistake he'd been making all morning, like going to town.

He'd left Jean a note wedged between the salt and pepper shakers—the whole story in a paragraph on the back of an envelope.

Nimrod sat on the seat beside him, head up, tongue bouncing in the corner of his mouth, tail charged by each word he uttered. "Worst of all," he explained to the dog, "running is really going to make me look guilty, but who'd believe I strangled her by accident?" The tail thumped dust from the front seat.

Road grime framed the windshield outside the wiper paths. Gazing beyond at the twisting road, Dutch couldn't remember it ever taking so long. "Suppose hate itself is a form of murder," he confessed. "Maybe it doesn't matter what you do, just what you think." He glanced at his companion. "Sound right?"

Anyway, he'd probably squandered any chance of escape. Dawdling in the rain, two hours flinging essential equipment into the pickup, and now, risking a stop at the Meat Market for food. Worst of all, he didn't know anything. Why hadn't he listened to the news? Had they found her?

"My picture's probably hanging in the Post Office and Charlie's sworn in a posse," he muttered. "Guys like Sam Lynstrom loading their .12-gauges with slugs."

Dutch couldn't remember the last time he'd seen clouds hanging this low and moving so fast across the land. "What if we're driving right into a trap?"

He'd done nothing to cover up and now his escape plans seemed puny and sure to fail. No one in Willow River ever heard of Vicky (Johnson) Murdock, but him. Wouldn't take long to figure that out. Maybe they'd sweat Jean. He'd confessed Vicky to her long ago. And Vicky's ex-husband, Carroll, knew everything. How many people had Vicky told? Every cop in Minnesota had his license number by now.

Dutch tightened his grip on the steering wheel, herding the old Dodge along. Wind whipped the dead grass and bare brush along the road.

The dog leaned over and licked his ear. "Stop it! Have you got any idea how many mistakes I've made? Didn't show up for work. Forgot to call somebody in for me. Left a body lying around where any idiot can find it. Murder's definitely not a career move for me, Pup."

He lifted his foot from the gas and eased the gearshift lever into second. The truck coasted toward a stop sign for the state highway. Traffic was light. He sat on a gentle rise overlooking Main Street and Market where Charlie Benson had his office. The rain had lessened and he switched off the wipers.

A green tractor pulling two wagons halted near a row of grain dryers at the Co-op Elevator. The driver climbed down, peeking under one of the canvas covers to see if his load was dry. Across the street at the Cenex station a woman pumped gas into her Toyota and further along Main Street shoppers hurried in and out.

"Looks peaceful enough," he told Nimrod.

The dog took a long juicy swipe at his face. "Maybe, as they say, it's too quiet." He eased the clutch. The Dodge crossed Highway 11 and entered the town.

* * *

Standing in the alley behind the Meat Market, Murdock didn't see Dutch slip into town. Might not have known him if he had, since they'd never met. Vicky brandished a photograph once when they had a fight. He tore it up. Hidden behind a pyramid of brown barrels near the rear door, he wasn't worried. This was the place Dutch would come, and so he would know him.

He'd nosed around town most of the day, talking casually with storekeepers, old ladies, and Davis the lawyer. Most talked openly, pleased to help Dutch's old Navy pal. He learned a great deal about Dutch, except where he was this minute, but every hunt has its period of waiting. Instinct said the Meat Market was worth an hour or so, then he'd try the Cleland home. By nightfall he'd run Dutch to ground and kill him. Of that, he was certain.

The spoiled child of a Tulsa physician and his permissive wife, Gordon learned early that the more you demand the more you get. Things like money, cars, sex with teachers. People are cowards. A taste of blood and you own 'em. Cleland too. Easy as pie.

He hawked and spit against the building. Do the guy quickly, but not too quickly, leave time enough for him to empty his bowels. Like dope, fear sharpens the senses. Cleland must die focused on his pain.

Tired of waiting, he squinted at the writing on the surrounding barrels: Lutefisk. Product of Norway. Smelled like some sort of rotten fish. Fitting place to deposit the remains.

The cold drizzle tightened the skin across his cheekbones, greasing his face to a faint glow and lending him an almost skull-like appearance. Longing lit his eyes as his mind wandered to Vicky when he first saw her five years before at a

Minneapolis hotel where he'd just scored a twenty-grand deal. She leaned across from her table and said wasn't it odd they were the only guests eating in the restaurant, and the food wasn't even bad. Later, upstairs, he tore off her clothes and she howled with delight. They were so alike, placid on the surface and turbulent beneath. In her it was all the more exciting because she maintained such a passive facade. Once she told him that each day of her life began the same, with no expectations, so whatever happened was a treat. He'd been her after dinner treat.

When she skipped after he'd disciplined her on Friday, he knew instantly where she'd gone. The butcher she used to brag about. What did she think? He'd let her just leave?

Murdock ran both hands through his thin hair. They came away wet and he wiped them on his pants. Sucker play sitting here any longer. Bastard could be miles away, running from the cops, as he would've done. He stood, straightening his legs, stretching out the cramps.

A crunching noise. Murdock ducked.

Dutch had his eyes on the gas gauge—one more thing he'd forgotten—as he brought the truck in from the alley, parking near the lutefisk barrels.

"Stay here, Nimrod," he said, jumping down. "I'm not riding two-hundred miles with a wet dog."

Water rattled from a rainspout. Dutch bent his head forward as he walked, flipping through his keys for the one to unlock the back door.

A soft noise in the gravel. The louder sound of water rushing in his ears.

Pain detonated at the front of his skull, surging backward, exploding down his spine. Something jammed his head to one side twisting it in a relentless ratchet, cranking until he heard popping inside his neck. Blind with pain, he felt his eyes swelling. The ratchet tightening, tightening. A sound of cracking vertebra. He wanted to cry out but his throat was a knot. There was an oily smell like sweat masked by cheap cologne. It flashed through his mind that what he'd failed to do with a handgun was now being accomplished by the fist of God. Struck down by some apoplectic seizure or maybe a brain aneurysm.

The keys slipped from his grasp as a black lake of pain drowned him, filling his ears, deafening him into submission. He felt himself ease into it, giving himself up to the endless embrace.

"Goodbye, butcher boy." A voice whispered so close he felt the damp lips touch his ear.

The words sent a jolt through his pain. If the voice had remained still, he might have died without ever knowing what happened to him. But the voice gave him courage. It belonged to a man not a disease, and a man could be beat. Red spots pulsed before his eyes and he tasted vomit at the back of his throat. There wasn't much time.

To stop his neck from breaking, Dutch drove his chin into his collarbone, locking bone against bone. The ratchet held tight but stopped turning. His hands came up and found the man's forearm. Clawed at it. Digging out chunks of flesh. His nails ripped. The man cursed him but there was no loss of strength or lessening of pain.

Driven by adrenaline, Dutch reached higher. He wanted the man's head. To drive his fingers into the eye sockets, find the root of his brain and rip it from his skull. The man's head was too far down. He clawed only wet hair, slick, hard to grasp. Painstakingly, he wound strands of it around his fingers until his fist was full. Using his own head for leverage, Dutch brought his arm up and forward, uprooting a fistful. The man screamed and staggered, slamming Dutch into the concrete building, grinding his face against the rough edges of the block, peeling skin from his cheekbone and using the wall to force his head around even further.

The salty taste of blood. He was going to die.

Both arms were pinned flat against the wall, his right leg, bent at an odd angle, trapped by something hard, cold. The barrel where he saved large trimming bones to bring home for Nimrod. He gasped for breath and thought about the bones, stripped clean of their meat, long and hard from the legs of steers. Squeezing his arm along the man's pelvis, he reached into the barrel though the monster still pinned his upper body tightly to the wall.

He groped for a bone, finally grasping a heavy femur. He couldn't swing it up where it would do the most damage. Only the man's legs were within range. He swung hard at a knee, arching his back as he did so to throw the man off balance.

The first swing caught him a glancing blow on the kneecap, enough to dislodge it. The ratchet man howled, realizing he couldn't protect himself with both arms locked onto Dutch's head. He loosened his grip to reach down and take the bone from Dutch's hand. The instant he felt the man's arm move, Dutch dropped to the ground and struck again, this time catching him at the ankles, toppling him backward, head slamming against the pickup's bumper. Struggling to his feet, Dutch gripped the bone with both hands and swung with his full body weight, aiming for the man's face.

The femur connected, bone on bone, shattering his jaw and skidding him headfirst along the bumper, limp body towed behind. He didn't get up.

Still holding the bone, Dutch stood over the man a very long time. It wasn't until Nimrod's incessant barking roused him that he let the bone slip from his fingers and staggered to the truck. He flung open the driver's side door. Nimrod bolted past and ran to where the man lay sprawled in the mud. Pawing his shoulder and biting his coat, the dog growled and shook the limp form.

"Who the hell is he?" Dutch pressed a hand gingerly to his face. It came away bloody.

Slowly, he shook his head. His brain seemed to slosh around inside. Jets of pain shot down his back, neck, right arm, and his face felt wire-brushed. His breathing was wheezy. Nimrod glanced up from the body and whimpered, then ran to Dutch and nuzzled his hand.

"Let's get out of the weather," he said. But the dog turned and looked at the limp form. "You're right. Can't leave him lying around." Dutch picked up the man's ankles and dragged him toward a lutefisk barrel. Lifting under the arms, he draped the corpse over the rim and upended him face first. Nimrod trotted off toward the back door, ears perked. Dutch followed.

Inside, Dutch moved as quickly as his unsteady legs would allow. First to the walk-in cooler where he packed frozen meats, cheese, and summer sausage into a cardboard box. Selecting two larger boxes he ran to the front of the store and loaded canned goods, candy bars, chips, sodas, fresh bread, potatoes, anything that caught his eye. In his haste, he fumbled several of the cans, and when they rolled across the floor he noticed the labels streaked with blood. The nightshades were drawn over the display windows and no one could see him running up and down the aisles, a mad shopper.

His pain deepened as he expended precious energy struggling with the food boxes. He staggered outside, dragging the last one along the wet gravel. Cans bounced into the mud.

The rain revived him slightly. Now, he thought, there's another reason to disappear. "Two people in less than twenty-four hours. I'm a goddamned serial killer," he laughed at his own madness. Two tours in Vietnam and never fired a shot in anger, now he'd taken to murdering people left and right in his hometown. He felt giddy. Of course, if he kept dumping bodies around someone was bound to get suspicious.

He reached into the mud to retrieve a can and his hand quivered as he read the label—sauerkraut.

He hated sauerkraut.

Chapter Seven

PINK PUFFS WRAPPED TIGHTLY around his finger, he carefully polished the brass nameplate tracing each letter in Carroll Monroe Johnson and, centering his ineffable name on his desk, sank back into a leather chair sweating like a common laborer.

All afternoon he'd been unable to shake the feeling something had gone wrong. He ate Tums and stewed. At three he caught a radio report of murder in Willow River. The nude body of an unidentified woman discovered in a wooded area outside town. Vicky, of course.

The radio said police had several leads. He might be one of them. Ex-husbands made good suspects, especially if no one in Willow River knew about Vicky and Dutch, and chances were they didn't. Vicky could be very discreet and Dutch would hardly brag it around.

He lacked an alibi, though his motive was weak this long after their divorce. They shouldn't be too suspicious. He'd smoked a little pot in college, what if there was a record?

Carroll Monroe Johnson got paid to make decisions. He wadded the used tissue into a tight ball, flipped it at the wastebasket, reached for the phone and punched the button for an outside line, bypassing his secretary. Information gave him the number.

At the dispatcher's desk, Marlene logged each call. Carroll Johnson's was number fifty-two. There'd been nothing like this in Willow River since the Co-op grain elevator fire in '61, but she'd already learned to tell cranks from legitimate callers.

She cupped her hand over the mouthpiece and shouted through the open door into Charlie's office. "I think you better take this one, Charlie!"

He glared at her through the door. She shrugged and he snatched the receiver from its hook. "Benson."

"Are you a policeman?" the voice said. Charlie rolled his eyes at Marlene.

"This is the Willow River Police Department," he said. "Who's speaking?"

"Carroll Johnson." It sounded like an apology.

"From?"

"Minneapolis." The voice hesitated. "I'm an executive with Central Data."

"Uh-huh."

"I'm calling about the death there," Carroll's voiced faltered. "Can you tell me what the woman looked like?"

"This is an ongoing police investigation." Charlie spoke in an official tone. "We can't release that information. Why don't you tell me why you called."

"My ex-wife is missing."

"Yes."

"I mean, I can't find her. We were supposed to have lunch today. She didn't show up."

"So you assume she's dead?"

"I don't know. That's why I called you."

Charlie sighed. "Okay. Give me a description."

"Tall. Natural blonde. Blue eyes. Thirty-seven years old. Quite good looking. Always neatly dressed. Polite."

"Just stick to the physical description. It's hard to tell if a corpse was polite."

"Oh," Carroll said. "Well, that's about it."

"Thank you, Mr. Johnson. Give me your number. We'll keep an eye out for her." Charlie was ready to hang up.

"She might have gone to Willow River," Carroll added.

"Oh?" His interest revived. "Why do you say that?"

"She knew a guy there."

"Who?"

"Dutch Cleland."

"Hold the line a minute." Charlie punched the hold button and shouted to Marlene in the outer office. "Pick up on this call and take notes." He reconnected. "Let's try a little something here, Mr. Johnson, just to make sure this isn't your ex-wife."

"Okay."

"Describe her hands and feet for me."

"Sure, if that's what you want." It seemed an odd request. "She kept them neat. Probably painted. Well manicured. Thin fingers. I always kind of liked her feet. Most people have unattractive feet but she used lotion. Kept everything soft."

"One more thing," Charlie paused. "How long were you married?"

"Seven years."

"As a husband you naturally knew certain things, physical things, that wouldn't be common knowledge, if you get what I mean?"

"Sure. But she didn't have any birthmarks or tattoos or anything." He paused. "There was a mole, though. Under her left breast. Fairly large."

Charlie hadn't forgotten the mole under that limp, sagging breast. "We'll check that out," he said in a noncommittal tone. "Tell me more about your wife's relationship with Dutch Cleland. What's her name, by the way?"

"Vicky. Victoria. Victoria Murdock, it is now," Carroll said. "She had an affair with this Dutch guy. I only met him once. It broke us up. She lives in Tulsa now."

"And you think she came back here to see Dutch?"

"I don't know. She called. Said she was going to be in town here and wanted to do lunch but she never showed. We

52

had a friendly divorce. I get a nice Christmas card every year."

"When did she call?"

"Saturday."

"From?"

"Tulsa, I guess."

"You've been very helpful, Mr. Johnson," Charlie said sincerely, "What I need now is a little contact information from you. Give it to my assistant. Later, we'll need to talk again. In person. Maybe tonight. Tomorrow, for sure."

"You want me to come up there?"

"I know it's a long drive, but I'm going to ask you to view the remains. We need positive identification."

The meeting was set for nine-thirty. Charlie put down the phone and drew up a legal pad, writing in bold, rapid strokes.

When he looked up a few moments later, Marlene was standing in the doorway. "This one wasn't another crank, was he?" Marlene said.

"Nope."

"Something solid?"

"Don't know yet." Charlie stood. "Check on this guy Johnson. Be discreet. Don't tell anyone it's part of the investigation." He strode to a small closet and dragged his blue jacket from its hanger but left his revolver in the cupboard. "I'm going out for a while."

Marlene followed him to the door, watching as he left the building and turned the corner to Main Street. Unlike most policemen, Charlie seldom carried a gun. Marlene had been with him a long time and wished he'd broken precedent this time. Every instinct told her their troubles were just beginning.

Charlie headed directly for Dutch Cleland's Meat Market. Rain slowed to an annoying spritz and anemic sunshine filtered through fast-moving clouds in the western sky. Seemed

53

to be warming up again. Charlie let his jacket hang open as he walked purposefully along the sidewalk, nodding absently to passers-by.

A connection between Vicky Murdock and Dutch Cleland gave Charlie all the circumstantial evidence he needed to question Dutch. Lots of ground to be covered before he could make an arrest, or even an accusation, but ideas exploded in Charlie's mind. One in particular—Dutch Cleland was guilty of murder.

The Meat Market, sandwiched between other two-story frame buildings on Main Street, had been recently remodeled into something Charlie thought common to chic, urban side streets. A stylish little shop with green awnings and recessed lighting. Not a place to get your money's worth. Charlie bought his meat at Lund's.

Seeing shaded windows at the front of Dutch's shop, Charlie swung into a narrow passageway between the Meat Market and a laundromat next door. It led to the alley behind and was just large enough for most men to move through at a brisk walk. Charlie wedged himself sideways, scraping his belt buckle on the wet brick. Reaching down to make sure the two-way radio was still in its holster, he turned his attention to the back door and found it locked.

The empty building and missing owner fueled Charlie's suspicions. More keenly than Dutch's neighbors, Charlie understood the human enigma—nice guys often do mean things. He'd spent thirty-five years peeking at people's lives and knew they aren't basically good or evil, they're basically both. But knowing their secrets left him alone with a maiden aunt and no close friends.

He toyed with the idea of using his flashlight to smash the lock and slip in for a peek but restrained himself. Just the kind of mistake Sheriff Mattson expected of him, breaking and entering, so he poked around outside instead. Nothing unusual except a smudged can of sauerkraut.

Searching for something to stand on to reach a window, he rolled a heavy wooden barrel against the wall, hiked his trousers and lifted one foot. Then froze.

The concrete wall was smeared with blood. Charlie dabbed it with his index finger. Tacky. Hardly unusual, blood outside a butcher shop, but fresh, when the place was closed? He carefully collected a sample, then climbed onto the barrel. Catching the high windowsill with both hands, he raised himself and peered inside.

It occurred to him that from inside his head presented a perfect target, silhouetted against the light. Happy thought, he chuckled. But would Dutch shoot him? They'd grown up together, after all. The kind of question you got answered when you least expected.

A heavy thud sounded behind him. Charlie spun, groping for the pistol he'd left in the cupboard. Balanced on an upended barrel, back against the wall, he focused on the noise and saw movement in one of the other barrels. A pair of feet, spread wide apart, pointed at the sky.

Feeling slightly ridiculous, he jumped to the ground, kicking his way through the stacks of barrels. Tipping the one with protruding feet, he pulled a body out by its ankles. A man drowning in his own blood.

Charlie knelt near the man's head, examining him quickly for injuries. Head down in the barrel, blood streamed upward from his facial cuts had filled his nose and eye sockets. Now it slopped over and ran down toward his ears. The man's sticky eyelashes blinked away the excess and he stared up at the policeman with pure hatred. His lower jaw, unhinged by some incredible force, dangled to one side. Only skin prevented it from falling into the mud.

"Take it easy," Charlie said, unable to imagine pain so excruciating. "You'll be okay. I'll get help."

He drew the radio from its holster. "Marlene!" he shouted. "Come in. It's me!"

A long moment of static, then her reassuring voice. "Go ahead."

"I'm in the alley behind the Meat Market. Call 911. Get an ambulance."

"You all right?"

"Fine," Charlie managed. "But I got a guy here with a busted face."

"Copy."

Charlie stared down at the pitiful creature, then removed his jacket and tucked it under the man's neck. "Help's on the way," he said, though he honestly believed it would be too late. "Don't move anything." He suspected a brain-stem injury.

Warily, the man's eyes held him, conscious and aware though the lower half of his face was detached. At last, he reached out and grasped the policeman's arm with surprising strength and drew him close.

"I ithen," he said, thickly.

"Don't talk."

"Lithen," he repeated, struggling to speak without the benefit of a lower jaw. "Duckth," he croaked.

"Sorry," Charlie replied. "Can't understand you."

"Duckth." He peered through Clinton's old, swollen eyes. "Duckth."

Charlie patted the man's arm. "You're going to be just fine," he said.

"Duckth," said the man.

* * *

The paramedics, an obese woman in skin-tight brown double-knit trousers and a gray-haired fellow with a ponytail and diamond nose ring, carted the injured man away to the St. Cloud Hospital for repairs. "Seen worse than that at bar close," the woman told Charlie. "Get just about everything in this job. Eyeballs gouged out hanging half way to their knees, teeth knocked up their noses, heads smashed so the brains

56

run out. We see it all. Car explosions and house fires are the worst."

Charlie cut her short as she launched into vomiting during CPR and all but ran back to the office. He'd borrowed the man's wallet, which wasn't exactly a gold mine of information, but did contain an Oklahoma driver's license and a Visa card. That was enough to find out that Gordon Murdock had a record. Even more illuminating, that record was sealed. Charlie wanted to know why.

And that name—Murdock. Hadn't that bigshot from the Cities just said his ex-wife's name was Murdock?

After three hours on the phone listening intently to Oklahoma bureaucrats explaining in detail why they couldn't be of any help to anyone, Marlene tracked down a detective with the Tulsa P.D. who seemed willing to talk. "Do me a favor, Charlie," she said. "Don't piss him off."

Charlie cleared his throat and lifted the receiver. "Detective Moe?"

"Call me Billy," a drawly voice said. "What's your pleasure?"

"My assistant says you're familiar with a Mr. Gordon Murdock. Just put him in an ambulance with the better part of his head knocked off. Can you shed any light on what he might be doing here?"

Billy Moe chuckled softly at the other end of the line. "No offense, Chief, but I'm just glad he's there and not here. As to what he's up to, well, could be just about anything knowing old Gordy like we do."

"We've been able to find out he's got a record, but it's sealed. Can you help me there?"

"Reckon not."

"You can't or you won't?" There was an edge in Charlie's voice that turned Marlene's head and drew a frown.

"You arrested him there . . . what's the name of that place . . . Willow-something?"

57

"No. No arrest," Charlie admitted. "Fight of some kind. Sent him to the hospital. Here in Willow-something, guys from Tulsa don't turn up too often in back alleys with serious injuries."

"No shit?"

"Can't we just talk man to man? All I want to know is what he's doing here. This is a small town. I'm the only full-time cop." Marlene nodded approval at what he thought sounded almost like begging. "Give me a hint what I'm dealing with. That can't be too much to ask whether records are sealed or not."

"What's your number?" Moe asked.

Charlie rattled it off and the Tulsa detective hung up.

Ten minutes later Charlie received a collect call from Billy Moe at a pay phone. He could hear traffic noise in the background.

"Know who you got there, Chief?" Billy asked. "You got yourself the Tulsa Vampire Rapist. That's what the media calls him. His first victim, Louisa Montero, a convenience store clerk—he took his sweet time with her. Afterwards he jammed a needle-nosed pliers into her neck and ripped out her jugular, milked the warm blood into the plastic cup from his Thermos and drank it. Our department's still got a gag order on because of the media, even though its been nearly a decade. Created such a panic we had two deaths when women shot their neighbors.

"Anyway, we eventually got the guy after three more rapes in which miraculously all the victims survived to testify. Old Gordy got life plus ten. Four years later one of those Clinton appointees on the bench commuted the sentence to life in a mental institution. Two years after that a board of psychiatrists with the very best of intentions, pronounced him cured and rehabilitated. I heard he got married. Somewhere he's got money, probably drugs. Beyond that, he lists his profession as "self-employed" and spends most of

his time hunting though he isn't allowed to own a firearm.
His folks are your typical liberal bleeders, you know, and I
heard they send him a generous monthly allowance."

"That's quite a story."

"Only if you don't like happy endings."

"A woman named Murdock was murdered here," Charlie
admitted. "Must be his wife. Which doesn't mean he's not
good for it."

"Have all her blood?" Moe asked bitterly. "Suppose
Gordy'd drain his own wife?"

"Doubt it. Anyway, she's got her blood. No sign of
molestation either. Domestic maybe, or somebody else
entirely."

"Well," Billy Moe said. "How many killers you got there in
Willow-something?"

Charlie hesitate a moment before answering. "You know,
Detective, I'm not really sure."

Chapter Eight

LEN DAVIS HAD ARRIVED AT CASEY'S half drunk but in good voice. Hammering through a raucous rendition of Hank Snow's "I Been Everywhere," Casey followed on the bass guitar and Mavis Faggering sang background soprano, same as in church. A thin crowd on vinyl chairs tapped their feet and smoked.

Len swung into the part about Fargo and Minnesota, letting his voice soar, and they all joined in drowning him out until they lost the words.

Casey recalled how Len wandered in with the guitar ten years before and sang "My Jamaica," a Charlie Pride tune. He'd never had anyone come in and burst into song before. Unnerving. Several regulars got up and left. On his way to throw him out, Casey noticed a table of high school teachers had joined in. Half an hour later he unplugged the jukebox and by the end of the evening Len was a hit.

Tonight he seemed preoccupied and drinking heavily so Casey set the guitar aside. Mavis had to leave and tend to the supper trade at Berkie's. He guided Len to a quiet spot at the bar. "What's up?"

"What'd you mean?"

"When's the last time you were in here on a Monday half in the bag before supper?"

"What happened to bartenders minding their own business?"

60

Casey wasn't offended. "Usually do," he grinned. "But I got an investment in you. You're a gold mine."

Len fumbled for a cigarette and Casey struck a match.

"Someone else gave me a light today," Len mumbled. "Hey! Where's that melon-breasted soprano got to?"

"Back to her griddle." Casey shoved two upside down beer glasses between his fingers, flipped them over and drew a draft into each. "Who gave you a light?"

"Oklahoma guy in Berkie's. Some creep looking for Dutch."

"What'd he want?"

Len sipped his foam. "Threatened me, the puke." Raising his glass, "Here's to liquid courage. Screw you, Mr. Murdick!"

"Tell Dutch?"

"Not yet."

Casey downed his beer in one gulp. "Still friends ain't ya?"

"Never got past the martinis after work, I guess. Anyway, couldn't find him."

"Probably home."

"Called there. No answer."

"Mrs. Cleland gone too?" A faraway look settled in Casey's eyes. "Hard to imagine a piece like her a school teacher. If they'd had that stuff around when I was in high school I might've graduated."

"Even for a bartender you're pretty rude," Len said coolly.

"Lighten up. Didn't say I wanted to jump her bones."

"Glad to hear it." Len jammed the half-smoked cigarette into an ashtray. "Jean Cleland's a very special friend of mine."

"Sure. I know." Casey said. "I only think she's nice to look at, that's all." He quickly changed the subject. "What did this western guy want, anyway?"

"Said he was Dutch's Navy buddy. I wasn't buying."

61

"Bet Dutch is getting sued." Casey nodded thoughtfully. "Western guy's a subpoena server."

"More like an ex-con."

"This murder's got everybody spooked," Casey frowned. "I'm sick of it. Your coming in tonight lightened the mood. Now they got this new stiff in an ally downtown. Hear that one? Guess somebody ripped his face right off."

Len fell silent awhile. He'd heard the rumor too. "Maybe I should drive out there," he said. "Funny nobody answers the phone."

"Foggy as hell." Casey mulled it over. "Say! Think this stranger could be the killer? Wow! Like the fugitive."

"He had both arms," Len grinned. "Spotted two news satellite trucks setting up across from the drug store by the tracks. Sheriff Lardass and old Charlie been pretty tight-lipped so far but things'll shake loose now with TV crews filming anybody dumb enough to talk to 'em. I've seen it before. This thing's about to go global."

"So maybe your mystery guy's just a crazy come for the show?"

"Maybe. But if he is, he's one cool SOB."

Casey helped himself to another draft. "Better get some more stock in," he chuckled. "Nothing like ghoulish excitement to work up a thirst. Going out there?"

Len placed his empty glass on the bar. "Right now."

He drove carefully through the thick fog toward the Cleland home. On the radio, warnings of a mega-snowstorm sweeping down the Rockies and roaring across the plains toward them. Outside the glass, nothing but clammy fog. Inside, the leather seats felt sticky and Len rejoiced in the familiar indifference alcohol bestowed upon his senses, yearning to close his eyes and float off into the sea of gray.

A short time later he stood at the back door. The booze wearing off; his heart labored and each pulse made his head ache.

The door opened.

Jean, dressed in blue jeans and faded sweatshirt, addressed him matter-of-factly. "I expected someone by now, but not you."

"Dutch around?"

She turned and walked away. She was barefooted and the sight of her slender, bony feet on the harsh tile pained him. He followed her to the kitchen where four loaves of freshly baked bread cooled on a counter near the window. The room was uncomfortably hot. He smelled more bread in the oven.

"Baking bread?" he asked, lamely.

"Six loaves so far, with the two in the oven." She looked drawn and tired. Bits of dough stuck to her thin fingers. Flour streaked the front of her blue sweatshirt. "Want some?"

"Sure."

She handed him a serrated bread knife.

"Hot enough in here to wear shorts," he said, pulling off his heavy sweater and tossing it onto a stool in the corner. "Cut you a slice?"

"No thanks."

"Baking all this for Dutch?"

"He's gone."

Len sawed the coarse bread into thick slices. Using the knife tip, he globbed butter onto a golden end piece. "Where'd he go?"

She shrugged, keeping her back to him.

"Jean?" No answer. "What's wrong?"

"He killed her, you know. That bitch."

He felt a sudden hollowness and set the bread aside. "What's going on?"

"I told you." She was crying now. "He killed her."

"Who?"

"Dutch."

"Killed who?"

"Vicky Johnson. Or whatever her name is now."

A piece fell into place. "Murdock, maybe?"

"Guess so."

"Man named Murdock was looking for Dutch in Berkie's today," Len said. "That's why I came out here. Tell Dutch about it. I didn't like him."

"He's gone. Are you drunk?"

"Who's gone, Murdock?"

"Dutch."

"Jean. This isn't getting us anywhere. Come here and sit down." He took her by the arm and motioned to the table. "Please."

She allowed herself to be led and pushed into a chair, her back to the window. The world outside black. "I'm so tired," she said, making no effort to wipe away the tears.

"Did you work today?" Len questioned gently.

"Left early." She hesitated. "When I heard about it."

"Can you tell me from the beginning?"

"Not much to tell." She straightened in the chair and wiped at the tears with her sleeve. "I knew it had to be Vicky. Maybe woman's intuition. So I came home. They beat him."

"Who?"

"Dutch."

"Dutch was here?"

"He was cleaning himself up. He was hurt, Len. Really hurt. Nearly killed. A man, maybe it was this Murdock, I don't know, attacked Dutch right downtown. Nobody came to help him. I never saw such horrible wounds. They struggled and Dutch said he killed him so I guess he's killed two people now. Vicky and the other one. Last night he said Vicky came back and that's why he was acting so dumb this morning, you know, because he'd killed her by accident and then didn't want me to find out because he decided to commit suicide after I went to school, and I just left, Len. I just left. How could I be so stupid? My husband's planning to blow his head off and I'm just getting ready for school and I was crabby because he said I shouldn't wear my boots or something like that."

"We need a drink." Len left the room, returning a moment later with a bottle of gin and two glasses. He poured them half full.

"What is it?" Jean asked, staring at the clear liquid.

"Martini."

"I hate martinis."

"It's not really a martini. Just drink it."

She made a face, then drank it like water. "I suppose Dutch never told you about Icky Vicky?"

"Never." Len held no illusions. His friend was no saint and had lived a man's life, but cheating on Jean seemed unthinkable.

"Kept his own council, that man." She ran a hand through her chestnut hair. "I'm a mess."

"You're beautiful."

"Liar." She brightened. "Thought you men talked to each other on your fishing trips?"

"We do," Len forced a grin. "Not always about women."

"I bet," she said, voice strengthening. "Why is it I picture you guys leering down some poor waitress' cleavage but too emotionally bound up to confide in each other about the women in your own lives?" She reached for his hand. "How'd I get in this mess?"

"You're in it," he said, crossly, "because Dutch was unfaithful."

She tightened her grip. "Even a sensible guy like Dutch can make a fool of himself." Arching an eyebrow. "In love affairs, Leonard, women have the upper hand."

"I don't care." Len couldn't decide what irritated him more, Jean defending a cheating husband or cutting him out when he was needed most. "You could've told me."

"Agreed," she said, evenly. "But it's my problem. Ours. And I don't love him the way Vicky did. They had passion or sex or something. What I have doesn't happen so often. Loyalty binds you to someone sometimes no matter what. Even betrayal can't break it." She read the skepticism in his eyes. "Sounds almost perverse doesn't it? Well, don't try and understand it."

In an odd way he did and pulled her onto her feet, wrapping his arms around her. Cheek pressing his chest, gradually she relaxed and he kissed her hair very softly but she didn't seem to notice. "Why would he kill her, Jean? It doesn't make sense." He felt her grow more tense.

"It was an accident."

"An accident? They said she was strangled. How does someone get strangled by accident?"

"Same way Len Davis gets drunk." Her voice cool, clipped. "Drink and drink until all of a sudden you're drunk by accident." She pulled away. "Anyway, he's gone."

She'd always disapproved of his drinking and said it cheapened him. He poured the remaining gin into the sink and asked her the important question. "Where'd he go?"

"How should I know?" she said. "Ran away. I made him sandwiches."

"Okay," he said, looking past her out the window at the darkness. Maybe she thought there was no depth to him beyond the bottom of a glass. "I'll find him."

* * *

A red-faced Charlie Benson held the telephone to his ear daintily, only the tips of his solid fingers touching the plastic. "Damn it, Sam! Did you ship the body to St. Cloud for autopsy or not?" He growled.

"How many hearses do I have?" Sam whined.

"Don't talk in riddles!"

"Well, I've got one! Just one."

"So?"

"So it can't be at the Hubbard funeral and in St. Cloud all at the same time!"

"In other words, you've still got Vicky Murdock's body there?"

"I just told you."

"Great! Glad you're not letting our little murder investigation inconvenience you."

"On the contrary. It's inconveniencing the hell out of me!"

"Listen, Sam." He took a deep breath. "I'd like to solve this case but I can't do it without physical evidence. Part of which is an autopsy. We can't have an autopsy until the body gets on the medical examiner's table in St. Cloud. So, right now, this case depends on you."

"Settle down," the mortician said. "Everybody knows Dutch did it!"

"They do?"

"Sure. It was just on the six o'clock news. Phillip Cleland wanted for questioning. Sheriff Mattson said so himself. Whole town's talking about it, and that other stiff Ben Lund found behind the Meat Market. Dutch must've gone nuts, killing all those people."

"First of all, I found the stiff behind the Meat Market. Second, he isn't a stiff. His name is Murdock, and he's doing quite well in the St. Cloud Hospital, which is where I wish his wife's body was, if a certain local undertaker would get the lead out of his ass and move her there!"

"It's after eight. I haven't even had supper."

"Fine, Sam." Charlie's patience ran out. "You sit there. Next time you want a police escort for one of your five-thousand-dollar funerals or beg for a little traffic control or double park that meat wagon of yours on Main Street, I'll remember you haven't eaten supper!"

"You don't have to get vindictive about it." Sam's voice was conciliatory.

"Are you taking her down tonight or not?"

"Calm down. I'll do it," Sam said, "but all I'll get is a sour stomach from one of those freeway drive-throughs!"

Carefully, Charlie held the receiver at a height of several inches above its cradle and dropped it. "Idiot!" he declared, to no one in particular.

Talk of food awakened Charlie's own hunger. He patted his hollow stomach. No chance. Should've been at the Cleland house hours ago.

He found a jacket, put it on and stretched the elastic waistband tight around his middle, holding his breath until the slider caught. The heartbreak of middle age. He snatched his Cenex cap from the desk, reached to turn out the light, then paused and went back to the cupboard above his filing cabinet. Slowly, he opened the oak doors.

Inside, the cupboard smelled of gun oil and leather. The .38, in its dark holster, lay on the second shelf. He hesitated, glad Marlene had gone home and the office was empty. Willow River had seldom seen Charlie Benson packing a gun, but Willow River had changed since morning. He put it on, and it felt good.

Outside, the night air was still and humid after the rain. The street was empty and dark as the sea, lined with well-lit houses that glowed like boats in a marina, doors locked now for the first time ever. Amber fog smoked under the street lamps and he wished for a fresh breeze to blow it off, blow everything clean.

He trudged down the steps listening to the hollow sound of his boots, shouldering the familiar, comfortable obligation he carried alone at night, on watch. Ordinarily now he'd patrol. Check alley doors, shine his spotlight in dark places, drink coffee from his Thermos, do the things a beat cop does. He preferred this to what he really had to do.

Charlie lifted the damp door handle and dropped into the squad's vinyl seat, switching on the high-intensity lamp above a dash-mounted clipboard. The interior smelled of grease from Bagg's. He logged the time—8:32—started the car, and drove slowly along Main Street toward the edge of town, then stomped the accelerator and barreled across the tracks, fog swirling behind.

* * *

Charlie hunched against the wind and tried quietly to fit one of the lost house keys into the Cleland's door, but it jammed. The door opened from the inside. If Jean Cleland was upset by her husband's predicament, Charlie couldn't see it in her face. Nor did she seem surprised to find him on her doorstep. If anything, she looked relieved, which slightly unnerved him. He'd expected shock or tears, but her face was calm, slightly pale beneath a tangle of brown hair, black in the dim light. Her lips moist, unpainted. Black eyes looked deep into his as she waited for him to speak.

Her composure gave the moment a sort of cheap drama that rendered trite anything he might say, and she seemed to understand this and take pity on him. "What took you so long, Charlie?" she asked, something of a smile on her lips. "What were you doing out there?"

"Nothing," He said. "Just fooling around with some keys I found. Don't suppose he's here?"

"Nope." She tugged at his sleeve. "Step inside."

He obeyed. "Where, then?"

"Honestly don't know," she said. "If I did, well . . ."

"You wouldn't tell me." He finished. "Just like the movies. Here's another line: 'It'll go easier with him if I find him first.' You'll have the sheriff out in the morning. Maybe the state cops. Foolish for him to run away and for you to protect him." The tone of his voice, neighborly and low-volumed.

"You're a good man, Charlie Benson." She reached up and touched his cheek. "But I can't help you."

Jean's stubbornness had sharpened her voice and Charlie's questions took a different tack. He'd seen Jean angry. "If you're not going to tell me where he is, then tell me why. Why does a man like Dutch up and kill somebody?"

69

Jean's lips turned a bright smile that never quite made it to her eyes. "Wish I'd had you in class, Charlie. Bet you despised poetry and fidgeted like a pup until the bell rang." The light tone faded. "Life has a poetic order sometimes and once the meter's set it stays consistent to the end. No surprises." She rubbed her eyes with both hands. "Dutch is that way—focused, consistent. Basically good. Man like that doesn't forgive himself easily. He couldn't have meant to kill her, but I suppose you don't care about that." Her voice trailed off.

"They had a love affair?" he asked. For some reason, probably because he knew them both so well, this hadn't occurred to him.

"Go home now, Charlie."

She looked through him, out into the fog, suddenly drunk with fatigue. "I'll leave," he said, smelling gin. "But I'll be back. Are you in class tomorrow?"

"Personal leave," she said, absently. Then perked up. "Don't worry. I won't leave town."

"Thanks," he said. "You're not my idea of a fun arrest."

"Charlie?" Tears filled her eyes. "Don't hurt him."

He stared at his shoes. "That's up to him."

Chapter Nine

NOT LONG AFTER CHARLIE ROARED out of town and disappeared into the heavy fog, Walleye pushed his tricycle onto Main Street. It was the only vehicle there except for Sam Lynstrom's hearse backed to the curb near the door of his funeral home. The street was wet and black and absorbent. The sidewalks were empty and the shops closed.

Walleye shivered. He usually stayed home after dark, pulled down the shades in the little house from mother, and waited for the light to return. But tonight he had no choice.

Certain things belonged to him by right. Things fast people left in ditches and alleyways and sometimes you had to fight for them. Last summer he fought the Boy Scouts. The new scoutmaster led his troop along ditches to find bottles and earn deposit money. Walleye defied them and they laughed. But Charlie Benson didn't laugh, and Charlie Benson talked to the scoutmaster. Things in ditches were his.

Walleye slipped the tattered piece of hemp around the center post of his tricycle just below the seat and tied it tight. The rope was at least ten feet long. Plenty for what he needed.

Sam Lynstrom's front door creaked as it opened, noise strengthened by the fog. A cart came out bearing the lady in a long black sack, with Sam behind, bent over, pushing. He jerked to a stop under the dark red canopy and swung wide the hearse's back door. Walleye kept very still, hidden in shadow under the hardware store awning. He remained motionless until Sam deposited his cargo, slammed the door and trudged back inside.

Walleye pushed the tricycle ahead, praying Sam wouldn't come out until he'd gone. The wheels were well greased. The bearings re-packed. It barely made a noise.

The dense air chilled Walleye's skin, drawing out the heat, but he knew it was being wrong that made him cold. Of all the things mother taught, first was Hands Off! She wasn't here now to ask about the lady. He'd found her. She'd looked at him first and her eyes asked why was she dead? This was not Hands Off! It was not.

The hearse's rear door was unlocked and opened easily. Using both hands Walleye pulled on the collapsed cart. It didn't move. Lavish curtains shrouded the windows and the dark air smelled mediciny. Feeling carefully along the cart's aluminum frame, Walleye found straps, like seat belts holding the cart in place. He loosened the buckles.

Walleye glanced toward the funeral home door. There was light inside. Voices. He pulled hard and the cart slid from the back of the hearse, legs springing down automatically as it emerged. He backed the tricycle around and tied the rope to the cart's aluminum frame. It stood higher than he'd imagined and his rope was barely long enough. She'd ride directly behind him.

A woman's scolding voice carried out into the night. Sam's wife. Walleye knew her. A big-boned woman with long feet and a sharp tongue. "I'll call Charlie Benson myself," she threatened. "I will! All the way to St. Cloud on a night like this? He must be crazy. You're no better."

"Fog'll thin out once I'm on the freeway."

"Vida Urbonis said on the TV that we're in for a real old fashioned blizzard. Killer storm out west aimed right for us."

"Too early in the year," he said. "Anyway, I'll be back before midnight."

"I'm calling right now!"

"No you're not."

"Oh, yes I am."

"I'm leaving."

Walleye heard footsteps on the wooden stair inside. He fumbled with the knot around the cart frame. There wasn't enough slack in the short rope to tie it properly.

"You get back here, Sam!"

The door squeaked.

"Sam Lynstrom!"

"Hush, for crying out loud. The whole town can hear you."

More footsteps.

"Fine. Go. See if I care."

"Please Lois. I've been busting my butt all day on Hubbard. Another one tomorrow afternoon. Just let me get on with it so I can get back and get some sleep."

"Fine! Kill yourself."

Walleye left the knot half tied, mounted the tricycle and pedaled away into the thick safety of the fog, legs straining against the load.

Over his shoulder he saw Sam's round head bowed at the ground as he walked around the hearse to the driver's side. He didn't look in the back. Behind the tricycle, the cart swayed dangerously with each rotation of the pedals. Walleye knew once he made the corner by the bank Sam couldn't see him in the fog, but he'd have to stop there and fix the knot.

At the corner Walleye veered sharply left. Unlike tricycle wheels, cart wheels swivel 360-degrees. The sudden change in direction caused the top-heavy cart to jerk, then lean. The slick plastic body bag and its contents sailed into the night. A thud, followed by a loud clattering as the cart, free of its load, turned over, dragging the tricycle to a halt. The noises echoed and died. Walleye held his breath. No one shouted. No one came.

Kneeling beside the bag, he fumbled in the dark for the zipper to see if she'd broken. It was underneath. He rolled her gently and unzipped the bag no more than necessary.

The face appeared more serene than it had this morning in the wet woods. Eyes and mouth closed now, almost artificially. She seemed kind of fake. Sam's work, he imagined. She was a pretty lady, but her skin was hard when he touched it, like wood.

Walleye was skinny. Too skinny to lift the lady alone. He lined the cart up alongside her and lifted just her top half, planning to ease the rest of her onto the cart after the top half was secure, but the cart rolled out from under and skidded against the curb. The body flopped back onto the street. More clattering.

The Willow River State Bank had recently installed the city's first Automatic Teller Machine. The device was chest high and stable. It gave Walleye an idea.

Just then Casey Andersen sped down Market Street in his Mercury Cougar. He had his mother in the car. Mondays he left the bar awhile and took her to Kensington for meat loaf. By eight o'clock he liked to be back sipping a draft to wash down her whining. She suffered from arthritis and phlebitis and her friends suffered from every ghastly disease known. After a couple hours of their sores and sorrows even meat loaf seemed inspirational. He hurried now to drop her off. Seven whole days before he had to pick her up again.

Casey didn't see Walleye at first, but Mother did.

"Look there," she squeaked. "Ain't it Walleye Wertz?"

Walleye struggled to lift a plastic bundle larger than himself onto the new ATM. Alongside, a cart of some sort trembled and clattered under its load. "What's he got there?" Casey strained to see through the fog. "Bag of bones?"

"Cans," Mother explained. "Don't suppose he has a cash card, do you?"

"Course not. He's an idiot."

"Read where this old bag lady in New York City died and left five million dollars to her cats," Mother said in a sharp tone.

Casey didn't answer. She ought to look in the mirror if she wanted to see a bag lady.

Moving fast, they left Walleye behind in a swirl of fog.

The ATM's narrow table was sturdy but not wide or long enough to support a body. Walleye hooked the gurney with his foot while balancing Vicky Murdock's corpse on the ATM table with both hands, back and leg muscles stretched thin, breath sucking through clenched teeth.

The black bag was slick and icy cold. Slowly, the gurney edged under her feet and legs, then finally supported her full weight. Walleye sat down on the curb to rest. His house was only three blocks from downtown. He'd make that easily if he tied her good this time and went slow.

She belonged to him and he knew what they were planning to do with her because they'd done it once before. They done it to his mother. Dressed her up pretty in a dress she never wore and sang and prayed and dug a hole and put her inside it. He came back the next morning to take her out but Charlie Benson said it was the law you couldn't dig. Sometimes Charlie Benson wasn't your friend.

Walleye knew something no one else knew. When anything is lost the one who loses it comes looking. The man who killed the lady would come looking too. Then he'd know him and tell Charlie Benson his name. Everybody would know his name.

Chapter Ten

WIND HISSED AT THE WINDOWS and Dutch hunched over the wheel as the old Dodge clattered through the predawn darkness three hours north of Willow River. Soft green instrument glow highlighted the pain in his face, and Pete Fountain played a mournful Dixieland tune appreciated mostly by the dog.

Dutch's head seemed weighted with fluid after the beating. When he moved it sloshed. The ratchet still gripped his neck and he feared muscles and ligaments had been forced so beyond normal elasticity they'd loosened from the bone, the head itself dislodged from its roots. Thankfully, none of his teeth were loose and now each mile he drove brought him closer to safety, good eye working tirelessly to keep them on the road. Long term, he feared his brain might've swollen and they'd eventually drill a hole in his skull to relieve the pressure.

He gripped the wheel and steadied himself, unable to relax since a pair of headlights appeared behind and kept pace for miles before turning off. Now the pavement was empty, the night unseasonably warm and humid. He worried the painkillers were wearing off.

After the fight his bleeding demanded a return home. Jean surprised him there in the bathroom picking bits of concrete from his cheek with a tweezers.

"My God!" Her face was ashen. "What happened?"

"Didn't expect you home so early," he said. "Left a note."

"I read it." She moved closer, placing a cool hand on his forehead, brushing the damp hair away. "Radio in the teacher's lounge described her and even in that silly officious way police spokespersons have of sounding scientific, I knew it was that woman, Vicky. And if it was her, then it was you so I came home."

"We should have a lot to say to each other." He looked at her in the mirror. "I should have a lot to say to you."

But for some time, neither of them spoke. Finally, he said, "I should say I'm sorry."

"We're beyond sorry."

"I know." He stared down at the sink, saw his blood, pink where it mixed with drops of water. "After you left this morning I went in the basement and got my .45. Imagine anyone less likely to kill himself than me?"

"No," she said, barely breathing.

"You saved me," he said, "Couldn't leave you a mess in the basement, then pretty soon I couldn't leave a mess at all."

Wary, she thought of what she'd taught her students an hour ago. Mary Hemingway driving from Minnesota to Idaho, watchful, worried, trying to judge the depth of her husband's mental illness and then finally to arrive home in good spirits only to be awakened early the next morning by the echoing blast of a shotgun.

"I won't try it again," he said with conviction. "Anyway, I'm like some dazed tornado victim, stopping every few seconds to wonder if it's really happening."

She nodded, watchful. "Right now you better tell me about this." Her fingers hovered near his mangled cheek.

"Some guy jumped me behind the Meat Market." He washed blood down the drain. "Nearly killed me."

"Why? Some kind of mugging? What?"

"In Willow River? No," he said. "Somebody's after me for Vicky."

"What happened to him?"

"Hit him with a bone." A hapless shrug. "Femur from Mrs. Swedberg's cow, I think."

"You're such a damn fool," she said, pressing a cheek against his upper arm. "Did he get away?"

"Nope," he said, turning to inhale the light fragrance of her hair. "I killed him."

"Dear God!" She drew back. "Who was he?"

"Don't know," he said. "It's crazy."

"What now?"

"I'm getting out, soon as I clean up." He touched his fingers to his tender cheek, steadily freshening with new blood. "Things are happening too fast. I need time to think."

"Time to think," she repeated.

He watched her in the mirror. "There's something else."

"What?"

"Not sure I can put it into words." He glanced away. "Sounds conceited." He stared back at his reflection. "This can't really be the face of a murderer, can it?"

She opened an oak cupboard and took down a plastic container crammed with first aid supplies. "Looks like the face of death right now. Let me get the bleeding stopped."

"I'm trying to tell you something."

She didn't want to hear it. "Did you kill her?" She reached around him to dampen the corner of a towel with fresh tap water.

"It was an accident," he said, allowing her to dab at his torn cheek. "Kind of."

"Explain that."

"Don't you believe it was an accident?"

"I don't know what I believe. Sometimes with us it's like forever, sometimes not. There's still some dirt in here. This is going to hurt." She brushed it out with the corner of the towel, not too gently. "Hold still!"

"Ouch! I am." He pushed her hand away.

"Don't you understand? It was a long time ago but it still hurts." Tears welled in her eyes. "You loved her. You did things with her. Lied to me. I didn't think you could do that. Now you kill somebody, well, it isn't such a stretch anymore. One deceit leads to the next and the next." She choked on the words. "People can lie to themselves and justify anything. After a while they aren't themselves anymore." Composing herself, she cut white tape into strips.

Awhile later she continued. "In the sixties I went anti-war. First we talked, then demonstrated, then unlawfully assembled. Less than a year later we did a burglary and burned some draft records. All in the name of politics or ideals or whatever, but it was really just junk. You screw up and can't admit it, so you build some wall of cheap principle to hide behind. I always knew I was wrong, I guess. Once I admitted it, I got on with my life."

He thought this over. "I didn't know that about the draft records," he said. "You never told me."

"I don't tell you everything," she responded. "Anyway, it's not the kind of confession a veteran should hear. Now I think those things we did muddied the water and prolonged the war. Got more people killed."

"You can't know that."

"I feel it," she said. "Don't you feel sad about Vicky?" The name fell hard from her lips.

"Yes," he said. "But there isn't as much guilt as there should be."

"Putting a gun to your head isn't a sign of guilt?"

"Insanity."

"Well, let's not have any more of it, okay?" Holding his chin, she guided his face close to her's for a final inspection in the light, then fitted a gauze bandage over the large abrasion on his cheek. "There," she said, taping the edges while he held it.

"Your hands are trembling," he said.

79

"I'm scared."

"Me too."

"Dutch. There's only one thing to do now. Call Charlie and tell him what happened."

"Is that what you did after the draft card thing?"

"No," she said quietly. "No guts."

"Me neither."

"But if it was an accident?"

Outside in the drizzle Nimrod howled. A high, piercing cry that sounded more like a wolf.

"I've got to get the hell out of here," Dutch said.

"I'm going with you."

"No." He brushed past her and limped down the hall.

"You still don't understand." She pursued him. "The real hurt came years ago when you told me about Vicky. I hated you." She caught his arm and spun him around. "Not so much for sleeping with her as for tricking me, making a fool of me so you could have your little adventure or whatever. I knew then you were an idiot, but I still loved you and there's no help for it. Now you're not leaving me again."

"Funny as it may sound, I don't think I ever understood the difference between love and sex," he said, brushing her tears aside with a finger. "I don't think half the country understands it, but this isn't draft card burning in the '60s, it's murder."

"We'll get Len. He's good."

"He's a tax attorney."

"He'll find somebody."

"And then what? It all goes public? We have a big trial? Can you imagine trying to teach after that? Don't be stupid," he said, growing cross. "If I was a drug-crazed lunatic they'd stick me in Stillwater for a half dozen years so I could be rehabilitated. But I'm not. I'm the worst thing you can be—a middle class white man who cheated on his wife and killed his girlfriend. I'd get a female judge and life plus ninety-nine years."

"You're not thinking," she said. "It's not like you to run from things."

"It's not like me to kill people either." He broke her grip but took a more reasonable tone. "I need time to think."

"How much time?"

"I don't know," he said. "A few days."

"What about me?"

"Stay here."

"To face the music?"

"They won't catch on for a while."

"Why can't we think someplace together?"

"No," he said, holding her tightly.

"I didn't leave when you cheated on me," she said stubbornly. "You think I'm going to dump you now? I'm going with!" She tore at his shirt.

Jean disliked compromise. Her heels were dug in now and he didn't have time to argue. "There might be a way," he lied, edging the leather vest from her shoulders. "Let's talk later. I need to hold you close as I can get," he said, deftly unbuttoning the soft blouse.

"That old trick," she protested, leaning back so he could kiss her neck. "There's no time."

"There's always time." He lifted her into his arms and carried her to bed, touching off the tension between them until it burned itself out.

Later, when she fell asleep, he slipped away, leaving her snug in the bed they'd shared so long.

Several miles beyond Nashwauk, the road straightened to a ribbon of rough pavement, stretching between scrubby jack pines, tamaracks, and aspen. Dutch settled back, easing the stiffness in his neck and shoulders. Thirty more miles. Maybe thirty-five. The odds steadily improving.

At first, it seemed a distant sound. Then the steering wheel jerked and pulled from his grip, nearly causing him to lose control. He jumped on the brake.

Nimrod, dozing on the seat, bounced up, whining. "Shut up," he scolded the dog. "It's only a flat tire."

He coaxed the truck forward several hundred yards to a grassy approach where the ground seemed firm, left Nimrod inside and jumped out. He removed the base, jack, and lug wrench from their brackets under the hood and set about changing the tire.

He couldn't risk showing a light and worked slowly in the dark. A trail of low clouds swung across the night sky, remnants of the rain. The air was heavy and oppressive, and the ground where he knelt soaked his knee. He listened a moment, rocking back on his heels to ease the cramps in his legs.

In the ditch behind him, brackish swamp water gurgled under a thin coating of melting ice. He was close to the Major Drainage Divide, where water begins flowing northward to Hudson Bay. The spare was buried under his supplies and he had to unload nearly everything to get at it, but no one came and thirty minutes later he was safely back on the road. The exertion had stretched his sore muscles to the limit but he felt a slight lessening in the stiffness.

He reached the cabin shortly after four in the morning, snaking the Dodge through meadow grass grown tall during summers of neglect. A small spruce had fallen across the road and he snapped it off with the bumper. The gnarled jack pine from which he hung his portable shower lay on its side in the clearing, fractured by a thunderstorm.

The forest sought to reclaim the open yard and brown grass grew chest high, thick with the dry remains of oxeye daisies decapitated by earlier frosts. Around the edges of the clearing the trees had thickened, dark spruce and the white glow of aspen and birch.

His foot pressed the clutch and he idled the truck, waiting in the trees just short of the clearing, alert for any sign of movement. Satisfying himself that no one waited in the dark beyond his headlights, he edged ahead.

The cabin was derelict—steps rotted, dead branches littering the porch, screen door cockeyed on its hinges. Only the thick pine planking of the main door remained intact.

Anxious to run, Nimrod stood on the seat pounding his tail against the dashboard. Dutch reached over and opened the passenger door. "Check it out, boy," he said. A moment later, he brought the truck up to within inches of the cabin steps and cut the engine. Waiting impatiently on the porch above, Nimrod swept twigs and pine needles with his tail.

"Looks like we made it," Dutch said, stepping out. Away from people and their noise, the dripping trees and the dull flapping of their dead leaves seemed unnaturally loud. The wind, high above the forest, touched only the tallest pines, sending down the melancholy song people describe as whispering. It was a lament to Dutch, and it promised danger.

He drew a long key from his pocket. "Hope the lock isn't rusted."

The cabin was a perfect hideout. One road, little more than a blaze through thick forest, appeared unnavigable, often was after a snowfall. Snow had been in the forecast repeatedly during the past forty-eight-hours, part of a dangerous weather system winding up over the Western Plains, a blessing if it closed the only road.

The lock on the door hadn't rusted, but seasons of neglect and dampness had swollen the wood. He dislodged it with a sharp kick. Inside, the stale air smelled of mouse turds. He fumbled in the darkness, bumping the table, feeling for the kerosene lamp. Touching the cool glass, he struck a match and held it to the wick, warming his hands over the flame for a moment before replacing the chimney and surveying the room.

Built of aspen logs, the cabin was a one-room structure no larger than a double car garage but vaulted ceilings of native pine, supported by log rafters, and a large covered porch with split-log railings, provided such a solid stance it appeared larger. Vicky first saw it covered in fresh snow and said it was a fairy-tale house. Even the lack of electricity, indoor plumbing, and central heating, failed to dampen her enthusiasm for their "Fairy Cottage."

Vicky had loved the snow and put great store in Christmas, often sobbing with uncontrolled holiday cheer. She hung a silver cross between her breasts and tears in her eyes, said if it hadn't been for Christ they couldn't commit adultery and get away with it.

The year the National Meat Packers and Locker Convention was held in St. Louis, he'd pretended to enter his hickory-smoked ham but took Vicky to Roatan instead. They'd bounced to earth aboard a DC-3 with an oil leak in its starboard engine. The Bay Islands of Honduras were selected because they feared places like Cozumel or Maui might find them walking hand in hand along some crowded beach only to come upon Mavis Faggering roasting her giant pink thighs in the sun. Adulterers leave nothing to chance.

Dust curled behind as the ancient aircraft's tail wheel dug the gravel airstrip and taxied clumsily to a halt near a brightly painted custom's shed with a tin roof. "Now what?" Vicky asked when they'd cleared customs.

The heavy air was dust laden from a narrow road that twisted off into dense trees and brush. "According to our instructions," Dutch said, "we take the local bus to the boat landing where one of the resort's watertaxis picks us up."

"What bus? I don't see a bus."

No bus arrived until after sunset, when they'd all but given up. It was blue and white and red and yellow and they'd named it Tormenta II. Vicky's breasts swayed and bounced beneath her silk blouse as it ground its way through the night over roads that snaked like dry river beds along the hilly coastline. Outside, a strange countryside slid by in the darkness, lingering in the senses and inhabited by noisy, melodious folk who shouted and sang and called to one another with Latin gusto and laughter. Weaving along past flickering doorways they listened in awe and smelled the sweet smoke of their fires and it struck them suddenly how far they'd come from home. "Did you know it would be like this?" Vicky asked.

"I knew reality isn't a travel brochure." He squeezed her hand. "Glad to have you to myself awhile."

"Well," she remarked, brushing dust from her chest, "you're getting me with frosting."

"I'll rinse you off first."

Tormenta II finally lurched to a stop and they inhaled the sea. Alongside their suitcases a moment later, they were dumbstruck by the unisonal barking of some outrageous Central American cricket. "No one here," Vicky said. Her hand felt clammy

"No boats either."

"Smells like rotten fish." She shuddered. "Shouldn't we hear the surf?"

"Must be a bay of some kind," he concluded. A bare bulb near the end of the rickety dock cast an anemic pool of light onto calm water, sloping lazily against wooden pilings.

"Snakes?" she whispered.

"No," he lied. Thousands died from snake bites when they built the Panama Canal. Or was it yellow fever? "Boat'll be along any minute," he told her confidently. "Captain's probably finishing his evening Salvavida."

"Salvavida? What's that?"

"Beer."

"Sounds like some kind of lizard." She shivered. "How do you know the names of beers in Honduras?"

"Old American Indian trick. Read the ads in the bus."

"Don't joke. What happens if the boat doesn't come?"

"We'll make mad passionate love on the sand. In the morning, I'll hollow out a canoe with my pen knife and catch fish for breakfast. You'll gather coconuts."

85

"Idiot," she said.

Moments later the engine sounds were unmistakable and a garish blue, white, and pink vessel slid under the light and gently bumped the dock. The name "Evelyn" hand lettered on the bow. "Senor Cleelan?"

"Yes. Si. I'm Cleland."

"I am Javier. This is the boat to Banyan Bay. I speak the English. Come now, please?"

Javier loaded the bags, able somehow to see in the dark. The boat, like everything else, had no lights. When it backed from the dock, Dutch offered Javier a cigarette to get a look at him. A handsome mulatto face bent over the flame of his lighter. A face filled with the warmth and serenity of the islands, graying a bit at the temples.

"Is it far to Banyan Bay?" Vicky asked him.

"Not far, missus."

Acquiring some night vision, Dutch soon realized they weren't anywhere near the open sea but threading a maze of small cays and sand bars inside some intercoastal waterway. Phosphorous winked in their wake, answered from above by eager stars set in a black, moonless sky. They rode for the better part of an hour in comfortable silence.

"Banyan Bay," Javier announced at last as *Eveyln* eased against the dock, but it remained invisible until morning when they stepped out into blazing sunshine and beheld a semi-circle of flawless green hills, trapping them against a trembling aquamarine sea that lapped clear and warm at their feet.

"I simply don't believe it," Vicky said, standing alongside Dutch on the veranda. "Air travel is a miracle."

"They gave this place no build-up at all." He looked at her and shook his head. "Wish I could take credit for dumb luck."

Vicky's eyes were on the beach, which began at the front step and curved in a long, unbroken crescent for several thousand yards. It came to a point at the end, beyond which the ocean was dotted with tiny cays, some sandy, others rich and green. A narrow footbridge led from the end of the beach to the first cay.

"Dumb luck or not, I love you." Vicky said, eyes brimming.

"What about breakfast?"

"I look at all this and I want to make love." She patted his belly. "You want to eat."

A hundred odd yards along the beach the Banyan Bay Club's main facility, a large clapboard tin-roofed building resembling a waterfront warehouse with a porch, stood ready to meet all their needs. It housed a bar, a rec-room (corner with ping pong table), small gift shop, office, restaurant, gaming area (corner where several locals played dominoes), and a porch hung with hammocks.

Meals were served when guests got hungry or when cook wasn't visiting her brother in French Harbor or taking a siesta under the giant banyan tree behind the kitchen. No menu. They ate everything from fresh lobster to iguana, following the dictates of their imaginations and stomachs. Guests kept their own drink tabs on scraps of notepaper.

After three days at Banyan Bay, it was hard to imagine having ever lived anywhere else. They already knew most of the staff by name but couldn't get an accurate count of the other guests, most of whom were scuba divers. They showed up for meals in pairs or small groups, usually with matted hair and damp swimsuits, often lugging complicated-looking camera equipment.

Eventually they concluded that the Banyan Bay Club was not built to serve its guests, but to leave them alone. Owners of the club, the Bradfords, were a retired couple from Alabama who ten years before had sailed into Banyan Bay and dropped anchor for the night. A reckless and brave couple, they never left.

On the fourth day, Vicky said, "Let's go snorkeling."

Javier held the outboard throttle wide open and the skiff danced at high speed across a choppy sea, slapping out sheets of white foam to crack against the tops of the chop. They headed for Half Moon Bay with a retired couple—Sam and Annie Murphy—who sat facing Dutch. Annie in the bow, Sam gripping the bill on his canvas baseball cap and eyeing Dutch's equipment.

"Where's your knife?" he asked finally. He had wild eyebrows and long, bony legs.

"What?"

"Your skin-diving knife," he said, clearly peeved. "Where is it?"

"We're just going snorkeling," Dutch explained. "No hunting."

He looked knowingly at Annie, who was fighting the wind, holding down a giant straw hat with one hand and using the other to hide vericose veins beneath a flapping towel.

"Snorkeling is a misnomer," he said, stirring Dutch's snorkeling equipment with his foot. "Skin diving is the proper term. Annie and me been skin diving since 1953. We carry knives." He swung a bare foot onto Dutch's upper leg, dripping slick gasoline and deck dirt. He had the toenails of a beast. "See that?" A ten-inch blade was strapped to his calf. He jerked a rubber clasp over the handle and shoved it butt-first into Dutch's hand.

"Impressive," he said.

"Stainless steel," Sam said. "Sixty-nine-ninety-five."

"Wow."

"Cheapest insurance you'll ever buy." He cocked his head and leaned closer. "Ever have a moray eel pop out of a hole and dig his teeth into your arm?"

Dutch shook his head.

"Only one thing to do when that happens," he went on. "Don't move a muscle until he lets go, then slash his head off! Morays got teeth like hypodermic needles." He snatched the knife away.

Dutch nodded, trying to picture himself holding still while a moray eel ground sharp needles into his arm.

"See this serrated edge?" Sam ran his finger over the saw-like points. "Know what that's for?"

Blank-faced, Dutch turned to Vicky for help. She gleefully studied the horizon. Again, he shook his head.

"Rope cutter," Sam announced. "Go through half-inch nylon in less than twenty seconds."

"Handy," he said.

"Damn right!" Sam bared a set of perfect dentures. "Knife's about the handiest thing you have underwater. How long can you hold your breath?"

Behind him Vicky giggled. "Don't know," Dutch admitted.

Sam grimaced. "If you don't know how long you can hold your breath, how do you know how long you can stay down when you make your surface dive?"

"Huh?"

"Underwater. How long?"

"Wasn't planning to go underwater."

"Then what've you got all this skin diving equipment for?"

"We're going to lay on top and look down," Dutch said, no longer caring if he liked it or not.

"Sam!" Annie called from the bow. "Did you remember my bag? The gray one?"

"What bag?"

"The gray one for heaven's sake! Sitting right inside the door. I told you to pick it up. Everything I need is in it."

Sam dug under his seat. "I'm not a pack mule, Annie. It's bad enough I had to lug all the diving equipment. Can't you get along without it?"

"Not that bag. I can't get along without that bag."

"Why not?"

"You know."

"Oh!" Sam spoke to Dutch behind his hand. "The wife's sixty-two years old. Still gets her period."

Javier cut the engine and they drifted into Half Moon Bay. Protected on three sides by high limestone cliffs, its calm water heavy and powerful. "Like green mercury," Vicky whispered. "But alive."

Vicky snorkeled lazily out into Half Moon Bay and it changed her forever. The sea with all its warm mysteries lost no time in becoming her personal discovery. She didn't know a trumpetfish from a trout or a sea anemone from a clump of crab grass but laid claim to them with the same innocent astonishment he'd discovered in her that first night in bed. He thought that before Half Moon Bay he could've broken with her. He'd said the things lovers say, but his heart had remained safely locked in a vault of self-restraint. He was still his own man, wise enough to love a woman without losing his heart. But he was a fool.

Later that afternoon, he found an opportunity to impress her and made the most of it. They'd lost sight of each other snorkeling after one strange new fish or another, and never a strong swimmer, Dutch swam farther and farther from the beach. He marked his progress by watching the bottom. Patches of coral on white sand, then waving grass or empty, rippled sand for awhile, then coral again. At the very edge of the bay something came into view that only a handful of men throughout history have seen—a sunken galleon. Its cannon visible in the sand. He counted eight. Then an even dozen.

Fearing some residual affect from the two beers he'd drank with lunch, he screamed for Vicky. "What's wrong?" she asked.

"Nothing," he said. "Just look down there and tell me what you see."

Her head popped back up almost immediately. "My God! It's cannons! Go down there."

"Pretty deep."

"But how can we be sure? You have to touch them."

"Must be twenty-five or thirty feet."

"Should I get Javier?"

"No," he said without hesitation. "Just give me a minute to get a deep breath."

"Were you listening to what Javier said at lunch about equalizing the pressure in your ears when you dive?" Vicky asked.

"Didn't make sense to me."

"I think you just use the nose pockets in your mask to pinch off the nostrils, then blow so your ears pop. Here." She guided his hand until his fingers found the pockets. "Try it."

He pinched and blew. His ears popped. "But will it work underwater?" he asked.

"Try it."

Dutch inhaled deeply and dove under the water, pinching his nose and popping his ears. Half way to the bottom he wished he'd let Vicky call Javier, until at last, he touched one of the cannon. Grasping it at the open end, he ran his hand over the rough iron, pitted by its centuries under the sea, then he kicked toward the surface.

"It looked almost as long as you," Vicky said as he caught his breath. "Can you believe this is happening? What now?"

"Tell the others, I guess. We can't just float around all day."

"Should we?" She pulled the mask down from her face. "What if there's treasure?"

"Then we'll need help. Divers, salvage equipment, things like that."

"Would they let us keep it?"

"Doubt it. Remember Mel Fisher? Found the *Atocha* gold but the Florida politicians kept robbing him. Bound to be worse down here."

"I suppose," she said reluctantly. "Maybe you can bribe somebody."

They yelled for Javier and the Murphys.

Sam Murphy was strangely quiet after coming ashore, and dropping his skin-diving equipment carelessly on the sand, retrieved a small book from his wife's bag and went off by himself to read. Convinced his sudden shyness was rooted in envy, Dutch said nothing to embarrass him further. Ten minutes later he discovered his error.

"I knew it!" Sam came screaming down the beach, waving the book above his head. "It's a fake!"

"What's a fake?" Annie wanted to know.

"Those cannon. Everything."

"Oh?" Vicky's voice had a frosty edge.

"It's part of a movie set. Says so right here." He held the book out for her to see. "Built in 1970. 'Don't be fooled into believing you've discovered sunken treasure, like some unsuspecting tourists when they've stumbled onto the old Shark Reef 'movie set.' See? Right there?" He pointed to the page.

Dutch looked at Javier, who was smiling and staring at the sand. "Javier?" he said.

"Si," he shrugged. "The cannon are made of cement. Halves only, sunk in the sand. But the happiness when you find them, is it not just as good?"

"Better," Dutch admitted, doubled with laughter.

Vicky never forgave Sam Murphy for exposing the truth and years later referred to him as that "arrogant little weenie" with the tourist book. But with Dutch she laughed about it, especially that night at dinner when they both drank too much.

Instead of brandy, the custom at Banyan Bay was to take a snifter of Jane Barbancourt, a fifteen-year-old Haitian rum, as an after dinner drink. Glasses in hand they strolled onto the veranda. The night sea slid softly along the sand, leaving flecks of phosphorus to sparkle and die.

"I'm going to cry," Vicky murmured. "I'm so happy."

Dutch felt it too, and her sunburned skin glowing beneath his grasp in the cool night air. "Can we just go on like this?" he asked. "On and on?"

She turned away as a land breeze billowed her flowered sundress and teased the flaxen hair at her neck. "That's up to you," she whispered. He caught the scent of aloe carried aloft with the evening cooking fires of the hill people.

There it was, the age-old question of commitment. "Lifejackets can't stop a ship from sinking," he said.

"What on earth does that mean?"

"Just that marriage is no protection against infidelity."

"So?"

"So divorcing one and marrying another isn't a solution," he said. "Just repetition. Can't we walk down to the hammock cay and just lie there until the moon comes up?"

"It's a new moon darling." She balanced her glass on the wooden rail and came closer, lacing her fingers about his neck. "We'll go later. Answer me now."

"You mean will I divorce Jean and marry you?"

She smiled. "Is that so terrible?"

Something made him tell the truth. "I just don't believe in divorce."

"But adultery's okay? Cheat on her but keep her?" Her voice remained soft as the night. "Isn't divorce more honest than that?"

He was confused. "I suppose, but I still don't believe in it. There's no sense to beliefs sometimes."

"Meaning you'd never divorce Jean under any circumstances?"

"I guess."

"What if she were the unfaithful one?"

"Even then."

"Wow." She seemed about to say something else, then retrieved her glass and sipped. Several moments later she said, "I like the dark here."

He said nothing.

"It's different. More personal, like hands under a warm blanket wrapping you up, protecting you from the light."

93

He waited a long time before she continued.

"We can stop talking about this if you like," she said. "I'm not mad or anything."

Vicky's aplomb was rooted in passivity, though he didn't know it then, and might not have understood how a person can create a philosophy that doesn't include disappointment. Passive acceptance of all things brought her peace, and she moved indiscriminately through the days, and eventually, through the men of her life. Later he realized she was so successful at it because she understood the quality men prize most in a woman, being a good listener.

They strolled arm in arm along the beach, across the footbridge to the hammock cay. She nestled against his chest and sighed, palm fronds rattling like windchimes in the breezes.

It wasn't an unpleasant memory, and Nimrod trotted along as Dutch strode to the wood box. Glancing inside, he said, "Plenty for tonight. A good fire will chase out the damp and the stink."

Minutes later, yellow flames licked the firewood spilling tiny puffs of smoke into the room as it ascended the chimney and sailed away into the darkness. The familiar smell reassured him. Gingerly, he lifted the shriveled corpses from the mousetraps and wiped droppings from the counter tops and then swept the floor. The chores kept him warm until the fire drove the chill away. He unloaded the supplies of food and tools.

An hour later the stove glowed, and he poured himself a stiff shot of Jane Barbancourt and settled into his favorite chair near the fire, dog at his feet. "What the hell," he confided. "I've had worse nights." Assuming an invitation, Nimrod sneaked his head heavily on Dutch's lap. "Tomorrow we better cut some wood," he said, resting back against the chair. "Just in case."

What had he done with the chainsaw?

The question nagged him.

He couldn't remember bringing it in. He looked around the room expecting to see it, in its yellow case, near the axes and bow saw. It wasn't there. When had he seen it last? He set his drink on the wood box and peered in the corner behind the stove. He remembered taking it out when he changed the tire.

"Uh, oh," he said. "It's back there in the ditch."

His firewood wouldn't last a day if it really got cold. He had axes and a hand saw, but if there was a blizzard followed by sub-zero temperatures, hand tools were slow. He might work all day just to keep the fire going, keep from freezing to death. Too many things in ditches lately.

He sighed heavily and threw one leg over the side of his chair. "Anyway, there's plenty of liquor," he informed the dog. "Weather's nice and it's too early for snow and cold. We'll worry about it in the morning." A moment later he was asleep.

*　　*　　*

Five hundred miles to the west over the great flat plains of the western Dakotas, a giant frontal system more than one thousand miles long churned slowly in a counterclockwise rotation driven by mild southerly winds. This enormous vortex drew frigid air from the Canadian plains southward, fueling the disturbance.

In Willow River and other towns on the eastern edge of the plains, people slept with their windows cracked. One last chance to breathe fresh air before a long winter.

From his apartment window on the second floor above the post office, Len Davis stared out over Main Street. There wasn't a great deal to see at this hour. He'd once described Willow River as a bustling little prairie town. He shrugged at the deserted street.

The newly installed amber street lights, pride of the City Council, grew dim as foggy night gave way to foggy day. Len wondered why he was up at all. His promise to Jean last

95

night that he'd find Dutch was an idle boast. He didn't even know where to start. Or if he should.

Len loved bachelorhood but had often been shocked by the casual infidelity of so many of his friends. Dutch's betrayal rankled most because he'd kept it secret, fooling Len completely. What kind of man kept a secret that well? The kind of man, Len thought, who'd be very hard to find.

He turned from the window, padded barefoot to the heavy oak entertainment center on the opposite wall and stabbed a power button. A red light appeared. Like the rest of the room's appointments, the stereo was expensive and tasteful, its deep tones wasted on another alarming weather report. Len frowned and jammed the CD button. K.D. Lang moaned she was down to her last cigarette.

When you thought about it, Dutch could be anywhere. Endless possibilities for an intelligent man with money who might fly to California, South America, hell . . . Russia!

Len remembered his coffee maker was set for seven-thirty. He strode to the kitchen and fiddled with the device, trying to back up the timer. Failing, he filled a teakettle instead and clanged it on the stove. In the jet age Dutch had a tremendous head start. Seven or eight hours to South America? Maybe five to the Caribbean. He might be watching the sunrise in Barbados by now. Imagine Charlie Benson chasing him to Barbados. Imagine Charlie in Bermuda shorts.

He'd been a fool to make Jean a promise he couldn't keep. And what if she'd been lying? Who'd know better than she where Dutch went? Come to think of it, who'd know better than he? He was Dutch's best friend, after all.

He had time for a shower before the water boiled. Bloody Mary wouldn't taste bad either. He hung his robe behind the bathroom door. He'd have to call Doris at home and cancel his schedule, which was light. No suit and tie today. Jeans and a sweatshirt.

He turned on the faucet, testing the stream for warmth. Sweatshirt?

The sweatshirt Dutch gave him. "Where the pavement ends and the north begins." Something else printed there too. He was cold that day in the boat. "Keep it," Dutch had said. "I can get another one next time I'm up at the cabin."

Len slammed the faucet shut, ran naked into the bedroom, flinging open his dresser drawers, pawing the neatly stacked piles of clothes. There, near the bottom, a gray sweatshirt. Screened between the words "Togo Joe's Bar" and "Where the pavement ends and the north begins" was a map. It showed a crossroads and the numbers of the highways that formed it. He sank back onto the rumpled bed. "Dutch, you clever devil. You didn't go far at all." He tossed the sweatshirt in the air. "Lawyers," he said proudly. "They hate us because we're all so damned smart!"

Chapter Eleven

THE DULL GREEN SQUAD CAR slid to a stop in front of a sign marked "Police Parking Only." A tired Charlie Benson rolled out from behind the wheel and stood a moment gazing up at the overcast sky. Where was the big snowstorm? The TV weather weenies plastered Megastorm on the screen. Like megaton, he thought. That should sell panty shields.

Jogging across to Berkie's for breakfast, he heard Marlene shouting from the Police Department steps behind him. "You better get in here!"

"Sausage and eggs," he called from the middle of the street.

"Your sausage is about to get ground, Buster." She held the door open, pointing inside. "Sheriff's on his way over and all hell's breaking loose."

"Great." He straddled the centerline. "What's his gripe?"

"Get inside. Want the whole town to hear?"

Charlie saw Tully Olson's old International Scout, two pickups and a John Deere parked in front of the café, otherwise the street was empty. He moved toward her shaking his head. "What are you? Paranoid?"

"Paranoid my derriere!" She growled. "Say, what is a goat-fuck, anyway?"

"Marlene!" He hustled her inside.

"Well, if people are going to say things like that to me, don't you think I should know what they mean?"

"Army term for a screw-up. Where do you hear things like that?"

"Mattson's description of the way you've handled the case so far." She grinned. "There was more."

"Never mind."

"'Tell that knucklehead you work for he better know where my friggin' corpse has got off to, per se!'" Drooping the corners of her mouth she looked dangerously like him.

Charlie tried not to laugh. "Did you tell him I ate it?"

"No," she said, keeping a straight face. "What did you do with it?"

"Sam Lynstrom hauled her to St. Cloud last night for the autopsy." He pushed her ahead of him into the room.

"No wonder he's spitting tacks," she frowned. "Told me he called St. Cloud first thing this morning and Miss Vicky never got there, and nobody can find Lynstrom." She toddled across to the coffee maker and poured two cups. "He's gonna be all over you for this goat-fuck."

"Quit saying that," he ordered, at the same time he thought how Marlene Winther was the best thing that ever happened to the Willow River Police Department. Dispatcher, researcher, friend. Knew more about rural police work than either of his two patrolmen and kept a secret better than most. She came from a large Willow River family that included half the town.

"Drink your coffee," she said, handing him a cup.

"Forget Mattson a minute," he said, motioning her to follow him into his office. "I need your angle on this thing." He'd shared his suspicions about Dutch with her yesterday after following the ambulance to St. Cloud and learning from Murdock that it was Dutch who'd assaulted him.

"You don't want to hear what I have to say, Charlie."

"Course I do." Wasn't like her to be taciturn. "Speak up."

She crossed her arms and leaned against a chipped, gray filing cabinet. "You don't want to hear it."

"Speak!"

"Fine," she said, drawing a breath. "You're blowing this investigation." She watched as he dropped into his chair, slopping coffee onto his lap. "Told you you wouldn't like it." She snatched a paper towel from the roll on the cabinet and folded it into a neat square. "Set it here. I've known Dutch Cleland since he was a boy. Used to shovel my sidewalk. Polite kid. Always liked him."

"So?"

"So, he grew up to be a nice man. I still like him. Maybe there's more to this than you think. More than just another love triangle."

"Like what?"

"I don't know." She leaned back again. "But that woman must have made him awful mad."

"Damn it!" Charlie sat upright, spilling more coffee. "People get mad all the time. They don't go around strangling everybody!"

"He didn't strangle everybody."

"No. He just beats hell out of the ones he doesn't kill." Charlie grumbled. "Or have you forgotten Mr. Murdock?"

"You asked for my opinion," she said. "Don't jump down my throat when I give it."

He stared at her a moment. "Okay," he said. "How am I blowing it?"

"By not doing what you told the sheriff yesterday you were going to do. Get physical evidence."

"That's before I knew Dutch did it."

Marlene sighed. "Charlie, that's what I'm trying to tell you. Everyone knows Dutch did it. But where's the proof?"

"His own wife admitted it!"

"Since when do wives testify against their husbands in America?" she asked, standing upright. "You don't have one shred of real evidence. Did anyone see Dutch Cleland and Victoria Murdock together Sunday night when this murder occurred? No. Is there a smoking gun, a bloody knife, a lead pipe with her hair on it and his fingerprints? No. Where are her clothes? Her car? You were ranting and raving around here yesterday because Sam Lynstrom suspected Walleye. Well, Charlie, so far at least Walleye can be placed at the murder scene. Dutch Cleland can't." She paused for breath. "The County Attorney isn't going to trial with a case that hasn't any evidence, so if I were you, Charlie, I'd quit being so proud of myself for figuring out who did it and start proving it. You might just find out you can't. Like I'll just bet you can't say for certain, even in your own little mind, that Gordon Murdock isn't a possibility. Convicted felon? Sadistic screwball freed by the system and no doubt in hot pursuit of his unfaithful wife? Lay that against Dutch, who obviously wasn't carrying on a long-distance affair with Mrs. Murdock in Oklahoma. So their relationship was dead years ago. Why kill her now? And from what you told me yourself, Jean Cleland didn't say much except it might have been an accident, and her husband was gone she didn't know where, and once upon a time he had a love affair with this babe. Are you following me, Charlie? And so what? Love affairs aren't illegal even if one party is murdered. It's murder that's illegal, Charlie." Her face opened in a broad smile. "Now, aren't you glad you asked me?"

"Thrilled. Least now I know where he is," he slurped noisily. "Under your bed."

"Only dust under my bed," she winked. "But then, I have the good fortune to work for you. If I didn't . . ." She let the sentence dangle, placing a cup to her lips.

"That's what I love about this town," he sighed. "Everybody's so cooperative. Honestly, Marlene, I haven't the foggiest idea why Dutch, a guy I've known most of my life, suddenly turned into public enemy number one. But physical evidence or not, I know he did it and so do you."

"Well, Chief Inspector, the real law should arrive here any second. What's the plan? More conjecture or are we going to start assembling some hard evidence?"

"Right now I have neither a body or a suspect. Find Sam Lynstrom, and I don't care if you have to turn this town upside down. Start with his wife. If he was scuba diving in the Azores she'd know how much air he had left." He swung his chair away and patted his stomach. "After his nibs is done chewing me out maybe I can get some breakfast."

The telephone rang.

"I'll get it." He lifted the receiver.

"Charlie?" Sam Lynstrom's voice wavered. "It's me. I got some kinda bad news."

"So help me, Sam, if you say you still haven't taken Vicky Murdock's body to St. Cloud I'm coming over there and feed you your teeth."

"It's complicated." He hesitated. "She's gone."

"What do you mean, gone?"

"Disappeared."

There was a very long pause during which Marlene tip-toed from the room. "Any second," Charlie said in a strained voice, "Sheriff Mattson's going to walk through my door. Explain this to me very carefully."

"I drove to St. Cloud just like you told me, but when I got there the hearse was empty. Maybe I forgot to shut the door tight or something, I don't know. Anyway, I drove all the way back on I-94 at ten miles an hour trying to find her. Couldn't see the southbound lanes 'cause of the fog, so when I got here I started all over again. Drove all the way back to St. Cloud at like five miles an hour. She wasn't there. Do you know how many dead 'coons there are between here and St. Cloud, Charlie? Then of course I was in St. Cloud again, so I had to drive back here. Took all night. Maybe somebody picked her up, or something ate her. She's gone Charlie."

Charlie hung up without a word.

Still sitting with his chin on his chest, the door burst open and Sheriff Mattson plowed through the outer office, two look-alike deputies sucked along in his wake. The sheriff rolled to a stop inches from Charlie's desk.

"I got a bone to pick with you!" Mattson blustered. "Bobby here," jerking a thumb at one of the look-alikes, who frowned menacingly in Charlie's direction, "says you never got my corpus shipped off to St. Cloud. True or false?"

"True," he answered, blinking. "I mean it's true that I didn't get it to St. Cloud but it's false that I didn't send it because I did."

"Talk English for crying out loud! Makes me out all kind of a fool when I don't even know where my body's at," Mattson continued. "Now I hear Dutch Cleland's gone and faux pas'd some hunter from Oklahoma named Merlick."

"Mur-dock," he corrected. "The corpse's husband, remember?"

"Whatever! I'm still running around like a toad with egg on his face," the sheriff asserted. "Where is she?"

"Sent Mrs. Murdock's remains to pathology in St. Cloud just like you told me," he said reasonably. "Assumed it got there."

"Don't assume." Mattson pounded the desk. "Don't assume nothin'! Don't act on your own recognizance! And don't forget who's running the goddamned County Sheriff's Department. It's up to me to know where the bodies are and which suspect is thumping the gourd of which other suspect!"

"You're right. I'm sorry," Charlie apologized. "We're not entirely sure what happened yet."

"Okay. Fine, fine. Now, what's the dope?" Mattson said more calmly. The deputies exchanged knowing looks. Their boss's ability to chew butt was legendary. "Lynstrom's meat wagon break down? Take her to the drive-in movies or something instead of the morgue? What's the deal?"

"Worse than that, I'm afraid. He lost her."

Mattson's frown forced his jowls to within an inch of his collar. "You tryin' to pull the proverbial wool over my eyes per se, or what? I told Marlene maybe you went into business for yourself here on this deal. Solve the case quick and get elected. That kinda thing. Now you're trying to tell me that Sam Lynstrom, whose been carting one stiff or another around here for twenty years, up and lost this particular one?"

"He left town with Mrs. Murdock in the rear and when he got to St. Cloud she was gone. Thinks he might've left the door open."

"Did he bother to look for her?"

"All night." Charlie shrugged. "Dark. Fog."

"So how many cars you got out now that it's light?"

"Only got one car. Mine. It's parked in front."

Unexpectedly, Mattson smiled. "Great to have you on this investigation, Charlie. Just great." He turned to the deputies. "I want every car we got, the uniformed reserves, the damn county mountie wannabes, the Highway Patrol, the friggin' Boy Scouts, and anybody else you can find, in a car right now on I-94 driving every inch of ground between here and St. Cloud. Seems like the Willow River Police Chief lost the corpus delicti that's the subject of this here murder investigation and when the press corps waltzes in here in no time flat and blasts the news across the airwaves of Minnesota, he's gonna need all the help he can get." He glanced back at Charlie and his smile widened. "I think you better prepare yourself for your television debut, Chief. You can give the same speech you're gonna give at your retirement dinner."

"You're going to tell the press?" He feared Mattson had gone full Hollywood.

"Course I won't tell 'em. That's why they're called reporters. They find out stuff. Already interviewed everybody in this one-horse town six times. Walleye Wertz's been on

104

the goddamn tube pickin' his nose so many times people in Minneapolis think he's the friggin' mayor."

"All they're getting from me is 'no comment.'"

"Like hell!" Mattson slapped his leg. "You'll be standing tall in front of those cameras right beside me and if the question comes up, you'll say the body's on the way to St. Cloud. One thing I asked you to do in this investigation, one thing, and what happened? Can't move one stiff ninety miles without dropping it in a ditch where it was probably dragged off by a pack a farm dogs and eaten. And if it snows, then what? Won't find it 'till spring. Nothin' left but the teeth, or maybe them fancy fingers and toes you're so fond of."

"Quite possibly someone picked it up and will turn it in," Charlie hoped.

"About the same time Billy Bob Clinton learns to zip his fly," the sheriff said. "Go on camera and say anybody out there with an extra corpse? Go ahead. They'll start a treasure hunt. Whole countryside crawling with Minneapolis yuppies in SUVs drinking goddamned mineral water and trying to be first in the scavenger hunt!" Sheriff Mattson moped his forehead with a monogrammed handkerchief. "TV's like testifying in court, don't volunteer diddly squat! Chances are nobody will ask because nobody's gonna think you're stupid enough to lose a corpse that's just barely cold. And call Lynstrom. His wife, too. Tell 'em both to shut up. One person in this town gets wind of it, we're dead."

"Don't worry. I'll keep the lid on."

"You better. Now bring me up to date on this Cleland perp." Sheriff Mattson had known Dutch as long as Charlie had.

"Gone. Soon as they wire Murdock's jaw I'm hoping we can get something solid," Charlie said. "Maybe he knew where Dutch was going."

"Doubt it. How about his wife? You talked to her last night, I'm told," Mattson said with an air of mystery.

105

Charlie was mildly surprised. He hadn't publicized his visit with Jean. The sheriff did have sources, he supposed. "She wasn't too cooperative," he answered. "If she knows anything, she's not telling."

"Well." Mattson nodded his head, seemingly pleased that Charlie had come away empty. "I'll be trying some friendly persuasion on her myself in half an hour. Until then, let's you and I get abreast of everything for these media pukes."

Charlie outlined his conversation with the Tulsa detective and with Victoria Murdock's ex-husband, Carroll Johnson. He explained Carroll was a man. The sheriff stuck his finger down his throat.

Mattson waited patiently until he finished. "Okay. Fine. Superb," the sheriff said. "You got further with this Murlick than I did. Knuckleheads in Tulsa gave us the runaround. Sealed records my ass! Karl. You know Karl my chief deputy? I want Karl to talk with both Murlick and Johnson. We're getting nowhere fast with physical evidence. No tire tracks. No vehicle to make them. No clothes. No murder weapon. No footprints except that idiot's, Walleye. We got his tire tracks, tricycle tracks I should say. So far we got a naked body and tricycle tracks. Take that to the media!"

"I've got a couple ideas," Charlie began.

"Fine," Mattson cut in. "Time is it?" He peered at his watch. "Let's hop over to Berkie's for a little breakfast, eh Charlie? You eaten yet?"

"No."

"Never face the press on an empty stomach," the sheriff advised, delightfully bouncing his belly in both hands. Noting Charlie's haggard look, he said, "Perk up! Misty Plopnik-Kowalski might be here." Charlie's face was blank. "Channel 11? Foxy babe? Big bazooms?" He cupped his hands. "Sat right next to her at a media dinner once. Cleavage a foot deep." He raised an eyebrow. "Watch your mouth. She's plenty damn tricky."

Twenty minutes later, after a hurried breakfast, they hiked back to the office, falling silent when they rounded the corner and spotted the media vans and satellite trucks with bright call letters, eagerly nosing the curb outside. In spite of himself, Charlie searched the crowd for Misty Plopnik-Kowalski.

If Mattson feared these pretentious young people, it didn't show beneath the sparkling smile now wedged firmly between his round cheeks. They rushed along, lugging mini-cams and battery packs up the steps, chatting noisily among themselves. Mattson slapped their backs and welcomed them to Pomme de Terre County, calling many by name.

Dodging a coiling wire, Charlie nearly fell over a long-haired young man with a diamond stud in his nose busy taping globs of microphones to a telescoping metal stand. "Hi," Charlie said, pleasantly.

The youngster glared at him. "Zip it, Fatso," he said.

Marlene stood on the far side of the room near the dispatch radio mesmerized by the Channel 11, Eyewitness News Team aiming cameras and lights at their star reporter, Misty Plopnik-Kowalski, who didn't appear thrilled at getting beamed via satellite from Willow River.

"I never thought it would be like this," Marlene whispered to Charlie as he approached, still smarting from his brush with the soundman. "They're all so young," she pointed. "Is that one a man or a woman?"

Charlie followed her finger. "An asshole!"

"Better not let the sheriff hear you talk like that," she scolded. "Here he comes."

Mattson joined them near the dispatcher's desk but kept an eye on the flower of microphones, opening wider as more and more duct tape was wound into place around the stand. He looked almost jubilant. Charlie shot daggers at Mr. Zip-it, but only Marlene seemed to notice.

107

"I'll start things off," the sheriff whispered to Charlie. "You come in when I cue you and make damn sure you don't say anything important. Don't slip up and say her name, stuff like that. Stay cool. And whatever you do, don't sweat. That's what got Nixon."

"Sure," Charlie nodded.

Sheriff Mattson stepped up to the microphone flower, positioning himself carefully. "Hear me okay?"

Heads turned in his direction. "Ready when you are, Sheriff," said a reporter.

There were four cameras on tripods, two balanced on the shoulders of other cameramen. All had red recording lights burning, recording every sound and action sighted in their merciless lenses. Charlie fidgeted though they weren't aimed at him. Sheriff Mattson only smiled broadly and began to speak in a genuine, straightforward manner. "If you don't mind," he said warmly, "I'd like to begin with a short statement about our progress on the case thus far." He paused. No objections. "Fine," he said. "As you all know, yesterday morning we discovered the body of a female victim in rural Pomme de Terre County. Her name, along with certain other facts, will be kept under wraps until the investigation is further along. I understand your responsibility to the public, and the public's right to know, per se, but my first responsibility is to the victim, her family, and the citizens of this county."

The sheriff waited a moment for this message to sink in, then continued. "Beyond that, we have several promising leads. We fully intend to make an arrest before the end of the week, and we are convinced this crime is the work of one perpetrator who knew the victim."

As he spoke, it occurred to Charlie how quickly the sheriff was able to switch positions. Only yesterday he'd ridiculed Charlie for even suggesting the murder might be local. Reporters shuffled impatiently. "Now, I'll take your questions," Mattson said.

"This suspect," a young reporter asked, "is he a local resident?"

"We haven't ruled that out, Kevin," Mattson answered, favoring Kevin with a knowing look.

Off camera Charlie turned slightly toward Marlene and slipped the mysterious keys into her hand. "Sheriff has a Chevy doesn't he?" he whispered, not waiting for an answer. "Slip outside while he's beating his gums and see if they fit."

"Charlie!"

"Shhh! I know its probably not him, but geez, I hate the pompous bastard. Check it out just in case."

"You are something," she slipped them quietly into her skirt pocket. "I'll do it just to show you."

"Fine."

A female reporter was addressing Mattson. "In fact, Sheriff," a woman said, "isn't there a statewide manhunt for Philip 'Dutch' Cleland, a Willow River businessman?"

"We'd like to ask Mr. Cleland some questions, yes," Mattson answered, "but I'm not in a position to say he's a suspect."

"But it's safe to say you don't want him for parking violations," a voice drawled from the back of the room.

Mattson joined in the laughter.

"This victim, whose name we're not allowed to know," asked Misty Plopnik-Kowalski, "was she raped or sexually molested in any way?"

"Not to my knowledge, Ms. Plopnik-Kowalski," the Sheriff said. "An autopsy is still pending. We'll know more in a day or two. I can tell you, the victim is Caucasian, approximately thirty-seven years old, and a resident of Oklahoma."

"Can you tell us how she died?" another voice.

"Strangulation."

"Was she beaten?"

"To some extent."

"But not raped?"

"We don't know yet." Mattson raised a hand, assuming a traffic cop pose. "Please. Let's not turn this into a sex crime until the facts are in."

"Don't you think people have a right to know if there's a sex offender on the loose up here?" Misty was clearly bewildered by the Sheriff's blasé attitude toward crimes against women.

"Of course I do!" the sheriff snapped. "But we don't know that yet." He regained his composure instantly. "I'll call a news conference the moment the autopsy report is in. Then we can operate from a basis of fact," he looked sternly at Ms. Plopnik-Kowalski, "not foolish speculation." An instant later his smile returned. Off-camera, Plopnik-Kowalski rolled her eyes.

Another reporter piped up. "We've heard from other sources that a man named (he read from a notebook) Gordon Murdock is also involved. Could you comment on his relationship to the victim and where he fits in?"

Without so much as a word of warning, Mattson motioned for Charlie to join him at the microphones. "You'll have to ask Chief Benson about that." But Charlie was rooted to the floor.

Seconds ticked by as heads and several cameras swung on him. He counted cracks in the linoleum. "Not much to say," he mumbled.

"We can't hear you!" Plopnik-Kowalski shouted, her sleepy on-camera eyes widening. "Step up to the mics."

Charlie might never have moved but Marlene jabbed his ribs, propelling him forward. Mattson took a step back to make room, then reached over and tapped the mics. "Speak right in here," he explained methodically.

"I said," Charlie began, "there ain't . . . isn't much to say."

"You'll have to do better than that," Misty Plopnik-Kowalski told him. Her sassy voice made it clear she thought him a rural clod in over his head. "What about Gordon

Murdock?"

"He's not a suspect," Charlie managed.

"What is he then?"

"The victim's husband."

"So her name's Murdock?" Plopnik-Kowalski was pleasantly surprised and the others wrote rapidly on their pads. Cameras zoomed in for a close-up of Charlie Benson's reddening face.

"Looks like," Charlie shrugged. "Might be Johnson-Murdock."

"Why?"

"She might not of changed it after the divorce. Or it might be Plopnik-Johnson-Murdock if she had like Plopnik for a maiden name."

Sheriff Mattson had been standing with his mouth gaping. Before Charlie could do any further damage, he elbowed him aside and regained center stage. "All we have time for now," he said hurriedly to the circle of growling reporters. "Call my office tomorrow. I'll have something for you then," he assured them, taking Charlie by the arm and leading him away. "We'll be in the chief's office," he called to Marlene, hustling Charlie in and slamming the door.

"What in hell did you think you were doing out there?" Mattson squeaked.

"Sorry," Charlie said, tired of apologizing.

All the day before they'd stonewalled the media, and Cedric Mattson intended to keep it up. Later, in his own good time, he'd hand them the solution wrapped just as he pleased. First, Charlie had to be brought into line. "Let me give you a TV truth," he advised. "Always lie."

It took a while for Charlie to absorb this dichotomy as he rarely watched anything but sports on television and got his news from newspapers. The cameras were bigger than he'd imagined. They'd been pointed at just about everyone in town the day before and when he did watch the ten o'clock news he was astounded. Reporters managed to interview every idiot in Willow River. People who'd never spoken to Dutch Cleland in their lives claimed to be his neighbor or life-long friend. "Lie?" he asked, eyeing the door, conscious of the commotion outside and the crews breaking down their equipment. "Just lie?"

"Exactly." Mattson beamed.

"What if they catch on?"

"They won't. And if they do it doesn't matter." The sheriff ran his hand back over his thinning hair. "Let me explain the media. TV is all show and no go. Lights, camera, action. Get it? Moving pictures. Most things are too complicated to be explained with pictures so they just skip the truth. Public accepts the myth that a picture is worth a thousand words and sponges everything off the tube like a calf at the tit. Like Rodney King." Mattson paused to be certain Charlie knew who Rodney King was. "Now your newspaper reporter, that's a different breed, per se, and you got to watch them. If they're any good they check on stuff and sometimes even collect facts. Don't lie to them unless you're sure they can't check up."

"I don't want anything to do with these people."

"Good." Mattson smiled. "Send 'em to me. Meantime, just do me a favor. Help us find Mrs. Murdock's body. Now that you've told everyboby her name they're going to know who to ask for, and if one of the brighter ones asks the M.E. when he'll be done carving her up, they're going to hear, 'What corpse?' from him, and then you're going to be the biggest dumbo cop since Barney Fife. Have a good day." The sheriff donned his campaign hat and stalked out.

Before Charlie could gather his remaining wits Marlene shouted, "Didn't you have a nine-thirty appointment?"

"Oh, yeah," Charlie faltered. "The first husband. Johnson."

"Can I question him?"

"Why?"

"He's gorgeous! If that's him."

Unhurriedly, Charlie walked to the counter where he could see out the front door. Marlene would notice how nonchalant he was. No reason he should care why she found a man attractive.

"Must be him," Charlie said. "Dresses like somebody who buys his clothes from Dayton's." Quick before he gets here, did you try the keys in Mattson's car?"

"Yes I did, and I almost got caught by one of those silly deputies hovering everywhere. Did you know they all wear the same sunglasses, even on cloudy days? Like a bunch of Secret Service agents. I suppose they think that's cool."

"Marlene! The keys?"

"Don't be silly. Of course they didn't fit."

"Shoot!"

Carroll Johnson was framed perfectly in the Police Department's glass doors, watching the last of the reporters file out. It felt good to stand up after the long ride. He'd been very careful to keep his legs straight in the car so his trousers would hold their crease. The suit was new—a light blue Palm Beach. The union tie, with white flecks, and the pink shirt were perfect accents. He'd bought the creamy Italian pumps the summer before in Miami—a poor choice for such a wet day.

There was another reason Carroll took his time— police. Not that he had anything to worry about. Not really. Smoked a joint once in a while at parties. Did a little cocaine, now that it was fashionable in Minneapolis. He was careful to make sure it didn't interfere with his professional life or his physical conditioning but couldn't quite shake that feeling of guilt he got when a squad car cruised past or he saw a uniform. Cops were such unenlightened dolts. Small town cops especially.

113

Marlene all but drooled. "I'm going to my office now," Charlie told her. "When gorgeous gets tired of standing around in the rain, send him in."

A few minutes later he got a closer look at Carroll Johnson, and had to admit, he was awfully handsome in a citified way. Wore white suspenders—though not to hold his pants up. Some men were becoming more and more like women, Charlie thought, wearing things designed to draw attention to themselves. He didn't think clothes made the man, and could not have told anyone what he had on right now unless he looked.

"Sit down Mr. Johnson," Charlie said, making no move to get up from his desk or shake Carroll's hand. "I won't keep you long."

"It's a tedious drive up here," Carroll observed.

"Yes," he agreed. "Ordinarily, our remoteness isolates us from urban crime. Ordinarily."

"I suppose," Carroll said uneasily, wondering if this big cop didn't suspect just about anybody from the Cities of being guilty of something unpleasant.

"This isn't painful for you, is it?" he asked. "Coming in to talk about your ex-wife, I mean."

"No. Our relationship was over some time ago. These things happen. We got to be friends. Love takes many forms." Carroll was quoting his therapist.

"I see," he said. It was hard to make the man out. "Love seems to have taken a rather brutal form in this case."

"I'm devastated," Carroll said.

"Yes. I can see that."

"You said something on the phone about identifying Vicky's remains? If it is Vicky."

"We think it is, but her body was moved to St. Cloud for an autopsy. Unfortunately, it's going to be awhile. Anyway, her current husband, Gordon Murdock, will make the ID. Unless you want to stick around for a few days?"

114

"I've got to get back to work." Carroll protested.

"We'll call you then as soon as we know anything definate," Charlie promised.

"Fine. Thank you."

"Can you help us with a few details since you're here?"

"Of course."

Charlie opened a file folder on his desk. "Your wife's full name?"

"Victoria Dean Johnson," Carroll recited. "Victoria Murdock now, I suppose. I gave all this to your secretary over the phone."

"I know. Think carefully now before you answer the next question. Can you think of any reason your ex-wife would come to Willow River other than to see Dutch Cleland as you told me on the phone?"

Carroll squirmed in the chair. "No. I guess not."

"Think about it," Charlie prompted, ignoring the man's discomfort. "No other possibility."

Carroll stared at his folded hands. "What else could it be?" he asked, lifting his eyes.

"Mr. Johnson, I just want to confirm what you told me on the telephone and make absolutely sure there's no other possibilities. Other people she might've known? Anything?"

"No. Nothing."

Charlie wrote on a piece of paper. When he finished he asked, "Do you know your wife's current husband? Gordon Murdock? Personally, I mean. Have you met?"

"Never."

"How about Dutch Cleland?"

Carroll hesitated, shifting his pale eyes toward the door. "Only met him once."

"Oh? When was that?"

"When he broke up my marriage. He came to my house. I threw him out."

"Physically?"

115

"No. Of course not."

"Assuming the victim is your ex-wife, can you think of any reason why Mr. Cleland would want to kill her?"

"No, not really," Carroll sneered. "What he usually did to her doesn't come under the heading of violence." A mirthless chuckle escaped his lips. "They were in love, I guess. That's what she said."

"What do you say?"

"It was a long time ago," Carroll shrugged. "Old news. Who cares?"

"Somebody did," Charlie said, standing. "She's dead."

* * *

Walleye had never heard the term rigor mortis in his life but appreciated his lady being stiff enough to stand upright in the corner of his fruit cellar. It was the only way he could get the door closed.

He was careful about the fruit cellar. More than half the chokecherry jelly, garden tomatoes, and his favorite spaghetti sauce remained in jars since Mother died. He ate from this nine-year-old supply sparingly, preserving it year after year. The lady leaned gently in a corner so as not to disturb the jars. He hoped the small room was cool enough. Dead things stink if they're left out. But like the tomatoes, she'd be okay here.

It was comforting to have her here. It was the feeling he got with a full sack of cans from ditches or two packages of peanut M & Ms in one day. Much to be done now and she wouldn't be here alone in the dark for long. It took time to know what to do. You had to think and think. Mother always said, stop and think. Stop and think before you do something. He did that.

Walleye smiled and flicked out the light.

116

Chapter Twelve

Safe in his garage, Len Davis listened to his car radio in stunned silence as reporter Cheri Py summarized Day Two: The Willow River Murders. The hunt was on for the mad butcher, Dutch Cleland, who still eluded police. Those in isolated rural areas cautioned to lock their doors, stay alert. Behind the wheel of his Midnight Blue 1964 Corvette, Len felt a bit criminal himself.

A daring plan had taken shape in his mind since finding Dutch's sweatshirt early that morning. From Jean he'd get directions to the cabin, dash there ahead of police, grab Dutch, who was probably in no condition to think clearly, and whisk him to New Orleans, the last place anyone would look. He had a college pal there who played trombone and kept a pad in the French Quarter. With Dutch safely stashed, he'd return to Willow River and prepare a brilliant legal defense.

Later, plea the whole thing down to manslaughter as it obviously wasn't premeditated. County Attorney was a thirty-four-year-old divorcee named Betty Linnmeyer who once sat in this very car and said he had cute ears. In fact, she'd done more than that in this car. He found the remote and opened the garage door, backing through a white cloud of dual exhaust into a gray morning.

He knew *every* curve and straightaway on the two-mile drive to Cleland's, and the Corvette performed magnificently, tires clawing fresh tracks in the wet gravel. Summers, when the road was dry, he liked to watch his dust curl behind and drift above the green corn, but nosing into a turn he toed back on the accelerator. He was an officer of the court. One thing to mount a spirited defense, quite another to risk criminal prosecution for aiding a fugitive. He let the car coast to a stop along the roadside and stepped out.

Gazing west over barren hills his eyes traveled further than he wanted. It takes a special person to endure the prairie's emptiness day after day. A person who wouldn't relish a stretch in Stillwater, even a short one. New Orleans was impossible. They'd be better off coming home and doing their best in court.

The law, he thought, is more a reflection of the public than the public likes to admit. The lawyer jokes they make are jokes on themselves really. Nobody forces them to hire lawyers or bring lawsuits. They do it out of their own hardheartedness and, like them, Dutch had only himself to blame. Now he'd face his jury, and Len would find a good criminal lawyer to defend him. In the end, the truth came out more often than not and Dutch must answer to it as everyone did.

Len wrapped the yellow windbreaker across his belly. Afternoon snow warnings up for significant accumulations. Blowing, drifting. The air smelled only of dead grass and freshly plowed earth. He dropped back into the car, this time driving on at a slower speed.

He approached Dutch's house from the east, winding the last mile in a giant question mark around the brown marsh. Pulling into the yard, he avoided the house and brought the Corvette into the tall grass behind the pole barn, why, he wasn't sure.

"Saw you coming," Jean called from the open doorway as he crossed the back patio. "Been watching the road all morning."

He didn't answer but stepped inside as she closed the door. The kitchen was spotless but her face still held its ghostly pallor, hair pulled away in a severe ponytail leaving shorter wisps behind to fluff at the roots. She wore a shapeless green bathrobe that only added to her gauntness. Bare feet. "You're not dressed," he observed.

"I don't feel good." The flesh around her eyes looked raw.

"You look like shit," he blurted. "Maybe I should call a doctor or something."

She grabbed him around the waist, pressing her face against his chest. "I just need a hug."

He responded, resting his cheek on top of her head. They stood like that a long time.

"I'm glad you're here," she said at last.

He held her at arm's length. "I'm going to bring him back to you," he said. "I thought of helping him get away but he's so damn guilty." He allowed this simple truth a moment to take root and then said, "Which doesn't mean so much as you might think in court."

"Explain that."

"Guilty people are really what it's all about you know. Not the OJ kind of deal where you have a weird jury of groupies, but courts which aren't really so much about punishment as symbolism." Her brows knit and he thought maybe he was starting to sound more lawyer than friend. "They make a statement against crime and criminal behavior, not against people. Judges want the law to prevail of course, to be a lesson, but this is Minnesota. Average convicted murderer spends less than twelve years in prison."

She turned and walked to the sink, fidgeting with a damp dishrag hung from the faucet. "You're missing the point," she said reasonably. "Dutch isn't afraid of prison. He's afraid of Willow River. Humiliation. Being contemptible in his own home."

She was right. He didn't get it. "So move," he said.

"Dutch leave Willow River?"

"What's a town compared to your life?"

119

She turned to face him, her eyes brightened and held onto
him. "Dutch leave Willow River," she repeated with a wan
smile. "He'll die first. This is Camelot. Oz, maybe."

"Talk sense." He wanted her to understand about the law,
how Dutch paid a fair price for what he'd done, then got on
with his life. "This isn't Camelot. Or English Lit. It's Willow
River."

"Only to you and me," she said, turning to gaze out the window toward the marsh. "Not to Dutch. And there are others.
Charlie Benson is one of them, I think. They have roots here
we can't begin to understand." She turned to face him again.
"You and I are kindred spirits. City missionaries to the sticks."
She came near a laugh. "But I suppose our converts don't
know they're in the sticks or want very much to be saved."

He thought she might be joking. "You can't believe Dutch
is more afraid of what people think than he is of prison, or
being hunted down, maybe killed?"

"I'd bet my life on it."

"Or his?"

"Yes," she said, pushing herself up onto the sink. "Even
his." She curled her legs and balanced, catlike, on the narrow lip. "Before we were married, I had big plans for Dutch.
Bet you didn't know he's got a masters from Columbia?"

Len was astonished. "Never asked," he said. "A butcher . . ."

"BA in history. MA Latin American Studies," she spoke
proudly. "Dutch can tell you the name of every dictator in
Haiti since 1804, or the last ten ruling parties in Venezuela,
or the most popular baseball team in the Dominican
Republic. But his best friend didn't know he got past high
school." She tucked the hems of her bathrobe behind her
knees to warm herself. "Ever meet a guy like that? Me neither, so I married him."

"And the big plans you had for him?"

"They all involved leaving Willow River," she said. "I was
living in Minneapolis then, and one weekend he came to stay

with me. We fought over it. Finally I gave him an ultima-
tum—me or Willow River." She rolled her eyes up at the ceiling. "Dutch went home."

"He did?" Len saw light in her eyes again and recalled her
curled like this at the end of the dock at Buttonbox Lake,
fishing pole forgotten across her lap, soft, husky voice rising
and falling with the rhythm of some tale. She was a born sto-
ryteller. "Go on," he encouraged, afraid the moment would
pass and the light fade again.

"I was devastated," she continued. "Especially at first.
Then I got angry. So angry I hated him." She reached up
and pulled a knot, freeing her hair to fall around her shoulders. "And my friends—those that knew Dutch—all took my
side. Called him a hick, small town jerk. I cried. Got drunk
once or twice. Started dating a guy who wore a Neru jacket
and played the harp. Benito." Combing knots from her hair
with her fingers, she paused to stare at Len. "Six months,"
she said, "Lost fifteen pounds and whenever Benny kissed
me I wished it was Dutch."

"You're making this up," Len teased.

"Honest," she said. "Every man I dated made me sick! I
finally got a teaching job, packed up and moved to Willow
River."

"Married Dutch and lived happily ever after," Len finished
the story.

"Not quite," she said. "Dutch wanted nothing to do with
me. Passed me by on the street like I was a lamp post."

Len shook his head in quiet disbelief.

"It was the middle of winter before I finally had it out with
him. Know what he asked me?" Len gave a blank stare.
"How did I like Willow River?"

"What did you say?"

"I said it was the most fascinating place on earth, and I
wanted to get old and die here."

"He didn't believe that!"

121

"Not a word of it," she said. "He just wanted to hear me say it."

"Balls!" Len reddened.

"Just what I thought," she chuckled again. "And don't kid yourself, the man was in love with me right down to his socks. He could never, never have been happy with anyone else but risked it to get me on his terms."

Len pulled at his ear. "But you're so . . ."

"Liberated?"

"Well," he said. "Independent. And I've heard you tell Dutch off good. Seen him back down. Some people think he's henpecked."

"He is, you sap!" She jumped down from the sink. "But I know better than to ever put his back against the wall, and I'm pretty damn good in bed. There's the secret to a perfect marriage."

"Then how could he run off with this Vicky broad?" The words were out before he had time to think. Jean didn't seem surprised.

"That's a story for another day," she smiled, absently. Turning serious. "You made me a promise last night. Are you here to keep it?"

"Yes," he said, with more determination than he felt. "How can I help?"

"I think I know where he is."

She walked toward him, around a cooking island where the stove was. She looked short without her shoes. "Don't toy with me," she said. "I've been racking my brain day and night."

"Wait here a minute."

He sprinted from the house, across the sloping lawn to his car. A moment later he was back inside puffing and holding up the sweatshirt.

"Here," he said. "He's here."

"Where?"

"Isn't it real?"

"What?"

"This map," he panted. "On the front, here." He shook the sweatshirt in her face.

"Looks like a bunch of lines and junk to me," she said, puzzled. "'Where the hell is Togo?'" she read the words. "'Where the pavement ends and the north begins'?"

"The cabin!" He saw she was still puzzled. "Don't you know your own cabin?"

The cloud lifted from her face. "The hunting shack," she said. "Someplace in the north woods. I've never been there. I don't do woods."

"But Dutch does."

"You're right. It's the kind of place he'd go, but how will you find him?"

"That's what I'm trying to tell you! With this map."

"A map from a sweatshirt?"

"Look at it!" He waved it like a matador's cape.

"Okay," she said. "Hold it still." She traced the lines of ink with her fingernail. "The roads have numbers. You believe this is a real map?"

"Exactly." His exasperation giving way to pride. "Screened to scale and everything."

"You're quite the detective," she said, a note of admiration in her voice.

"Thanks. But before I go roaring off into the backwoods, tell me again about last night. Did you help Dutch with his packing?"

"No," she said. "I made the sandwiches."

"Did you see him pack?"

"Just from the window," she shrugged. "Cans of gas, saws, axes . . ." Her eyes widened. "Oh, my!"

"Women!" He threw the sweatshirt at her.

She hugged him. "You can find him."

"Bet on it," he said.

123

"Take my Jeep," she offered. "You'll need the four-wheel drive."

"What about my car?"

"We'll hide it in the pole barn. Cover it up with something. I'll drive the cattle truck for a few days. Say my Jeep's in for repairs or something. Come on," she said, shaking him, breasts trembling beneath the robe. "I'll help you put the car in."

"Hadn't you better get dressed first?" he said, embarrassed by her sudden lack of modesty.

She looked down at the bathrobe, gaping almost to her waist. "What's the matter?" she said. "Am I starting to sag?"

But she was speaking to his back, as he made quickly for the door.

* * *

Seven miles away, on the other side of town, Charlie Benson stood in LeRoy Immelman's dead corn talking to himself. "I have my doubts," he admitted. The slight breeze created a mysterious rustling.

The cornpicker had stripped the ears and bent the brown remains to earth. If this was a field of dreams, Charlie thought, there was nowhere left to disappear. The finality of harvest, like death, left nothing worthwhile behind except memory, maybe regret. The perfect setting for a cop with doubts.

He strolled, stepping over flattened stalks as he moved to the crest of the hill and gazed down at the town below. The silver water tower loomed above the trees. He'd climbed it once on a dare. Dutch had probably done it too. Marlene was right. He'd forgotten the first rule of investigation— impartiality. You don't lead the evidence, you let the evidence lead you.

He had a log of bias in his eye. No one in Willow River except Charlie himself had ever taken a life, killed another human being, except maybe those who went to war, and that was different. If Dutch killed Victoria Murdock it changed things forever. He'd been so shocked by the concept he couldn't see around it. He was afraid, in fact, to consider the other possiblities for fear he might be deluding himself to save the town from becoming, in his own mind, like everywhere else. If Willow River wasn't safe, then there was no safe place. That's why he killed the burglar that night long ago, to send them a message. Don't bring that garbage here. We'll punish you as quick for a box of bandaids as a bank heist because we're able to protect ourselves and we'll do it at all costs.

If Dutch killed Victoria Murdock there was no protection. Rot within. Charlie knew Marlene was telling him he'd gone there ahead of the evidence, maybe to do what he'd done in the drug store, make an example of Dutch. Maybe he'd never cared about evidence because he'd never planned to bring Dutch back alive.

Charlie Benson had his doubts. He shoved both hands in his pockets and turned to go, jangling a set of keys that didn't fit anything.

Chapter Thirteen

DUTCH AWOKE. THE ROOM WAS freezing cold. A foul-tasting paste coated his tongue and the roof of his mouth. He'd slept seven hours in the chair, yet was exhausted, depleted—his neck cocked at an odd angle.

He'd been dreaming of wolves with plastic faces, like Halloween masks. They'd encircled him with fixed smiles and gaping mouths filled with bloody teeth. His feet were weighted. He couldn't run. Behind the circle of wolves, Vicky's form rose atop long, naked legs. He watched in horror as dark hairs sprouted from her upper body, spiraling wormlike toward the ground. She called his name, slowly chewing it from her mouth until it took form, dripping dark red onto her bare breasts.

Dutch leaned over the arm of his chair and vomited onto the floor. Nimrod rose from his spot by the stove and sniffed the vomit, licking the chunks.

"Get away!" Dutch screamed.

He struggled to his feet and steadied himself, then stepped over and opened the door. "Get out," he ordered the dog. Nimrod slunk from the room. Dutch crossed to the cupboard, bent down and filled his mouth with cool water from a plastic cooler, then spit into a metal basin. Behind him the sour vomitus steamed in the cold air of the cabin.

He went to the stove and with a small metal shovel scooped ash from inside, sprinkling it onto the mess beside his chair. He shoveled until the smell was gone then started a fire.

"Good morning," Dutch said later, peering into a small mirror above the basin, now filled with hot water for shaving. "You look like I feel."

Nimrod dozed on the freshly scrubbed floor, his head resting on his crossed paws. The rhythmic sound of his breathing clearly audible above the crackling fire.

"How about some music?" Dutch asked the dog, who lifted his head momentarily and thumped his tail. "Maybe we'll hear the weather."

The ancient battery-powered, ten-band short-wave hummed as he searched the AM dial for a clear signal. ". . . reminder from the National Weather Service," a male voice said. "A major winter storm is likely by late afternoon or early evening today. Heavy snow watch has been extended to include all of northern and central Minnesota, with accumulations of ten to twelve inches possible, beginning this afternoon and continuing tonight."

"That'll keep Charlie Benson busy for a while," Dutch said, glancing out at the first flakes arriving ahead of schedule. "We'd better get ready, too," he said, frowning at the near empty woodbox.

Outside, he couldn't shake the dream image of Vicky. How should you remember the people you've loved when you don't love them anymore? Or the people you've murdered?

The truth was he remembered Vicky mostly in Roatan. He remembered the morning they sat on the tiny veranda outside their cabana. He had his feet up drinking a mid-morning Salvavida. Vicky was reading from a stack of what-to-do brochures.

"How about this one?" she'd asked. "'Unique adventure for the sportsman. Hunt the illusive iguana in his native habitat.' Habitat is spelled h-a-b-i-t. 'Weapon and canoe provided. Guides available.' How about it? Wanna test your skill against the big lizard, Dutcho?"

"Get a life."

"Chicken, eh? Well, here's another one. 'Scuba to adventure.' Has a picture of a woman with hardly anything on except a tank."

"Let me see that."

"Hands off. Pay attention. 'Our certified instructors will take you on an actual scuba dive after only one hour of lessons in the hotel pool.' What pool? 'Slip beneath the gin-clear waters into a world of underwater adventure and beauty. One hundred and thirty five dollars, U.S.' Sounds fun. What do you think?"

"Already had my underwater adventure. Pass the cigarettes."

"We're not sitting here all day drinking beer and smoking cigarettes. I want to do something."

"Keep reading."

"Here's one. 'X-rated picnic. Spend the day on your own secluded island. Swim suits optional. We provide the boat ride, deserted island, hammock, and shore lunch. The rest is up to you.' Sound romantic?"

"How much?" he asked, imagining Vicky's long naked form stretched out lazily on a deserted beach.

"Thirty-five dollars."

"Let's do it."

"Not so fast." She looked down from her perch on the porch railing. "I see we're pretty quick to make up our minds when the event involves nudity for only thirty-five dollars. Care to comment?"

"On the nudity or the thirty-five dollars?"

"Don't be flip."

"Is this the old 'Do you just love my body' question?"

"Yes. It is."

"I've always hated that one."

128

She threw the brochures.

They'd boarded the boat late that morning carrying a dirty Styrofoam cooler and snorkeling gear. Javier gazed longingly at Vicky in her one-piece black swimsuit and punched Dutch in the arm. "Bueno," he said, cranking the engine.

The X-rated Island, or large cay, was no bigger around than two city blocks. Its center dominated by rugged palms and low, thorny brush. Sea grape crowded the beach and dappled the dark limestone rock. Javier landed them near a small beach and forced them to wade ashore so *Evelyn* didn't scrape her bottom on the scattered bits of rock and coral. There was a fire pit, wood stacked nearby, and of course, a hammock.

They watched Javier backing cautiously into deeper water. "Sunset," he called. "Come to this place." They waved. Grinning, he turned and headed out to sea.

Vicky waited near the hammock in the conservative black bathing suit. Any second she was going to slip it off.

"I know what you're thinking!" she said.

"Not at all," he answered, straightfaced. "It's past noon. I was thinking about what's to eat."

"Oh?"

"Sure. See what's in the basket."

She shrugged and dropped to her knees, prying away the Styrofoam cover. "Wine," she said, tossing a bottle onto the sand. "Sandwiches. Plantain chips. Two mangos. Some hard cheese. Whew! Stinks. That's about it. Wait. What's this?" She held up a lidded jar and cracked it open, sniffing. "Yuk! Horrible old fish eggs."

"You don't like caviar?"

"Never tried it."

"Then how do you know if you like it or not?" he'd snapped more harshly than intended.

"I don't like chilled monkey brains either," she said. "And I've never tried them."

"Hardly the same thing. It's immature to have such a strong dislike for something you've never tried. After all, it isn't going to kill you to taste it."

"So I'm immature?"

"I didn't say you were immature. I said you were behaving in an immature way."

"Yes you did. You called me a name."

"No, I didn't."

"You're not my father, you know."

"Meaning I'm old enough?"

"Oh no, I didn't say you were old, just acting like it. I'm surprised you don't watch me at dinner to be certain I eat all my vegetables." She shook the jar of caviar in her fist. "Or do you?"

"Don't be stupid."

"Now I'm stupid?" Her voice, bitter, even menacing, remained modulated. Only her eyes flashed with real anger and for an instant he felt their hatred.

"Are you going to try it or not?"

"You like caviar?" She pulled out the waistband on his swim suit. "Here! Have some!" She dumped it down the opening and stomped off along the beach.

Awhile later, after washing out the swim suit and ironically becoming the only naked person at the X-rated picnic, he set out to find her. He'd cooled down and started thinking how lonely she must be sitting somewhere, probably on the other side of the island, sulking.

Following her course clockwise around the island, dodging tide pools and jumping deep, ankle-twisting cracks in the limestone, he reached the backside. Vicky wasn't there. Five other people were.

They weren't part of the deserted island fantasy. What if he'd been tracking Vicky naked? Furthermore, the three elderly women and two men picking shells didn't seem the least bit surprised to see him.

"Good afternoon," he said in a foolish attempt at civility.

They remained stooped. A middle-aged lady wearing an offensive straw hat said, "Hello," in a rather offhand, disagreeable manner.

"Where did you all come from?" he asked.

"Sussex," said the hat lady, straightening.

"Sussex what?"

"Sussex, Great Britian, of course."

"Oh. Well, this is supposed to be a deserted island," he informed her.

"In point of fact, it isn't, is it?" She examined the broken conch in her hand, then dropped it back on the sand. "Besides the young girl sunbathing here when we landed, there are the five of us and now you. Hardly deserted. In fact, considering its modest size, this island boasts a current population density roughly that of Hong Kong. Wouldn't you say so Edward?" She said, turning toward a pale man stooped several feet away.

"Precisely," Edward said to the ground.

"How'd you get here?" Dutch asked, noticing no boat in evidence.

"Boat, naturally."

"Where is it?"

"I must say! You Yanks are a bit presumptuous. You don't lay claim to these islands, do you?"

"No," he admitted.

"Run along, then. There's a good chap."

He'd learned what he needed from them anyway. Vicky had been spotted.

The backside of the island was mostly a mixture of sand and rock, unshaded and blistering away from the cooling breeze. Scrubby foliage crowded the water, narrowing the beach to little more than a path inhabited by swarms of biting gnats.

Vicky was nowhere in sight. Dutch continued on around until he arrived back at the private, abandoned beach. The wine, lunch, and wet towel he'd hung over the hammock, were all where he'd left them. It occurred to him that per-haps—since he'd gone in a clockwise direction around the island as she had—Vicky had circled in the same direction. The simplest way to find her was to walk back, counter-clockwise, the way he'd come.

He set off again, sweating now in the blazing afternoon sun, and circled the island twice more. He didn't see Vicky. He didn't see the contentious British beachcombers. The gnats were still there.

Back at the hammock, he uncorked the warm wine and sipped it from the bottle. The solution was obvious. Vicky, angry with him, had come around the island a second time and stopped to talk with the Brits. They'd told her he was a rude, obnoxious jerk. She agreed and they invited her away with them in their boat, wherever it was hidden. He was now alone on the island. There'd be no X-rated picnic, or any other kind. The cheese had melted, and the caviar, which had been the cause of this whole mess, was destroyed, along with the day. He'd sit alone on the beach until Javier cruised in at sundown.

An hour later, tired of brooding, he decided to make a final circuit of the island—jogging this time. The trip took less than ten minutes and was fruitless. He resigned myself to the hammock, and a nap.

At dusk, someone shook him awake.

"Better get up," Vicky said. "I hear the boat."

He blinked at her silhouette against the setting sun. "Thought you left."

"Left what?"

"This island."

"Don't be ridiculous. How could I do that?"

"With the English people."

"What English people?"

"The bloody beachcombing English people!"

"You must've been dreaming," she said, faintly amused. "This is a deserted island."

"Are you trying to tell me you've been on this island the whole time? That you didn't see anyone else when you walked around to the other side? That you didn't leave me here all alone?"

"Yes, to one and two. No, to three."

"Then you're lying. I searched every inch of this island!"

"The middle?" she said, folding her arms.

"Middle?"

"Yes, the middle. The center of the island."

"Brush and scrub. Nothing there."

"Don't be silly," she laughed. "There's a clump of beautiful palms. Lots of warm sand. Someone's even put up a couple more hammocks and built a small table. It's very homey, secluded. I spent the afternoon there." She paused, giving him a hard stare. "While you napped instead of coming after me to apologize."

Javier found them waiting there on the deserted beach.

After guiding Vicky up and over the stern ladder he turned to Dutch, grinned and winked. "You seem tired," he teased, imagining God only knows what kind of debauchery.

That night they'd made up to each other for what they missed on the island, but somehow it wasn't the same. Every fight leaves a rip in the fabric of a relationship and he never got over that dumb picnic. Hadn't got over it yet.

Three days later they left Banyan Bay. Javier squinted across the helm and early morning sunshine sliced the bay. A fresh crop of pink-white vacationers lined the hard benches along *Evelyn's* port and starboard sides. "Early plane from Tugoose (Tegucigalpa)," Javier whispered. "Hoosiers for Anthony's Key. We ride them along."

Vicky was braless in a simple khaki dress and the golden hues of her skin and hair created a union of cloth and flesh, except for her eyes, which shown like beryl. They carried

133

fresh drinks—rum with ice and lime water. "Looks like you folks travel in style," a female Hoosier volunteered. "Honeymooners, I bet."

"How'd you guess?" he said.

"Anybody could tell that," she said. "We're from Gary. That's in Indiana."

"I knew it," he said.

Already, the sun drew salty beads of sweat from his back and neck and he longed to take his shirt off and dive over the side into the aquamarine water.

"Where you folks from?" the lady asked.

"Minnesota."

"Twenty below zero in International Falls. Came over the TV just before we left."

Dutch gazed across the water, searching the small islands and cays for a beach and hammock.

"I'll always remember you just like that," Vicky whispered. "Your face set, looking out to sea."

"I was looking for our island."

"Why?"

"I don't know." He ran his fingers gently along her forearm, petting the bleached hair. "Maybe because I'd like to do that part over again."

"I'm tanner than you," she teased, holding her arm next to his. "And I'm a blonde."

"Weird genes."

"Dutch?"

"What?"

"Are we ever coming back here?"

"Don't know."

She stared at Javier's back a moment. "Suppose it's crazy, but I've lived so much in just a few days." Her voice grew distant. "It's not right to go away and never see Javier again, or Half Moon Bay, or ride in this rickety old boat. We're like aliens, called home before we've had time to explore the

New World. Not fair. I don't want someone else to sit in our hammock and watch the sunset."

"We're just tourists," he said finally. "Tourists go home."

"You're such a romantic," she smiled.

"Sorry."

"Wasn't this the very best time of your whole life?" She spoke in a low voice so the others wouldn't hear.

"It was good," he said, cautiously. "Like everything with us. It's over too quick."

"Whose fault is that?"

"Senor Dutch!" Javier called, pointing to the bow line.

Pleased to be treated like an old salt, Dutch brought in the line as *Evelyn* cleared the pilings and made her way up channel. The water was clear enough to make out the bottom and he watched a filefish nosing the current. Overhead gulls swung, white kites in blue space.

"There's no place I'd rather be right now," he told Vicky as he dropped back down beside her. "And nobody I'd rather be with. I just wish this boat was pointed the other direction." She returned his drink. "Just one more Salvavida and one more sunset."

"Funny," she said. "I don't even know what that means."

"Javier, what's Salvavida in English?"

One hand on the wheel, he lifted the lid on a large locker. "This," he said, taking out a life preserver.

"Now that's a good name for a beer."

"Si."

"Should've taken a couple back."

"No problem." Javier pointed to the ice chest.

"Just two," he said. "While we wait for the bus."

Too soon *Evelyn* slid alongside the dock, bouncing softly against a row of old tires, and Javier helped them unload the luggage. Dutch shook his hand and Vicky hugged him. They watched in silence until the old boat rounded the point and disappeared.

He thought Vicky might cry but she didn't. He made a seat for her with an upended suitcase and lit a cigarette.

"What day is it?" she asked, tugging the khaki dress above her knees and tucking it between her bare legs.

Peering at the date window of his watch, he said, "The twenty-sixth."

"Not the date. The day."

"Wednesday, I think."

"I didn't know that."

"Well, it might be Thursday."

"You're not sure?"

"I have a calendar in my wallet."

"Never mind." She held up a hand. "I'm glad you don't know. In a few hours we'll always know. That's how we live, by the clock. When we're home tonight, Javier will be having a game of dominoes." She stared at the two bottles of beer. "We shouldn't have taken his Salvavida."

"Well," he said, stroking her hair. "I guess he figures we need it more than he does."

If he'd known then how true those words would ring today, maybe he could've saved a life, even two. Or maybe not.

After the morning cutting chores he realized they still needed more wood. Dutch had eaten little during the past forty-eight hours, not uncommon for him. He often fasted, unintentionally, for a day or two, then developed a ravenous appetite. He sat before a plate overflowing with fried eggs, onions, potatoes, and chopped ham, shoveling food into his mouth without regard for his earlier nausea. Nimrod watched with interest, sitting upright, close to Dutch's elbow.

"Our main concern is the chainsaw," Dutch explained between mouthfuls. "We've got a lot more wood to cut before the storm hits." He tossed the dog a scrap of ham. "Won't be easy." Nimrod nipped twice at the morsel and swallowed. "More?" He speared a fresh slice. "Eat all you want," he said. "Before this is over I'll have to hitch you like a mule to drag logs."

A couple medium-sized poplar should do it until after the storm. Then the temperature would drop. He'd be gone by then.

Chapter Fourteen

IN BARELY TWENTY-FOUR HOURS the media had transformed a quiet prairie town into something Charlie termed "manufactured hysteria." Already that morning he'd heard from a psychic in Arizona, the mayor (she called six times), each councilman and two of their wives, and some fifteen-year-old producer at *Inside Edition*.

He stared now at a row of blinking lights and then back up at the window. It was snowing steadily.

"Marlene. Come in here a minute, will you?"

"I'm busy as hell, Charlie."

"Phones can wait."

Marlene didn't like doing more than one thing at a time. Only her head entered the room. "What?"

Standing so long in LeRoy Immelman's corn something came over him. A mental switching, tracking his energies in what he hoped would be a more productive direction. "Close the door and sit down."

"The phones."

"Forget the phones!" Two windows overlooked the street, and he paced between them, seeing only the floor. Below, sparse traffic and swirling snow slipped silently by. "You had quite a bit to say to me before, and I've been thinking about it. Now, I don't want you to take this wrong, but you got me having doubts." He glanced up, suspecting a smirk, but saw none. "I'm still ninety percent sure Dutch is guilty. Had op-

138

portunity and motive, even if the motive has aged somewhat, and he ran. If he's innocent why not stay and fight?"
Charlie shook his head. "He's running from a guilty con-
science as much as from punishment."

"I thought you said you had doubts?"

"I'm coming to that," he said. "You're right about the lack
of physical evidence. We don't even have a body. Unless one
of those calls was Mattson?" She shook her head. "So right
now if we find Dutch we can't even arrest him. Good thing
he doesn't know all he's wanted for is leaving home without
permission." Charlie chuckled. "So, I'll do what you said, get
Victoria Murdock's body back (don't ask me how) and then
work at finding real physical evidence while we're looking for
Dutch." He paused to gaze outside. "In the middle of a snow
storm."

Marlene held her tongue.

"That still leaves the doubt. But mine is different from
yours," he said, absently working the rusted damper on the
old fireplace. "I'm going to bring up a load of wood in case
the lights go out. Dutch was younger than me. Once when I
was a senior we had to scrimmage with the freshmen, lame
idea the coaching staff had to start them early on being
killers. Anyway, I lined up across from Dutch and he looked
up at me with those innocent freshman eyes and said, 'Take
it easy on me, okay Charlie?' and I creamed the little bugger.
I mean laid him out, stomped him with my spikes and blood-
ied hell out of him." He turned his back and stared out at the
blowing snow.

"Why?"

"Teach him a lesson." Charlie shook his head and kept his
face away. "Maybe I'm doing it again. Anyway, you were
right and I don't want to keep making the same mistake.
From now on we'll let the evidence do the talking."

"So he gets the benefit of the doubt?"

"Yes, but I'm still betting he did it."

139

"I'll get back to the phones."

"No," he ordered. "Make a new recording—due to the high volume of calls and so forth—then send everything to the machine and bring in your shorthand pad. You and I are going to find Vicky Murdock's body."

Marlene made the necessary arrangements and was back in ten minutes. Charlie had run an electric razor over his stubble and put on a fresh shirt. "Much better," she said.

"Sam Lynstrom has a funeral today but I want you to track him down again on his cell phone, beeper, or whatever gizmo he's got down his pants and have him call me on the City Council phone next door. Then get on our phone and call Mattson. Make sure they haven't found her. Then call Sam's wife and find out what time she says he left for St. Cloud." He waited a second while she caught up with her scribbling. "Then get both our so-called patrolmen in here. Time they learned how to do something besides roust drunks and jiggle door handles."

"You don't think Lynstrom took the body?"

"Sam isn't that clever." He started for the door. "Get on that right away. I'm going down for the wood." He paused in the doorway. "You see Marlene, this body deal ain't such a mystery. It either got in Lynstrom's hearse or it didn't. If it did, they would've found it out on I-94. Half the cops in Minnesota are looking. Who'd be dumb enough to steal a corpse from a ditch? Leaves just one other possibility—it never left Willow River. And if that's true, then someone stole it from Lynstrom without him knowing. Now, who'd do that? Who wouldn't want that body for evidence? Dutch, of course, maybe Murdock. Might explain why Dutch beat him senseless. In fact, add Murdock to your list of calls. Friendly reminder I'd like to talk to him when he feels up to it. So there you have it," he said. "All the possibilities." Oh, and remind me to try those keys in Murdock's Surburban."

As his footsteps echoed across the outer office and down

the stairs she thought how pat answers annoyed her. Outside the triple-glaze window tiny flakes drifted left and right, attracted like gnats to the glass, colliding and melting.

* * *

One hundred fifty miles northeast, the temperature plunged but not a single snowflake. Wheels humming under an alabaster sky of flat formless clouds, Len outran the storm. He'd rather outrun the radio, which spewed warnings and repetitive accounts of disaster in western and north-western counties. Travel advisories unlike any he'd heard from both the National Weather Service and the State Patrol poured from the speakers. Everyone in Minnesota ordered to seek shelter immediately.

He was comfortable that no storm sustained his ground speed of sixty miles per hour so he held his foot to the gas, traveling mostly north now instead of east, crossing the storm's front. Highway 65, a direct link to the Twin Cities, was usually steady traffic. In the last thirty minutes he'd counted four cars, locals heading for cover.

Three hundred people just ahead in the town of McGregor might be all that stood between him and oblivion, he thought. After McGregor there was nothing for a hundred miles but tamarack swamps, peat bogs and stunted jack pine. His rump was sore and his bladder ached. A brief rest stop in McGregor seemed prudent.

A solitary snowflake struck the windshield. Then another. And another. Each in turn melting to benign drops of water. He switched on the wipers.

Snow is ice, he recalled. Water vapor condensed on a nucleus, say a speck of dust in the atmosphere, then crystallized by falling temperatures to become delicate hexagonal structures of complex beauty. Len smiled. The snow intensified, but the rubber blades squeegeed it away. On the edges of the glass flakes froze and became ice again. Slowly, two small glaciers grew from the melting and refreezing and

141

hardened. Each swipe of the wipers was shortened. The blades thumped, packing the ice. Len adjusted the heater control, forcing more air through the defrosters. Another five minutes of this and he'd be unable to see the road.

Rapid ice buildup on the windshield didn't frighten him. Every Minnesotan has been forced to stop and scrape. But scraping is time-consuming work, with McGregor still a good ten minutes away. He'd already escaped one close call at Jean's, hiding in the pole barn under a canvas tarp with his Corvette, shivering, until Sheriff Mattson and his men left.

They'd arrived in two polished squad cars—lights but no sirens. A small parade of police power designed to frighten Jean. It hadn't worked. She allowed them to search the house without a warrant and later told Len the whole thing was "goofy." Mattson did the "good cop," "bad cop" routine just like the movies, playing both roles himself and sometimes getting them mixed up. Finally they drove away and Len crept out of the barn. She fixed sandwiches and boiled rutabaga for lunch.

When he was ready to leave they stood together just inside the back door.

"I keep saying goodbye to everybody," Jean said. "Have you got your sandwiches? Only two Cokes?"

"Not a picnic, you know," Len complained. "Quit fussing."

"It's a long drive." She took his hand. "I should be going with you."

"Impossible," he said flatly, though moved by her burning need for action. He'd seen the color flow back into her cheeks as she helped load the Cherokee. "Take you if I could," he said. "But Charlie Benson and even that dipshit Mattson would miss you the minute you left town. No one's watching me."

"I know," she said, hopelessly. "I'd lead them right to Dutch, but I'm so tired of being left behind."

"I'll find him and bring him back," he said. "He'll listen to reason, I promise."

"Darling Len." She squeezed his hand. "Wish I shared your confidence in Dutch's good sense. What about the weather?"

"That's what four-wheel-drives are for. Besides, these warnings are inflated most of the time. Remember Mega Storm '91? Big hype for a couple feet of snow. TV producers love natural disasters. Terrify their own mothers for a Neilson point, if they had mothers."

"Get going," she said, but kept his hand. "Promise me?"

"What?"

"If it does get bad, I mean a real blizzard, you'll turn back." She squeezed until it hurt. "Promise?"

"Okay, okay."

"Can't all be hype. Two people missing and presumed dead in Milbank, South Dakota. Caught that when Mattson was here," she said. "Milbank's close to the border. This thing's headed our way."

He'd kissed her cheek then and dashed out.

Ahead, visibility dropped to only a few hundred yards but he maintained speed. The wet pavement wasn't slippery. If the snow kept on he'd engage the four-wheel-drive. After all, snow is a natural phenomenon in this country and one learned to put up with it, or play in it. He'd driven in worse.

He pushed the play button on the tape deck and Harry Connick, Jr.'s, mellow voice filled the warm interior, accompanied by the buffeting wind outside. He switched on the headlights. The easterly wind, gusting at high speeds, made it difficult to hold the wheel with just one hand.

He stabbed the eject button and caught the word "blizzard," followed by a lengthy explanation, delivered in earnest two-minute warning style, of snow depths in feet, winds reaching tremendous velocities, and dangerous cold. Blizzards, the blitzkrieg of snowstorms.

143

Some time now since he'd seen another vehicle. Occasionally there were white-outs—sheets of snow so thick he drove into them like stationary walls. He switched on the foglights.

The boxy Jeep handled poorly in the wind. Unlike his sleek Corvette, the Cherokee stood high and square, exposing its flat surface like a sail. Len's grip on the steering wheel tightened, jerking left and right to hold to his side of the highway, like driving an open umbrella.

A draft chilled his ribs. The wind had found its way inside, spitting jets of snow around the door handle and window crank. He remembered seeing water in the bilges on a fishing charter once in Florida. "All boats leak a bit," the captain had said, amused. "It's not enough to sink us." Later, safe on the dock, he'd felt quite foolish. Here too, where was the danger? The snow inside would melt.

Visibility worsened. He measured it by the number of yellow lines he saw on the road ahead—two. During white-outs—none. He'd lost sight of things alongside the highway, even electrical poles. In storms like this he'd heard of people driving straight through a small town without seeing it. Snow was sticking to the pavement, dancing serpents of white smoke squirming in the wind. He reduced speed.

Under the hood, the V-6 engine would be sucking snow up from the road. If the snow melted, as it had on the glass, then froze, could it entomb the engine in a block of ice? He reduced speed again, no faster than a walk, and shifted into four-wheel-drive.

Was it his imagination, or had the engine temperature gauge dropped? He shut off the heater fan, listening. He didn't like the four-wheel-drive noise.

What if a car came up on him from the rear, moving fast? He'd be rear-ended. What if it was an eighteen-wheeler driven by some maniac from Tennessee. He jammed the emergency flasher button with the heel of his hand. A futile gesture.

He had to get off the road. Pull up somewhere and cover the engine. Get away from the highway before he got creamed. His back ached and his hands were sweaty. It would be dark soon, and already he'd lost sight of the road most of the time. Instead of looking ahead, he looked down to see the yellow lines. Before long he wouldn't be able to see them at all, then he'd just sail off into the white spume until he hit something or rolled into the ditch.

His best bet was a secondary road where he could put his back to the wind, tie a cover over the engine and wait out the storm. He brought the Jeep right, onto the shoulder, crawling along to avoid the ditch, feeling for it with the tires.

Time dragged. He saw nothing, not even a road sign. The Jeep rocked in the wind. The snow beat at the windows. The engine sounded like its cylinders were filled with gravel. On the radio, the static stopped and a man's voice said quite clearly, "The North Oaks Animal Rights Support Group meeting tonight has been cancelled." More static. ". . . blizzard." Static. Len said, "No shit?" and something silver passed by the window to his right. He stopped the Jeep. Shifted to reverse. Edging backward, he saw a mailbox and stopped.

Len jumped the armrest and slid across to the passenger's window, peering out at the mailbox. It was only inches away, jiggling violently atop a wooden post. He couldn't read the name, but the red flag was up. Whoever they were, they had mail—and a guest for dinner.

Len looked down at the ground. Had these people placed their mailbox to the left or the right of their driveway? Or across the highway from it?

He brought the Jeep forward a few yards. Saw nothing. Went back past the mailbox again. Still nothing. Across the highway then. Directly across? Or at an angle? Think about it! You didn't put a mailbox in the middle of nowhere. Make a decision. The Tennessee trucker was coming, wearing a quilted vest, grinning around an unlit cigar, listening to country-western music, bouncing along at sixty-miles an hour, black smoke pouring from his stacks. They'd tell the story at truckstops. The story of Len Davis—the man in the little red Jeep. "Did he ever return? No, he never returned. The man in the little red Jeep. He rides forever 'neath the streets of Boston. The man in the little red Jeep."

Len pushed open the door and struggled to his feet. The driveway had to be on this side of the highway. No one was stupid enough to put their mailbox across a busy highway. He couldn't see it but the drive was here, probably only a few steps ahead or behind.

He zipped the light jacket to his neck, turned up the collar and stepped out from the sheltered side of his vehicle into the swirling gale of snow. He gasped as the wind sucked breath from his throat but bent his head forward and moved on. Angling right, he found the edge of the road and followed it ahead, leaning heavily against the wind to keep his balance.

Snow blew up his nose and into his eyes. It came from the side, from below, sharp, hard as sand, driven to a deafening roar by the blades of a wild wind machine. His eyelids fluttered in a vain attempt to beat away the tears and ice. Grit blew into his mouth, tasting of tar. His feet ached from the cold, and he had on the wrong shoes—loafers over thin argyle socks. He'd lost the road.

He fell to his knees, feeling with his bare hands. The sloping ditch was replaced by solid ground. His fingers dug into the gravel. He had found the driveway. Just in time.

Len turned toward the Jeep.

It was gone.

* * *

Four cubes of clear ice clanked into the heavy highball glass followed immediately by a generous, amber splash of

Jane Barbancourt. "Shame to spoil this with Coca Cola,"
Dutch told the dog, and drank.

Unshaven, uncombed, but dressed comfortably in a navy
sweater and khaki trousers he sat near the stove, firelight
through the isinglass casting tropical orange patterns on the
floor. He saw Vicky hugging her knees while he rubbed
lotion across her arched back. A sand crab scampered for
cover under a rotting palm frond, bits of shell and blowing
leaves littered the beach. Beads of sweat stood out on his
forehead. Was the cabin overheating, or was it the rum?

Outdoors, nature gone nuts. "Bet they're dying like flies
out there," he told Nimrod. A real blizzard. Maybe as bad as
the Great 1940 Armistice Day Blizzard his father told about.

"Good dog," he said, pouring rum into his bowl. Nimrod
sniffed, lapped gingerly, sneezing. "Can't drink alone. Sign
of alcoholism."

Rum took the edge off his fear.

A short walk from the cabin's front door stood a pumphouse, a more modern building built of tongue and groove
cedar topped with green shingles. It housed the well and
plastic water containers he needed to fill. The cabin had no
running water. He couldn't see the pumphouse any longer
through the snow but foolishly he'd stacked most of the
wood there before the storm. All day he and Nimrod worked
—felling, hauling, and splitting.

He drained his glass. "Stay here, pup," he ordered, uncoil-
ing a nylon rope beside his chair. "If I'm not back in ten minutes, bring me that bottle." He rose unsteadily to his feet and
tied one rope end around his waist then crossed the room
and tied the other to the door handle. Donning his parka,
Dutch stumbled into the howling storm.

Gale force winds swept through the naked trees in raging
gusts and a mournful cry halted Dutch in his tracks. Clothing
snapped against his body loud enough to be heard above the
howl. He knew instantly this was a storm to be feared.

147

Unlike hurricanes, blizzards aren't named but this one had plenty of personality. He pulled on his mittens and cupped them over his mouth to steal a breath. Driven mad by the wind, snow struck everywhere at once. The covered porch offered little protection and windows set securely into the logs were opaque with packed snow and brown grass ripped from the earth. He could not see his own feet. Beyond, in the yard, a white tidal wave sucked light and heat and oxygen from the air, replacing it with stinging ice.

The snow descended on warm ground but accumulated so rapidly very little melted. Dutch heard the moaning of weakened trees forsaking their roots and thumping into the snow. And like the trees, his body wobbled atop the porch threatening to topple.

Dutch turned back to the door and untied the rope. He no longer trusted it. The wind velocity threatened to tear the latch away or shove him hard enough to rip the entire door from its hinges. Instead, he attached the rope to a huge center upright on the porch, but thoughts of carrying in the water jugs now seemed ludicrous. He'd spend energy only on wood or the storm might easily accomplish what the ratchet man and the cops had failed to do.

Like an encumbered astronaut on the surface of the moon, he moved clumsily down the steps and into the churning yard. He quickly lost sight of the cabin lights and did not see the pumphouse. He fought down his panic, fearing the rope would pull loose and he might veer off, missing the building. He remembered a storm the year before much milder than this. A farmer leaving a tavern drove to within several hundred yards of his barn before his truck stalled. He managed to get out and walk. They found him next spring face down, twenty feet from the barn door.

There were a hundred stories like that, so common a person became insensitive to them and allowed the same thing to happen. The day before he'd been ready to kill himself and now he struggled to survive. The capriciousness of the human character. He struck the pumphouse with his right shoulder.

The trip back seemed less painful and frightening but netted only one armload—six pieces. Enough for an hour. Dutch went eleven times and added frostbite to the mess already made of his face. In the mirror, he found himself unrecognizable. No need then for plastic surgery to hide his identity.

He reached again for the bottle and poured. Another long night. He shouldn't be drinking really, because drinking only gave him a false sense of well-being that soon degenerated to melancholy and self-pity. He'd tally his regrets and end up feeling nasty as hell.

* * *

Len crawled ahead on all fours like a dog. His knees had torn through his thin trousers and the fresh wounds cut by frozen gravel collected dirt. His hands too, were cut and bleeding. He doubled them into fists hoping to warm them, cursing his stupidity for leaving his gloves on the seat in the Jeep. As if that were the worst mistake he'd made today.

Leaving the Jeep was the kind of mistake made only by the feebleminded. "You are, Mr. Davis, the most hebetudinous blockhead I've ever had the misfortune to instruct," Dr. Clemet Canavor said to him in law school after three dull answers in succession. Old "Cadaver" sent him scurrying for a dictionary after class to look up hebetude, and Len decided then that getting called a dope so well you weren't sure of it, made you doubly dull. And here he was, at it again. This freak. This end-of-the-world, nuclear winter, Armageddon, freak of a snowstorm. Len resolved to sue the whole goddamned Weather Service if he lived.

Mercifully, his ears had stopped stinging and gone numb. He supposed that was the first stage of frostbite, or the final stage before they turned black and fell off. He ignored them and crawled forward, one idea locked in his head—it could-

149

n't be much further. If he hadn't gone far from the Jeep to begin with, then it couldn't be far back. It just seemed like it was taking a long time, unless of course he'd crawled right past the Jeep and not seen it. Entirely possible. Visibility was zero, stinging snow and dirt stabbed his eyes into little more than running sores.

He dug under the packing snow to feel the place where the gravel shoulder met the raised pavement of the highway. This took time, moving left and right until he found it and then found it again to be sure he wasn't deluding himself or that the pain in his hands weren't enough to trick him into feeling something not really there. In his mind he drew a picture of the highway without the snow and everything was clear. Jeep sitting alongside the road on the gravel shoulder and the highway with yellow lines down the middle and a nice clear fog line at the edge just where his hand was now, and everything in its place just like it should be.

He was there too, crawling along in a perfect line directly for the Jeep. Just a few yards ahead. He could stand up, take a few quick steps and be there.

He'd parked almost on top of the mailbox and left the engine running. The heater fan humming, pumping warm air into an empty space of glass and steel. Dear God, if only his hands would go numb he'd never ask for another thing.

Len Davis thought he heard himself crying and then Bing Crosby was singing "White Christmas." Words and melody fading in and out. A final irony. Or was it just the wind in the highline wires?

The top of his bare head struck the Jeep's front license plate as the last notes died away. He hugged the bumper, resting his cheek fondly against the frozen chrome and rubber. "There you have it," said a faint, clear voice from inside. "The old crooner himself for all you folks out there enjoying the first snow."

Len thanked God out loud because he had to say some-thing, but the words were barely out of his mouth before a new thought overpowered him. Out of old city habit maybe he'd locked the door. When he got out did he unconsciously hit the electric switch and lock all five doors?

With his cheek against the bumper, he felt more than heard the engine running. The vehicle offered a windbreak and he edged along to where he could see the driver's side door handle. The only way to find out if the door was open was to walk over and try it.

He crawled over.

He gripped the handle to pull himself erect but quickly bent again, keeping his head below the level of the roof where wind sliced across with the force of a beheading ax. Bracing himself against the quarter panel, he reached for the handle with something that looked remotely like his right hand. Bloodless fingers, swollen and tight, small hairs bleached and brittle, div-ots gouged from the skin around the knuckles. Deep scratch-es should've been bleeding but weren't.

He hunched there a moment, just staring. "How do you define success?" Dutch asked him once on a flat-calm lake soaking in the August sun drinking beer and not doing a whole lot of fishing.

He'd felt trapped into the stock answer—family, job, cars, house—things. But finally he managed to say, "Guess I'd define success as happiness."

Dutch had only shook his head and asked if he wanted the sandwich with the mayo or the horseradish. Today he'd define success as opening the door.

He placed his hand on the latch, but his fingers wouldn't curl. Maybe it was locked anyway. He took the fingers with his other hand and bent them, hooking each in turn beneath the latch and jerking.

The door opened. He grinned and cracked his lip.

*   *   *

151

Walleye wasn't afraid of storms. He wasn't afraid of anything once he was inside the house, but he didn't think it was right to leave the lady naked. Even in a plastic bag.

Rummaging through mother's dresser he clutched underthings in one hand, with the other pressed a blue dress against his breast. It matched her eyes, he thought. He wasn't sure about underthings. Mother had been modest and he'd never seen much of her in underthings and wasn't entirely sure which piece went where on a woman. Maybe the dress was enough. He didn't wear underwear sometimes if he forgot.

Draping the blue dress over his arm, Walleye opened the door to Mother's closet and selected a pair of black oxfords she'd always thought comfortable. He'd forgotten stockings. No one dressed without stockings. Your feet got warm and sticky in shoes without stockings. He snatched a lacy pair of white anklets.

He carried things high, like he'd been taught, so nothing dragged on the ground. In the fruit cellar the lady stood inside her bag in the corner. Painfully thin and pale, Walleye nevertheless possessed surprising strength. He unzipped the bag and peeled it away to the lady's bare ankles. Hugging her just below the rump, he lifted Victoria Murdock clear and rested her back against the shelves, barely rattling a crowded row of sweet pickles. The dress went over her head, though the stiff, unyielding arms nearly wore him out, bending and twisting and shoving. Lucky it was a short-sleeved dress. Stockings were easier. Shoes were not. He left the laces untied and one heel out.

Stepping back, Walleye admired his handiwork. Thoughtfully, he stuck his tongue out and chewed it. Something was missing. Jewelry. And a touch of perfume might improve her odor. Evening in Paris. A small dark bottle beside Mother's hairbrush and red plastic combs. Yes. Pearls and Evening in Paris.

152

Chapter Fifteen

STURDY WIRE STITCHED BETWEEN Gordon Murdock's teeth secured metal arch bars along his gum line on both sides of his broken jaw. Someone had yanked one of his incisors to make a feeding hole and today the nurses allowed him solid food, puréed pork chops sucked through a large straw. Lying in a narrow hospital bed, he'd focused on only two things: the impending death of Dutch Cleland and the unwitting assistance of the man standing awkwardly in his doorway. Both now contingent on the weather.

Snow was falling at a rate beyond Murdock's experience. His view of the landscape restricted to a brick wall, white flakes swirling in all directions, including up. "If it's so impossible to drive in this shit how'd you get here?" he asked Carroll Johnson.

It took Carroll time to answer. What Murdock said sounded more to him like "Ifisso imposuble todrivenisshit howdyagether?" Carroll had only stopped by out of curiosity. Get a look at the current husband, the big ex-con from Oklahoma. He told Murdock, "Of course as a native Minnesotan, I'm quite proficient at winter driving. The funny old policeman told me where you were. I guess that jaw is pretty painful."

"'uck the jaw. The guy killed your wife."

"Your wife."

"Our wife then." Elastic bands criss-crossed the outside of his mouth and saliva filled the trough in his lower lip, caus-

153

ing him to slurp at it after nearly every sentence. "I need a ride back to that town. My Suburban's there. All my stuff."

"Oh," Carroll said, wishing he'd made it out the door ahead of this request. "Well. I was really on the way back to Minneapolis. Business, you know. Just wanted to stop in, see how you're doing even though we've never met. This isn't the kind of thing I usually get involved in, as you might guess. It's your affair, and Vicky's of course." Carroll was considering a stop downtown for a topcoat. When things got him down he liked to shop. Perhaps a town the size of St. Cloud had an acceptable men's clothier. "I really should be running along."

"Sure. Go ahead," Murdock slurped. "Guy murders your wife and beats up her husband. What's that to you, eh, big shot? If you were still married to her maybe you'd be lying here sucking lunch through a 'ucking straw."

"You're suffering now. Striking out. Pain does that. In any event, I'm hardly to blame."

Murdock raised his bed and neither of them spoke as the motor whined. "Dutch Cleland killed Vicky," Murdock stated plainly. "Is that important enough to you that you can sit down for two minutes and listen to me?" Murdock's skin-enfolded eyes were unavoidable.

"Of course," Carroll said. "I just don't have time to drive you all the way back to Willow River." He crossed to the chair by the window and sat on the edge.

"It's hard for me to talk," Murdock said. "But I think pretty good. Lying here thinking and thinking. First, did you see Vicky?"

"See her?"

"Her body."

"No."

"Did they ask you to make an ID?"

"Yes, but later. Some sort of bureaucratic snafu. About what you'd expect from small town law enforcement." He sighed. "Out of their depth, obviously."

154

Murdock nodded. It made him dizzy. "I thought that too, at first," he said. "Old Benson found me behind Dutch's butcher shop and got an ambulance. Came down here with me and asked a bunch of lame questions. Said Vicky was being brought here and he'd like me to have a look at her when I felt up to it." Speech was an effort for Murdock and the pain in his jaw was considerable.

"Did you?"

"No. And nobody's mentioned it since."

"So?"

"So I asked the nurses and a couple doctors. Know what they said? No information." Murdock slurped and spit into a green emesis basin. "So I asked one of the housekeeping girls. Figured they clean everyplace, even the morgue. The word comes back, two stiffs in there. Some eighty-year-old guy. Emphysema. A kid who croaked from a cancer. Story about it in the paper. Nobody else. No Vicky."

Carroll was puzzled. "What's it mean?"

"You gotta understand how the law works," Murdock explained. "I been through the system, see? All about provable stuff. Evidence. Depositions. Witnesses. Vicky ain't nothin' anymore, just evidence. So the old cop tells me to ID Vicky ASAP before the Medical Examiner starts to carve her up, but when I ask I get the stall. All of a sudden nobody knows nothin'. Bullshit. Something's going on."

"Maybe they just changed their minds," Carroll suggested. "Identified her by other means."

"She'd still be here somewhere for the autopsy wouldn't she?" Murdock rested his head on the pillow. "I been thinking about all the possibilities. They ain't that many. If she isn't here, she has to be in Willow River, right? But they got no morgue there. She's gotta be stinking by now. And don't turn away like that. Use your head. Benson might've stashed her in his deep freeze but I doubt it. So what's that leave?"

155

"A guy under the influence of pain medication with too much time on his hands," Carroll said rather directly, standing to go.

"That's what you think? I got a high on?" Murdock attempted a grin but when the lips pulled back away from the wires and rubber bands it looked to Carroll more like a snarl. "Sit down. Your two minutes ain't up yet."

Carroll refused to sit, but remained at the end of Murdock's bed. "Vicky's dead. What they've done with her body doesn't concern me. The case is already well-documented in the media and I think it's pretty clear Dutch is guilty. There's too many people involved now for any small town cop to ball things up. Sheriff over there said he expects an arrest before long. I feel like hell about Vicky, but it's over. She's dead. When you get a date for the funeral, let me know, I'd like to send a substantial gift of flowers."

"No shit?" Murdock said. "A substantial gift of flowers. Cleland murders your wife—ex-wife, I'm sorry—and you're gonna send flowers?" Murdock couldn't figure it. Guy didn't appear stupid. Even had a good physique on him. What was he scared of?

"I'm sorry," Carroll repeated. "It's all I can do now."

"Really," Murdock said, trying to push himself higher on the bed. "I know something else we can both do. We can stop Cleland from getting away with it."

"It's not our business." Carroll was becoming exasperated. "He's not going to get away with it, anyway."

"Listen to me," Murdock said more strongly. "He took Vicky. That's why she ain't here. Maybe he killed her in a fight, I don't know. She left home because she was mad at me about some issues and she came running to him and who knows where it went from there? Maybe he told her to get lost or his wife got wise. Must've done something to piss him off and they got physical and he snuffed her. He panics and runs. Then later he starts to think, you know, when his head

156

clears. Maybe he talks to a lawyer. Anyway, he finally figures that nobody saw him so he goes back for her but the dummy on his tricycle gets there first and screams for the cops. So he stays cool until he sees a chance to snatch her." Murdock slurped. "Think about it. By now he's got her at the bottom of some half frozen lake with a goddamn tractor tied around her neck. No body, no case. He's unavailable for a while, then resurfaces and says he wonders what all the fuss is about. He was just hunting."

"Who'd believe such a story."

"Doesn't matter. In the system, you gotta have proof. No body. No proof. The guy's off."

There was a certain amount of rudimentary logic to Murdock's ravings, but the idea that Murdock wanted to involve him was more than annoying, it was dangerous. "I suggest you relate your suspicions to the police," he said.

"They already know," Murdock asserted. "They got no corpse to use as evidence of a crime and they got nothin' else. Week from now they'll still have nothin' and by then this whole thing will be a done deal. Cleland's lawyers will get the law off his back and Cleland will be home wrapping hamburger paddies until the whole thing blows over. And where you gonna be? Sittin' in your big city office kicking yourself in the ass 'cause you let the bastard get away with killing your old lady?"

Carroll had no idea what became of Vicky's body. Murdock's wild theories had a certain street-smart logic but what was the guy really getting at? "It still has nothing to do with us."

Murdock made his grotesque attempt at a smile again and seemed almost friendly. "You smoke?"

"Of course not," Carroll said. "Anyway, this is a hospital. You can't smoke here."

"Cigarettes in my shirt." He pointed to a small closet on the opposite wall. "Lighter's there too. I'm gonna tell you the truest thing you ever heard."

When Carroll returned, Murdock wedged the filter in the black hole between his teeth and lit up, smoking with no hands. "Before I begin, I'm gonna convey something to you. Cleland's home free now. You got to understand that. He walks. Nobody touches him except you and me." It was almost as if Murdock preferred it this way. "He's got Vicky someplace they'll never find her. All this media hype will go away when there's no body. Pretty soon they'll be back to countin' pimples on Jesse Ventura's lardy ass and a year or two goes by and nothing happens and finally the whole deal's blown over, just like I said. Understand?" He waited until Carroll nodded. "Now, here's the deal. We ain't cops. We don't have no silly rules to play by, and I got a plan to take the guy down." He meant kill of course, but it wouldn't do to spook the dude too soon. He needed him. Murdock was in no condition to drive, let alone face Dutch again.

During this speech Carroll examined his own reasons for wanting Dutch caught. There were more than he'd thought at first, and they were old, deep. "I might be persuaded to go along," he said. "However, I need some assurance our involvement will be limited." He slid Murdock's lighter from the metal bedside table and flicked the cover open and closed in a methodical series of sharp clicks, allowing the ideas to take shape in his mind slowly and with perfect precision. Unlike Murdock, his hatred for Dutch had festered for years though he'd plastered it with poise, covering the most sickening and chronic wound of all —she couldn't kiss him. What she said was, "Kissing you makes me puke." "I don't intend to ever be identified with this business in any way, understand?" he told Murdock. Ten years of marriage, of risking his career to see her advanced, of pumping everyday to keep himself fit, and then kissing him made her puke. She said it matter-of-factly in the kitchen. "Tell me how we find Dutch when the police can't. How we get to him without so much as a whisper of our presence being

heard or suspected or even imagined, then maybe I'm in."
Carroll set the lighter on the table. "Don't light any fires you
can't put out."

Murdock was mildly shocked by the dude's suppressed
venom but encouraged by his apparent sudden lack of scru-
ples. Maybe he even had brains to go with it. "Nobody disappears except in the movies," he promised. "The little
wifey, Jean, knows where he is. She's used to covering for
him but we'll crack her."

"How?"

Murdock retrieved the lighter. "I know how to handle
women."

"So I've heard."

* * *

In semi-darkness Charlie sat slumped atop the service
counter. Outside, the storm revved, moaning at the windows, flinging branches, dirt, and snow against the building.
The electricity had failed at 5:09, stranding the minute hand
just above Vern Palmquist's ear. Vern was a doctor of chiro-
practic who served two terms on the City Council and later
donated himself as a clock. There was something restful in
having a familiar bald-headed man with two chins smiling
down on him from the wall.

Charlie wondered if Dutch ever had Vern adjust his back.
Something to ponder, like motives for murder. Why does a
guy kill his lover years after their affair ends? Killing her during makes sense, or when they break up. Killing her years
later he'd never heard of.

Marlene came in carrying a candle.

"Ah, Lady Macbeth!" he sighed with great drama.
"Whyfore did he kill her now after all these leagues?"

"League is a distance, dope, not a time," she said, pouring hot candle wax into a puddle beside him. "I think
Murdock did it with the nylon stocking in the ditch."

159

"Maybe." Charlie slid over to give her room. "But if the Tulsa cops are right about him, he's too clever to stick around. He'd be long gone."

"Really? Another gifted prognostication by the wizard who said it wasn't going to snow." She crossed her eyes, sucked at her cheeks and puckered her lips to make a fish face. "Go down the basement and start the generator, I've got no radio. Here's a flashlight."

"Any other orders?"

"Phones are still out but I doubt there's anything you can do."

"Call the telephone company?"

"Very funny. Get in the basement."

Charlie heaved himself down and obeyed.

Outside, the combination windows rattled in their aluminum frames and the wind whistled mournfully through the screens. Above, something was slapping hard against the building. It gave Marlene the creeps and the room seemed void suddenly without Charlie. They were in for a long night, but maybe it was a blessing. For a few hours at least, Willow River could be just another prairie town caught in a snowstorm, not a murder scene. She didn't know why that should be so soothing, the storm might be an even more vicious killer, after all.

The lights came back on but with a pulse. Charlie nagged the City Council every year for a new generator. She heard him trudging up the stairs. "Bunch a tight-fisted, skin-flint Swedes. Surprised they don't have a mule down there walking in circles."

"Generator on the fritz?" she asked, politely.

"Call that piece of junk a generator? Try the radio. If it works, see if Bobby's got his ears on." Bobby Brown was one of Charlie's two full-time patrolmen. He worked the night shift, and part-time days as a mechanic at the Cenex garage.

160

"You had him working an extra shift today," Marlene said. "And he usually sleeps in the afternoon."

"Usually sleeps on the job," Charlie responded. "Maybe the storm woke him."

The radio hummed and popped. She keyed the mic. "Patrol One. WRPD. Patrol One. WRPD. How do you read? Over."

Charlie leaned on the high counter that separated the dispatch station and Marlene's desk from the rest of the room, close enough to grab the mic if Bobby answered.

"Patrol One. WRPD. Do you read?" Marlene looked up at her boss. "Sleeping like a baby."

"WRPD. Patrol One." A deep, resonant voice came from the speaker. The kind of voice you imagined calling in air strikes on the Viet Cong. "Read you five by five. Over." The voice really belonged to a man in his thirties, barely five-foot-seven, who wore cowboy boots with elevated soles.

Charlie reached for the mic. "It's Charlie, Bobby. Can you come in a little early tonight?"

"That's a negative. Over," the voice said, void of emotion.

"Why not?" Charlie could feel his face getting warm.

"Ten-seven. Over."

Charlie gave Marlene a quizzical look. He refused to learn the ten-codes. "Supper," she whispered.

"After supper, then?" He was doing a marvelous job holding his temper.

The response was some time in coming. "Switch to land-line. Over."

"Bobby! You dumb shit!" Charlie erupted. "It's the middle of a blizzard. Land-lines are out. Are you coming in or not?"

Another long pause, during which Charlie glared at the radio and Marlene picked an imaginary hangnail.

"Do I get paid overtime?" the voice inquired.

"I don't flipping believe it!" He flung the mic in Marlene's lap and stalked off.

"Affirmative, Patrol One," Marlene said into the mic. "But I'd skip the ten-seven if I were you."

"Roger your last," Bobby said, glad to be talking with Marlene again. "ETA five minutes."

Marlene clicked the mic twice and tossed it on the desk. Bobby could get under Charlie's skin faster than anyone on earth, and she had only five minutes to calm him down.

She found him in the closet rummaging for his fur cap. "On the shelf right above your head."

"Oh."

"I know why you're mad."

"Of course," he said. "You know everything."

She snatched the cap from the shelf and handed it to him. He took it slowly, deliberately. "The snow stops you from running Dutch to ground so you're all frustrated and ungratified."

"Okay, Dr. Freudenstein."

"I'm serious," she said. "This is too personal with you and you better decide once and for all if you're a professional or not."

"Not," he said under his breath, jamming the cap on. "Where's my choppers?"

"Did you hear what I just said?"

"I answered you. I'm giving the guy the benefit of the doubt. That's enough."

"That's not what they're paying you for."

He turned on her. "That what you think? It's about money? Teachers used to make three-thousand a year and they actually taught kids something. Country docs got paid in chickens and eggs and came by your house late Sunday night to see your sick child. Courts stood for justice and cops didn't look at murder as a case to solve but a wrong to right." He retrieved the leather mitts from a cardboard box on the floor. "I'd rather be a gifted amateur than a pro any day."

"Well, you've got the gift of gab, I'll give you that."
Marlene shrugged. "Where do you think you're going in this
storm anyway?"

"Out."

"Don't be silly. Dutch isn't out in the storm."

"No, but others might be," he said. "Besides, it's what
they pay me for, remember?"

Chapter Sixteen

THE STORM WAS OVER. Beneath her long overcoat Marlene clutched the warm donuts to her breast, though it was hard to crawl with one hand. Snowdrifts exceeded fifteen feet, according to Dean Pixley on MNN. The shortest blizzard with the most snow in Minnesota history— twelve hours and 37.6 inches. There were semi trucks on Highway 11 with only their stacks showing.

She rolled onto her back, feet in the air, and slid to the sidewalk. To her right, City Hall's granite steps were blown clear all the way to the door and she mounted them with determination. A sixty-four-year-old woman with a midriff shouldn't work this hard for a half dozen squashed donuts, but they'd been up all night.

Brushing caked snow from her coat and hanging it near a heat register, she found Charlie asleep at his desk, a dozing hobo with a day's growth of beard graying his face. "You'll get a stiff neck lying there," she said.

He remained so motionless she drew a quick breath, reminded of the summer he contracted a strange illness they thought was polio, but wasn't. "Get up," she said, pinching his toe. "I brought you a treat."

"Oh, it's you."

"Donuts."

He lowered his feet into a waiting pair of Sorels. "I'm starved," he said, standing.

"Clean up first. You look like something the cat dragged in."

He groped around in the cupboard until he discovered a bottle of Aqua Velva and doused his head with it.

"What've you got against water?" she asked fanning the air.

Charlie threw the empty bottle at the waste basket. "Still digging out on Main Street?"

"Sounds like a snowblower jamboree. Elton Bolick had the city garage door up and diesel smoke billowing out so I suppose he finally got the plow going." She opened the donut bag and laid out two flattened glazed donuts on a napkin. "Day old. Hardware Hank sign went right through their window and one of the newspaper racks from in front of Berkie's is up on Sam Lynstrom's awning, or what's left of it."

"Death toll's what I'm worried about," Charlie said. "They'll be finding people all day. Got Bobby out on snowmobile. Should be checking in before long."

"Eat," she said. "Phones back up?"

"Off and on like before."

She poured them each coffee from the white coffee maker on his filing cabinet. "Did I tell you about Milly Wayne?"

Mouth full, he shook his head.

"Called earlier. Guy from Iowa out on 11 last night headed to Fargo. Slides off the road, sits in his car until it runs out of gas, then starts walking. After God only knows how long, he ends up in the middle of Buttonbox Lake. Thinks he's a goner out on the ice when he spots Duane Jorgenson's fishhouse. Breaks in and gets the stove going. Nothing else to do so he opens the hole and hauls in six crappies. Strolls up to Milly's this morning big as you please, knocks on the door and wants to know if he cleans the fish will she make him breakfast. When she called they were playing double solitare. He needs a lift. Suppose they ate the fish."

"Hope not," he said. "They're evidence. Iowa guys aren't licensed to fish in Minnesota."

"Very funny," she said, getting up to answer the phone. "It's Bobby."

Charlie washed down the last bite of donut and picked up the receiver. "Where you at now?"

"Laundromat. Back door got jarred open. Drift in here tall as the extractor. Land line's okay though."

"Don't check the phones, check people, roads, accesses to homes. Move fast in case somebody's trapped or hurt."

"Yeah. Got it. Might actually be a guy missing," Bobby said hopefully.

"Who?"

"You know Doris Rayden-Bergdung, that women's libber with the big nose? Wears clogs all the time? Works for that dink lawyer, Davis?"

"Everybody knows Doris. What happened to her."

"Nothing." He sounded peeved. "Ran into her walking in the snow in her stocking feet. You know Charlie, she ain't exactly bowling with all ten pins, anyway I was expressing concern about her welfare, like I'm supposed to, and she engages me in this lengthy conversation during which I discover her boss, Davis, took off late yesterday in his little 'Vette and disappeared. What do you think about that?"

"Not much."

"Pretty suspicious if you ask me. Right before a storm. And Rayden-Bergdung says she overheard him calling Mrs. Cleland too, just before he left."

"Are you sure? Go back and talk to her again. Find out if she overheard anything. Try to be nice."

"Okay," Bobby said. "Securing premises here first."

"Forget the washers and dryers. Make a quick sweep around town then talk to Doris."

He set the phone down as Marlene stuck her head in again. "Lady out here just spent two hours on a snowmobile getting in from her farm to see you."

"What lady?"

"A Mrs. George Carlin," she said. "Won't talk to anyone but you."

"What's she want?"

"Ask her why don't you?" Marlene got frazzled when too many things happened at once. "Go right in Mrs. Carlin," he heard her say, "but don't expect much."

Mrs. Carlin, gripping a brown paper sack, entered the room with a look of reluctant determination. She had the rangy appearance of the hard-working farm wife, face heavily lined and clear of makeup. Beneath a full skirt she wore heavy wool slacks and Charlie caught the smell of early morning barn chores. She halted several feet short of his desk and waited.

"Mrs. Carlin?"

She nodded.

"Please sit down and tell me what this is about."

She eyed the chair suspiciously and perched on the edge. "Been watching the news," she began. "Guess you're the one I have to talk to. Ain't you the one who's out to get Mr. Cleland?"

"We aren't out to get anyone, Mrs. Carlin," Charlie said. "Mr. Cleland is wanted for questioning. Afraid that's all I'm allowed to tell you."

"Didn't come for you to tell me. Came to tell you. Fifteen miles on the back of Lyndon's snow machine," she said firmly. "And I got sacroiliac trouble. But I come to tell you." Manly hands spread open the sack and withdrew a photograph set in an old-fashioned iron frame. "See this here?" She held it up for him.

Charlie saw a nice-looking young man in his mid thirties wearing a dark suit. He looked prosperous.

"That's Wesley," Mrs. Carlin explained. "Our boy. Ever been to Memphis?"

"No," he said.

"Wesley lives there," she said, as if Memphis was pretty much the center of things. "With his wife and three girls."

167

"Nice looking boy," he said.

"Wesley was thirty-three here," she said, turning the photograph so she could see his face. "Taken just after he finished dental school." Her eyes grew misty. "Eleven years after he should've been dead."

"I see," Charlie said, no idea what she was talking about. "Have children, Mr. Benson?"

"No. I'm a bachelor."

"Sorry," she said, genuinely. "Harvey and I just had the one boy. Wesley. I couldn't have any more children. Female problems," she confided. "When that happens, maybe you pin all your hopes on the one."

"So he's a dentist?"

"In Memphis," she said. "Studied at the University of Minnesota and come back to the farm summers. Helped Harvey with the planting and worked another job in town. Costs a lot, these colleges."

He waited while she put Wesley back in the bag.

"Wesley worked for Mr. Cleland at the slaughterhouse," she said finally. "Got a fair wage. Three summers he worked, boning hamburger meat. You been inside there, Mr. Benson?"

"Yes. Several times."

"Then you know the place where they bone the meat?" She wanted to be sure he understood. "Where they all stand and cut it off the bones so it can be ground up?"

"I know the place," Charlie said.

"Suppose a policeman has to study first aid?"

"Yes," he said, watching her closely.

"Maybe you know what the femoral artery is?"

"Yes. I do."

"Do you know what happens if it gets cut?"

"You bleed to death rather quickly," Charlie answered. "Like cutting your jugular vein."

"Wesley cut his femoral artery," Mrs. Carlin said, looking down at the bag. "He's a dentist now."

168

"Guess I don't understand."

"That's why I came out," she said, "so you people would understand. Wesley cut himself at Mr. Cleland's slaughterhouse. The doctor told us Wesley lost almost four pints of blood and should've been dead. But Mr. Cleland took shop aprons and wadded 'em up between Wesley's legs and applied pressure to the femoral artery and made Wesley stay awake and hold it while he carried him out and put him in his car and drove twenty miles to Pomme de Terre County Hospital, where they got an emergency room." She paused to see if Charlie was listening. "They said Mr. Cleland drove at speeds over one hundred twenty miles per hour, Mr. Benson. I'm surprised you didn't hear about that, being a policeman. The Highway Patrol officer who chased Mr. Cleland told me he could barely make the curves doing seventy. I talked to him at the hospital when Wesley was in surgery, and he said only a crazy man would drive a hundred and twenty on that road." Very carefully, she folded the bag over her son's photograph. "I'm surprised you never heard about it," she said.

"I did hear about it, Mrs. Carlin," he said softly. "I'd just forgotten."

"Harvey and I, we don't forget."

"I think I know now why you came here," he said. "Thank you."

Mrs. Carlin rose from the chair and nodded to Charlie. "You can't believe everything you see on the TV," she told him. "But if Mr. Cleland done what they say, well, I wanted you to know he also saved a life once." At the door, she paused. "Thank you for listening to me. It was all a long time ago, but we don't forget."

When she'd gone, Charlie remained at his desk, too tired to move. Marlene entered the room several minutes later and plopped a pile of phone messages on his desk.

"Who was that?" she asked.

169

"Wesley Carlin's mother," he replied.

"Who's Wesley Carlin?"

"A dentist in Memphis."

Some days you were better off not talking to Charlie Benson at all.

* * *

Dutch had no telephone line to be brought down and no electricity to fail. He had enough oil for the lamps and wood for the fire, though the wood had to be cut. He bitterly regretted the lost chainsaw. He'd eaten handfuls of aspirin for his badly blistered hands, aching back, and sore face.

When he awakened in the morning, he longed for a hot shower. And a plan, he thought, itching his scalp gingerly through matted strands of tender hair, oily with sweat and dirt. "I smell like an outhouse with a shallow hole," he informed the dog, who only wagged his tail.

In the beginning he'd wanted time to think. He knew now that somewhere along the line he'd decided never to go back. Simply disappear. How does a person disappear these days when everybody's got you on a list?

"Hello there! In the cabin!" A man's voice just outside.

Dutch fumbled for his shotgun, flung open the door and confronted two bundled hulks standing in the waist-deep snow of the yard.

"Hey man, you deaf?" inquired the larger one. "We've been calling all the way up your drive." He spotted the shotgun. "No need for artillery, Man. We're friendlies."

Staring in disbelief Dutch soon realized the authorities weren't likely to arrive on foot dressed in outfits undoubltedly secured from a Salvation Army clearance rack. It took a conscious effort to bring his nerves under control. "Quite a storm," he managed.

"Goddamn winter wonderland," the man replied. His eyebrows were white with frost.

170

"How'd you know I was here."

"Heard a truck night before last. Don't nobody come up this road we don't hear 'em, man."

"Who are you?"

The man turned to his companion and they shared a quiet chuckle behind thick scarves layered around their heads. "We're your neighbors. Sally and Dylan."

This revelation took time to soak in, until he remembered the two hippies who'd long ago built a crude cabin a couple decades too late for the sixties. Harmless enough. "Might as well come in out of the weather," he said, his heartbeat coasting back to normal.

"Thanks," Dylan replied. They marched into the warmth of his fire and stood, dripping.

"Wouldn't you know," Dutch said, thinking fast and setting aside the shotgun. "Drove all the way up here for a little hunting and ended up in a snowstorm."

Dylan unwrapped his scarf, shook it near the stove and hung it to dry. A gray ponytail protruded from under his dirty red stocking cap but his face lit with a warm smile that twinkled in his blue eyes. "Sure," he said. "Do you ever drink beer?"

"Not for breakfast."

"Sally likes it on her Marshmellow Mateys," he said. "I take it from the bottle."

Not knowing what else to do, Dutch pulled two bottles of Sam Adams from the refrigerator.

Meanwhile, Sally decided to unveil and Dutch was surprised to find her attractive in a scrub-faced, sixtyish way with braided brown hair and a lightly freckled complextion younger than her years. Apparently, the natural life had its advantages. He just hoped she didn't ask for Marshmellow Mateys.

"I like your wood stove," she said in a quiet voice, hanging her scarf next to Dylan's. "Functional but ornate. You should oil it more often."

She glided then to the cupboard, and opening the correct door, drew out a beer mug. "I like a glass," she explained.

Trying not to give offense, Dutch said, "You seem quite at home here."

"Why shouldn't we?" she replied.

Dutch could think of no answer to this.

"He doesn't remember," Dylan explained to her.

"Remember what?" Dutch asked.

"Giving us the key and telling us to move in."

It didn't seem like the kind of thing he'd forget, but Dutch stood mute some time before asking, "When was this?"

"1979."

And then he did remember. They were so young, living in a tent with nothing more than a few hand tools and a Time/Life do-it-yourself book, attempting to construct a cabin. Winter coming on, he'd offered them the use of his place until spring. He'd never known if they took him up on it or not.

"Now I remember," he said.

"We've got your key here," Sally offered.

"Keep it. I'm leaving soon as the weather clears."

"Gonna try for Canada?" Dylan asked. "Won't be easy. Spent Vietnam there. Got friends there still."

"Canada? What for?"

"Borders' only about sixty miles. Won't be easy. Only two roads and they'll be covered on both sides."

"Covered?"

"Sure, man. The fuzz."

"Why would I care?"

Dylan took a long pull from his beer. "Because your name's still Philip "Dutch" Cleland isn't it?"

"Yeah."

"The Butcher of Willow River?"

Suddenly, the close cabin air felt like cold steel.

* * *

172

Len Davis sat up with a start and looked out the windshield. The engine had stopped running. Sunshine beamed across the snow with eye-watering brilliance and it was very cold. Placing his hand on the plastic heater duct he found it still warm. The fuel gauge read empty. He rubbed his eyes and tried to think.

Overnight, things had been restructured and magnified by the storm. Telephone poles stretched like shadowed crosses on a white field. Fences had tails. Slough grass, once golden brown, stood in white shocks along the highway and oddly enough, the Jeep sat on the one piece of ground almost clear of snow. He could see for miles under a flat blue sky swept clean of clouds. Time to move.

Len removed a five-gallon jerry can of gasoline from the hatchback and emptied it into the tank, slopping carelessly. Moments later, the engine alive again, he munched a Snickers and planned his next move. Nothing like waking up alive as a good first step to a successful day, he thought. The highway, nonetheless, appeared impassable even to four-wheel-drive. He wouldn't mind seeing a snowplow. He reached over and tried the radio.

Music on two stations. A third came in so well he was forced to turn down the volume. "This is Lynn Dean, with the news," the voice said, in a poor imitation of Paul Harvey. "Good morning, Minnesotans! Did we have a blizzard last night, or what? Some roads in Aitkin County won't be cleared of snow until tomorrow, or later, according to a highway department spokesman. How about those snowplow drivers, huh? Out since dawn. Hundreds of motorists stranded across the state and here in Aitkin County dozens of cars are abandoned in ditches. This may prove to be the worst November snowstorm in recent history, followed by record cold temperatures dipping into the low twenties. That's below zero, folks! And if you're sitting in your car waiting for help, don't count on it. And don't forget to crack a window for safety."

Len glanced at his fuel gauge. Less than a quarter. Couple hours. Barely time enough to think things over.

He'd backed the Jeep into the side road so the front end faced the highway. The land was mostly flat here and he imagined that under the snow it was a peat bog. The few trees in sight were stunted, some bowed by the heavy snow until their tops touched the ground. It was a lousy place to get stuck.

About a mile off to his left, something moved. Wishing for binoculars, he opened the door and stood on the running board. A moving cloud of snow. He strained to see. It had to be a plow.

A moment later he saw it clearly, blaze orange behind a white waterfall, closing at high speed. "Come and get me!" he shouted, grinning. Seconds later he realized the driver, sitting high and warm in his giant orange plow, had no intention of stopping. He was a government employee and rescues weren't his business. He plowed snow, and in a few seconds would pass within several yards of Len's front bumper, dumping thousands of pounds of it right onto his lap. They'd find him in the spring.

He dropped back inside and slammed the gear-shift lever into reverse, door hanging open he blindly backed the Jeep, all four wheels spinning, until it smashed against something solid, snapping his neck. The plow roared past, showering the Jeep with stones, gravel, and a thundering avalanche of snow. Len swore at the unseen driver as the windshield slowly spread into a web of fine cracks.

He leaned out and stared at the highway. The plow had gone. The Jeep's door was sprung. He had crashed into something. The engine had died and he was probably stuck.

He glanced up through the broken glass just as a line of cars streamed by safely in the snowplow's wake. One of the drivers smiled and waved. Len gave him the finger.

Chapter Seventeen

THE BUTCHER OF WILLOW RIVER spent the morning listening to his options as explained to him by two middle-aged hippies. To hear Dylan and Sally tell it, the sixty miles to the Canadian border might as well be six thousand.

"Know where you're comin' from, Man, but there's still just the two roads," Dylan said, displaying two fingers. "Couple deputies with a Thermos and a radio, you're dead meat." He grinned. "No offense about the meat."

"Duluth has an airport," Dutch suggested.

The Duluth airport was tiny, they explained. "Wouldn't even get your bag checked in before they'd have you," Sally predicted. She'd fastened the end of her hair braid with a yellow bread tie.

Thick patterns of frost glittered on the windows and outside the dazzling mid-day sun deceived them with an image of warmth. The mercury hovered at seventeen below zero. The stove ticked and the log walls popped as they expanded. All morning Dutch wondered why his visitors remained, lending a hand with chopping and shoveling.

"Got to be something I can do," Dutch said, deciding maybe they'd come to gloat.

"Look," Dylan began. "This ain't our business but you're sort of organizationally challenged, you know? This isn't Hollywood. Everybody gets caught. You'd be in jail now if they didn't have to plow the roads first."

175

"No," Dutch said, shaking his head. "It's safe here. Nobody knows this place."

"Think like law enforcement," Dylan urged. "They don't believe you disappeared. You just went somewhere and they got to figure out where. That's easy. People usually go somewhere they know, just like you did. It's not some dude in a trenchcoat tracking you down. It's a computer nurd looking you up."

"But there's nothing to find," Dutch insisted.

"Did you buy this place under an assumed name or a dummy corporation or something?"

"No. Of course not."

"Then there's a deed with your name on it, right? They send you tax statements, right? Computer's got your address, phone, Social Security number. Whether you wear briefs or boxers, Man!"

Charlie Benson didn't have a computer Dutch thought, but Dylan's logic was flawless, everybody else did.

Dylan guzzled beer and continued. "The BCA, State Patrol, the County Mounties." He belched. "All on your case." He waited until he was sure it had sunk in.

"Okay," Dutch said finally. "So now what?"

Dylan exhaled a long noisy breath. "They'll be here tonight. Tomorrow for sure."

"So I can't fly or drive? Can't walk sixty miles in this weather. So what do you suggest, surrender?"

"We been thinking it over." Dylan glanced at Sally and grinned. "Still got that snow machine in the shed?"

"Far as I know." Dutch hadn't ridden in years. "Don't know if it works. Anyway, taking a snowmobile cross-country isn't much better than walking."

"Unless," Dylan said, "you've got groomed trails and frozen lakes. Once in a while maybe you run along some county road someplace. Everybody and his brother will be out the next few days showing off their new machines. You'll blend in."

176

Minnesota maintained a system of groomed trails, complete with warming houses and trail signs, which wound hundreds of miles through largely uninhabited lands. In another day they'd be crowded with snowmobile enthusiasts from across the state. A storm like this was just what they waited for.

Dutch thought it over. Sixty miles on clear trails was an easy morning ride. "Okay," he agreed. "What happens once I'm across the border? Southern Ontario's nothing but wilderness."

"The Jacksons," Sally said simply. "They're in Arbor Vitae. Twenty miles past."

"Friends?"

"Muhammid Jackson and Tuesday," Dylan explained. "They can't come back to the States for a while." He shrugged apologetically. "Muhammid's okay, but keep an eye on Tuesday. Like, I never sleep there."

"Great. Why would they help me?"

"We'll call 'em."

"You have a telephone?"

"Sure." Dylan helped himself to another beer and backed up to the fire. "We got to do business, you know?"

Dutch didn't ask what kind. Anyway, something deeper gnawed at him. "Pardon me for asking," he said, "but why are you helping me?"

Dylan took a long pull on the beer. "Winter we lived here at your place was the coldest in nearly twenty years. Ten days over New Year's it stayed forty below zero." He shook his head and grinned at the ceiling. "Holy shit did I cut wood!" The smile faded. "We'd a died in that tent."

Dutch still wasn't satisfied. "But you know what I did?"

"Only what was on the tube," he said, then chuckled. "Man, they must've got that picture of you from your high school yearbook!"

"You got television too?"

177

"Hardly. No electricity," Dylan reminded him. "Togo Joe's got three TVs at the bar now. We shoot pool there Fridays. Only thing to do here except fuck."

Dutch studied their faces. "No one-armed man running away or anything, you know. I did it."

"Figured that," Dylan replied.

"We aren't stupid," Sally said, leaving her chair by the stove to open the refrigerator. "Imagine a butcher's got pretty good lunch meat," she said. "I'll make some sandwiches."

He didn't expect her to be domestic.

She stacked meat, cheese, lettuce, bread, and an onion on the counter. "Don't suppose I could kill anything," she went on, taking a sharp knife from the drawer. "Even when the birds eat my strawberries."

"She feeds table scraps to the goddamn wolves," Dylan offered.

Dutch glanced up, saw their eyes avoid his, clearly they did expect an explanation. "I'm not ready to talk about it yet," he said slowly. "Let's just say I don't handle betrayal very well."

"Gets lonely up here," she continued, gobbing butter onto the bread and layering it with the cold cuts. "When you're by yourself a good while you learn not to be judgemental." She stepped back, admiring her handiwork. "I make a good sandwich. Me and Dylan talked it over last night during the storm. We'll get you out. After that." She shrugged. "It's up to you."

"Met your wife back when," Dylan said suddenly. "Why didn't she come with?"

"She wanted to," Dutch said. "Wouldn't let her." A wave of guilt swept over him. Not only had he left her to face the music but a killer storm. "She's back home sticking up for me," he said simply.

The aging hippie pulled his pony tail over his shoulder and set the empty beer bottle on the counter. "Lucky to have a woman like that," he said.

178

"Yes," Dutch replied. "Took me a while to figure that out. Maybe I could use your phone and call her."

"Forget it," Dylan said. "They'll have your phone tapped by now."

This wasn't what he'd expected, that people would help him. "If I had it to do over again," Dutch said. "I'd take her with me. My wife I mean."

"Don't worry about that now," Dylan warned. "She's safe enough and we need to map you a route out of here."

When he got to Canada he'd call her, phone tap or no phone tap, and then she'd meet him someplace and maybe they'd start over.

* * *

Carroll Johnson never thought of himself as immoral. His recreational use of cocaine and marijuana notwithstanding, he attended church every Christmas and Easter, put his change in the Salvation Army pot, gave the United Way, and even sent an annual check to a shelter for battered women. But he couldn't remember any time in his life he'd felt this loose and powerful.

Murdock handed him the roach for a last drag. The air inside the Suburban was blue with the pungent smoke. They'd been on a bender since the night before and Carroll couldn't remember the drive from St. Cloud to Willow River earlier that day. He remembered a motel room and snorting breakfast. Murdock seemed to have an endless supply.

"Do you feel as good as I feel?" Carroll asked. Like thousands of Minnesotans, Carroll had a strong appetite for drugs. They were childishly easy to get and the state's left-wing judicial system all but looked the other way.

"What I wanna feel is something soft in my hands," Murdock giggled.

Carroll sucked the roach down until he felt it burning his finger, then stomped it out on the floor. "I'm up for it," he said.

179

Murdock slipped the Suburban in gear and they covered the last mile quickly, thanks to four-wheel drive and a county snowplow, which had cut a narrow path up the Cleland drive. "I'm going to kiss her," Murdock said. He'd insisted on driving even though he blacked out occasionally from the combination of painkillers and dope. "Take off all her clothes and kiss her everywhere. What's wrong with that? Kissing is nice isn't it? Guy kills my wife, beats me up, what do I do? Turn the other cheek, eh, Carroll baby?" He puckered. "I kiss my enemies!"

"Well, don't kiss me."

"I won't kiss you, Carroll baby. You hold her while I kiss her." He jammed the lever into park. "Be nice I'll let you kiss her too."

They stood weaving on the back patio and Carroll couldn't stop laughing. Murdock hissed for him to quiet down but the image of Cleland's naked wife filled his head, standing with her hands on her hips while they pecked her like birds. Lips, their secret weapon. Their truth serum. Tell us what you know or be subjected to unauthorized kissing! And what could she do? Call 911 afterwards and report a kissing? He bellowed again.

"Will you shut up?" Murdock whispered. "If she doesn't open the door we can't get in."

Carroll tried to compose himself. He pictured Murdock kissing the woman with his wired jaw. All lips and no tongue. At least he couldn't bite her.

Magically the door swung open and the woman who confronted them was taller than he'd imagined, wearing blue sweats and white high tops. The sweat shirt, a full size too large, had its sleeves rolled up and beneath he saw large breasts heaving. She'd been working out. Sweat glistened on her forehead and her dark hair was tangled. Somehow this made it better.

Murdock slammed his body against the door and threw her off balance. An instant later he had her across the chest.

"Don't fight," he said from behind. "Just came a'kissin'." He kissed her hair. An ear.

"Tell us were Dutch is and we'll leave," Carroll said, suddenly uncomfortable with the wild look in Murdock's eyes. He'd promised. Kissing only. If she relaxed everything would go fine.

Jean Cleland's eyes were on him instead of Murdock. She was terrified but he thought he saw something else there too. Stubbornness. What if this wasn't easy? Murdock wouldn't want any stubbornness.

Murdock seemed uninterested in information. His head bobbed around her face and neck, smacking loudly. "Kissy, kissy," he said is a syrupy voice.

Jean held very still, tucking her chin to deflect his grotesque mouth. The rich, sweet smell of his breath brought tears to her eyes. "You better let me go," she advised.

Even Carroll laughed at this. She really was a schoolteacher. "We're conducting an investigation," he said. "If you don't cooperate," his voice broke high. "We'll just kiss you until you do. Where's Dutch? And don't lie."

Murdock squeezed one of her breasts. "Lots left to kiss."

His touch made her shiver but she remained still, rigid. "Take your hands off me!" she ordered, glad she'd worn a sport bra under the sweatshirt.

Murdock hugged her under both arms, squeezing one breast in each hand until she moaned in pain. "Kissy, kissy," he said. "Answer the man before I take your pants down."

"I don't know," she gasped.

He stared at Carroll Johnson and pursed his lips. "She doesn't know. Like we came here for that? She doesn't know!" He squeezed until her moans turned to screams. "You know, bitch! You know. Pull her pants down," he ordered Carroll.

Carroll obeyed not so much out of fear of Murdock as from the look of real terror in Jean's eyes. If she was going to tell them anything, it was now.

The sweats slipped easily across her hips but stuck on her high tops. Beneath she wore thick Spandex shorts.

"Layered like a nun," Murdock cursed.

Struggling to free herself from the sweats wrapped around her ankles, Jean caught Carroll with a knee to the nose, out of reflex more than any planned defense.

"Ow!" he cried, probing with his finger. "Blood." He rushed around the kitchen searching for a mirror.

"Cool it," Murdock ordered. "It's a bump. Get her pants down the rest of the way."

"Do it yourself."

Carroll reached across the telephone to tear a square from the paper towel holder and bumped the answering machine. A red light blinked.

"Give me a hand," Murdock said, dragging Jean toward a butcher block where he planned to finish what he'd started.

"This is Charlie Benson," the machine said in a hollow voice. "Sent Sy out to open your road. Hope you managed the storm okay. Stay home. I'll be there in a little while."

Carroll glanced out the frosted window. "Damn that cop," he said, searching the road.

"Who cares?" Murdock grunted, hooking his thumb under the waistband of Jean's shorts. "Maybe he wants to kiss you too. But nobody's going to ever kiss you like me."

"You ugly faggot!" It was all she could think to say. "He'll shoot you."

"What if he's on the way?" Carroll asked.

"So?" Murdock was preoccupied. "Don't you like to play kissy with me? I might be offended."

"I don't know where Dutch is," she lied. "But Benson thinks I do. That message has been on the machine at least an hour. He'll be here any minute."

"She doesn't know anything," Carroll said. "Let's get out of here."

Murdock struggled with the waistband. "Bullshit."

Carroll was beginning to sober up and Murdock had left the keys in the Suburban. "You're on your own," he said, dashing out the door.

Of all the ways this could've gone, the worst Jean realized, was to be left alone with Murdock. Anyone could see he was mad. The other man, though appearing physically stronger, was obviously the weaker. The awful, grunting mouth pressed on hers.

Murdock had selected the one place to lay her where an array of weapons was holstered and ready. Bolted in a stainless steel rack alongside the solid butcher block were four knives and a cleaver. As Murdock worked on her tight shorts, Jean's hand closed around the black-handled cleaver.

The bone-splitter, which Dutch honed to perfection, made a scraping noise as she drew it and the tallowed whites of Murdock's eyes widened slightly. She felt him draw a breath as her hand, heavy and high, swept downward at an angle to the man's exposed neck.

Murdock smiled. A fist like a piston slammed her wrist, streaking pain down her arm and opening her hand in reflex. The cleaver arched away and clattered harmlessly to the tile. "You're a murderous bitch," the man said quietly. "Must run in the family."

He mounted her and smiled again. "How's that feel?"

Outside an engine roared to life and she felt the man's heavy body stiffen. The sound of tires spinning. The crunch of snow as they took hold.

"That chickenshit son-of-a-bitch!"

Jean prayed silently.

Murdock hopped to the floor and caught her by the neck. "I'll be back, baby. Keep it warm."

He was gone as quickly as he'd come. The door left open, smoking against the dry cold. Tears sprang to her eyes bringing relief and an even deeper terror. She knew it was true. He'd be back.

* * *

Walleye had perfumed the lady, discarded the plastic body bag, and moved her upstairs onto Mother's bed. He closed the heat registers and opened one window a crack to cool the room, which was at the back of the house away from the kitchen where he spent most of his time. He'd stuff towels under the door to stem the draft.

The lady seemed comfortable lying on the creamy spread. One of Mother's handmade afghans, the Christmas one zig-zag green and red, warmed her feet. He removed her shoes but left the stockings.

Her face no longer frightened him, even at night. He loved her like Haitian lady. But Haitian lady had never lived —he knew that—but she comforted him when he held her mohagony head in his lap and stroked her wide nose. When her wooden face got dry he'd squeeze rich, white worms of grease from the pores of his own nose and rub it in gently to restore her sheen.

The new lady was bigger. She had arms and legs. She might even be the very best treasure he'd ever found. "You can be my friend," he told her. Walleye never had a friend. "Maybe my girlfriend." Was it goofy to talk to a dead body?

Walleye perched on the bed beside her. Maybe the lady had eternal life coming pretty soon, he thought. He'd learned a great deal about eternal life at Mount Carmel Lutheran Church where he cleaned the basement and rang the bell sometimes on Sundays. He listened to the sermons. Most of it was hard to understand but not eternal life. That was the best part of religion. You lived forever even after you died. The kind of an idea he might've had himself, and it surprised him the fast people had even come up with it.

The problem with eternal life is you never know when it starts. First you have to die they always say. But if you keep sticking people in the ground how will you know if they get the eternal life or not?

Walleye slid off the bed and gazed down lovingly on his sleeping lady, remembering her eyes. Large, like a hornet's. Hornets had big almond eyes out of proportion to the size of their heads same as drawings made by the people who believe in aliens. He knew this because he looked at a lot of things through the magnifying glass on his Swiss army knife.

But Walleye had decided not to open her eyes again. She'd sleep now until she woke and breathed again and opened her big almond eyes and saw him. Saw him first of all. Then they'd probably get married and have a little boy who'd never have to hear people say he was an idiot. Never.

* * *

Berkie's Cafe opened almost on time, along with most of Willow River's small businesses. Trade was brisk. On his way to Clelands, Charlie dropped in to pick up a couple club sandwiches and some chips. A peace offering to Jean. Besides the weather stunk and she might not have thought about food.

While Mavis wrapped the sandwiches in waxed paper he flipped open the menu. It had a fresh insert.

****TODAY'S SPECIAL****
Butcher Burger...................$3.95
(A delicious quarter pound of finely
ground beef, hand-pattied by the
Butcher of Willow River personally)
Your chance to eat history!

"Christ, Mavis," Charlie growled. "Is this necessary?"
She shrugged. "I'm in business."
"You got no way of knowing if Dutch pattied these burgers," he said. "It's fraud. Nobody'll buy 'em."
"Sold eighteen already before lunch." She tossed his sandwiches on the counter. "Should've ordered a couple yourself. Comes with fries and a shake."

Well, he thought, no worse than KQWR Radio, known locally as "Queer." This morning they'd begun an ad campaign featuring Murder Tours of the "Butcher Shop" where the brutal slaying took place, (although tourists couldn't go inside to see the actual knives and saws used to dismember the body), a drive-by of the Butcher of Willow River's home, and a nature hike, weather permitting, to the spot where he dumped the body. Included in the price were complimentary beverages in the fifteen-passenger van rented from Bagg's Auto and a stop in the alley behind the Meat Market to see the blood-soaked gravel where Gordon Murdock was butchered.

Charlie headed for the door. How long before they came out with the T-shirts and ball caps?

The streets had been cleared of snow, except for a thing at the east end of Main Street that resembled Mount Hood. A front-end loader with hard snow packed against the rims of its giant tires worked ceaselessly to clear the bank parking lot, its backup warning alarm a constant reminder that life had returned to normal. Snow was something they knew how to handle. Who knows, he thought, maybe "Butcher Burgers" and a "Murder Tour" helped them handle the rest.

He sped toward Cleland's.

The club sandwiches were cold when he arrived and the place seemed deserted when he knocked. He couldn't see anything in the kitchen window except a dim section of room which held a butcher block and hanging pans.

"Dammit Jean!" He used his fist this time. "It's Charlie! Charlie Benson!"

What was she doing? Hiding?

A shadow crossed the peephole, finally. "It's Charlie Benson, Jean." He held the bag up. "I got sandwiches." The woman was paranoid. The deadbolt drew and he opened the door himself. "Were you asleep?" he growled. "It's below zero."

186

She allowed him to pass and quickly locked the door. Her hair was wet. "Shower," she said.

Her voice seemed dull and he noticed too that she averted her eyes as if his own gaze stung her. Seeing her like that and barefoot, dripping under the oversized white robe, he softened. "Here," he said, holding up the sack of frozen sandwiches. "Eat."

"What is it?" she asked, moving listlessly to the cupboard for two plates.

"Clubs and chips." He peered into the sack and without thinking said, "Could've got Butcher Burgers."

"Huh?"

"Never mind," he said, silently cursing his big mouth. "Looks like you've had company."

"What?"

"Fresh tracks on the road."

She hesitated. More than anything she wanted to tell someone, ease the disgust and ugliness still gripping her, but Charlie was the last person she'd choose. Ill at ease around women, he seemed to live to hunt and fish. Horded his bachelorhood, and as far as she knew, never had a female friend under the age of sixty.

"Two men came here, Charlie," she began. It was too much to bear alone. She told it to him like an unpleasant story she might read in class, without emotion, letting the facts speak for themselves. At the end she added her opinion that the men were high on something. When she looked up she saw his sandwich lay untouched and her revulsion transplanted on his face in a manner she knew didn't bode well for those men when he found them.

"Murdock," he said. "Gordon Murdock. Had him and let him go. I need your phone." He brushed past her and dialed. "Marlene. Put a description on the air of Gordon Murdock's Suburban. Get the license. Call Sheriff Mattson and tell him. Then have Bobby start looking around town. Check the motel. What? Tried to rape Jean Cleland. That's right. Just a while ago. Bobby's not to approach him alone. Make that clear to the half-wit. Almost forgot. Your friend Johnson's with him. Get a description out on him too, and his car. Impress on everybody that this just happened and they can't have gotten very far. Chances are good we'll catch them. Call me here for the next ten or fifteen minutes. Got all that?" He slammed down the phone.

His next move surprised Jean more than the look on his face. "Damn you!" he said. "This is your fault."

"Mine?" She backed away.

"Yes, yours. You know where Dutch is but you're too smart or too smug to tell me, right?" He towered over her. "Who do you think gave Murdock that face? When he sees Dutch next he won't wait. He'll just kill him. That what you want?"

"No. But you want me to betray him. I won't."

"Are you really that naive?" He cocked his head, not expecting an answer. "We'll find him anyway. Sheriff Mattson's men are looking, when they're not digging some knothead out of a snowbank, so's the Highway Patrol and the BCA. It's only a matter of time. Can't you see it's better if I find him first?"

"Better for Dutch if he got out of this town and never came back!" She was close to tears.

"All right, Jean," he sighed. "But use your head. I've known Dutch a long time. We weren't best buddies, but neither am I going to come up on him and stick a .38 in his ear. One of Mattson's pissant deputies, or some state cop, may not see it that way. Neither will Murdock." He waited for an answer. "Do you hear me?"

Jean's tears ran silent down both cheeks. "I heard you, Mr. Benson."

She wasn't going to tell him anything, though he'd played on her vulnerability and felt low about it, too. "I'm not your enemy," he said gently and dropped onto the stool near the phone. "Maybe you'll talk to Dutch. He might call. Tell him it's hopeless. That's the truth. If he wants to face up to this, I'll come get him personally. No back up, nothing, just me and him. No hoopla in the media. Will you tell him that?"

"You'll never see him again," she answered and the light went out of her eyes. "And neither will I."

He knew she was ready for him to leave now but the most important question hadn't been asked, and damned if he wouldn't ask it no matter what she wanted. "I have a couple more questions," he began. "Won't take long but you're standing there all wet. I can wait while you get dressed."

"No. Finish."

"It's not easy. This affair, I mean this thing with the other woman. You knew about it?"

"Yes. Later."

"But you and Dutch patched things up?"

"More like we rebuilt."

Charlie wore an old fur hat with earlaps because he hated baseball caps and everybody wore baseball caps. He'd shoved the hat to the back of his head when he came in, now he took it off and smoothed down his chopped gray hair. "See, that's what bothers me," he said, genuinely puzzled. "No heat of the moment. Doesn't seem possible. Maybe you understand it."

She stared vacantly at the beige wall hoping he'd leave. She shouldn't have told him anything. Especially about Murdock. It just made her more vulnerable. More a cripple.

"This case is attracting so much attention partly because it's so odd," he said. "Who murders his girlfriend years after their affair is over? I know this isn't something you're comfortable talking about, but the quickest way to be rid of me is answer."

Too many questions. "Ever watch the TV news?" she asked.

189

"No more than I have to. Just the headlines."

"That's enough." She picked up a cold sandwich and bit into it without looking. "I haven't taken a survey or anything, but the crime they seem to feature most is domestic violence. Especially violence against women."

Charlie thought he saw where this was going and opened his mouth to protest but Jean cut him off.

"Wait," she said. "I thought that too, once. Men, those violent bastards abusing the weaker sex, but that's too simplistic. These stories are all much the same. A family splits up, a girlfriend leaves, there's a divorce, somebody doesn't love somebody anymore. Whatever. Some kind of betrayal. Then they make the news. A woman is beaten, stabbed, shot. Sometimes a whole family. Little children shotgunned in their beds. We're all shocked as hell until we hear it again and again, then it's not shock anymore but fear, distrust. We lose confidence. Get scared of each other." She frowned at the food in her hand. "Many times the violence erupts months or years later. I couldn't figure that out either. Why wait? That's your question isn't it? 'What took you so long, Dutch?'"

He heaved his heavy shoulders into a shrug that looked more like a linebacker taking a stance. "She jilts him. He kills her. That I understand," he said. "Sorry to be so blunt. But she jilts him. He kills her years later. That makes no sense."

"Sure it does," Jean answered, her voice strengthening. "Because this isn't about murder, it's about betrayal. Murder's a crime like mugging somebody or rape. When you came I was in the shower. I've been there since those animals left." Her body shook suddenly under the robe. "Locked all the doors, even the windows, and scrubbed until I almost bled, but it wasn't until just before you started banging on my door I realized I was okay. I was going to wash that man's dirty hands from my body because that's all he got, the outside of me. And that's it, Charlie. That's the answer. Betrayal is an inside job. It rips your heart out and shakes your faith in yourself. You'll heal up from a beating but nothing can leave you with a ball of hate like betrayal. I learned that firsthand."

"From Dutch," he said needlessly. Their roles seemed reversed. "I've read the surveys. Men do most of the killing. You can't tell me women aren't betrayed as often as men."

"Course not," she said. "But women have different ways of getting even. A woman is more likely to hurt in a way that keeps on hurting. Taking the kids, the money, replacing the man with another. Men do those things too, but I think they're more likely to strike out physically, almost instinctively."

"Maybe you should teach sociology," he suggested. "Murder's against the law. Betrayal isn't."

"Sure it is, Charlie." She drew a piece of cold bacon from between the slices of smashed toast and dropped it to the plate. "We just don't obey those laws anymore."

Charlie had never really cared for Jean Cleland. Didn't care much for schoolteachers generally. But here she stood, barefooted, damaged in ways he couldn't even imagine and lecturing him on the one thing he thought he understood pretty well—human frailty. "Well," he said, standing, "I gotta do what the law says. Even so, two wrongs don't make a right. Dutch has to pay for what he's done. Like you said, he betrayed you and you didn't kill him. You even stayed married to him."

She pushed the plate aside and smiled in an absent way. How straightforward he was. "I'm a woman. We're used to living with double standards." She looked down to find she was standing in a small puddle of water. "Okay if I get dressed?"

Charlie figured if he ever found a woman with this much grit and brains he'd settle down. Trouble was, women always wanted to change a guy. "One more question," he said. "Then I'll leave. Where's Len Davis?"

191

This caught her by surprise and she hoped it didn't show on her face. "Is he missing?"

"Left town sometime yesterday according to the Rayden-Bergdung woman." Back on his feet now, hat on. "Funny coincidence Dutch's best friend, and yours, suddenly disappears same time he does. Before I put out a bulletin on his car, stir up a lot of needless speculation, why not tell me where he went? Only want to talk to him."

Jean pictured Len's Corvette safe under an old tarp in the pole barn. "Good luck," she said, suppressing an odd desire to gloat. Charlie's "bulletin" wouldn't do much good.

A moment lapsed before Charlie spoke again. "I don't understand your attitude. Expected more from an educated woman."

"Just like you to be patronizing." She rubbed the last of the tears from her cheeks. "I'm also a wife who loves her husband."

"What you're doing isn't helping him."

"We've been through all this," she said, moving toward the door.

"Yes," he said. "I hope you know what you're doing. I'm not your enemy."

"Is that all?"

"Not quite," he said more calmly. "Don't worry about Murdock. My hand is going to close around his neck before he ever has a chance to make good on his threat. That's a promise. And here's another: I'm going to find Dutch, with or without you. Think about it. That just leaves Davis, and by God I'm going to get him too if he isn't buried under a snowbank somewheres."

* * *

Outside McGregor, one hundred miles south of Dutch's cabin, Len Davis was buried under the snowbank left by the plow. But what the hell, he was alive. Little comfort as he swung the short-handled camp shovel. His back sore from bending and swinging, bending and swinging.

He'd cleared the front tires and luckily the undercarriage was almost on dry ground. The snowplow had flung a ton of packed, rolled chunks of hardened snow up to form an impregnable wall between the Jeep and the road. He planned on writing a letter to the Minnesota Department of Transportation. A lawsuit wasn't out of the question.

He'd cleared a path three feet wide, chest high. Several cars and a milk truck had gone by while he labored. The drivers stared curiously out at him and some waved in a neighborly way. None stopped to help.

With the camp shovel he moved about a quart of snow with each shovelful, and even at that he was forced to move slowly, careful not to lose the load. The blade had no curled sides like a sand or scoop shovel. The snow simply slid off.

"You bitch!" Len swore, flinging down the shovel and straightening to ease the crick in his lower back. "You horrible little adulterated short-handled bitch!"

* * *

Carroll Johnson's breath came in short, wheezing gasps that sounded like a wimpering dog. His head felt like a pumpkin filled with sand. Worse than anything he'd largely sobered up and remembered perfectly what they'd done. Murdock, who crouched beside him in the snow, either was still high or just didn't give a damn.

A dark blue Chevy Blazer with a silver police badge painted on its door moved cautiously around the back of the motel parking lot. The man inside was looking for them. That was certain. Through the frosted passenger window he saw the rifle racks. They were full.

"He's going to see us."

"Shut the fuck up," Murdock cursed.

Murdock had driven the Suburban behind a massive snow mountain and covered it with white sheets stripped from

193

their bed in the motel, trying to make it appear as part of the snow mountain. Carroll thought it just looked like a Suburban with a sheet over it.

The Blazer stopped and the man got out. He was uniformed rather well for a hick cop and carried a short-barreled shotgun, stock jammed against his hip. Carroll had no doubt it was loaded. He squirmed deeper into the snow ignoring the bitter cold. He wanted to burrow deeper still, until the snow covered every inch of him.

Murdock gripped the black handle of a 9mm Ruger. His cupped hands making an even groove in the snow as they followed the moving policeman. Carroll was afraid Murdock would shoot even if the cop didn't see them. He knew now there was no way out. He'd simple snorted his life away in less than a day. His office, his secretary, probably his house. All gone. There was only one reason for this cop to be looking in this parking lot. He knew them by name. What a fool he'd been. What a fool he was!

To their immediate left and slightly behind the prowling policeman another man appeared. Carroll recognized him. The motel desk clerk, Danny Dohrmann. He approached rapidly without cap or coat. "If you wanna see the room it's now or never," he said loudly, holding up a pass key with a large wooden spoon taped to it. "I gotta go get the towels and sheets from the laundromat. Would you believe they even stole the sheets? Say, what you lookin' back here for? You don't think they're dumb enough to hide in the parking lot in broad daylight do you?"

"We check everything," said the cop. "Leave no stone unturned."

"Yeah, okay Kojak but I'm freezing my balls off here."

They both got into the Blazer and drove around front. Carroll watched the muzzle of Murdock's pistol ease forward and rest in the snow.

Chapter Eighteen

IN THE GATHERING TWILIGHT, the reflective lettering seemed to come out of nowhere. Bringing the Jeep to an abrupt halt, he peered between the windshield cracks at the welcome glow of neon—Samuel Adams Boston Lager. Civilization. Togo Joe's Bar.

Until he'd seen the tavern lights he hadn't realized how lonely he'd become since the day before, how starved for humankind, how thirsty. An array of trucks, mostly pickups and covered four-by-fours flanked the building on three sides. Dead deer were strapped to about half of them. To the far right he counted seven snowmobiles, their windshield's heavily powdered. He climbed out and stretched.

On closer inspection, Len realized Togo Joe's wasn't a haven but the kind of place that makes a motorist shudder when he drives past. A wooden porch with sagging roof stretched the building's full length and cedar planking formed a clapboard exterior. There were two small casement windows, each with a neon sign visible through frost and dirt. Len swallowed hard and flung open the door, instantly enveloped by a cloud of steam as subzero air vaporized in the doorway. He stepped from the swirling cloud into an overheated room flush with noise, smoke, and drunken laughter, aglow with blaze orange.

He inhaled odors of tobacco and whiskey, burning wood and urine. It made his nose run. Four orange Indians shot pool at a table they'd leveled with a crushed beer can and somewhere near the back George Jones sang mournfully above the cursing and rattling colored balls. Len squeezed into a place at the bar between a man and a woman facing away from each other.

A fifty-five-gallon barrel stove lay on its side cradled precariously on thin metal legs, puffs of smoke belched from a dozen cracks and holes. The collie-faced woman on the next stool leaned against his arm as he caught a bartender's attention.

"Gin tonic," Len said.

"Say again," he shouted, haggard and short-tempered. The noise was deafening. "Gin and tonic water!"

The bartender snatched a half empty bottle of Johnny Walker from the shelf. An odorous, orange-clad man to his right spoke loudly. "So how's he doin' now?"

"Haven't heard," another answered. "Looked stone dead when we found him, that's for sure."

"Won't catch me crying," the first man said, thumping the bar. "Should've known better than to fall asleep up there."

"Snow broke his fall or he'd be dead," said the other. "Way it was we drug him nearly two miles on a piece of cardboard 'till we got to the truck and pitched him in back. I'd rather haul a deer outta the woods any day."

"Where'd you take him?"

"Bigfork."

"Break his neck, or what?"

"Got me."

The bartender slopped Len's drink. "Three-fifty," he said.

Len put a twenty on the bar. The woman had been steadily snuggling against him, as if by accident. He had no room to move and felt her bumpy spine rubbing rhythmically against his upper arm.

Finally she turned and said, "You're pretty soft." When she smiled, there were gaps between her front teeth, and her breath stank of pickled eggs.

"It ruins your muscle tone," he said.

"What does?" She frowned at him.

"AIDS."

She stiffened and whispered something to the man next to her. He cursed, and Len ignored them both.

The bartender returned with his change. "Maybe you can help me," Len said. "I'm looking for a guy. Has a cabin around here. Dutch Cleland."

"Never heard of him."

"We're supposed to hunt together tomorrow, but I lost his directions." Len shrugged. "All these roads look alike."

"Can't help ya."

"Can't be that many cabins near here," he persisted. "Early forties. Sort of sandy-colored hair. Six feet. Drinks a special rum. Barbancourt."

Len saw the spark of recognition in the bartender's eyes. And something else, a growing skepticism.

"Where'd you say you was from?"

"Minneapolis." Len thought the lie more convincing than the truth. "Been invited up here five or six times, but you know how it is." He shrugged. "Finally made it."

"There used to be a guy came in here asking for some oddball rum." The man looked Len over carefully. "Never knew his name. Could be him."

"I'd call him," Len said, "but he doesn't have a phone. Sure would keep me from looking like a fool if you know the way out to his place."

"Never been up there myself." He shrugged. "Marty might know." He pointed at the other bartender.

Len watched him walk the length of the bar where Marty was busy mixing a line of drinks. He shouted something and jerked a thumb over his shoulder. Marty nodded in Len's direction.

Len sipped at his drink and ordered another before Marty, a taller man with pock-marked cheeks, approached. "You ain't going to get where you're going tonight," he told Len.

197

"Why not?"

"Snow up to your ass, that's why!"

"I've got four-wheel-drive."

"No good in snow that deep." He shook his head. "Hang you up in no time."

"Everybody else seems to be getting around okay," Len said, sweeping his arm around the room.

"They park and walk in." Marty explained the obvious. "On snowshoes. Got any?"

Len smiled. "Not with me."

"Make you a deal," Marty said. "You buy a pair from me, I'll give you a map to that cabin, if it's the one I'm thinking of."

Len noticed pairs of snowshoes mounted to the wall, assumed them to be part of the decor. "Fine," he said.

Marty disappeared behind a partition, returning a moment later with the snowshoes. "Genuine Canadian babiche in these," he said.

"Huh?"

"The laces." He strummed them with his fingers. "Babiche. Hand made."

"Expensive?"

"Two-forty."

"Two hundred and forty?"

"You don't get these at K-Mart." Marty was insulted. "Want 'em or not?"

"It's only money," Len said, reaching for his wallet.

"I'll draw you a map," Marty produced a pen from his pocket and drew up a bar napkin, quite pleased with himself. Len ordered another drink and Marty gave it to him on the house to seal their bargain.

"Be careful you don't fall down in those," Marty said, setting the drink before him.

"Why?"

"Can't get up." He reached across the bar and clapped Len on the shoulder good-naturedly. "Like a turtle."

Len finished his drink and carried the snowshoes to the Jeep. The night air was icy vapor, thick and hard to draw in. He cranked the cold engine several times before it caught, then drove away to the east, the bar napkin with its map to Dutch's cabin spread carefully on the seat beside him.

Within fifteen minutes, he was totally lost.

* * *

The other bartender's name was MOM, Melvyn O. Mahelich. MOM and Marty they'd been since childhood. Grown together, hunted together, got laid by the same whore together and at the same time. Since Len went out the door this was the first chance they'd had to talk.

"Sell those display snowshoes to that rube?" MOM wanted to know. Squatting in the sticky ooze behind the bar they sliced frantically at cardboard boxes of cheap whisky to hurry the restocking. They made it now during hunting season or not at all. Business sucked the rest of the year.

"Should've asked for more than two forty," Marty shook his head of greasy blonde hair. "Who's he trying to kid? Never been hunting in his life. Some Yuppie in an L.L. Bean sweater."

They both laughed. "But you remember this Cleland?"

"Sure. Stringy guy. Offered to buy a case of some certain rum he liked and have it put behind the bar especially for him. Kiss off! I said. Next they'll be wanting glasses for their beer."

MOM grabbed him by the arm and pulled him closer. "Don't you recognize that name? Cleland?"

"Huh?"

"That's the guy on the news. The Butcher of Willow River. Dutch Cleland. I'd bet your ass."

"Can't be."

"Why not? This is a perfect place to get lost and our little Yuppie buddy isn't up here hunting, said so yourself, so what's he doing? Maybe looking for old Dutchy?"

199

"Cop?"

"That soft-bellied runt? No way. Smelled like lawyer to me, a buddy maybe." MOM rested two bottles of budget booze on his upper leg. "Anyway, who cares? What I wanna know is, how much reward are they offering?"

Marty's pock-marked cheeks spread in a delighted grin. "You clever son-of-a-bitch!" He spoke admiringly. "Never heard of a reward didn't start with at least ten thousand."

MOM returned his smile. "Little hunting of our own in the morning? Say just before sun up?"

His friend clapped him on the back and they returned to work with new energy.

* * *

Seven miles away, Dutch poured the rich, dark liquid slowly over ice. Its aroma carried him back to Roatan and the darkness Vicky said was different, like warm hands inside a blanket. That night, which led to their X-rated picnic fight the next day, was the seed of everything that finally went wrong, down to this very day, this very hour.

They'd spent the night in a hammock on the cay watching the stars as the earth slipped slowly beneath and the warm waters of the bay hissed gently on the sand. In the hills above, the smoke of a hundred charcoal fires drifted on the night breezes until their coals dwindled and the night was empty except for the soft silk of her hair and slow wind of her breath upon his bare chest. Even now he could smell her and it was the piquant scent of skin.

Tomorrow Dylan promised to be over early so they could see to the snowmobile. If it started, he'd be gone. He really believed it now.

The rum bottle rested on his knee as he sat near the fire. He spun it slowly, counting backward fifteen years to calculate the date it was poured into oaken casks for aging. This very quart of liquid would've been in the Caribbean that day.

Some things aged better than others, he thought. It outlasted her and maybe it would outlast him too.

He drank.

* * *

The road took a sharp, ninety-degree turn to avoid a large outcropping of rock. The Cherokee went straight.

Even at twenty miles per hour, the impact flung Len sharply against the steering wheel, snapping his head forward, crumpling his legs painfully into the lower dash and taking his breath away. The Cherokee trembled a moment on its nose, then dropped back onto all fours. Another few feet and he'd have collided with rock instead of deep snow.

He pushed back from the steering wheel and cautiously drew a breath. Miraculously, he seemed uninjured.

Driving in circles for the past forty-five minutes he'd decided the bartender's map was a fake but he knew Dutch was close by. No mistaking the recognition he'd seen on the bartender's face. He knew Dutch all right, and given time, Len would've found him.

He crawled out through the window dragging the snowshoes behind and sank waist-deep in snow. He struggled toward the road, deciding not to try the snowshoes until he reached solid ground. The sky above was dark and overcast. A night wind had come up since he left Togo Joe's, and while it was nothing compared to the blizzard, it swirled the dry snow in tiny tornadoes, stinging his face.

This time he'd dressed for the weather, putting on every scrap of clothing he could manage. He'd learned something at least, and pulled the wool scarf up against his face. On the road, he dropped the snowshoes and tried to get his bearings. The only direction he hadn't searched was north, away from Togo. If he walked in that direction now, and was wrong, he'd be moving further from what passed for civilization, deeper into the wilderness. He looked down at the road, hard-packed with snow from the plows. No need for snowshoes here. He'd walk awhile, north, then if he didn't find Dutch, give up and go back to the bar. It was no more than five or six miles away.

He thought of tossing the bulky snowshoes, but the idea of losing all that money made him hang on. He walked north.

A short distance from the buried Jeep he spotted a trace leading back into the woods. Following it no more than fifty or sixty yards, he came upon a tarpaper building about the size of an enlarged outhouse. Around the corner from the door a fifty-gallon propane tank. Len screwed his eyes shut and prayed it was full.

Up to now, Len thought, he hadn't done many things right. Ignored the weather, smashed up Jean's Jeep, wasted two days getting here. Time now to start using his head. He reached over and knocked on the propane cylinder. Sounded full.

From his pocket, he withdrew a small fingernail clipper and went to work on the door. A metal clasp and padlock held it securely but the wood underneath was soft and flaked away quickly as he worked.

Five minutes later, he was safe inside.

Chapter Nineteen

CARROLL JOHNSON WATCHED THE DOOR and Gordon Murdock leaned on the motel's registration counter in a lazy, powerful manner. A pose not wasted on the motel's clerk, Danny Dohrmann, who knew exactly who these men were and wondered why there's never a cop around when you need one.

"Thought we'd get out and see the local sights tonight," Murdock lied casually. "What happens in this town after dark?"

"Same thing as happens before dark," Danny answered, bitterly. He'd seen all kinds here. These two were trouble. Old Man McWhirter better install one of those bullet-proof windows or he was going to be short one employee. His only defense now was to act cool.

"Nothing?"

Danny made a show of setting aside the magazine he was reading. "Wednesday night's church night. Catholics have a spaghetti supper, there's choir practice, senior citizens got bingo," he said. "Ain't no strip tease or nothin'."

Murdock's grin was metallic. "So when they're not out killing women, they're in church," he said, marveling at the beads of sweat already visible on Dorhmann's upper lip.

Danny didn't think Murdock looked so tough and the guy with him had the jitters. "If you don't like it here maybe you should move on."

"Plan to," Murdock said pleasantly. "Soon as I talk to somebody named Walleye." The dummy knew what key crime scene facts, if any, the cops were withholding. "So, where's he live?"

"On the moon."

Murdock didn't seem to hear this response. "Is this the switchboard?" he asked.

Danny nodded, tense and watchful.

"If I call from my room, the little light comes on here by the number?"

Danny slid his chair back against the wall and nodded again.

"Isn't that clever," he said, reaching over and lifting it with both hands, placing it gently on the counter.

"That's motel property," Danny protested.

"No shit?" Murdock raised the entire switchboard above his head and slammed it against the counter. "So," he said reasonably, "this then must be destroying motel property?"

Danny's eyes widened.

He flung the remains of the plastic device directly at Danny's head. He ducked too late and was struck a glancing blow on the temple before the unit shattered against the wall.

"Then there's destroying smartass motel clerks."

Frozen to the chair Danny felt blood trickle across the corner of his left eye. Murdock hopped the counter and took him by the hair. "We've never been properly introduced," Murdock said. "What's your name?"

Danny told him.

Murdock pulled his hair so his head tilted back and he examined Danny's laceration closely. He forced a finger painfully into the cut. It came away bloody and Murdock printed the letter "D" on the wall above Danny's head. He dipped again for an "A." There was nothing Danny could do but whimper. "Before I get your named spelled out,"

204

Murdock said, "I'd like you to tell me exactly where Walleye lives and how I might get there."

Danny rattled off the street address and precise directions.

"Excellent," Murdock said. "Now let's talk about the rest of your life." He dipped and printed the letter "N." With his left hand he eased Danny's body up by the hair until his nose touched the wall just below his name. "Life is short, Dan. Life is short." Murdock tried for more blood but the cut was closing up. He squeezed until it ran freely. Danny moaned. Murdock wrote "R.I.P." on the wall. "I spent most of my life on the wrong side of the law, Dan. Prison, you know, all that. Won't bore you with the details of my misspent youth, but one thing I've prided myself on Dan, one thing I'm really proud of. Know what that is?" He pressed Danny's nose harder against the wall until it seemed ready to snap. "It's this Dan. Every single pukey little punk who ever finked on me, I found 'em later. Know what I'm saying? Don't you think that's something to be proud of, Dan?"

He didn't wait for Danny response and jockeyed his head violently against the wall. "Every single one," Murdock said. "So when we leave here you won't call anybody. If fact, you'll fix your face up nice and stay right here in this little office until I come back. Half hour, maybe. The most important half hour in your life, Dan. And when I get back if you didn't go anywhere or talk to anybody or make any sort of fuss, well then Dan, you and I'll just say 'bye-bye' forever. Would you like that?"

It seemed a loaded question to Danny.

"It's okay to answer yes," Murdock said fairly. "I understand. Just remember, investing a half hour in keeping your mouth shut now will earn you a lifetime of sleeping nights. Get my drift, Dan?"

"I ain't moving until you get back."

"Smart boy," Murdock said, hopping back across the counter with easy grace.

Danny Dorhmann decided even after they were gone that broken phones were broken phones and what could he do about it? The guy was obviously crazy. He had enough problems. Anyway, he could go get the cops later. Much later.

Outside, Carroll Johnson wasn't so sure. "He'll report this. Don't kid yourself," he predicted.

"Eventually," Murdock said. "Eventually. But by then we'll have finished with Walleye and be long gone."

* * *

Only the kitchen light burned in the little house. Murdock remained outside awhile, watching. Streets were empty. Houses snug against the cold, white ribbons of smoke from their chimneys bent by the stiff northerly breeze. Apparently the retard valued his privacy. All the shades were down.

The street on which Walleye lived was only one block long, the first full block of homes south of Main Street. Walleye's house could be accessed by an alley and there Murdock left the Suburban and Carroll Johnson. The engine was running and two blasts on the horn meant time to leave. Johnson should be able to accomplish that much. He wouldn't be any use with Walleye.

Murdock rapped firmly on the back door, standing knee deep in undisturbed snow. Either the dummy didn't have enough sense to shovel or was too lazy.

The inner door opened a crack and Walleye peered at Murdock through the frosted glass of the storm door, still closed between them. "Who are you?" he asked, voice muffled.

"Danny at the motel sent me," Murdock answered pleasantly, opening the outer door. "I just want to talk to you. Walleye, right?"

"Ervin. I don't talk to strangers."

"Not even for money?" Murdock's attempt at a smile seemed to repel Walleye, so he placed a foot on the threshold.

206

"Don't come in!" Walleye said loudly. "Don't come in." He banged the heavy door hard against the man's foot.

Murdock thrust Walleye aside and strode past him into the kitchen. "Shut the door and come here," he ordered.

Walleye obeyed, standing with his back pressed against the cupboard. He was scared. *Mother didn't allow anyone in the house.* Even when he was little and she baked cookies and laid them on newspapers on the kitchen table and he wanted the other boys to taste them, no one came in the house. It was the rule. "You can't come in the house," he said.

"Shut up!" Murdock rapped Walleye on the head with his knuckles. "Pay attention. I'm going to ask a question. You answer it right, we go on to the next one. You lie or give me lip, and I do this again." He rapped Walleye a second time.

Walleye staggered, clutching his aching head with both hands. An elbow caught a spice rack on the wall and sent it clattering to the floor. He pressed his back harder against the cupboard. Always before the kitchen had been a safe place. Nothing bad ever happened here. He was too scared to run.

"How come you're telling people that body you found had satanic crap around it?" Murdock began the questioning.

Walleye had never heard the word satanic. "Charlie Benson is my friend," he told the man. Everyone knew Charlie Benson.

Murdock reached out and snatched Walleye's left ear, twisting until he felt warm blood oozing between his fingers. "I asked you a question," he said evenly. "Why'd you say that?"

"I didn't say it," Walleye cried. "I didn't say it!" The root of his ear seemed dangerously close to popping from his skull.

"Maybe you didn't." Murdock released his grip. "I bet you're almost too dumb to lie." He leaned closer. "Isn't that right, Dummy?"

Walleye felt hot tears on his cheeks and the trickle of blood running along his neck. He'd learned to be brave about pain. Mother said he was a brave boy when he got shots and had doctor tests and did clumsies in the street with his trike. "I'm not fast people," he said.

"You're an idiot! And idiots ought to keep their mouths shut." Murdock pinched Walleye's lips together. "Understand?"

Walleye nodded.

"That's better. Now, I want you to tell me from the beginning what happened when you found that lady's body." Murdock stepped left to the table and swept a porcelain salt shaker into his fist, tossing it in the air and catching it again and again. Walleye feared he might drop it and reached out. Murdock flung it against the cupboard inches from Walleye's head. Pieces of Mother's shaker, one of the bluebirds he'd bought her for Christmas the winter she died, struck Walleye's cheek. This was bad. No breaking. Breaking was bad. He ran for the bedroom.

The man caught him by the collar and spun him around. Their faces nearly touched. He didn't want to see the man's eyes. Like pig eyes. If you climbed the fence and fell in with the pigs they'd eat you. Grandpa showed him on the farm. Made him watch the pigs eat corn. They had dead eyes. Pitiless. He squirmed against the man's grasp. "Don't eat me," he begged.

In spite of his uncontrolled anger and the power it flooded through his body, Murdock laughed. "You're the dumbest little bastard I've ever met," he said. "If you don't tell about the woman you found, I will eat you. Rip your liver out and eat it raw."

Walleye didn't want to be eaten by the man's odd, tightly pinched mouth. One of his front teeth was gone, leaving a dark hole. Best give him what he wanted so he'd go away. Leave him alone with his lady. He wouldn't tell the man about the lady in Mother's bed.

"It was the day before yesterday," Walleye said. "Monday." He prided himself in knowing the days of the week. He could say them not only forwards, but backwards too. "I was hunting. The road that goes by the lake. On a hill. People leave stuff in ditches and by the lake I find money sometimes. People drop it from their clothes."

"Get to the point," the man growled.

"I saw white plastic by the woods. It was wet. I never liked woods." He could feel the man's grasp relaxing as he told the story. "I walked in high grass and got wet. I forgot the plastic when I saw the lady. No clothes. Open eyes. She has the same tooth like you."

"What are you talking about?" He pushed Walleye away.

Walleye pointed to one of his own front teeth. "Like this," he said. "No tooth here, on the lady."

"Quit saying 'lady.' Her name was Vicky."

"Vicky?" The name didn't seem right. Mother's name was Lydia. It suited her. Vicky did not suit the lady. But it was better not to tell this to the man.

"She was my old lady," he said. "What did you do after you found her?"

Walleye stared at the floor. He didn't want the man to know. But finally he told the truth. "I went pee-pee," he said.

"Pissed yourself?" The man laughed. "Christ."

"A truck took me to Charlie Benson."

"And you never saw any satanic crap around there?"

Walleye didn't understand, but he knew this idea made the man angry and mean. "No," he said positively.

"That's what I figured." He seemed to be more calm now. "What's that smell in here?"

Walleye shrugged. The kitchen always smelled the same to him.

"Smells like something crawled in here and died," the man said, walking toward the back of the house, toward Mother's room.

209

"No!" Walleye shouted. "Don't come in!"

Murdock brushed him aside and tried the door at the end of a short, dim hallway. When it swung open he was sent reeling backward by a blast of odor so foul he tried to breathe from his mouth, drawing air in gulps. He switched on the light.

Vicky was on the bed, made up in old clothes and childish socks. The flesh on her face had begun to decompose. The little ghoul had kept her around like some piece of junk he'd found in a ditch.

The sight of Vicky's corpse aroused no pity in Murdock, only anger. A man didn't like to see the woman he slept with laid out like that. Smelling her rotting flesh, seeing lips he'd kissed stretched across her teeth in a ghastly grin. Only a ghoulish little freak dressed up a woman like this and kept her for a toy.

He turned from the bed and went for Walleye.

Walleye ran.

* * *

Casey was accustomed to Charlie Benson stepping inside the bar to eye the customers, but usually at closing time. He could count on one hand the number of times he'd served Charlie a drink. Tonight Charlie strolled up to him and ordered a beer. Sign of the times, no doubt. Even the cops were letting their hair down.

He drew a glass of his cheapest draft, in case this was on the cuff, and set it close to the policeman's thick hand. Casey cared little for cops, small-town or otherwise, but Charlie wasn't a bad sort. Strict about the one A.M. closing time, fair if a fight broke out or some kid slipped in on a fake ID. Cops could be pricks in a small town if they wanted to.

"Good crowd tonight," Charlie observed, looking around the room.

"Storm brought 'em out," Casey explained. "Some people need an excuse to drink. Been like this all day."

The tall beer glass lost in Charlie's hand as he raised it and drank. "Time for a few questions?" he asked, too politely.

"Nothin' but time, Chief."

"Dutch Cleland been in here during the past week or so?" Charlie began.

"Never does come in much," Casey replied. "Picks up a bottle on the Off Sale side once in awhile," he said, pointing to the package liquor store adjacent to the bar.

"How about Len Davis?" Charlie continued pleasantly.

"Sure," he said, wondering where this was leading. "Len's in here most afternoons."

"Lately?"

"Can't say." Casey shrugged and stared down at the bar, avoiding Charlie's eyes. "Comes and goes."

"This isn't idle curiosity," Charlie said more forcefully, his gray eyes searching Casey's face. "I've had a lousy day, a lousy couple days, and I'm tired. I want to go home. Be nice if I only had to ask you these questions one time."

"Monday," Casey said. He didn't appreciate the threatening edge to Charlie's voice but swallowed his hostility.

"What time?"

"After work." He pushed away from the bar and leaned against the cash register table. "Around six or seven."

"You talk to him?"

"Sure," Casey said. "We talked."

"What about?"

"How am I supposed to remember that?" Casey protested. "Get off it. Len's a friend of mine. You know he ain't got nothin' to do with this thing."

"Davis is a friend of Dutch's," Charlie snapped. "You're a friend of Davis. Dutch is gone and Davis is gone. Not a coincidence. If I knew where Len Davis was, I wouldn't be talking to you."

"Yeah, well everybody around here knows everybody else," Casey said. "It's a small town and people should mind

211

their own business. Mine's running a saloon. You want Len, go look for him. He's not in here." Casey turned and walked away.

For a moment Charlie did nothing. Sunday morning he'd taken his aunt to the First Lutheran Church where Casey was one of the ushers. They'd said good morning. Casey had teased him about dating an older woman. They'd all laughed. It was a small town and they did all know each other.

Then again, people will always surprise you. He strolled to the light switch near the front door and brightened the room as he did at closing time. There were catcalls. Several people shouted "Very funny!" One guy yelled, "Hey Charlie! Your watch set to Greenwich mean time or what?" People laughed.

"This establishment in closed." Charlie's tone left no room for doubt but he added, "By order of the Willow River Police Department."

"Come on, Charlie!" a voice said.

"I mean it! Everybody out!" He drew his nightstick and struck it against a table. "Now! Let's go!"

Calling many of them by name, he herded them through the door until the room was empty. Casey, standing alone by the bar, screamed at him. "You're nuts!" Charlie closed the door and locked it. "You won't get away with this!" Casey kicked over a chair and started toward him.

It never entered Charlie's mind to hurt Casey, but when he saw the bulging eyes and the flaming red face he quickly closed the distance between them and smashed his fist into Casey's open mouth. The force of the blow, struck just below the nose, split his upper lip and showered blood in its wake. A second later he was unconscious, lying on his back among the scattered chairs.

Charlie stood over him, awed and more than a little frightened Casey might be dead. Years since he'd struck anyone

212

in anger, and even then never a person he'd known well. *What do I do now*, he thought, *say I'm sorry?*

He stared down at his fist, which was beginning to hurt, and saw three of his knuckles were bleeding, skin split to the bone. He walked behind the bar and stuck the injured hand deep into the ice maker then reached up with his free hand and drew a beer.

Casey remained unconscious a full fifteen minutes, during which time Charlie gave thanks no one had witnessed the fight—if it was a fight. When he'd gone to turn up the lights and close the bar, his intentions were simple. Show them the law still had its teeth and get Casey's attention. By the look of things, he was a failure all around.

When Casey's eyeballs finally rolled back toward center, Charlie was ready with a wad of cotton he'd found in a first aid kit behind the bar. "Here," he said, handing it over. "Stick this behind your lip. Facial cuts bleed a lot but they're never as bad as they look."

Carefully, Casey slid the cotton behind his split lip and staggered to his feet. "I think my teeth are loose," he said.

"Sorry I hit you."

"I'm going to sue your ass. I'll sue you back to the stone age." Head spinning, he quickly sat down in the first available chair. "You know that?"

"Probably win too," Charlie said, retrieving his beer. "If anyone believed your side of it."

"You hit me!"

"That's your story." Charlie smiled. "Mine might be different. A policeman defending himself against an angry bar owner. Pretty common story."

"Not around here it ain't."

"Have it your own way." Charlie reached for his handcuffs. "Stand up and place both hands on the bar."

"Why?"

"I'm going to arrest you."

213

"You can't do that," Casey said, making no move to get up. "I didn't do anything."

"I know," Charlie said pleasantly. "And you'll get a chance to tell all that to the judge. Without witnesses of course, it'll pretty much come down to your word against mine. But Judge Emmert's a good egg. I bring him a drunk and disorderly every couple weeks. Usually just gives 'em a thirty day suspended and a fine, unless the arresting officer wants to press it."

"So first you beat me up, then you frame me," Casey complained. "That's police harassment."

"No. That's not harassment," Charlie said. "Harassment is when the town cop comes in here every night and busts anybody who even looks like he's going to drive down the block after two beers. Harassment is when your place gets such a bad record your dramshop insurance premium bounces up to five figures. Or when the Liquor Control Board gets so many complaints on Police Department letterhead, they finally pull your liquor license. That's harassment."

"I won't forget this," Casey said, standing. "What is it you want anyhow?"

"Word for word what Len Davis said to you Monday night."

"We joked around, same as always," Casey rubbed his jaw. "He ordered his usual."

"And?" Charlie prompted.

"And we talked about the murder, like everybody else."

"And Dutch?"

"Yeah. Dutch."

"What time did you say that was?"

"After work. Five-thirty. Six," Casey recalled.

"At five-thirty or six o'clock Monday not even I knew Dutch Cleland had any connection with this killing," Charlie said. "How'd you and Davis know?"

214

"We didn't." Casey touched his lip. "Ouch! I need some ice for this." He walked behind the bar. "I only said Len and I talked about Dutch and about the killing. I didn't say we put the two together."

"So what did you say about Dutch?"

"Len told me some guy named Murdock was around look- ing for Dutch," Casey said, drawing a handful of ice from the bin and wrapping it in a bar towel. "Len thought the guy was after Dutch or something. I told him to give Dutch or his old lady a call. But he left. Said he'd go out there instead."

"And you're sure this was Monday night?"

"Yeah," he said, holding the ice to his upper lip. "Positive."

"You could have saved yourself a lot of trouble if you'd simply told me this in the beginning," Charlie said.

"Why should I?"

"Because I asked you nice," Charlie said. "And because it's important."

"Big deal."

"Anything else you've seen or heard? Anybody else in here asking questions? People acting suspicious? Anything?"

"You mean Monday night?" Whenever he spoke he blew blood bubbles.

"Monday especially, but anytime."

"Saw Walleye Monday night," Casey said. "Maybe he done it. Had something big up on that new ATM in the bank lot. Crazy little bastard."

"Probably a sack of cans," Charlie mused.

"That's what the old lady said. You still going to arrest me?"

"No." Charlie started for the door. "But if I were you, I'd say I tripped and fell against the bar."

"Fat chance," Casey said as Charlie went out and shut the door.

Outside, Charlie sat in his car waiting for it to warm up. He shouldn't have hit Casey and he'd catch hell for it, but if

Len Davis went to see Dutch on Monday that explained a lot. Len must've gone somewhere with Dutch or gone somewhere after him. Either way, he knew where Dutch was hiding, and two people are easier to find than one. Tomorrow the Willow River Police Department is going to turn this town upside down and shake it until something drops out. He shifted the car into reverse.

His hand throbbed. He should go home and soak it but something nagged him about Casey's description of Walleye at the ATM. Why the ATM? When had he ever seen Walleye out after dark? He checked his watch. *Still early. Greenwich Mean Time. That was a pretty good line*, he thought. *Must've been Erik Billig. He had a quick wit.* Time for a quick visit with Walleye Wertz before turning in. It was on his way home.

*   *   *

Charlie Benson followed fresh footprints in the snow until he reached the back door of Walleye's tiny house. Lights were on inside behind drawn shades. He knew Walleye was easily spooked after dark and knocked gently. "It's Charlie Benson, Walleye," he called. "Open the door."

He spotted an old fashioned dead bolt screwed to the door on the inside and more out of habit than hope he turned the knob and pushed. It was unlocked. Surprised, he poked his head inside and shouted, "Hey! Walleye! It's me, Charlie."

He heard the faint ticking of the old Seth Thomas Walleye had restored. Charlie stepped inside. "Walleye?" He lowered his voice. "Where are you?"

Three paces into the kitchen Charlie smelled the unmistakable stench of death. All the more frightening here in a kitchen mixed with strong scents of cinnamon. A wooden spice rack lay on the floor, contents scattered. Near the window a table set with one place. A thin splattering of blood across the white plate, silverware, plastic table cloth. Charlie drew his revolver. Two blooming plants on the sill. The source of the evil smell originated deeper inside the house.

Cautiously he crept down a dark hallway, heavy flashlight up resting on his shoulder. He cocked the revolver. Avoiding the light switches and edging forward, he silently cursed the rustle of his nylon jacket. Each foot placed well and firm, he strained to hear any telltale sound above the ticking of the clock and his own labored breathing.

Toe of his massive rubber boot against the bedroom door, he shoved it open with a sudden scrape that echoed in the house. The smell engulfed him like heat and his beam of light picked up Vicky Murdock's corpse stretched out on a bed, dressed in outdated clothes. With the flashlight handle, Charlie flipped the switch, flooding the pathetic shrine with orange light from a shaded lamp.

A straight-backed chair was placed near the bed facing Vicky's head as if a friend or relative had sat there to comfort her. It was of course far too early in the decomposition process for Vicky's face to be anything near a skull, but Charlie felt he saw it anyway asserting itself beneath the rotting flesh and drying skin. He holstered his flashlight. Mrs. Murdock wore an old lady's dress buttoned to her neck, stretched along her body to mid-calf. Her perfect toes hidden by frilly white ankle socks.

Hand over his mouth, Charlie stepped closer. Draped around her neck a strand of fake pearls, and under her head, straw-like hair spread evenly against the white pillow, gaudy earrings shaped like half moons but neon pink. It appeared someone had attempted to color her pale lips with a garish red lipstick then made a clumsy attempt to wipe it away.

"Dear God," Charlie muttered.

Walleye wasn't there. He spotted an open window. Did he run, knowing Charlie would punish him for stealing the corpse? Charlie holstered the revolver. Vicky Murdock's remains, now seventy-two-hours old and unrefrigerated, required immediate attention. He imagined the press account and who'd be blamed when he called Sheriff

217

Mattson. First he had to find Walleye and put the little rascal on ice somewhere.

He searched another bedroom and the small living room. Peeked upstairs in the attic. Checked a pantry and several closets. Walleye had vanished.

The wooden steps leading to the basement were painted haze gray and worn by years of treading feet. Charlie transferred his weight slowly from step to step and felt the wood sag in protest. Damp, musty air. The whirring rattle of a furnace fan. The familiar mechanical noise eased his tension.

"Come on, Walleye," he coaxed. "I'm not mad. Quit fooling around now and come out. Let's talk."

His foot touched an old rag rug at the bottom of the stairs. No light switch on either side, he drew the flashlight and swept the beam in a slow arc around the room. Cement floor. Exposed joists hung with ancient plumbing and frayed wiring. Someone had strung clothesline back and forth to his immediate left. Opposite, a row of mismatched barrels filled with aluminum cans, tin, glass, and plastic. The furnace blocked Charlie's view of the rest, one large open room. A low door beneath the clotheslines, undoubtedly a fruit cellar. He pulled it open and sprayed light inside. Empty except for cans, jars of vegetables, fruits, and berries lining the homemade shelves, and a black body bag on the floor. He must've stored her here awhile.

Charlie exhaled a long breath and backed out. Moving around to the back side of the furnace something brushed his ear. A string. He pulled it and a bare, low wattage bulb lit the basement, casting deep shadows that swayed as the bulb danced at the end of its cord. The basement was empty.

Chapter Twenty

THE SUN ROSE IN THE SOUTHEAST, lighting a world brittle with cold. A forest of frozen white sticks. Inside the cabin the fire had gone out and Dutch awakened to pounding noises and Nimrod's sharp yapping. Stretching his head through the opening of his sleeping bag, he shivered uncontrollably, fighting consciousness.

"Wake up! It's Dylan."

Gathering the folds of the bag around his neck and making an effort to breathe the cold air, Dutch invited the hippie to enter. He burst in behind a wave of stinging cold. "Lock your door," he adivsed, stomping snow from thick boots. "Try and remember you're a fugitive."

Dutch sat up inside the warm bag. "I heard you," he said. "Anyway, the dog stands watch."

Nimrod wagged his tail, licking ice chunks from Dylan's choppers. "Vicious hound."

"He knows you."

Shedding two outer layers, Dylan kicked open the stove door and peered inside. "Fire's almost out." He stuffed it with fresh wood. "Expected you up and ready."

"Sorry," he said. "Put some water on for coffee while I dress."

The younger man nodded, dumping fresh water into the pot of used grounds as Dutch hurried into his clothes. "I'm going back," he said simply. "My wife, everything is there. Friend of mine's a pretty good lawyer. He'll tell me what to do."

Dylan studied him. "Make this decision last night?"

He shrugged. "Back of my mind all along, I guess. Just needed time to think really. I've got to go back." He stared directly at Dylan. "Sorry if I put you and your wife to any trouble."

"She ain't my wife. Just friends."

"Oh."

"She called the Jacksons last night and they said okay for you to come. Have to call 'em back, I guess. You sure? I got oil and fresh gas outside. Don't suppose you thought to put fuel stabalizer in that snow machine before you stored it. Brought my tools, even scrounged a new oil filter. Couple hours we'll have her running."

The disappointment in Dylan's voice was understandable, Dutch thought, because there's reward for Dylan in beating the system. His own urge to run was strong, too. "Will you help me get it running even if I head into Togo and call the cops on myself?" he asked.

"If that's what you want. Be sure though, like a parachute jump, you know? Leave the plane you can't turn back. The System might drop you on your noodle." Dylan poured fresh coffee and slurped, eyes sparkling through the steam. "You're salty, I'll say that for you, Man."

On the rock ridge above the cabin, MOM and Marty, clothed in white camouflage garments, squirmed like snow allegators until they'd concealed themselves behind a fallen jack pine. Each cradled a high powered rifle across his forearms and automatic pistols were strapped to their belts. The Butcher of Willow River was a vicious killer and they weren't taking chances. Half the night, they sat drinking and talking themselves toward courage. To shoot first and bring him down.

"From here we've got a perfect field of fire," MOM whispered. "No back door." He grinned. "Gopher in a hole."

"What's the plan?" Marty was eager, and like most of MOM's friends, obedient and fiercely loyal. "We gonna call him out?"

"Don't be dumb. Want him to hold up in there behind those thick logs? Take weeks. We wait 'til he comes out to piss or something then we fire a volley over his head and order him to freeze. If he so much as shakes the dew off his lilly, we pop him right there."

"Sweet!"

MOM knew it wasn't just his hunting and tracking skill that made him the natural leader. It went deeper. Some locals hated city vacationers and were fed up with eking out a living on land which couldn't support anything but aspen. They were tired of enduring a climate too cold in winter, too humid and thick with bugs the rest of the time and they looked to MOM for leadership because he did more than talk. He'd invented the Homestead Property Rule. MOM believed Homestead property entitled you to full property rights, but vacation property was subject to local "tax." A full tank of propane might be liberated or a nice set of tools, anything handy and portable. Marty and a few others appreciated such original thinking and followed MOM while the sob sisters sat on their bar stools, whining and pissing away their welfare money.

MOM pondered the deployment of his force and discovered it lacked strategic initiative. He'd concentrated too much in one position. "See if you can't slip around back of that big spruce there along his drive, see it?" MOM ordered. "Catch him in a cross fire."

"What if he spots me?"

"Go left. Behind the cabin where there ain't no windows." MOM shook his head. "Do I have to tell you everything?"

Marty slithered off at high speed, digging knees and toes into the snow. A few minutes later he was in position and MOM settled down to wait.

Dutch's morning routine seldom varied. "I'll scramble up some eggs when I get back," he said pushing through the door without a coat. The air had a bite but he was going

221

home. Even the prospect of prison failed to dampen his spirits. He'd fallen asleep just before dawn but not until his mind was made up. What he told Jean was true - he needed time to think. Tossing in his bunk he'd hit upon something that hadn't occurred to him - he wasn't going to die for Vicky. He may be forced to trade freedom for captivity but was prison much worse than years at sea in a narrow hull with three hundred sailors? And wasn't there some value in doing the right thing even if your motives were tainted by self-interest? He waded through the deep snow of the yard and unzipped his pants.

* * *

Less than two miles away, Len Davis awoke sore and confused. He tossed aside the pile of filthy blankets and old newspapers he'd slept under and swung his legs over the side of his wooden bunk. A small propane stove kept the shack above freezing during the night and now he hoped the absentee hunters had stashed some canned goods for emergencies. Wasn't that northwoods etiquette?

These particular hunters were stingy assholes, leaving nothing but a plastic bag containing several teaspoons of old coffee. The shack had no plumbing and no water. "Great," he said, rummaging the cupboard until he found a dirty aluminum pot.

He packed the two-quart pot with fresh snow he scooped a safe distance from the shack, placed the pot on the heat and smiled proudly as water drops hissed against the stove's metal skin and burst into steam. He'd solved the basic human need of shelter, warmth, and food. He lit a cigarette. The first one in the morning tastes good after the hacking and spitting.

The pot of snow melted, netting three tablespoons of semi-clear liquid with suspended solids. He strained it through a paper towel and repeated the distillation process during the next hour until he produced nearly two cups of liquid. He added coffee from the plastic bag, boiled the combination and drank the result. It tasted like boiled bark with a zing.

Through the thin walls Len heard a series of rapid-fire shots. Were they machinegunning the deer? There'd been shooting since dawn but this was close, less than a mile he guessed.

Draining his cup, he decided to walk toward the shooting. Local hunters might know Dutch's cabin.

* * *

When the shooting stopped Dutch pulled his face from the snow and struggled trembling to his feet, supported by the corner of the porch. Two strangers dressed in camouflaged white suits had just shot each other across his yard.

The man to his right, who'd been concealed behind a fallen pine, was slumped holding his side and howling like a wounded animal. The other man was tangled in the lower bows of a large spruce only yards away and remained quite still. Dutch decided they might've been shooting at him but missed somehow.

"Amateurs," Dylan said from the doorway. "After the bounty."

"On me?" Dutch was dumfounded by this and remained standing, uncovered. "You mean there's a reward?"

"Naw," Dylan said, grinning. "Zip up, man." He bounded down the steps toward the motionless body. "Doesn't mean these cretins knew it."

On the rock ridge the wounded man cried, "Somebody help me! I'm bad shot!"

Dylan kept moving toward the other man. "I know the one up on the rocks," he told Dutch. "MOM Mahalich. Owns the local bar, works as a game warden sometimes and logs when he's broke. Real prick." Still grinning Dylan rolled the other man over with his foot. "Marty Taylor. All the Taylors are idiots and married their cousins or screwed their

223

sisters, or their fathers did." He glanced at Dutch. "I ain't never had so much fun."

MOM's bullet had entered Marty's body near the clavical and traveled through soft tissue, mushrooming nicely until it hooked the heart muscle and its arteries, exiting under his arm. The exit wound left a jagged hole and a large quantity of remarkably red blood steamed in the snow.

"Just so you know, you fucking idiot," Dylan called up the hill, "Marty's dead. You shot him square in the chest, probably right through the heart."

"It was an accident," the man whined. "It's his fault."

Dutch realized he meant him.

"We're just law-abiding citizens trying to apprehend a fugitive," he hollered. "God! I'm bleeding bad. You better help me, Dylan, you hippie bastard, or I'll say you were aiding and abetting. You'll do time!"

Dylan retrieved Marty's rifle and brushed it clear of snow. "In that case," he said, sighting the weapon carefully at MOM, "I'll blow a nice round hole in your fat, brainless head. When the cops get here they'll see the two of you shot each other, which is what happened anyway."

"You better not," MOM warned. "You people are supposed to be non-violent."

"Get your ass down here before I'm forced to destroy another sixties myth."

"I can't walk!"

"Hop!"

Dutch was afraid Dylan would shoot him and started for the ridge. "I'll get him. There's a first aid kit inside."

* * *

When Len came up the trail he spotted Dutch and some guy with a ponytail carrying a third man up the steps. The third man was bleeding profusely and crying. There was a fourth man dead in the yard.

"Hi, Dutch," he said and all three froze. "Kind of a busy morning?"

* * *

Dylan treated MOM's wound and Len fired questions. Dutch found it impossible to concentrate. Len had always had an appetite for details and the questioning went on for nearly two hours until the lawyer finally lapsed into brooding silence.

The sudden episode of mindless violence outside had stirred in Dutch memories of Vicky's betrayal and he drifted back into the wreckage. They'd made such a mess of it in the end. It plagued him for years and he was angry because they managed a satisfying physical intimacy until one night she brought him to Nightingale's for a farewell dinner and confessed to have taken a lover.

He hadn't believed her at first and later thought her heightened lovemaking beforehand was a result of her bold deception of him. There'd been a scene then at the club and he settled into a kind of lover's pathos which gradually deepened into self-pity and finally blossomed as hatred. Striking out at Vicky first in word—he called her a slut—then by confessing to Jean because he thought that might hurt. Nothing worked of course and Vicky, further along the path to recovery, invited him to her house to begin the healing process, and in a moment of insanity, he accepted.

Shortly after eleven o'clock on a Sunday morning he arrived at Vicky and Carroll Johnson's suburban home in a subdivision called Doverwood. He'd never been there. The Johnson house was a boxy bilevel like all the others, its open garage door the prominent architectural feature. He pulled up and sat staring. Vicky owned two hundred feet of green garden hose, two upside down bicycles and a partially used case of Valvolin just like everybody else.

Solemly she'd opened the door and ushered him into an atmosphere of bereavement. Her funereal costume—consertive white blouse buttoned to the neck over a black, mid-calf skirt and dark nylons—muted her figure and the lack of jewelry lent a puritanical air. She'd pinned her hair back in a bun.

"We're all in the living room," she said.

"I came early, hoping we'd get a few minutes alone."

"You're the last one here." She closed the door and led him up five carpeted steps toward a large living room with steeped ceiling. It smelled of candlewax and lemon furniture polish. "You told Jean?"

"Yes."

"Good."

"She didn't come?"

"She would never come to anything like this."

On the drive from Willow River he'd imagined them together. Carroll, the powerful husband, cockholded and bitter. The new man, Bill Prestly, who'd come with his wife Gloria. They had several children, he'd forgotten how many, and listened for kid sounds.

"This is Dutch," Vicky announced to the gathering, treating him as an acquaintance.

A grandfather clock taller then a man gleamed to his right, its silent pendulum the only moving thing. The coral carpet was freshly vacuumed.

"We're all here because we love each other," Vicky said in a throaty voice. She picked up a Bible from a small table near the fireplace and folded it into the crook of her arm and stood very straight. She kept her head slightly bowed.

Dutch slid into a straight-backed chair next to the pendulum.

"I mean that with all my heart," she promised. "It's because we all love each other—isn't that ironic?—we face such heartache. God wants us to show our love for each other now and get everything out in the open to begin the healing process."

226

These words rolled glibly from her tongue and the audience received them with benigned expressions. Carroll leaned back comfortably on the couch next to Gloria Prestly. Bill Prestly sat alone on a forest green loveseat recently vacated by Vicky. (The burgandy pillow was left in the position she always preferred to keep her back straight.) It wouldn't have seemed unreasonable for them to have gotten up a few hands of whist as if unaware they'd gathered because Vicky was sleeping with everyone in the room, with the possible exception of Gloria.

Gloria, a lumpy moon-headed woman, sat on the very edge of the couch, feet together, bouncing lightly. Not crying but sore-eyed and solemn. Her face was blotchy red and edged with an almost-green pallor.

"These past few days have been difficult for me too," Vicky continued. "I've examined my heart." She bowed her head and reverently opened the Bible to a place she'd marked with an index card. "I want to read something." There was a pause while her finger ran along the page. "Here it is," she said. "From Romans: 'We know that in everything God works for good with those who love him.'" She looked up and her eyes misted, forcing a trembling smile. "That says it all. It's why we're here, to make something good out of our love for each other."

The Reverend Vicky was a new character and her happy bumper sticker religion pierced the gathering's facade of sophistication so Dutch asked, "Am I the only one disgusted by this evil invocation?"

"I'm warning you Dutch," Vicky said in a strident voice. "Don't ruin this."

"Ruin it?" Undoubtedly, the scene was planned to the last detail. "You mean I'm not suppose to mention that you are married to Carroll over there?" He pointed and acknowledged with a solemn nod of the perfectly manicured head. "That for the past five years you've also been sleeping with me, and we've recently discovered you're also sleeping with Bill, here to my right." He smiled at Bill. "Sorry we haven't met."

"You're dragging it in the gutter," Vicky said, clenching her teeth.

"Some people might say we are the gutter."

"Yes," she said, shooting a venomous stare, "small town pukes like you!"

"Let's calm down," Carroll said reasonably. "We're all adults here."

It was time for someone to say that. "What's the use of beating around the bush?" Dutch asked. "We're all in trouble for screwing Vicky."

"Not me," Gloria cut in.

"Glad to hear it."

"Not me either," Carroll said, frowning. "I'm her husband."

"What about you, Bill?" Dutch asked. "Nothing to say?"

"Bill and I are very much in love." Vicky volunteered for him.

Gloria sobbed.

Bill shifted his brown eyes from Vicky to Gloria and back again.

"I was hoping Bill might speak for himself," I said.

"He doesn't have to," Vicky squeaked. "This is my house, and if you don't like it, leave."

"Never mind, Darling." Bill held up his hand. "I'll be glad to speak for myself if Cleland shuts up long enough."

"Who are you anyway?" Dutch wanted to be rude.

"William L. Prestly," he said with a thin smile, sunlight catching the line of his toupee. "I sell Toyotas."

"More offshore cars than anybody in the Twin Cities," Gloria announced.

"This is my house too," Carroll broke in, rising from the couch to confront Dutch. "I'm reluctant to set rules of behavior, this is a unique situation and emotions run high, but I won't allow a shouting match." Thumbs behind his suspenders, he strode like an Alabama lawyer to the darkened bar behind the couch. "Let's take a breather and I'll mix some drinks."

Dutch believed the only ingredient lacking in this powderkeg was alcohol but all embraced the idea, even Vicky. Gloria wanted a grasshopper. Carroll didn't know how to mix it and Bill told her to pick something simple so they could get on with it. Vicky had Chablis. Bill poured for her. Dutch asked for rum and got whiskey. Carroll was about as good at bartending as he was at grasping reality.

"How do you think the Vikings look this year?" he asked Bill.

"Like usual," he responded. "All defense and no offense."

Carroll nodded agreement.

Gloria asked Vicky where she'd found her lovely chenille drapes and then left the room to call the children, being babysat by her sister in Brooklyn Park. Dutch imagined how Gloria explained the gathering to her sister, or wasn't she curious? Maybe this kind of thing went on all over town and he'd never known about it.

"Was everyone happy with where they were sitting before?" Carroll wanted to know. "There's plenty of chairs. No reason to sit in the same place if you don't want to."

Dutch took Carroll's place next to Gloria. "I'm Dutch Cleland," he said, giving her his hand.

She smiled thinly. "Gloria Prestly." She held on. "I shouldn't be here. Someone told me you were married too. Why isn't your wife here?"

"She takes a very dim view of this sort of thing."

"Oh!" she said. "I do too, ordinarily. But don't you think Vicky's been very nice about it? Inviting us here and everything?"

"Personally," he said, "I view Vicky as little more than a common slut."

She disapproved. "It's not our place to judge others."

"Why not?"

"It isn't right."

"Why?"

"Well, because how do you know that what you think is right? I mean, right and wrong is such a gray area."

"It is? You mean you don't think it was wrong for Vicky to sit here in the same room with you and say she's in love with your husband? The father of your children?"

"Well, actually, only two of them are his children," she said. "We were both married before. But I see what you mean," she hastened to add. "If you don't mind my asking, aren't you cheating on your wife too?"

"Don't get the wrong idea. I'm no better. Maybe worse, but. . . ."

"If you two are finished visiting," Vicky interrupted, "Bill and I have something to say to Gloria."

"Oh?" Gloria sounded surprised and a little flattered. She smoothed her denim skirt and sat up straight.

"Certain things need to be said openly," Vicky explained, turning to Bill. "Have you told Gloria you're in love with me?"

Bill seemed suddenly fascinated by his shoes.

"Bill?" Vicky chided, gently.

"We haven't talked much about it," Bill said, "since I told her I was seeing another woman."

"Well, that's what we're here for. To talk about it." Vicky had a way of inclining her head forward, almost bowing, that at first seemed humble and later reminded Dutch of a King Cobra. To Gloria she said, "You've been married before. You know that sometimes things don't work out. Bill and I can't help the way we feel about each other but that doesn't mean we feel any less love for you or Bill feels any less love for the children." She clutched the Bible table. "There are many kinds of love, all genuine, but we've decided our lives would be better, happier, if we were together. We only have one life. I don't think you'd want to keep Bill just for the children's sake, would you? Hold him back? How can that help? You see that, don't you?"

"No," Dutch said.

"Dutch. Please shut up!" she snapped without looking.

"Don't listen to this crap," he addressed Gloria. "Didn't you and Bill have a good marriage before Vicky came along?"

"I thought we still had a good marriage," Gloria said, somewhat perplexed.

"I mean, are you happy? Do you fight? Does he beat the kids, or what?"

"Listen here, Cleland!" Bill slapped his hands down on his knees. "I've legally adopted Gloria's children and I've always treated them like my own. You better watch your mouth!"

"I don't think Dutch meant to hurt your feelings," Gloria consoled him.

"She's right," Dutch said. "If you're happy parents and you had a good thing going until Vicky came along, what's the problem?" They both had blank looks. "The problem isn't you, it's Vicky."

This simple truth exploded in the room and Vicky barely controlled the muscles in her face and eyes aflame, she said bitterly, "You hate me because I made a fool of you. The simple fact is: I don't love you. So, grow up!"

Dutch rose from the couch and moved as close as he dared. "No Vicky. You didn't make a fool of me. I made a fool of myself." He snatched the Bible. "Don't talk about love. In the Biblical sense, you've known every man in this room, almost simultaneously. That isn't love."

"Damn you Dutch!" Vicky shrieked. "Get out of my house!"

"I've every intention of leaving, when I'm damn good and ready!"

231

"Carroll?" Vicky spun around. "Are you going to let him talk like that?"

"She's right, you know," Carroll told me. "This is her house."

"Yes," Dutch said. "Everything here belongs to Vicky, doesn't it?"

"I'm leaving!" Vicky announced, and bolted from the room. A moment later a door slammed. Carroll stood helplessly looking around the room, as if he might find her somewhere under the furniture, then hurried away.

"Now's your chance," Dutch told Bill. "Take Gloria and get the hell out of here before Vicky comes back. Pick up the kids and go home."

A few minutes later they left without a word and he never saw either of them again.

When Carroll brought Vicky back into the room, Dutch stood by the door like some actor who'd waited too long before his exit. Vicky repeated her order to get out and this time Carroll backed her up with words that sounded rehearsed.

The old pickup carried him further from the city and the band around his heart loosened. In the weeks and months that followed, he grew a fine hatred and remembered always the mindless clicking of the tires on the pavement.

By Christmas that year he'd lost fifteen pounds and performed daily routines in robotic boredom. There was an awful feeling nothing was resolved. Daydreams of killing her grew into serious plans worked out in painstaking detail only to be rejected later when she wasn't worth killing or it was discovered killing was wrong.

On December 26, Jean, who decided to forgive him, explained certain facts of life. Most important, the hating of Vicky had ruined him more efficiently than Vicky herself, and Jean advised him to forgive and forget.

Two days later Bill Prestly called from his car dealership in Wayzata.

"She's gone," he said.

"Vicky?"

"Yep."

"Where?"

"Oklahoma."

"I'm surprised you called me," Dutch told him.

"Well, Cleland," he said. "Suppose there'll never be any love lost between us but I've had time to think. Last fall you did me a favor. On days when Gloria and I fight or the bills pile up or the damn kids flunk something, I think maybe I should've gone off with her, but then I figure you know, she won't be happy with this new guy either."

"New guy?"

"Name's Gordon Murdock," he said. "Met him at one of those hotel seminars she does. He was having dinner at the next table or something and invited her over. They ended up in the sack and a month later she divorced Carroll and left for Tulsa."

"How do you know all this?"

"Carroll told me."

"You guys buddies now or what?"

"Same hairdresser."

There was more to ask but he couldn't think of it now. "Carroll's better off rid of her too," Dutch said.

"Maybe. But he doesn't see it that way."

"Oh?"

"He's not too fond of you."

"How's that?" Dutch was mildly stunned. "He can't blame me for Vicky running off with this Murdock, or whatever."

"Figures you started it all. Besides, he never met Murdock."

"Well, don't suppose Carroll and I were destined to become pals."

"Yeah," Bill said. "Don't worry. He's not the homicidal type."

"And you?"

"Nope. Far as I'm concerned she's history."

And so he believed, until a few days ago.

Chapter Twenty-One

SITTING CROSS-LEGGED ON MURDOCK'S BED Carroll Johnson knew he'd never been in so much trouble. He was a wanted man. They'd eluded the Willow River authorities and taken a room under fake names in Sinclair Lewis's hometown of Sauk Centre, but so what? His life was over. He'd snorted it right into the toilet and the cause of all his misery slept beside him, snoring loudly through a wired jaw. He stared at the drawn features, smug even in sleep. The sight filled him with loathing.

"Get up!" He shook Murdock. Butt-kissing his way up the corporate ladder, enduring every kind of abuse to his pride, sweating to stay fit—all for nothing. The motel room had one double bed and he'd slept in it with Murdock, luckily too stoned to remember. He reached for his laptop. "Wake up!" He snatched the pillow from under Murdock's head. "Was Vicky online?"

"What? No. She never touched the stuff."

"Computers! I'm talking about computers."

"Oh. Yeah. She was nuts for computers, you know. They got some pretty kinky stuff on there. She showed me."

Carroll's fingers clicked the keys. "Address?"

Murdock gave it, then asked, "What's going on?"

"I need our friend Cleland's Social Security number and I'm guessing Vicky has it on file. Her password?"

Murdock rose on one elbow, grinning. "Her measurements."

Carroll typed them in and waited. "It'll take me awhile to go through her files. Got a few hours of hacking after that— airlines, rental cars, credit cards, that kind of stuff. Maybe he's got a little hideaway down in the Caribbean somewhere. Whatever leaves a trail. With luck, I'll have something solid on him by lunch."

"So you're up early and all gung-ho." Murdock sounded wary. "I don't get it?"

"You've made me an accessory to an assult." Carroll returned his stare. "There's just one way out. Find Cleland, and quick."

"Got news for you." Murdock stretched his thin lips across his teeth. "If you do find him, you're about to be an accessory to something much worse."

"No matter," Carroll said. "I've figured a way to fix it so Mr. Cleland takes the blame for all of it."

"How's that?"

Carroll wagged a finger. "Wait until the time comes. Wouldn't want you to get tired of me."

Murdock stared straight into his eyes. "Don't get too clever for your own good."

"This is for my own good," Carroll said.

Murdock chuckled and seemed satisfied. "We'll see."

* * *

Marlene watched Charlie Benson's massive frame lumber up the Police Department steps, a slump to his shoulders. She doubted he'd slept at all since discovering Walleye missing last night, and here she stood, bearer of more bad news.

"Had your breakfast?" she asked, easing into it.

He ambled by toward his office. "Not hungry."

"We need to talk."

"Come in then," he said without enthusiasm.

She waited until he'd settled comfortably. "Wish we didn't have to have this conversation," she began, "but you're fired."

236

Charlie yawned, squeezing his eyes shut. "Good. I need the rest."

"I'm not kidding."

Something in her voice brought him up short. "Oh?"

"Casey."

"Shot his mouth off?" He shrugged. "Guess I should've expected it."

"Of course you should've," she said more forcefully. "Last night I had calls from two members of the City Council, Mayor Heather Janski, and Sheriff Mattson. Not to mention various friends and neighbors. You're quite notorious. And I might add, stupid."

"Marlene."

"Don't Marlene me!" She stomped her foot. "Fighting in a bar like some common hooligan! What got into you?"

"Into me?" Charlie sat up straight. "Did it ever occur to you, or any of the city mothers, that I might've had my reasons?"

"No," she said flatly. "You walk into someone's place of business and order his customers out the door, then beat the propretor senseless. Are you on drugs?"

"Wanted some answers."

"Well, you got 'em. Our illustrious mayor is busy upstairs typing your pink slip. I know because I've been up there twice trying to talk her out of it. You'd be gone already but the lamebrain can't type and her adminstrative assistant, Faye Gordon, is getting her hair done down at Betty's for her cousin's wedding. Your life hangs by a curler."

She was beginning to worry him. "Even Janski's not dumb enough to fire me right in the middle of the biggest murder investigation in Willow River history," he declared.

"Sure she is," she answered. "Now, do you want me to fix it or not?"

"How?"

"Will you do exactly as I say?" Her heavily lidded eyes held a motherly sternness.

"Apologize, right?"

"For starters," she nodded. "To Casey, the mayor, and of course Councilman Sanders' wife, Lorna."

"Who?"

"Casey's sister and she's extremely upset. So upset she couldn't even work. She's the bookkeeper at Cenex. Her friends are upset, and their husbands. So you apologize to her first."

"What a tangled web we weave," he said. "And after my apologies, then what?"

"Then I bring in our secret weapon."

"Which is?"

"Who, not which. Enough for now. You'll find out when the time comes," she evaded. "Get on the phone."

She was right, of course. You pop one barkeep in the nose around here and offend half the town. Maybe she planned to get the WCTU ladies on his side. He straightened his blotter and reached for the telephone directory.

"By the way," Marlene said. "Vicky Murdock finally arrived safely in St. Cloud for autopsy. I pushed the staff meeting back half an hour so you'll have time to grovel. And Sheriff Mattson called to say you're sick in the head."

Marlene swept from the office and headed directly for her own telephone. She delighted in crisis. It was the only thing left these days that really got her blood up, like a good romance novel. In her own directory she found Jean Cleland's number.

"Lorna Sanders called me a brute," he told Marlene after his last phone call. "Later though she reckoned she had a forgiving heart and would go to work after all. Casey got his lip taped at the clinic and her forgiveness hinged on my apologizing to him." Half way to the door, Charlie zipped his jacket. "The rest were easier. Janski said 'we'll see' and Casey said 'screw you.'"

"Where are you going?"

238

"Cenex. I got an idea."

"Are you going to talk to anybody?"

"No. I'm going to put air in my tires." He adjusted the .38 on his belt. "What's the matter with you? Our job is to investigate crime."

"I suppose," she granted, "but this is tragedy more than crime, so remember how many people are up early drinking coffee and talking about how dumb you are. Don't be brusque. Don't set yourself against people. Don't hit anybody!"

"It's my job," he said, stubbornly.

"I know." She moved close and hooked his arm with hers. "It's just that you've known Dutch all your life. Don't go after him like he's Jeffrey Dahmer."

He returned her squeeze and rubbed her hand, noticing the swollen arthritic joints. "Maybe it's because I've known him that I've got to find him myself. I don't care if he ends up with six weeks and a fifty-dollar fine. It'll be over. People can go back to being like they were."

Marlene walked to the door and opened it. "Get out there then, just remember you're not Dirty Charlie, okay?"

* * *

You can't drive a mile in Minnesota without seeing a pole barn. Charlie likened them to anodized aluminum tents, and the Cenex, which sold fertilizer, fuel, and pizza was a blue and white steel building so ugly your eyes yearned for a plowed field or a thousand acres of blank snow.

Part of the "new" Willow River, Cenex and a late-night service station called "Tank 'N' Tummy" were constructed along Highway 11 to capture the tourist trade, what little there was of it. He disliked not just their prefabricated look but the gung-ho attitude of those who believed new buildings were progress.

He maneuvered the squad close as the heaped snow would allow and bounded through the front door. "Hi'ya

239

Charlie," called an eager young man stacking blue jugs of windshield de-icing juice.

"Boss around?" he asked.

"In back," the boy, Shag, answered. "Hey, Charlie. You on this murder thing?"

"Yep."

"Wow!"

"In fact," Charlie said, "I'm going to want to talk to you about it when I'm finished inside. Hang around."

"You bet!"

Charlie threaded his way through the dusty displays of miniaturized tractors and snowblowers toward the offices at the rear. He feared his reception in Bill Miller's office might be less cordial than the wide-eyed greeting he'd received from Shag. Miller was a City Councilman. With luck, Marlene had already called him and smoothed things over.

Miller glanced up from his desk as Charlie came through the door, putting on a big smile and motioning him to a chair. Charlie declined.

"How's my favorite policeman this morning?" Miller asked through a row of shining teeth. "Come to pay your bill or arrest me for murder?"

"Depends on the size of the bill," Charlie replied.

Miller suddenly turned serious. "Bad business."

"Murder is pretty bad."

"Well, that too, but I was referring to this thing with Casey." He gnawed the end of a pencil. "We'll help you smooth it over, of course. Having lunch with him today, some of us on the Council. Emotions run high at times like this."

Charlie stood silently, his feet firmly planted.

"Your coming in to see me this morning is a good first step," Miller went on. "But you need to talk to Casey."

"I did." Charlie focused on the bald spot atop Miller's head. "Came about Dutch Cleland."

Miller frowned at Charlie's shoes. "Give it a rest," he said. "Sheriff Mattson's problem."

Charlie drew a breath and plunged ahead. "I need to know if you saw Dutch on Monday. If he came in here for gas or anything."

"This simply won't do," Miller said, slapping the pencil onto his desk. "Going around giving people the third degree."

Marlene didn't understand why he'd punched Casey. "I need to ask these questions, Bill, because they help us understand where Dutch might've gone. We want to find him and we don't know where he is."

"Let the police handle it," Miller said. "I've got work to do."

Charlie opened his mouth, thought better of it and stalked out. Miller wasn't interested. Murdock and Johnson tried to rape Jean Cleland and most likely killed Walleye but boosters like Miller feared bad press more than low corn prices. Maybe they thought Jean was hysterical and Walleye got what he deserved.

On his way to the car, he found Shag sprinkling de-icing salt along the sidewalk.

"Didn't take you long," the young man observed.

"Waste of time," he said, giving the boy an insider grin.

Shag nodded. "Sits in his office most days. I'm the leg man around here."

"Just who I want to talk to," Charlie said, confidentially. "Sell any gas to Dutch or Len Davis Monday?"

"Clelands have a bulk tank," he said, sharing a trade secret. "We go out there and fill it once a month."

"Davis?"

"Yeah. He was in here, but not Monday. Tuesday, I think, before the storm." He set aside the bag of de-icing salt. "I remember 'cause he was driving Mrs. Cleland's Jeep. The Cherokee. Gnarly machine. She used to be my English teacher. Made us read John Milton. You know him?"

"Isn't he the druggist in Kensington?"

241

Shag laughed and slapped Charlie on the back. "You're all right, Mr. Benson."

"Tell me about Davis."

"Not much to tell," Shag gazed up at the ice blue sky. "Didn't say much. Bought some gas and left." He thought for a moment. "I got the sale kind of screwed up 'cause he had this can with him, and he started filling it himself after I'd already rung it up."

"Large can?"

"Yeah, I guess. Extra ten bucks worth."

"Did you get a look inside the vehicle?"

Shag shrugged under his jacket. "Well, sort of," he said. "It's hard not to, you know, when you're standing right there filling the tank."

"Of course," said Charlie. "What was inside?"

"Camping stuff, looked like. Snow boots, shovels, junk like that." Shag shook his head. "Who'd go camping this time of year?"

"I don't suppose he told you where he was going? Or bought a map? Anything like that?"

"Nope. Just paid and left."

"You've been a big help, Shag." Charlie placed a hand on his shoulder. "I won't forget it."

He turned to leave but Shag caught his arm. "Can I ask a question?"

"Shoot."

"Do you think Dutch butchered this woman, like people say?" Shag loosened a piece of ice with the toe of his boot. "Somebody said she was ground into hamburger and they got a batch of it down at Berkie's. I don't believe it. But how'd you like to find a toenail in your cheeseburger?"

"I found the body, Shag," Charlie said firmly. "All the toes were present."

"That's what I figured," Shag said, disappointed.

* * *

242

They sat on straight-backed chairs in a semi-circle around Charlie's desk—on his left Patrolman Bobby Brown, short-haired, athletic, his blue uniform immaculate. Very close to Bobby was Patrolman Ed Lund, skinny, big-eared, wearing the uniform of an auto mechanic with "Ed" embroidered over his left pocket. Marlene had drawn up a chair a distance away. All were quiet and rather stiff. The door was closed. It was their first staff meeting.

Charlie coached them in a fatherly tone. "The past three days are the worst I can remember in this town," he said, looking at each in turn. "Two people dead and a woman assulted in her own home. Mood's pretty bleak. Our job to change it." He swiveled his chair and pointed to a large job assignment sheet tacked to the wall behind him. "Read that," he ordered.

Marlene, who'd read it when she hand-lettered it, read it again. Ed Lund read it aloud, until Bobby elbowed him in the ribs.

"Questions?" Charlie said when they'd finished.

"Two people?" Bobby Brown said. "Two people are dead?"

"Walleye Wertz."

"Did we find his body too?"

"No."

"Shouldn't we be looking then? According to your sheet there I'm supposed to pick up as many volunteer firemen as can get off their regular jobs, cut the shore ice and drag Wilson slough for some kind of vehicle this Murdock chick might've driven, right?"

"Right," Charlie said. "What's the question?"

"Well," Bobby said. "Who cares?"

"She had to get here somehow," Charlie explained, "Edge of that slough's a logical place. The storm wiped out any tracks. Just look around shore where it could've been pushed."

"There's more ice now than there was a few days ago."

"It's thin. It'll cut fast."

"How do you know that's where the car is?"

"I don't." Charlie placing a fist against his forehead. "That's why I'm sending you out there."

"Waste of time if you ask me." Bobby complained.

"Nobody did," Charlie said flatly.

Bobby slumped in his chair. Hard to know what Charlie was thinking these days. They should be looking for Walleye. He might still be alive.

Not to be overlooked, Ed Lund cleared his throat. "Yessir," he began, addressing Charlie formally. "I got a question too. I got to call every county sheriff in Minnesota on the phone and ask 'em to look out for Mrs. Cleland's Jeep Cherokee." He paused while the others stared at him. "Well. I got two questions." He looked around as if waiting for someone else to ask them.

"And?" Charlie prompted.

"Well... How many counties are there in Minnesota?"

"Eighty-seven."

"That's a lot."

"Eighty-seven."

"I got to call all of 'em? One at a time? And be done by one o'clock?"

"Yes," said Charlie. "The other question?"

"It don't make sense," Ed observed. "We can just broadcast..."

"No," Charlie cut him off. "We're using the telephone so this can be done quietly." He rose to full height and leaned across the desk. "This department, and no one else, will apprehend Dutch Cleland. Is that clear? No talk on the radio."

Ed said, "I hate talking on the phone."

"Anything else?" Charlie asked. It hadn't exactly been a Tony Robbin's moment.

244

"I just got one more thing to say." Bobby rose from his chair. "You shouldn't of punched Casey in the nose." Bobby liked Casey and the barman often let him drink on the cuff.

"It was the mouth, Bobby. I punched him in the mouth, and I apologized. All of you get to work now so I don't have anyone else to apologize to."

They marched out and Marlene said, "They think you're crazy, you know."

"You?"

"I'm afraid you're not." she said, crossing to the large assignment sheet on the wall, "I've worked with you long enough to know you've already baked the cake." She tapped the paper. "You know where Dutch is, don't you?"

"Not that hard to figure," he said. "We've got a four-wheel-drive vehicle loaded with camping gear driven by a guy who knows where our suspect's hiding. A woman who's helping them and also knows. What's that say to you?"

Marlene read her assignment from the sheet. "Marlene to investigate lakehome/land/cabin purchases—Cleland." She turned back to face him. "You love this, don't you?"

"Start with courthouses in northern counties," Charlie said. "You'll have to be very persuasive to get the bureaucrats moving."

"And what will you be doing?"

"Packing my gear."

"A man of faith. Do you really think Dutch would stay here in Minnesota?"

"Why not? Worked so far, unless Murdock finds him before we do. Don't forget Walleye."

Marlene nodded. "Hurry and pack then Charlie, and don't forget your shotgun."

* * *

Mrs. Willeke, Amy to her friends, inherited Ernie's Motorcourt when her husband died in '71 shortly after they built the freeway and by-passed the motel. The freeway killed him and she didn't have long left herself. People without gall bladders seldom lived to a ripe old age, even though no one knew what the gall bladder did, exactly.

The guests she attracted these days were very much like the two in seventeen. Homos.

Ernie had been a high school principal for thirty years until the schools were lost to anarchy. When he retired and bought the motel, he installed a modern intercom system similar to the one at Sauk Centre Central High and it piped music into the rooms. It also listened if you wanted it to.

She'd begun listening after Ernie died, out of loneliness at first, then curiosity. She'd learned the word jackshit. Two boys from the University of Alabama used the word extensively when they spent a night on their way to NDSU in Fargo. She liked the word because it wasn't very Minnesotan and foreign swear words didn't seem as dirty.

The intercom control box hung inside Mrs. Willeke's apartment at eye level around the corner from the office. A poor place really because if the outside door opened, or the motor on the Coca Cola machine kicked in, the sounds could be heard clearly in every room of the motel, unless the switch was in broadcast position, which it was most of the time, but not now. She was listening to Room Seventeen. She was terribly curious about Homos.

"I'm writing as fast as I can!" Carroll complained hotly. "If you'd shut up I'd get it copied a lot faster."

"You won't be able to read it anyway," Murdock predicted. "I can't even read it on the screen."

"That's because this is a Dun and Bradstreet report," Carroll explained. "Codes and abbreviations."

Mrs. Willeke heard a loud sigh from the room, followed by a clunk. One of them must have dropped something or they might be destroying her property. They certainly had some sort of unauthorized machine in there. She'd found a dildo once in Number Eight, in the bathtub. She kept it, but never told anybody.

She listened awhile before they spoke again. She'd been tempted to screw up the volume a touch, but had learned better over the years. The intercom system was old and emitted static into the room if you fiddled with the controls.

"So? What've you got this time?"

"Real estate."

"Big deal."

"The house in Willow River. Slaughterhouse and stockyards. Retail facility. A fourplex of rental property. Eighty acres of forested land in Itasca County. A condo in Minneapolis valued at sixty-thousand. Why would he want a condo in Minneapolis?"

"Wait! What was the one before that?"

"The eighty acres?"

"That's it!"

"What?"

"That's where he is. Hiding out in the woods."

"How can you know that?"

"Because that's where I'd be."

Mrs. Willeke toggled the switch and sent a flow of music, the greatest hits of Patti Page, back into the room. It wasn't wise to leave the music off for long or they got suspicious. A few minutes of quiet here and there could easily be attributed to the management being too busy to change the tape.

"We're getting out of here. Now!" Murdock said.

"What if you're wrong?" Carroll asked. "Itasca County is two hundred miles from here."

"I don't care. If I have to listen to "How Much Is That Doggy In The Window?" one more time, I'll go nuts," Murdock growled through his teeth. "Besides, you've got the exact location of Cleland's land there, don't you?"

"No," Carroll answered. "But I think I can get it from another source. Problem is, it's going to come out as a

247

bunch of southeast corners of this and northeast corners of that. We'll need a map."

"Pick one up on the way," Murdock said, heading for the door. "I'll turn in the key."

When the Suburban swung out and headed toward the freeway, it wasn't the first time Mrs. Willeke had seen guests check out abruptly. Maybe they had a fight. She wondered if homo couples fought about the same things regular couples did?

Mrs. Willeke plunked herself down behind the counter, thumbing a copy of "Globe." What if they'd done some damage down there? They acted suspicious, she thought. The beat-up one was outside before with a can of Christmas tree flock spraying his license plate. If she went down there and looked right away, and if there was damage to her property, the police could still catch them. They couldn't have gotten very far. She'd never heard of the town they were talking about, Willow River, which might be some kind of code word. Homos had those.

* * *

The Willow River Police Department's second history-making staff meeting was surprisingly productive.

"Bobby?" Charlie yielded the floor to his young patrolman.

"Can I smoke?" Bobby asked, tapping his shirt pocket. Marlene frowned and shook her head. "Fine. Like I told you on the radio," he turned his attention to Charlie. "The car's in Wilson's slough, white Pontiac Grand Am rental." He consulted a slip of paper. "License number GIY-406. Rented at the Minneapolis/St. Paul International Airport on Sunday last by a Mrs. Gordon Murdock of Tulsa, Oklahoma. Want me to call it in to the county?"

"Already done," Charlie said. "County forensics people on the way and my guess is they'll find her clothes in there too. You didn't see them?"

Bobby shook his head. "Full of mud, Charlie. Nearly froze to death out there." He rubbed his hands.

"How about the key?"

"Still in the ignition."

"Sure?"

"I know keys when I see keys."

Charlie rested back in the chair. *Must be different keys,* he mused. "Some physical evidence anyway, and gives Mattson something for the cameras," he said, turning to Ed. "What'd you come up with?"

The older patrolman squirmed in his chair, unable to find a position where he didn't end up face to face with his boss. "I did like you told me," he said, defensively. "Tried to call....well, I did call eighty-seven county sheriffs, but half of 'em weren't around. Some said they'd call back. Twenty-six said they'd watch for the Jeep. I got it all written up. Marlene's gonna type it."

"You should try and read his handwriting," Marlene said.

"Do it later," Charlie snapped. "I got a feeling there's bad news."

Color drained from Ed's face. "You said to call all eighty-seven counties," he stammered.

Charlie closed his eyes. "Tell me you didn't call our own county. You didn't call Sheriff Mattson?"

"I think he wants to talk to you," Ed said, so quietly they could barely hear.

"Ed. Why did I want you to call them individually? Remember?"

"Because you didn't want anybody to find out?"

"Who didn't I want to find out?"

"Sheriff Mattson?"

Marlene came reluctantly to his aid. "No use crying over spilt milk," she reminded Charlie. "I'll call Mattson and make some excuse. Anyway, finding the car will help."

Ed, speaking almost to himself, said, "I forgot."

"I called the courthouses," Marlene confirmed. "Good news. Just before I walked in here I heard from the county clerk in Grand Rapids. Phillip Cleland owns eighty acres in the northeast corner of Itasca County, near Togo."

"Fits with what Shag told me about Len Davis packing Jean's Jeep with camping gear," Charlie said. "Looks like they're together. Any buildings?"

"Checked for phone, electric service, other utilities," Marlene said. "Nothing listed. Land taxed as forest land. No mention of a house or cabin but the clerk said it's not uncommon in isolated areas for buildings to go up and never get recorded until much later, usually when the property changes hands."

Charlie suppressed a growing enthusiasm. If Dutch had been here all along, just a three or four hour drive away, this whole deal was about to blow. "When we're done here Marlene, call the Itasca County Sheriff's Department and see if they'll drive over for a quick peek." He smiled. "Who knows? Might get lucky."

The meeting broke up and Charlie sent Bobby and Ed back out in search of Walleye, more convinced than ever they'd not find him alive. With the discovery of Vicky's car and the disappearance of Murdock and Johnson, there was plenty of keep Mattson out of their hair. Charlie talked with him earlier. Mattson was so happy to get Vicky Murdock's remains back he seemed oblivious to Walleye's fate. "Serves him right," he'd said. "Running off with people's corpses. Wouldn't surprise me yet if the little bugger didn't do the whole deal. Ain't wasting my resources to find him. Just about everybody in this damn circus has disappeared. First the killer, then the corpse, the two ex-husbands, and now the idiot who found the body. Goddamn nightmare. Only found back two of 'em, if you count the car. And that's another thing. You should've called me for the 'film at eleven,' per se. Looks good, big crane hoisting a dead broad's car from an icy lake, water running out the doors and windows. Really plays. All we get now is a dirty wreck in the impound lot. No action, per se. You got to conceptionalize all the angles."

Charlie knew Mattson would've been right there, standing by the lake, our hero Fatso Cop. At least they'd talked on a more professional plain, with Mattson even solicitous about Charlie's Casey troubles at City Hall.

"Jennifer Holker. She's the lady from Itasca County," Marlene said, striding in suddenly. "Just called back. Somebody with the e-mail address 'carrollj@ibm.net' requested an on-line plat of Dutch Cleland's eighty. You better get moving buster, looks like Johnson's got the jump on you."

"Not necessarily," he said. "No telling where he and Murdock are."

"That brings me to Amy Willeke."

"Please don't add another character to this drama."

"Owns a motel in Sauk Centre," Marlene continued unabated. "Checked in two 'homos,'" she said. Sounds like Murdock and Johnson. She overheard conversation in which they mentioned Willow River and somebody hiding in the woods and it all sounded perverted to her so she thought she'd better call Willow River to find out. Want my opinion, she's kind of a busybody, but it's a break anyway."

"Maybe," Charlie said. "If they're in Sauk Centre then you're right, I better get moving. That's half way to Itasca County."

Marlene didn't appear worried. "If it wasn't for our secret weapon."

"That's the second time you've said that this morning."

"Don't get mad," she said. "But if one person could smooth everything over with Mayor Janski and lead you straight to Dutch would you grant that person a special favor?"

"Depends."

"No, it doesn't," she said, leaving no room for argument. "YES or NO?"

"What's the favor?"

251

"The person in question accompanies you."

"Marlene!" He had to go right for Dutch now or Murdock would get there first. "Okay. Who?"

"Jean Cleland."

"Oh, shit! I knew you were going to say that." He didn't have time to argue. "Okay. Don't call the Itasca County Sheriff. Jean knows exactly where Dutch is and I don't want anybody else around when I get there."

"Not even back up?"

"Won't need any."

Chapter Twenty-Two

CIRRUS FILAMENTS OBSCURED THE SUN'S PALE TWILIGHT and pinked the white land and the white trees. Dutch turned reluctantly from the patch of sky framed in the window crosshairs and faced the world inside. Three men currently held his life in their hands: a hippie, a bleeding bartender, and a lawyer who liked gin.

"Should've thought of that before you had me bid the job," Dylan accused MOM in a loud voice.

"I'm supposed to know your pickup has bald tires?" MOM reclined on the futon with his bandaged side supported by a line of pillows. "Man, that's your problem."

"If you'd stuck to our deal it wouldn't have been anyboby's problem!" Dylan said even more loudly.

This was the third dispute since lunch and again Len mediated. "Could we just agree you're both somewhat at fault? MOM, as contractor, should've informed bidders of the possibility of competition and Dylan, as bidder, should've waited until he had contract in hand before investing in any equipment upgrades."

"Eighty-nine bucks each I paid," the hippie complained. "Not only did he stiff me on that load, which was supposed to be forty cases of beer and fifteen hard liquor, but never gave me the other loads he promised. No wonder the beerman doesn't stop here anymore. He probably stiffed him!"

"It's too far north," MOM corrected. "Doesn't pay to drive way up here for a few cases. Anyway, what was I offering

253

you? Twenty bucks! You ain't much of a businessman if you buy two hundred dollars worth of tires to make twenty bucks. Guess you better stick to being a hippie!"

Current disagreement notwithstanding, it had been a productive day. MOM's bleeding slowed to a soaking trickle. Dylan brought the snowmobile back to life and rigged a sled behind it for Marty's frozen body, wrapped in bed sheets and ready to transport. All that remained was to determine who had rights to the person of one Phillip "Dutch" Cleland, Butcher of Willow River.

Even in his wounded and weakened state, MOM claimed Dutch for himself, insisting that although he'd shot the wrong man, he'd still made a successful citizen's arrest and should be allowed to take Dutch in. Dylan said, "In a pig's eye!" Len claimed authority as an officer of the court. Dutch just wanted to go home. Now that he'd decided to give himself up, no one would allow it.

"Please!" Len begged, "Any more fruitless discussion and it'll be dark."

"So?" MOM inquired. "Scared of the dark or what?"

"I wanted to be half way to Willow River with Dutch by now, not sitting here debating somebody's old tires."

"End it right now then. Crank the snow machine up and take us all down to the bar and I'll call the cops. Drinks on me."

"Absolutely not! Dutch already decided to surrender himself before you blundered in, killing the trespasser who accompanied you on this vigilante foray." Len paced the small space between the stove and outside door. "Get this straight. If Dutch were to go back with you or you were to go back alone and call the police and inform them of his whereabouts, he couldn't turn himself in, which is key to his defense. Judges look kindly on fugitives who surrender and express remorse, especially at sentencing time. I won't have my client jeopardized so you can spend the next twenty years bragging in a saloon!"

Ironically, it was Dylan who asked the first sensible question. "He put his finger on it MOM? You want bragging rights?"

"It's all I'm gonna get." Earlier, Len convinced him no reward existed, which was true.

"What could that possibly be worth?" Len wanted to know.

"Lots," MOM insisted. "Remember D.B. Cooper? The first American highjacker? Bailed out over the Oregon woods. Strolled into a local bar afterwards—can't remember the name of it—and ordered a beer. Guy who owns that place is a millionare today. Tourists mob the joint and it's as much in the middle of nowhere as my place. Don't tell me! Bragging rights is better than a reward."

"Bullshit," Dylan said. "Cooper's bones are still hanging in some big fur tree."

"Some believe that too," MOM replied reasonably. "And when they go looking for him, and the suitcase with the money, they all stop at this guy's bar. I'm telling you, no way I'm backing down on this deal."

Len stopped and stared at Dylan, who shrugged. Back to square one.

"Doesn't matter," Dutch said almost to himself.

"What doesn't?" Len asked.

"About Cooper and bragging rights. All that."

"Why?"

"He was famous because he disappeared. Mystery brings tourists. No mystery here once I'm in custody. Week from now something else will be in the headlines and business at Togo Joe's will be right back to normal."

This quieted them, though Dutch disliked the evil gleam he saw in MOM's eye.

"True enough," Dylan said, nodding with delight.

"Unless," Dutch continued, "I really do disappear." He hoped Len knew him well enough to suspect his deception.

MOM propped himself on his elbows. "What you saying? You're gonna run for it after all? Thought you was all remorseful and full of Christian repentance?"

"I am, but Len's the one who's convinced a judge will sentence me light. I'm not so sure, and it's my life not his."

Such reasoning appealed to MOM. "And you're a white man," he added. "No white male gets a fair trial in the People's Republic of Minnesota."

Dutch stared hard at Len, willing him to keep quiet. "Got a brother in the Orient." Len knew Dutch had no brothers. "Works for a Japanese company. Wouldn't mind spending some time over there. He'd get me a job."

Len caught on. "I won't stand for it!" he said.

Dylan looked confused.

"What if you get caught?" MOM suddenly worried.

"That's up to you," Dutch said. "You can let Dylan take you into Hibbing to the hospital. Marty too. You tell them about an unfortunate hunting accident. Dylan backs you up. Tomorrow morning I'm part of local legend and you're on your way to unheard of profits. Of course, I'd expect you to hire Dylan to bring in the booze and as a token of your honest intent, pay him for the tires."

"Deal," MOM said without a second thought. He dug out his wallet and handed Dylan two crisp hundreds. "See how easy I am?"

Not so easy, Dutch thought. His luck needed to hold. At first light they'd walk somewhere to a phone and by the time MOM firgured out he'd been tricked, it would be too late. Nothing was likely to happen before then. Outside now bitter cold had swept the night clear of everything but stars.

Len clued Dylan later and he seemed eager to pull one over on MOM. An hour later he spun the snow machine down the drive with the bar owner clutching his middle and Marty on the sled behind. A desultory sight hardly of this world and the absolute silence that followed lulled Dutch and Len into a strange sense of mutual peace.

They ate well after cutting wood and then Dutch told him the whole story, his seduction, romance and final betrayal, talking far into the night. "That's pretty much it," he said finally, placing both hands on his hips and rotating his torso side to side. "Except the actual deed, of course, when I killed her."

Len wasn't satisfied and his leg had fallen asleep. He limped to the stove and tossed a split log onto the hot coals. "Listen old buddy," he said, frowning deeply. "Too many years went by. Why kill her now?"

"All night I'm pouring my heart out and all you're worried about is time." Dutch groaned. "Missed the whole point. Is it night or day?"

Len hobbled to the door. "Tell you when I get back."

Outside, he unzipped his pants and looked up at the stars. No hint of dawn and nothing stirred. The earth stopped spinning during the night and froze in place. His exposed part steamed, surrendering its heat to the subzero air. He shivered uncontrollably and stared at the hole he'd made in the snow, glad for this moment away from Dutch. People don't kill other people if they're sane. Somewhere along the line Dutch slipped a gear, falling in love with some trollop and brooding for years until he killed her.

Len zipped his pants. He'd go in and get the details. Make Dutch understand the law's passion for them, how they're dissected and microscopically examined in court to prosecute and to defend. Every moment. Every thought. Every motive.

He scraped open the door. "No sign of dawn yet," he said. "Making coffee?"

Embraced by the warmth of the room, he shuddered. Neither of them had slept but he wasn't tired, though a deep weariness settled over him, combined with watery eyes from the fire and cigarette smoke.

257

"What are you waiting for?" Dutch asked, fiddling with the flame under the coffee pot.

"An answer. A reason that makes sense."

"What makes you think there is one?"

"Because there has to be."

"Nothing like a man with an analytical mind," Dutch said, shaking his head. "You think I have a bunch of logical reasons listed out somewhere? I'll just give them to you and it'll all make sense?"

"Suppose not." He lit a cigarette to kill the taste of too many cigarettes. "You're different from a lot of guys I know. Always in control. I've this picture in my head of you choking Vicky with one hand and talking on your cellphone with the other." He dropped into a chair by the fire. "Can't imagine you getting worked up enough to kill anybody."

"That's not your problem, Len. Your problem, like everyone else, is you're a hypocrite," he said without rancor.

"What are you talking about?" Len straightened himself. "I didn't kill anybody."

"Sure you did. Milo Anderson."

"Milo is quite well and living in Athens, Alabama."

"Yeah?" Dutch said. "Because you ran him out of Minnesota. You and the Bar Association."

Len shook his head. "Brought it on himself."

Dutch dropped into a chair and hooked a leg over the armrest. "He's in Alabama because you got him on the six o'clock news accused of some pretty serious stuff."

"All of which he was guilty."

"Yes," Dutch said. "Vicky was guilty. So am I."

"I didn't kill Milo Anderson."

"Really? Right now Milo Anderson's a dead man, walking the streets of Athens, Alabama."

"If anything, I feel sorry for him. He could come through that door right now and I wouldn't lay a finger on him."

"Good," Dutch said. "Then you know exactly the way I felt about Vicky. I thought the same thing until I put my hands around her neck."

With his foot, Len lifted the handle and opened the stove door, tossing his cigarette inside among the cherry-red coals. "You didn't mean to kill her?"

"In my mind I had her dead years ago. Sunday the dream came true, that's all."

"But you didn't know you were going to do it?"

"No."

"Then it wasn't premeditated. No Murder One. I'll talk to the County Attorney and plea bargain this thing."

"Okay, but we do it straight. No insanity defenses or lawyer tricks. I tell it all and hope they give me a fair shake. Haven't felt worth a damn in years until this past couple days and I think I'm more sorry for hating her than for killing her. That's the truth and I'll tell it."

How far, Len wondered, would truth go with a jury? Good question since they seldom heard it. "Fine," he said. "All that remains then is for you to tell me exactly what occurred Sunday evening. Every detail. Start at the beginning and tell it in your own words and leave nothing out."

Dutch's hair appeared mussed and oily. His clear eyes clouded with worry. "I've tried to make light of it in my mind, you know? Keep it from settling in on me. Talking about it makes me sick."

"You don't have a choice," Len answered with vigor. "By the time we're finished you'll tell this again and again. Might as well start now."

Dutch shrugged.

First of all, it didn't start Sunday, it started Saturday. Vicky called him at work. The phone rang and there she was, and the years melted away. "Please don't hang up," she said. "I've a very good reason for calling."

He hung up.

It rang again almost immediately and he let it go nine, ten times before finally picking up, "This line's equipped with Caller ID," he threatened.

"I'm not trying to remain anonymous," she said. "Please don't hang up. You're the one who told me to call."

"What?"

"You said once that no matter what happened between us if I ever needed you, all I had to do was ask." Her voice softened, grew more intimate. "Remember?"

It was true, of course. He'd said it. Said it in bed after a night of forever promises.

"Didn't want to call but I'm in serious trouble," she went on. "I'm at the Radisson South in Minneapolis under your name, Mrs. P. Cleland. Please come."

A hotel room with Vicky.

He hung up.

The next afternoon he went into town to check his machinery. Business was good and a couple hundred thousand in beef aged in the coolers. Maybe she knew his habits, who knows? Anyway, he came out the back door and found her there in a rental car with the wipers going.

A low wind chilled him to the bone and he froze there watching heavy clouds pile up above Our Own Hardware. She stepped out and stood in the rain. Black heels and long military style coat same color. Leaving both hands in her pockets, she let the rain soak her hair. Even wet, it remained thick.

He waited for her to speak but she just stood silently composed, rain glistening on the coat, her cheeks, hair. So oblivious it was obviously an act.

"What do you want?" he croaked.

"You can't even be polite," she said in a low voice. "You hate me so much after all this time?"

"Don't bother with you at all. What do you want?"

"Are we going to talk out here in the rain?"

"You won't be here long."

"Dutch." She spoke his name. He fished the keys from his pocket.

Inside she immediately took an interest in the stacks of wholesale canned goods in cardboard boxes, touching the giant steel handle on the new walk-in cooler, petting the hamburger patty machine.

"I'm not here to give a tour," he said.

"I'm not here to take one."

"Fine. What do you want?"

It wasn't in Vicky's nature to give a direct answer when she meant to be persuasive. "You know I'm married again?" she began.

"Yes."

"It's not working out."

"Surprise. Surprise."

"I don't blame you for being sarcastic," she said, strolling toward the front of the store. "I loved him in the beginning."

"Like you loved Carroll, me, Bill, and now?"

"Gordon. Gordon Murdock."

"And how many more?" The old feeling gnawed at his insides. "Actually, I don't wonder and I don't give a damn. Get the hell out of here."

"Think I wanted to come to you of all people?" She kept moving away, almost to the display windows facing Main Street. "He hurt me. Friday was the worst." She crossed her arms just under her breasts and shuddered. "Nearly killed me."

"Not my problem." She didn't have a bruise on her. "Must not've hit you in the face." He laughed when he said that.

"No," she said, hanging her head.

"Beat you where no one can see the bruises, I bet."

"I don't expect you to care. I know you hate me." Tears. "All I want is a safe place. Give me the keys to the cabin and you'll never see me again. Promise."

He didn't know why she'd come with this story but whatever the reason, it couldn't be good for him. "Think back to yesterday when you called," he said. "I didn't want to talk to you. I didn't invite you here. I don't want anything to do with you. Go away. I sold the cabin anyway."

"I don't believe you."

"Vicky! Leave."

"I know for a fact you didn't sell the cabin. I checked."

"Checked?"

"There are ways."

"Well, there are two ways out of this store - a front door and a back door. Garbage goes out the back, unless you want some real bruises to accompany your imaginary ones."

She listened to this with stoic indifference. "You talk like that because I hurt you," she said softly. "Because you still love me."

Unable to touch her, he grabbed her coat at the shoulder and twisted the material in his fist, marching her out the back door into the rain. Though her feet barely brushed the floor, she remained agonizingly passive and stood exactly where he planted her outside, saying nothing. He jumped in the pickup and roared away toward home.

Across the railroad tracks by Highway 11, he glanced in the mirror. She was tailing him. The last stretch of pavement before his turnoff was that short piece up Wilson Hill and he stopped there, pulling the truck well off the highway. Vicky's small rental glided in behind and when she didn't get out he walked back and opened her door. "Where do you think you're going?" he asked.

"With you."

"No you're not. I'm going home."

"Then give me the keys to the cabin."

He reached inside and snatched her car keys. "You're done following me. The cabin, like all my property, is off limits to you." Winding up, he hurled the keys far into the wet

262

woods. "When you find those keys, use them to get out of here."

"I'll follow you on foot," she said as he stalked back to the truck. "I'll come to your house. It isn't far. I know that."

The pickup dug two trenches in the gravel and he sped away. A mile further along he pulled in at Gormann's grove and concealed the truck in the trees. It's high ground there and he could spy out the road without being seen. Beyond the trees lay a cornfield, harvested stalks pointing north. He cranked the window down and sat smoking, no idea what to do if she followed. Head her off he supposed, before she got to Jean.

After nearly an hour nothing moved on the road and Dutch climbed part way up a tree, dousing himself with cold rain from the dead leaves. Even from a height he saw nothing, and not seeing her made him more frantic than seeing her. He hopped in the truck and drove back.

Vicky's car was abandoned. He grabbed an old umbrella from the pickup's gun rack and shook out the dust, ducking beneath and starting for the woods.

An hour before sunset darkness had invaded the trees, quieting the wind and forcing him to fold the umbrella and step carefully around deadfalls and pockets of oozing mud. He tried to remember where he'd thrown the keys. It didn't seem they could've gone this far. The sodden leaves along his way were undisturbed. Vicky might very well have taken the road to town and he thought of turning back, but only for a moment. He felt her presence, oppressive as the chilled damp air.

A ravine cut sharply away to the left and he angled down sideways, running uncontrollably to the bottom where he halted, chest heaving. Vicky sat on a stump several yards away, long naked legs crossed above the knee. She'd unbuttoned her coat, her sole garment.

"I've been waiting," she scolded mildly.

263

Her semi-nakedness stimulated the latent hatred. He seemed ripped apart inside, enraged and at the same time so consumed by passion he lost the ability to speak or think coherently. He wanted to scream obscenities and smash her with his fists and, in the same instant, he prayed she'd wrap her arms and legs around him and with siren voice beg for his love. A moment later, his internal struggle ended and the space of air between them seemed washed and his mind was crisp with simple resolve. His legs and arms grew powerful, wonderfully strong. She was no match for it.

He didn't hurry, and closed the distance between them with measured step. His hands were slim steel and folded evenly around her neck. Her face registered mild surprise and then astonishment. Fear came too, but late.

Truthfully, she died pretty much as she'd lived—passively. No struggling or screaming. A low-keyed kind of dying. For Dutch, it was like straggling a tame rabbit, without blood or excitement. Nobody should die that easy.

He lost track of time then awhile. Later, sitting next to her body, he noticed no bruises. She'd been lying about the beatings. Not that it mattered. Maybe she'd really meant to seduce him after all. This struck him deliciously funny and he sat in the wet woods laughing aloud.

Eventually he took her coat, where he found her car keys, and put it with the rest of her clothes in the rental car. Discarding her there naked had a finality he liked. Before climbing out of the revine he collected the umbrella, suddenly facinated by its steel end spike. He balanced it in one hand like a dart, aimed at her gaping mouth, and stabbed downward. One of her front teeth broke off nicely half way up. The ease with which he abused her was a surprise and a thrill. Finally, he'd defeated her.

Later on, he pushed the car into Wilson's slough, where it sank and he ruined a perfectly good pair of boots. It wasn't until he stood again on dry ground along the ditch that he felt remorse. He broke down then and wept. Everything seemed terribly confused like microfiche scrolling faster and faster until he was dizzy. His anger evaporated. The thing that had just happened couldn't possibly have happened. He toyed with the idea of going back again to look at her because it was clear to him now that she wasn't dead, not really. She'd fallen maybe and knocked herself unconscious. That happens. How could she die that easily? No one died that easily. Hadn't he killed huge steers and hogs, even chickens? Didn't he know what it took? Even chickens flopped, sometimes for minutes and minutes. Why didn't she flop?

His knees were weak and he stumbled and sat along the ditch and cried. He didn't go back in the woods and after a while lost track of time again.

Later, he drove home for dinner. He didn't know what else to do and he couldn't focus on anything so he pretended to be normal, to reclaim his life. Maybe if he could do that the world would recover itself and all the fuzzy edges would sharpen again.

That was how he remembered it.

"You killed her because she took her clothes off and you thought she was going to try and seduce you?" Len barked. "All the prosecuting attorney has to do is show a picture of Vicky: tall, blonde, built. You're toast. Life without parole. Who'd believe a guy turns that down?"

"What's the matter with you?" Dutch shook his head. "She humiliated me."

"You showed her!" Len strolled to the window, hands clasped in his best courtroom pose. "Maybe insanity is the best defense for you." Outside the sky had gone gray above the snow, preparing to greet the sun at last with cloudless dawn.

"I'm going to be frank with you," Len continued. "Prison's a given. You tell this story to a jury—male, female—won't matter. Guilty. You got a twenty-five percent chance of draw-ing Judge Wendy Braun and she's merciless on abuse cases. She locked this guy up for eighteen months because he lost his job and missed nine child support payments. You gotta get another story. I mean it."

"Was he sorry? The guy who missed his child support?"

"What?"

"I'm sorry as hell about Vicky," Dutch confessed. "Not that she's dead, but that I did it. When you said before that I didn't mean to kill her you were right. I was trying to kill her, I mean, well, I can't explain it. I wanted her dead and I had her and it felt good but there was a second toward the end when I thought I'd stopped just in time, you know? That feel-ing you get sometimes that you're falling but you jerk just in time? It shocked me when she dropped. I panicked. It was-n't anything like the killing I've done. I didn't understand it."

"Well the jury will understand it." Len shrugged. "Remorse helps but it won't get you off."

"You mean I can't kill people and get by with it?"

"People?" Len scratched his matted hair. "Haven't killed anybody else, have you?"

"Actually, I think I have," Dutch said.

"Who?"

"Don't know for sure. Murdock, I think. Jumped me behind the Meat Market. Clubbed him with a bone."

"Jean told me about it. Was Murdock," Len confirmed. "Doubt if you killed him, though. News like that gets around in a hurry."

"If I didn't kill him, he'll try and kill me."

"Unlikely," Len said. "He's probably in a hospital some-where just glad to be alive."

"Maybe."

*   *   *

They stopped a mile south of where the old logger said Dutch Cleland owned a cabin and Murdock covered the

266

Suburban's hood with a thick blanket to muffle the sound of their approach. He'd finally lost it, Carroll believed. "You don't really think this is going to work?" he asked, tying down his side of the blanket.

Murdock moved in quick jerks, head up, alert for the slightest sound. "We gotta sneak up, quiet." With a long hunting knife he cut holes so the radiator could suck air.

Sneak up in a four-thousand-pound truck, tires crunching? On the running board, Carroll knocked snow from his boots and climbed inside. Murdock was already behind the wheel, anxious to get moving.

"We've got to drive with the windows down," Murdock said.

"It's twenty below zero."

"Sound travels in the woods. Listen for him. See how much noise we're making ourselves."

"Listen for what?"

"Anything. Maybe he's chopping wood, slamming doors, scratching his behind. Hell, I don't know! Just listen."

Carroll listened as Murdock edged the truck ahead in four-wheel drive, plowing snow up over the running boards. No tire track since the storm, but he noticed tracks made by at least one man walking and a snowmobile that must've been towing something. He pulled the earlaps down on his fur cap. Even at this snail's pace he was freezing to death.

"How you gonna hear anything with your ears covered?" Murdock barked.

"Well, I can hear you plain enough. Yell a little louder why don't you?" He played a dangerous game with Murdock, certainly the most dangerous he'd ever played, but with luck today he'd come out on top.

"Listen!" Murdock hissed. "Hear that?"

Carroll didn't hear anything. "What?"

"A scraping noise." He turned off the ignition.

"You're imagining things."

"Listen!"

There was a noise. Someone shoveling snow. He heard the scrape of the shovel, then a pause before the scraping began anew. Distant, but not too distant. "I hear it," Carroll said. "How far?"

"Half mile at most."

"Long walk."

"We can chance the truck awhile longer, but don't bang against anything or start yodeling," Murdock warned. He believed yodeling and consumption of rhubarb endemic to northerners.

"Right," Carroll said.

Black trunks slipping slowly past the window, here and there colored by the green of a spruce or balsam layered in snow. The scraping noises originated from off to the left.

"See those tall spruce?" Murdock asked. Carroll nodded. "That's where we pull up and leave the truck. I got an extra shotgun and a 30-30. You gonna carry one?"

Carroll was ready for this question. "I'll take the shotgun. It's better for close up work." Let Murdock figure out what that meant.

Murdock shrugged. "Suit yourself."

The bushy spruce were large when they drew up close and Murdock cut the engine. No one spoke. Murdock was engrossed now in the hunt. The final stalk before the kill.

"You can't just shoot him on sight, you know," Carroll said.

"Oh?"

"I'm serious."

"Shut up. Get the shotgun out and be quiet about it."

Later, struggling a long time through snow above their knees, they dropped down and crawled on their bellies, winding around clumps of barren alder brush. It was light now and to Carroll it seemed they must be terribly exposed—dark stains on a white tablecloth. Anyone with eyes would surely see them. Without tall grass or foliage for cover, only the bare alder stalks hid them. He burrowed deep in the snow.

Murdock too, kept his head low, slithering and stopping every few feet to rest on his elbows and look ahead. Carroll followed close behind, cradling the shotgun and keeping an eye on the soles of Murdock's boots to gauge his progress. Murdock had carved a skull and cross bones into each heel. It seemed such a childish thing to do.

Murdock pointed to a high ridge of rock, mostly buried in snow, signaling they should move toward it. Carroll nodded.

Below the crest Murdock stopped and motioned Carroll to crawl up beside him. "Look there!" he whispered. "See that?"

It took Carroll a moment to make out the green roof covered in white except along the edges, and the deep brown of stained logs. A cabin hidden beneath the pines. "This belongs to Cleland?"

"That's his pickup to the right there," Murdock said softly. "I'd bet on it."

"We've got to be sure."

"We will be." Murdock drew a large pair of olive-green waterproof binoculars from one of his oversized pockets. "Won't take long," he said, bringing the glasses to his eyes.

*　*　*

"Well, we found Togo. Again," Charlie said, half to Jean and half to himself. "Big deal."

"Park over there," she ordered, pointing to the right.

"Why?" he asked.

"Because cruising up and down this road isn't doing anything but packing the snow. We need directions."

He obeyed. "More time wasted. Shouldn't have taken you along in the first place."

Jean sighed. "I'm a terrible handicap, but if you'd turned left back there like I said we wouldn't be in Togo again. We need to ask directions."

"There's nobody to ask."

"Drive back to that bar. Togo Joe's."

269

"Bars aren't open at seven thirty in the morning."

"Well," she said, "it's the first time I've been in a town so small there isn't even a grocery store or a gas station. You want to take another look at the map?"

"Might as well."

She spread it on the seat between them. He marveled at her composure and the flush in her cheeks. Joining forces had been a tonic for her and she'd stuck up for him back home, insisting he remain on the case. Jean and Mayor Janski were in the same book club. He was quite certain they read deep, dark novels in which men were always villainous scum. Even so, in his heart, he was damn glad to have her along.

They'd borrowed Bobby Brown's Blazer. Bobby's baby. He'd lectured them on the dos and don'ts and in some fanatical devotion to cleanliness had treated the seats with a silicone-based vinyl care product. Their backs were sore from fighting to stay upright but sometime during the four-hour drive they'd become a team. Now he stared hopelessly at the map. "We can't go all the way back to Nashwauk. Over thirty miles, but there's nothing here, not even a store or a gas station."

"Wonder where people do get gas and groceries?" she said.

"Good question. Isn't another town within twenty miles and nobody's going to drive that distance every time they need a quart of milk." He produced a pen and drew a circle around Togo. "What else we got around here?"

She squinted at the map. "Rauch, Greaney, and Celina. All pretty small."

"Which is closest?"

"Celina."

"Let's try it. Beats sitting here and if there's anybody around I'll even ask the directions myself."

In tandem, their rumps slid right as Charlie pulled the Blazer back onto the highway.

* * *

"When you finish eating," Dutch said, "take off."

Len shoveled eggs into his mouth without looking up. "I don't know why I'm so starved."

"Dylan brought the snowmobile back while you were enthroned in the outhouse," he said. "Gassed-up and ready to go. Sally even packed lunch. He's coming back later with a plow so he can get the truck out for me. They really turned out to be nice neighbors."

"What about MOM, that idiot?"

"Bellowing at some kid doctor when Dylan left him. Wound's not too serious. Already making plans for the Butcher of Willow River Display behind his bar. Wish I could see the look on his face when he finds out I've given myself up."

"Don't be surprised if he appears as a prosecution witness," Len said between mouthfuls. "Guys like that know how to massage the system." He wiped the last of his egg yoke from the plate with his toast as Dutch slipped into a heavy coat. "Got any more toilet paper?"

"You just went."

"I know. Rapid digestion. Always go after I eat."

Dutch produced a fresh roll from under the cupboard. "How can you sit out there so long in this weather?"

"Helps me focus," he said, heading for the door. "And don't rush me. I'm planning your defense."

"How reassuring."

He appeared in Murdock's powerful binoculars almost like a television closeup, head bobbing in and out of the frame.

"Who the hell is that?" Murdock whispered, thrusting the glasses at Carroll.

Carroll got only a glimpse of the man's face before he turned and followed a well-worn path off into the trees. "Never saw him before," he said.

"Well, I have."

"Or think you have. Face it, Murdock. We're in the wrong place."

"Bullshit! I've seen that guy."

"So what are we going to do? Lay around here in the snow until you finally figure out he was the gas station attendant in Sauk Centre or whatever?"

"No!" Murdock jerked the binoculars away. "When this guy comes back from shittin' in the woods I'll get another look at him. Seen him before."

Len came bouncing out of the trees finally, and Murdock studied him through the glasses. Pink stocking cap with a tassel. Groovy. A name went with that face but he couldn't remember. They'd have to wait.

"Let's go," Carroll said, impatiently.

Murdock scowled, his wired jaw aching with the effort. "We're going to wait here." He left no room for argument.

Inside the cabin Dutch had been busily packing a few necessities for Len to take on the snowmobile. His fingers worked the backpack tie. "I packed you light," he said, smiling. Len was going ahead to break the news before Dutch showed up. "Wear the helmet."

"I was thinking," Len said, backing up to the stove. "How come there wasn't something inside you that hollered at you to stop when you got your hands around Vicky's neck? How come you didn't stop just in the nick of time?"

"Another treasure of outhouse logic?"

"Guess so, but I know you. You're not an evil man. Hatred and heat of the moment aside, I still can't picture it." If he couldn't get an answer to this question then how could anyone believe Dutch was really sorry? "Please," Len said. "I have to know."

"I'm not sure I can explain it." Dutch shoved his hands into his pants pockets. "Not sure I understand it myself. I wanted to kill her but didn't know I would until it happened.

272

Does that make sense?"

"Sort of."

"Used to have fantasies of her suffering or dying but I wasn't responsible. She'd get caught dealing drugs, be beaten to death by mobsters, have a love affair with an AIDs carrier, or get fat as a pig." A mirthless chuckle. "Sounds like kid's stuff doesn't it?"

"I don't know. Pretty hateful."

"It was." He thought awhile. "She robbed me, Len. Took something away from deep inside. I lied and cheated to love her and she made it feel good. Stole my integrity, I don't know."

"Integrity?"

"You know. A little sleeping around, little lying, little cheating." His clear eyes seemed suddenly bright, piercing. "Ever gone a ways down that road, Len? Maybe allow one of life's pleasures to get out of hand?" He avoided the word alcohol.

"So your appetite for her was so insatiable you lost your integrity and felt the only way to get it back was kill her?"

"Little corruption goes a long way, I guess. One day you're fooling around and the next you're lying to keep it secret. Pretty soon you're changing loyalties, redirecting your finances, giving of your time. Finally it falls apart and you turn to hate. What's so hard to understand?" He swung the pack across the room and it dropped near the door. "That part of my life is over. Let's go."

The door opened and it was snowing again. In the trees a point of light glinted on glass.

* * *

Miles away, he lingered by the edge of the frozen lake near a young balsam, resting. A billion snowflakes parachuted from the sky colliding soundlessly with the earth around him, billowing onto the flat, lime-green needles of his cover. He was uneasy with the calm windless snowfall.

273

It muffled sounds, carried no scent to his uplifted nose, floated no warnings. Death came quickly in the deep forest, stalking, as he so often stalked, with a certainty born of relentless pursuit, of killing the weak and running to ground the unwatchful.

He blended perfectly with his surroundings. Gray and white coat, flecked with snow, concealed him against the white background, the gray outcroppings of rock and darkened bark. But these things were no comfort to him. On such a day the sudden explosion dropped his mate dead at his feet, the warm red flow of her life melting the snow. He'd left the pack then, roaming alone, a solitary hunter.

His pale blue eyes were almost white as he watched the lake. Only a few of his kind remained alive in Minnesota, and while he had no way of knowing, he was among the oldest of timberwolves. He stood nearly three feet high at the shoulders and weighed almost ninety pounds, thanks to good hunting since the first snowfall.

The falling snow thickened, obscuring the pine-studded island where he planned to spend the night sleeping on a mat of pine needles between some large rocks he knew. But he'd wait for the snow to let up. He had learned patience. Learned not to be caught in the open, out on the ice. These past few days he'd eaten well, surprising a young moose and bringing her down easily, as he'd done in the more carefree days of his youth when he was dominant among the pack.

High above the still land the wind freshened, a haunting breeze brushing the tree-tops. He stood quietly, sniffing the air. The falling snow, confused by the sudden wind, scattered across the frozen lake and he could see the island again. The wind swept upward, back into the white sky high above the earth. Its mournful sound in the trees died away. The island was gone.

The breeze reassured him. There was no danger. Cautiously at first, he stepped out from the tree-line, picking his way carefully along the steep bank to a spot where a small creek ran into the lake. Here he paused for water, where there shouldn't be running water.

He drank his fill, then placed a front paw on the thin ice and transferred a portion of his weight to it. The ice sagged, then snapped and broke away, falling into the hole where the creek entered the lake. He shook his paw vigorously. Another danger, and this one too he'd experienced before, during other long winters when snow came early and lay heavy on new ice. Patches of open water sometimes survived even the subzero weather of January.

He climbed easily up the embankment, his long legs lifting his body well above the snow, carrying him away from the lake back toward the deep woods. Several miles to the south, close to a seldom used log cabin, was a cedar swamp where deer often hid in the thick branches. A skillful hunter on a day like this, when there was no wind to carry his scent, could sometimes creep into the cedars and surprise one of the young deer. If this failed, the cabin was worth a look. Sometimes men left food about, or penned their chickens.

The island would've been the perfect place to sleep until the snow let up. The small cave he knew there contained a good matt of pine needles for warmth. The primal urge that drove him would bring him back again soon to see if the ice was safe.

Later, in the hush of the cedars, he inhaled the sharp, cold air in deep drafts, ignoring the frost left on his snout and fur when he exhaled. From somewhere, further along the rock ridge toward the pale sun, he caught a scent of woodsmoke. Too distant to be visible, close enough to be frightening. The strong, familiar smell meant only one thing—men were nearby.

For some time he remained hidden in the trees, watching the open rock ridge which rose from the forest floor like the snow-capped spine of a dinosaur, only to dwindle away again a few hundred yards further on. Nothing moved over the open ground. He listened for footsteps or the telltale snapping of a frozen twig - anything that might signal danger. There was nothing, not even the thump of a rabbit's foot in the snow or a whisper of wind in the pines.

Now it was safe to move closer, searching the air for the man-scent, and for prey. Always the hunt to exploit the weak or young or old. Uncover an animal trapped in deep snow unable to run. His thin legs were barely impeded by the snow as he moved diagonally across the rock-ridge, loping toward the smell of smoke coming from Dutch's cabin.

The risk was great hunting this close, but a heavily traveled deer trail paralleled the rock ridge on the opposite side from the cabin. The ridge shielded the white tails and allowed them to move swiftly from the thick cover to the large cedar swamp for fresh browse. If he could lie downwind, perhaps in a crevice of rock, and wait patiently, his chances were good.

He looked up at the sky. Already the sun was above the horizon. Days were short. Sunrise came late and he preferred to hunt during the daylight. Nearby a small stand of immature spruce had taken root in the rock. Most would wither and die in some dry year, but now they offered excellent cover and he moved toward them.

Before he'd gone far something caught his eye and he dropped in the snow, eyes searching the forest below the ridge. A strong scent of deer. He crept to the edge of the rocks and there below stood a yearling who had wandered from the trail, following a line of thin browse until it was disoriented. A moment more and the young deer might find the trail or one of its herd might return. An angry buck with a full rack of horns was a formidable foe even to the largest timber wolf.

Gathering his legs beneath him like powerful springs he inched forward, eyes focused intently. The juvenile deer stood facing away, its white tail flicking in nervous spasms.

He found good traction on the rock ledge as he leapt through the air, landing less than a yard from the startled deer. It in turn leapt to the side but struck against a small aspen and momentarily lost balance. It was enough. The wolf caught the yearling by its throat and in one powerful thrust tore the hide away and severed a large artery, soaking the snow with spays of rich blood.

Death came swiftly and soundlessly in the soft snow. An efficient death which served a purpose as old as life itself.

Once he'd eaten his fill he sat awhile, then ate again. Now it was time for the frozen lake and the pine island. Then he could rest and be alone, watch the moon light the snow and savor the stillness of a cold night. Secure in loneliness.

Two hours later, he appeared, a four-legged ghost at the edge of the lake. There he stopped high on the bank, dropping into the thick snow and resting his head on crossed paws. The snow was a warm carpet. His sides heaved from the tiring run he'd made to the northeast out of the sparsely populated forest surrounding Dutch's cabin to the edge of Pooquette Lake.

During the past few days, he'd touched corners of three large Minnesota counties—St. Louis, Itasca, and now Koochiching. He didn't know this, of course, being ignorant of political boundaries. He cocked his head and nipped at the soft snow, snapping his teeth together in a clacking noise as he ate. White flakes stuck to his snout

*and dusted his whiskers. The dry snow yielded little mois-
ture and served only to taunt his thirst.*

*Down the bank where a small creek joined the frozen
lake there might yet be running water. This he would
investigate. He stood and sniffed the clear air. During the
last half hour a stiff northwesterly wind arose, causing the
hard powdery snow to swirl and dance in lively rhythms.
It stung his eyes but carried no scent of danger, and he
preferred wind to calm, poor visibility to good. He was
made for this weather and this place and it concealed him
inside it's snowy cloak.*

*He picked his way carefully down the bank to the place
where the creek entered the lake. The snow was very
deep. The white drifts smoothed the land and hid its
imperfections. The gully and ravine and rock of summer
was now a flowing ocean of shimmering crystals. The
long legs and snowshoe-like paws failed him. His belly
plowed a deep wake in the white sea.*

*Under the snow, the creek crept out into the lake form-
ing a narrow pool at its edge no larger than a beaver's tail.
The water was clear and cold, ringed with fragile ice like
translucent paper, and he bent forward just touching his
nose to the liquid, drinking quietly. He braced his front
legs apart, holding himself steady over the opening. His
ears remained alert, cool eyes searching the distance
between him and the pine island rising green and warm
from the frozen lake. It drifted in and out of his vision as
the snow was driven by the gusty wind tugging at his thick
winter coat.*

*Lifting his nose to the wind he let out a long mournful
cry, and like the last sound on earth it was carried away
and was lost in the whistling pines and creaking branches
of an empty forest.*

*The weather would turn even more cold now with an
arctic wind drawing frigid air down across the northern*

plains. Time to seek shelter. He loped off across the ice in the direction of the pine island.

Snow lay thick and heavy on the ice. His large paws pounded silently against it, sending up a fine powder which caught in his fur. The days of eating had strengthened him, and he glided easily through the soft, heavy snow.

Underneath, frail glass.

Days before, patches of open water could be seen between the land and the pine island, but now a glaze of paper-thin ice and new snow hid them. If the wind had come earlier and swept the ice clean perhaps then a pair of discerning eyes might have seen the danger. Or perhaps the snow would not have fallen so evenly, pressing so heavily on the brittle ice.

He panted slightly now as the island, a green mirage, appeared before him. The warm bed of pine needles beckoned. His long legs stretched out and his speed increased. His chest heaved with exertion. Head down, tail pointed, blood pounding through his body, he flew - a whirlwind of white powder. In his face, his cool eyes, a look of satisfaction.

There was no warning or sound when the lake opened and swallowed him. Nor did he cry out. No one was there to see him slip beneath the surface.

By morning the small hole in the ice had frozen shut and snow covered it completely, stretching away white, unbroken as far as the eye could see.

Chapter Twenty-Three

"There!" Murdock shouted, dumping the binoculars in the snow, fumbling for his rifle. "It's him! It's him!"

Murdock was right about sound in the woods. Dutch and Len heard him clearly as they walked side by side toward the snowmobile. Instinctively, Dutch dropped his pack and pushed Len forward to shelter behind the woodshed.

Two shots rang out in close succession. One struck harmlessly in the snow. The other tore a large jagged hole through the calf muscle of Len's left leg. He continued to crawl closer to the side of the building and did not cry out.

"Murdock?" Len asked, mouth gaping.

"Who else?" Dutch examined Len's wound. "He shot you."

"No shit."

"Hurt?"

"Not really. But look at the blood!"

"How'd he find us?"

"Who cares? Are you planning to let me bleed to death?"

"Just calm down," Dutch said. He didn't feel calm himself. "Can you run?"

"How in hell should I know! I've never been shot before."

"Want to try it?"

"Why?"

"I thought if you could run, I'd say something to keep Murdock occupied while you sprint to the cabin for the first aid kit. Then get my shotgun and pop off a couple rounds and I'll run to the cabin."

"That's your plan?"

"Yeah."

"Why does it have all that running in it?"

"You want to walk over there?"

"Let's surrender."

"Don't be stupid. Murdock's here to kill me. He isn't going to leave any witnesses, especially lawyers. Get ready before the pain and bleeding get worse. Ready?"

Len nodded, wide-eyed.

Dutch cupped both hands around his mouth and shouted, "Hey! Is your name Murdock?"

Not original, Len thought, and bounded across the deep snow of the yard like a wounded deer and burst through the cabin door before Murdock fired again, a tardy report that ended with a dull thump as spent lead was absorbed by a log. He ignored his leg a moment, searching desperately for the shotgun which he'd last seen leaning in a corner near Dutch's bunk.

He found it alongside the dresser but unfamiliar with guns, he was forced to concentrate on what must be done to fire it. Listing these steps in his head, he bravely stepped out the front door and onto the exposed porch. When he pulled the trigger, nothing happened. More shots rang out and Len felt the bullets pass close to his ears and strike the end logs by the door. He retreated inside, unhurt but trembling.

"Load it first!" he heard Dutch calling from the shed.

When he stepped out on the porch a second time, both he and Murdock fired simultaneously. Dutch crashed through the door before the smoke cleared, Len at his back.

"Close," he said, gasping.

On the rock ridge south of the cabin, Murdock felt he'd been betrayed. "If we'd both fired at the same time we might've got him," he seethed at Carroll. "What's the matter with you? Still think it's a hunter's cabin?"

"I think you've just shot an innocent bystander and we both better get out of here."

"He's no innocent bystander. I recognized him. That's Davis, the lawyer."

"You shot the guy's lawyer. Brilliant!" He pounded the snow. "We're as good as dead."

"For a guy who's suppose to be so smart, you're pretty dumb." Murdock growled. "What'd you think Davis is doing up here with Mr. Public Enemy? Huh?"

"What difference does it make? You just shot him."

"We," Murdock said, jabbing a finger at Carroll's chest. "We just shot him. Davis is here to save his buddy Cleland and that makes him an accessory, or worse. In other words, he's fair game."

Carroll rolled onto his back in the snow and stared up at the twisted canopy of bare branches. The way out was clear and the time for it had come. He sat up and loaded the shotgun.

"Tight?" Dutch asked, checking the tension of Len's bandage with his finger. "I can loosen it."

Len shook his head, trickles of perspiration running freely from his forehead. His cheeks were hot and he was sure his complextion must be mottled and strange, like a man dying of his wounds on a battlefield.

"Don't worry." Dutch patted him on the shoulder. "Looks worse than it is. Bullet passed through your calf just like a paper punch. You lost a little meat, that's all. Bleeding's almost stopped and unless there's an infection or something, the only thing you'll have is an interesting scar."

"It hurts," Len whined. "Get me some aspirin."

"Aspirin thins the blood. You need yours to thicken just now."

"How about a shot of whiskey?"

"This isn't Hollywood, Sundance. No booze. We need to keep our wits about us. We're not out of this yet." Dutch patted him again, then crept to the window, peering cautiously through the tan curtain. "Can't see him."

"Let's surrender," Len said.

* * *

On the map Celina is a name and a small white circle. On the map legend, as Jean quoted, it's marked "unincorporated." In reality, Celina is a grocery store with two gas pumps.

"This can't be it." Charlie sounded less convinced each time they'd driven past the tiny crossroads store. "There's no sign."

"I don't want to tell a trained investigator how to do his job," Jean grumbled, "but if you'd stop the damn truck long enough for me to get out and ask, we'd know where we are. Of course, I can see the tremendous advantage to meandering up and down the back roads of northern Minnesota, allowing criminals, even if they are my husband, sufficient time to escape. You see, I actually want you to catch him so he'll come home with me and pay his debt to society and we can just get on with our miserable little lives. Before any of that can happen, of course, you have to stop this truck at that store so I can get out and ask directions! It's the smart thing to do so I can see why you might reject it."

"You sure are long-winded." He pulled in near the store's front door and slammed on the brakes. "I'll wait here," he said, jamming the gearshift lever into park and revving the engine to keep warm air blowing from the heater.

A bell rang softly somewhere in the back as Jean stepped inside the Celina Store. It felt good to be out of the truck and away from Charlie. She couldn't rid herself of guilt for cooperating but Murdock frightened her enough to trust Charlie.

"Good morning," said a soft female voice.

Jean turned and saw a tiny woman, bent with age, smiling at her between jars of Cheese Whiz. The old lady's eyes sparkled in obvious pleasure at seeing an attractive young customer so early in the morning.

283

"Hi," Jean said, returning the smile to establish quick rapport. "Can you help me? I'm looking for a man."

"My goodness," the woman said. "A girl as pretty as you shouldn't have to look very far."

"Thank you," she acknowledged with a nod, "This man's my husband."

"Oh?"

"Dutch Cleland. He...we have a cabin near here. I'm looking for it."

The old lady puzzled a moment. "You don't know where your cabin is?"

"Never been there. My husband and I...well, we've had some difficulties." Jean didn't have to fabricate the pain in her eyes.

"You've nothing to explain to me." The woman ripped a piece of narrow paper from the ancient adding machine on the counter. "Here," she said. "My name is Sylvia. I'll draw you a little map. I know your husband quite well. Comes here often. Summers I pick blueberries on the rock ridges around your cabin. Do you like jerky?" She uncovered a glass jar. "Here. I'll treat you."

When Jean brought the map out and related her conversation with Sylvia, Charlie was skeptical. "Sure the old gal wasn't off her rocker? We've been down all these roads."

"She lives here Charlie."

"Which way is north on this thing?" He turned the slip of paper upside down. "This doesn't even make sense."

"You drive," she said, snatching the paper from his thick fingers. "I'll interpret the map. You don't need north and south. We aren't exploring for the National Geographic Society. Turn left when I tell you to turn left and turn right when I tell you to turn right."

Clearly the woman had no idea what direction they were headed and the only thing worse than taking directions from a woman was taking directions from two women, but he slipped the lever into reverse and backed the truck onto the main road. "Now what?"

"Straight up that hill," Jean said confidently.

They sped away raising a cloud of powdery snow to swirl and settle again to the pavement.

* * *

Lying on his back, left leg packed in ice and slung onto a large cooler, Len was in the perfect position to observe the vaulted ceiling and speculate on Dutch's new dilemma. The more the poor bastard wanted to give himself up the more it seemed someone violently wanted to stop him. He shifted his weight to the other hip. Ouch. But Dutch had no other choice, did he?

"Still painful?" Dutch asked from his spot by the window.

"Throbs."

"Sorry."

"Not your fault," Len said. "How come you don't knock out the glass in that window?"

"Huh?"

"Knock the glass out. So you can shoot."

Dutch laughed. "It's twenty below zero. Except what's in the woodbox, all our wood is outside. I'd just as soon not freeze to death before he shoots us."

"They always do that in the movies. Knock the windows out, I mean."

"They always get away from the bad guys too." Dutch smiled. "But I'll be damned if I can remember right now how they did it."

"They wait until dark, open the secret trap door in the floor and sneak off into the night. Of course, you'd have to carry me." Len smiled then too. "You never leave your side-kick behind."

"Sorry," Dutch said again. "No trap door."

"I'm too tired anyway."

Turning, Dutch slid down along the wall and sat on the floor, staring curiously at a small bow saw which hung on a hook behind the stove. "But I could cut a hole in the floor," he said.

"Wouldn't that be colder than an open window?"

"No," he said. "The cabin is skirted with half-inch plywood. It's much warmer under there than outside." He leaned his rifle against the logs and stood up. "But what would I do with you?"

Len struggled onto his elbows. "I was just kidding. You don't seriously think you can cut your way out of here? He'll see us."

The smile widened on Dutch's face. "No," he said. "He won't see us. We'll come down inside the skirting, crawl to the back, knock out a section and disappear. He'd be sitting there watching an empty building."

"We'd be on foot."

His smile faded. Len was right. How far would they get? He couldn't carry Len through the deep snow and if he left him behind Murdock would surely kill him.

"I'll think of something," he said. "The hole's a good idea anyway. Let's cut it just in case." Keeping away from the windows, he lifted the bow saw from its hook. "If we cut between the floor joists, it shouldn't take long."

On the ridge Murdock too was tired of waiting. "Listen carefully," he said, breath hissing like a teakettle from the hole in his teeth. "I've got an idea."

Carroll beat his mittened hands together to keep them from freezing. "What?"

"There's only so many ways out of that cabin. The front door or the windows. We've got everything covered except the two windows on the other side there." He pointed to the left. "Crawl around to that long ridge. See it? Then plant yourself as high up as you can get. When I see you're in position, we'll both open up with everything we've got."

"What good's that going to do? Those logs are two feet thick."

"Not the logs, genius. Door and windows. Let's make sure they're as cold as we are. Who knows? Might get lucky and blow a piece of glass in someone's eye." Murdock's thin lips spread apart. "Move out."

Carroll welcomed the opportunity to get away and wormed quickly off to the left. This fit his own plans.

Murdock watched him go, wondering if Carroll had even an inkling of what was to come in the next few minutes. Unlikely. The man was a fool. Did he seriously think there would be any witnesses? That he'd allow anyone such power over him? Anyway, the guy was annoying. He turned his attention to the cabin. Time Cleland found out who he was up against. "Hey!" he yelled. "In the shack! Listen up!"

No answer came from behind the thick plank door.

"You hear me in there?"

Dutch chuckled. Murdock had a speech impediment and the reason for it suddenly occurred to him. While it may be coming back to haunt him now there was no reason Murdock should think they were cowering inside like a couple twitching rabbits. "Speak clearly!" Dutch shouted. "Sounds like you got a mouth full of marbles!"

A train of curses rumbled from between Murdock's clenched teeth but he managed to keep his finger off the trigger until Carroll had finally worked his way to the ridge.

"I'm going to give you something for your mouth Cleland," he said as loudly as jaw wires allowed. "You and your little buddy have five minutes to step out on that porch. No weapons. Then we go see the sheriff."

Dutch spoke softly to Len. "Move closer to the wall. He's about to start shooting." To Murdock he called, "Sounds reasonable. Come on down for a cup of coffee first. You must be cold lying out there in the snow."

The response was about what Murdock expected. Cleland was no easy mark but this time he'd be more careful and kill him at the first opportunity. "Last chance! I'm counting!"

To Len, Dutch said, "When he opens up it's going to seem like all hell's breaking loose in here. Cover your head, keep down and be cool. Noise and broken glass never killed anybody, okay? Unless he's got a bazooka, the logs'll save us."

Len nodded, pressing his back hard against the warm logs and drawing his wounded leg up closer to the wall. "This what I missed by going to college and dodging the draft?" Len asked.

"Kinda," Dutch answered. "Get ready now."

Almost on cue the first volley from Murdock's carbine shattered the window closest to them, spitting glass and bits of wood across their backs and down their necks. Len screamed in spite of himself. He was shocked at the damage done by the mushrooming lead bullets as they found plates, glasses, shelving, kerosene lamps. Dust and fragments of pink insulation floated in the room. His senses seemed heightened and the smell of burning wood had been replaced by the smell of dust.

Carroll's shotgun opened up and the window on the west wall above the stove blew apart in one sudden burst and steel pellets pelted the stovepipe, leaving it full of holes. Dutch rolled to his left and fired wildly through the open window, panicked by this unexpected blast from the west. The realization that Murdock had someone with him came hard. Dutch was ready to face Murdock alone, even eager for it, but confronting two enemies might make a critical difference. It simply hadn't occurred to him they might be killed.

The bullets came again. Dutch heard the shotgun clearly now, firing from the ridge west of the cabin. Another window shattered. A can of baked beans exploded, spraying its contents in a fan-like pattern against the wall. He smelled kerosene. Luckily none of the lamps were lit. He ignored his strong urge to stand up and fire the rifle.

Len's head was lost inside his coat. "How you doing?" Dutch hollered at him.

One section of the stovepipe separated, hung in midair a moment, then clattered to the floor producing a cloud of black, strong-smelling soot. Len buried his head deeper inside the coat.

"Destructive bastards, aren't they?" Dutch commented.

For a moment Len did not respond. When he finally did, his voice came from deep within his clothing. "They?"

"Murdock's got someone with him. Somebody's firing from the ridge to the west."

"Now can we surrender?"

"Sit tight. When they're done wasting ammunition we're going to have some fun with 'em."

Len brought his eyes above the coat collar. "We are going to have some fun with them?" His eyes widened. "Please tell me you haven't decided we should attack."

An empty tin cup launched vertically from the table at the same instant an angry swarm of pellets came across from the other side and caught it, plastering the cup at a right angle like it was a prop in a magic act. Another bullet struck the plastic hook holding Len's pants to the end of his bunk. The pants crumpled to the floor. Len stared at them. They didn't seem damaged, though the plastic hook split into several pieces, part still held to the bunk by the nail.

The sight made Len furious. "They shot my pants," he told Dutch.

"Hell," he replied, laughing. "They've shot you."

Len brought his head out from under the coat. "Where's the shotgun. I'm not going to let them shoot my pants."

Carroll had been pumping and firing the twelve-gauge just as Murdock told him, aiming at the windows. Now the shotgun was empty. He slid back from the crown of the ridge to reload where he was hidden from Murdock and those inside the cabin.

After he reloaded he'd be expected to crawl up and fire again until the magazine was empty. Then, no doubt, Murdock would want him to do it a third time, and a fourth and a fifth. And then what?

He listened.

Murdock had stopped firing too.

He heard Dutch's voice, clear and strong in the intense quiet that followed their last volley. "You fellas are making an awful lot of noise out there and you shot up a perfectly good can of beans, but I should think by now every neighbor in five miles is on the way here, along with the sheriff and twenty deputies."

Murdock fired two rounds and Carroll heard them strike the cabin.

"Where'd you park your car, Murdock?" Carroll listened again to Dutch's unhurried voice. "Not up on this road, I hope. It's a dead end. No way out. First vehicle that comes in here will block you tight. You weren't that stupid, were you Murdock?"

Of course he was, Carroll thought. And I'm stupid enough to get caught with him.

Murdock opened fire. Carroll heard the tinkling of glass. He couldn't imagine there was any glass left to break.

Again, all was quiet.

Carroll slid further down behind the ridge. He looked at the shotgun laying across his lap and pushed it off into the snow. Maybe there was an easier way then killing Murdock, which he'd been planning for two days. Less than twenty feet behind him the ridge dropped straight into the ground and disappeared. There the forest was thick. A man could walk upright without being seen.

It was so simple. Carroll crawled to the edge, dropped down and walked away, never looking back.

One thought pounded inside Murdock's head—shut Cleland up! Shut his big mouth! Make him crawl, and when he died make sure he knew who put him down.

Murdock smiled and took aim at Dutch's pickup parked alongside the cabin. He squeezed the rounds out evenly, one at a time, blowing a tire, punching a hole in the radiator, collapsing the windshield, smashing the headlights.

"Maybe you should start worrying about your own car," he yelled.

Dutch looked from Len to Nimrod, who'd remained under a bunk since the shooting began, and shook his head. "I feel about that truck the way you do about your pants," he said. "But we can't let him know it."

Raising his voice again so Murdock could hear, he said, "I hope you're not still upset about that little disagreement we had back in Willow River the other day, Murdock." Another flurry of bullets poured through the window. "You really should work on controlling that temper," Dutch shouted in return.

"Why do you keep egging him on?" Len asked.

"To keep him shooting. A few shots in the woods this time of year, even in this weather, is expected, but enough rapid firing from one direction is going to bring someone around for a look."

"I hope you're right," Len said.

"Besides, he might lose his cool and show himself, and that would suit me just fine."

Lying in the snow, his carbine smoking, Murdock too was getting wise. It was a stand-off. He wasted ammunition while Cleland let time work to his advantage. He'd have to tip the balance. Find Cleland's weak point.

Murdock picked up the binoculars again and examined the cabin. Door in the front. Windows on three sides. What was on the fourth wall? Nothing. Logs. If he came up from behind, Cleland was blind. Nice little fire back there and the place would go up like a cardboard box full of straw.

Two loaded clips lay in the snow next to his rifle. He picked one and slammed it into the magazine, sliding carefully back away from the ridge.

Something cold and hard touched his neck just below his right ear.

"One of two things is going to happen now," a gravely voice said from above. "Either you're going to keep very still and place both hands behind your neck or your head's going to gain some weight."

Murdock froze, bringing both hands to the back of his neck where they were roughly handcuffed together.

"Good boy," Charlie Benson said.

Chapter Twenty-Four

CHARLIE BENSON STOOD ON THE PORCH outside Dutch's cabin and drew a deep breath, then kicked open the door.

Len Davis was lying on his back on a rag rug near a wood stove, right leg propped on a large green cooler. A dog sat next to him. Looking up and seeing Charlie, the dog wagged his tail. Slightly to his right there was a jagged hole in the floor.

"This is absolutely the worst day of my life," Len said. "I hope you're in radio contact with somebody. I need a doctor."

Charlie held a shotgun in his hands, which seemed to be trained casually in Len's direction, but the policeman's eyes darted around the room. "You're under arrest," he said offhandedly. "Where's Dutch?"

"Dutch?" Len seemed puzzled. "Would that be Dutch Cleland?"

"Wouldn't smart off if I were you."

"Why not?"

"Because you're in enough trouble."

"Being arrested, you mean?"

"For starters."

Len laughed. "You can't arrest me, Charlie."

"I already did."

"What for? Getting shot? No law against that, though I think there should be."

"I'm arresting you for harboring a fugitive," Charlie said.
Len yawned. "Sorry, up all night. This is Dutch's place. I
didn't harbor anybody. I'm just visiting. You'll have to arrest
me for visiting a fugitive."

"Shut up," Charlie said. "Where is he?"

"Will you relax? He's giving himself up."

From outside they heard the high-pitched bark of a snowmobile engine coming to life, throttling up, down, and up
again. The significance of this spread across Charlie's face as
he spun toward the door. "Thought you said he was giving up."
The snowmobile roared past the cabin and down the road.

"Guess he changed his mind," Len said.

Charlie reached the porch an instant later and brought the
shotgun to his shoulder, both eyes locked on the hunched
back of the retreating form aboard the snowmobile. An easy
shot.

His finger squeezed the trigger as another form took
shape in the middle distance between him and his target.
Jean. Her head square in his sights.

The shotgun kicked against his shoulder as it fired, its
close pattern of deadly pellets punching empty sky. Jean
smiled. The snowmobile could be heard winding up and
shifting to a higher gear.

"Big deal," Charlie said. "Where's he going to go?"

Behind him, Murdock, handcuffed to the porch railing,
lifted the rotten spindle from its mounting and eased the
handcuff chain free. He aimed the spindle at Charlie's head
but missed and clobbered him in the back between his shoulder blades. Charlie lost the shotgun and Murdock caught it
easily as the policeman went down and brought it to bear on
Dutch's retreating back. The snowmobile, negotiating the
narrow drive, was still in range.

Murdock grinned and closed one eye.

The eye widened and his hands fell away limp, shotgun
toppling from his grasp at the sound of Charlie's .38 echo-

ing in the trees. Jean lowered the revolver and Murdock screamed, a girlish, high-pitched sound.

Charlie lifted his head in time to see Murdock sink to his knees, both hands on his crotch.

"Ouch," Charlie said, struggling to his feet. "Lucky that railing was rotten or he'd broken my back. Please give me the gun, Jean."

"Bitch shot me," Murdock complained.

"Drop your pants and I'll have a look."

Murdock's pain overcame his modesty and Charlie examined him there in the yard, kneeling in the snow. "Well, Gordy. She shot one of your nuts off."

"Bitch!"

"One'll get you by where you're going."

"I need a doctor." Murdock stuffed a scarf between his legs to stem the flow of blood and buckled his pants. "I want a lawyer."

"Got one right inside," Charlie said. "But if it turns out you shot him too, I hope you don't own anything you wanted to keep."

"I was making a citizen's arrest and he got in the way."

Charlie nodded thoughtfully as he reattached the handcuffs, this time behind the back. "Scares me to think you might get away with this. Scares me even more you'd do Walleye like you did and not have to pay the price."

"I don't know what you're talking about. Aren't you going to stop my bleeding?"

"Those county lab fellas went over Walleye's little house with vacuum cleaners and a pound of fingerprint dust." Charlie shook his head. "Guess you must've worn gloves. Didn't find a thing. Trouble is, snow works even better than mud for casting. Did you know that? We got three nice casts of a right foot and two of a left. Sheriff Mattson told me there's a skull and cross bones carved into the heels," he chuckled. "You ain't really that dumb are you Murdock? I

295

mean, you didn't carve that in your boots?" Charlie pushed him backward into the snow, yanking his foot up by the boot lacing. "Well now, what have we here?"

Murdock howled. "That's abuse! I got a witness."

Charlie turned to Jean. "You mean this woman you tried to rape? How about if I give her the gun back?"

"Get me a lawyer, I said!"

* * *

Dutch followed Dylan's route to the northwest which would lead him across the wasteland of Koochiching County toward Lake of the Woods.

The lake is so large, encompassing so many thousands of acres, dotted with hundreds of uninhabited islands, it's virtually impossible to search without employing an army. Lake homes and cabins deserted this time of year would surely yield a warm fireplace and room to hide the snowmobile until the weather improved. He'd decided against giving himself up until people quit trying to kill him. He'd also decided against Dylan's idea of the Jacksons in Arbor Vidae. Winnipeg was better.

There was a lady in Winnipeg who once promised him anything. Delores Erickson's only son Kevin, Dutch's boat engineer, died in Vietnam and Dutch drove to Winnipeg when his tour ended and told her how it was. A boy barely nineteen shouldn't return to his mother's arms in a coffin and she needed the whole truth of his death to square it with his life. She'd transferred some of the love for him to Dutch, and they'd written regularly and visited most summers. She was old now, but she was also like family. If he made it to Winnipeg, he'd made it. She'd help with a car and anything he needed.

Dutch roared along logging roads and narrow trails due west toward Lake Pooquette. The Minnesota-made Arctic Cat growled and lurched as it jumped deadfalls and uneven ground. Through the smoked Plexiglas helmet the trees and frozen sloughs flashed by quickly. The vibrating tips of his silver skis barely touched earth and his narrow escape from the cabin added to the exhilaration. The hot engine and subzero wind cut him off from the subtle sounds of the forest and he felt that if he leaned back and pulled the handlebars, the racing sled would lift up and fly away.

His speedometer read forty-five. The route ahead was clear for several miles and he twisted the throttle, surging forward and the needle reached sixty. Speed demands complete concentration and its reward is emptiness, and it leaves even fear behind.

High on a wooded bluff Dutch passed Five Island Lake, then slowed considerably to cross the Valley River which was really little more than a big creek, finally entered Koochiching County unnoticed.

The danger he faced now came from the land not his pursuers, if there were any. Maneuvering a snowmobile in uncharted woods, deep with snow, is foolhardy, and he stuck to trails whenever possible or made only short runs between lakes. Plentiful and often connected by portages, Minnesota's frozen lakes form a bed of wind-driven snow and become snowmobile race tracks in winter.

In a clearing surrounded by white cedar so thick he couldn't see ten feet into them, he let up on the throttle and the sled coasted to a stop. He dismounted. As the crow flies, he'd traveled little more than eight miles, but his odometer recorded seventeen.

He popped the helmet from his head and methodically inspected the sled, then lit a cigarette. He wasn't the least bit cold. Electric hand-warmers helped and so did adrenaline. He drew smoke deep into his lungs and held it before exhaling. They couldn't let him alone. He sailed down the drive and there she was, his Jean, looking small and frail in her parka. He couldn't stop even for her. Not even to ask why she was there. He refused to think about it now.

The cigarette left him dizzy and he flipped the butt into the snow. When he'd dismounted the sled he switched off the engine out of habit and now he wondered if it would start. He grunted, and turned the key to the on position. He pulled the plastic handle and the engine coughed, breathed a small cloud of blue smoke, and came alive. He swung his leg over the seat, squeezed the clutch and sped away through the trees without looking back.

An hour later, he waited under the lime-green branches of a young balsam overlooking Lake Pooquette. A wide bank of clouds had blown in from the west bringing a light snowfall. He watched as the wind freshened and the harried flakes all but obscured a small pine-covered island near the middle of the frozen lake. He'd turn north here.

Removing his right glove he unzipped his parka a few inches and reached inside, producing a silver compass mounted on a clear plastic board. Dutch clicked the outside bezel slowly counterclockwise until a red arrow lined up exactly with the degree setting he'd selected, then he looked up across the lake. Perfect.

He hesitated to pull the starter rope and disturb the hushed snowfall. His fondness of snow, its cleanness, was a new freedom and on the high bank alongside the hidden lake he watched the snow drift to earth and he believed anything was possible.

He smiled.

Vicky liked snow. One of the first things he remembered respecting about her—she never apologized for Minnesota. "They make me sick with their complaining," she said. Vicky liked snow, and sun, and steak, and cottage cheese. She liked him. Liking things is the ultimate indiscretion.

He pulled the starter cord and the engine purred.

Locking his knees and leaning back, he rode the sled down the bank and onto the ice of Lake Pooquette. The ice appeared safe but he decided to run the sled parallel to shore awhile to be sure.

The snow was deeper here, drifting down from the bank. Intermittent flurries increased to a steady squall slanted by the wind, obscuring his view of the lake. The snowmobile handled sluggishly in the deep snow.

Ahead, leading from shore toward the center of the lake, he discovered a set of wolf tracks, filling with snow. Dutch smiled inside the helmet, there weren't many left. The tracks were a good omen. If an old wolf with better winter survival skills than he had, found this ice safe, why was he puttering along?

He twisted the throttle and leaned his body to the left. The sled dug its track into the snow and sped off across the lake, white rooster tail in close pursuit.

Dutch bent his body forward like a jockey, keeping his head behind the small plastic windshield. The handlebars jigged sharply left and right as the skis and front suspension reacted to the sudden changes of the lake's surface. Deep snow. Packed snow. Clear ice with a skim of snow.

It took all his concentration to steer the sled along the track of the wolf. Out in the open the wind was strong, pressing against his clothing and fanning the snow in dusty curls across the tracks.

For an instant, when the snowmobile left the solid ice, it seemed as if speed and momentum would carry the sled across the open water safely to the solid ice beyond. But seeing the danger, Dutch pulled back on the handlebars as if reining in a horse. His weight shifted to the rear and the machine's nose came up, bringing it down dead center in open water.

Skis pointing at the sky, it sank.

The force of the impact crumpled Dutch down and forward onto the seat and instrument panel. His head, safe inside the helmet, drove through the windshield causing no more pain than a slap but his legs were trapped against the firewall, heavy boots lodged under the metal cowling. He

299

registered more surprise than pain and things moved incredibly slow, like in a dream, and there seemed plenty of time.

The snowmobile sank slowly out from under him. He felt it rub against his legs as it went down. He knew he was in the water now, but didn't feel wet or cold. Instead, he seemed strangely buoyant for quite some time and the only real difficulty was his mental slowness, a lethargy which he couldn't shake though he knew it was important to make quick decisions.

Above, he saw the hole in the ice, no more than ten feet across. The underwater world wasn't dark but clear and sharp as he studied it through the air bubble of his helmet. He observed the underside of the smooth ice, unblemished, the color and texture of mercury. He drew a breath.

Water seeped beneath his layered clothing, unimaginably cold. He drifted further and further from the surface, soundlessly. He was dizzy. Gurgling noises sounded like tiny explosions and silver bubbles passed him on their way to the surface. He held very still to escape the cold. The surface receded until it was a great distance away and he seemed to be looking at it through a lighted tunnel. Terrific pain ripped his ears, followed by freezing explosions inside his head. Instantly, there was nausea and dizziness.

His back landed softly in the fine silt bottom of Pooquette Lake. Next to him was the snowmobile, sitting upright, magnified and gleaming, enlarged in the underwater world. He turned his head slowly. A wolf lay sleeping beside him.

He closed his eyes momentarily but only to rest them, never to surrender to the dark. He was heavy but if he was light he could swim to the surface and draw sweet air deep into his lungs.

300

Chapter Twenty-Five

CURTIS RYLANDER HAD THE SLOPING FOREHEAD OF AN APE. He also had a bad complexion, skin craters ripe with raw zits and pus-laden whiteheads. Curtis wore a stocking cap, even in summer, to hide his head. The zits were another matter but his job as track inspector for the Soo Line Railroad helped. He worked alone.

Late Friday afternoon, Curtis was inspecting a section of track across County Road 4 several hundred yards south of the Willow River Welcome Sign when he noticed evidence of illegal activity. People were fascinated by railroad tracks and this often led to destructive behavior, such as placing foreign objects on the tracks, opening switches, stealing railroad property. Curtis attended mandatory company seminars on the recognition of such behavior and the means to combat it. Therefore, when he saw numerous new railroad ties cleverly arranged to form a tiny dwelling in a ditch along the right-of-way, Curtis Rylander knew just what to do.

He hopped from the orange four-door pickup parked on the rails a few yards from the tie house, and drew a long pry bar from the bed. The bar had come in handy more than once.

Curtis eased himself quietly through the deep snow until he was within arm's length of the tie house. He listened awhile but heard nothing. Kids were an uncontrolled menace on the right-of-way and when you tried to deal with them the

state rose up in their defense. You weren't allowed to prosecute them but you were allowed to pay millions to their
lawyers if the little bastards hurt themselves.

Down on one knee, Curtis inserted the pry bar under one
of the ties that formed the roof. Very gently he lifted and
swung the tie into the snow. The opening it left was no more
than a slit but Curtis saw a human foot, and not a child's. He
wished then he'd made a call on the radio and asked for
help. Holding his breath, he removed the second tie and saw
the man clearly.

He was lying in a bed of filthy rags, newspaper and cardboard. He looked more like roadkill than a human being,
face so dirty the whites of his eyes shown.

"Get out of there!" Curtis commanded.

"I ain't doin' anything. You better not touch me."

Curtis then threw back his sloped head and laughed. "I
know you, you little shit! You're Walleye Wertz, aren't you?
Retard with the big tricycle, rides up and down taking things
from ditches. So now what, you start living in a ditch? Come
on out of there. I ain't gonna hurt you."

"I got a ornery man after me."

"Ain't nobody around here but me. Get outta there.
You're half froze to death, Dummy. Move it. This is railroad
right-of-way. You got no business here."

Walleye came out only to shoulder height and peered cautiously in all directions. His feet were frozen and it hurt dread-
fully to stand on them. After Murdock's attack he'd built the little shelter and hid there in safely and total darkness. It was too
small for him to do much more than crouch. Gazing across the
frozen fields at the remains of the winter sunset blushing the
sky, he saw a few thin clouds spread with burnt orange.

"Take me home now," Walleye said.

"Go on your own steam," Curtis ordered. "I ain't your
chauffeur, Dummy. Can't you see I got my high rails on?
You're trespassing. Start walking."

Walleye did as he was told, wading through the deep snow, up and out of the ditch.

* * *

Carroll Johnson managed his usual appointment at Gasquet's that following Monday, entering exactly on time and nodding pleasantly to the receptionist, who seemed slightly more interested than on other occasions. He wondered if she felt his energy. There's a dynamic in men who've lived certain things and Carroll believed women can sense it, like a thin odor of testosterone.

He exchanged the usual pleasantries with Gasquet and finally settled back in the chair, closing his eyes. He'd taken a quick snort in the Men's Room and now just wanted to be still and feel it rule.

The truly ludicrous thing was that absolutely no one knew except Vicky. Even Murdock hadn't suspected. Such a clever street-smart fellow left absolutely clueless. The irony shook him so deeply and joyfully Gasquet was forced to pause a moment before continuing to message his scalp. My God, what fools they all were.

Carroll supposed, if you thought about it, everyone had simply struggled to come to the obvious conclusion. Dutch most of all. Sad though, the shallow minds, the gullibility.

Was it only eight days ago?

Yes. She'd called a week ago Saturday and the idea flowered so perfectly, so flawless and just he could hardly breathe. Following her to Willow River the next day without being seen proved childishly simple, watching from the old Scout camp while Dutch strangled her and removed the evidence, simple too. Dutch had saved him the trouble, except it turned out he was a flop as a killer. Murdock survived and so did Vicky. Carroll wondered how the guy made any money killing animals when he was so clumsy at it.

After Dutch pushed Vicky's car into the slough and drove away, Carroll watched her stand up and rub her neck. Even standing alone in the trees she was an arrogant bitch. She strutted in circles bare-ass naked, searching for her clothes. When he showed himself she only strutted all the more and asked for his coat.

"Aren't you even surprised to see me?" he'd said.

"I'm never surprised to see you, Carroll." Her voice was little more than a croak. "If Dutch Cleland thinks he's going to get by with this he's crazy. My throat feels crushed. He could've killed me. Where are my things?"

The rest was easy. She was half way there anyway and he'd more than enough strength in his hands to finish her, and unlike Cleland, he waited until her breathing stopped and even then he squeezed and squeezed. He felt high. She'd died twice in a day and if it had been in his power he'd have resurrected her and killed her over again. It had a certain impudence that rivaled his most exhilarating fantacies. All those years she'd squeezed him and now he was even, and no one would ever know.

There'd only been that one moment when he discovered the missing keys. He'd panicked, tearing through the ditch, the trees, even rolling Vicky's body over in case she was lying on them. They were nowhere and he couldn't hang around searching forever. He had to get away. Luckily he kept a spare ignition key in a magnetic holder inside the gas door. Anyway, he reasoned, if he couldn't find the keys what were the chances the cops would find them?

Water tingled against his scalp. Dutch had done everything to prove his guilt, including the most important thing of all, believe it himself. Carroll couldn't hold the laughter inside and Gasquet finally scolded him. "Mr. Johnson. You're quite naughty."

"Oh, Gasquet," he said. "You have no idea."

His howling laughter carried out into the reception area where Linda turned her head and frowned.

* * *

304

Summer

Out on Buttonbox the crappies were biting. The final stage of Sheriff Cedric Mattson's political campaign kicked into high gear with a fish fry in Prairie Park. He was a shoe-in. Marlene thought Charlie should grow a handlebar moustache for Pioneer Days, coming in August. Dutch Cleland had committed murder and got away with it.

A great many people who hardly knew Dutch became experts on the case, making themselves available to the various electronic and print media, all of which had now entirely forgotten the story. Once in a while a passing tourist asked about it.

The last real news of Dutch was a four-minute segment aired on *CBS Evening News* late in the year. It was never followed up by the other networks. The syndicated show *Current Affair* did send a crew in May and aired ten minutes or so of locals mugging the camera and shaking their heads and telling how they'd all been intimate friends with the Butcher of Willow River.

Charlie arrested Murdock but when Walleye turned up all they had against him was his assault on Jean Cleland and Jean suddenly refused to testify and told Charlie privately that shooting Murdock's ball off was good enough for her. What was the use of a lengthy trial which would probably just result in a wrist slap anyway? Carroll Johnson was questioned briefly and released. In fact, because of his position with Central Data and the Willow River City Council's belief their Police Chief was overzealous, the City apologized to Mr. Johnson in writing, fearing a civil lawsuit. The Council also voted unanimously to place a letter of reprimand in Charlie's personnel file and dock him one weeks' pay.

No trace of Dutch or his snowmobile were ever found. As a result, Dutch achieved legend. In a ramshackle tavern outside Togo a man with the unlikely name MOM, boasted of a gunfight he'd had with the Butcher, barely escaping with his

life. Oddly, he was supported in this claim by Len Davis.
Charlie couldn't understand it.

Even Canadians liked to tell the story, and "Sledding with
Dutch" T-shirts were abundant in the border tourist shops of Fort
Francis and International Falls for awhile where an employee at
Boise Cascade swore he witnessed Dutch and his snowmobile
cross the Rainy River into Canada during the graveyard shift.

Charlie had his own theories about what happened to
Dutch, but kept quiet about them. He'd pretty much given
up talking about the affair at all, except to Len. Charlie and
Len became friends in an odd sort of way. They didn't visit
in each others homes or go fishing together or anything like
that, but they shared a greeting always and often lunched
together at Berkie's.

A civil court finally declared Jean Cleland sole heir to all
joint property and she sold everything, even their furniture
and Dutch's collection of restored butcher blocks. One report-
edly brought a price over ten thousand dollars. If she believed
any of the stories about Dutch, she never said so. After the
Fourth of July holiday, she left Willow River for good.

Charlie spoke to her briefly beforehand.

"Thought maybe we'd become friends," he said, noticing
she still wore her wedding band. "We'll miss you."

"Don't let's start lying to each other now," she said. "I
hate this town and it isn't too fond of me."

"St. Paul, I suppose."

"Maybe later. Going to spend some of Dutch's money and
get off someplace warm and humid and eat until I'm fat."

He'd left her standing on one foot and she didn't appear
the least bit sad or sorry about things. Her strange dark eyes
seemed lit with passion for some new life more pleasant than
the one she left behind. It was as if she'd forgotten her husband entirely.

For his part, Charlie Benson was left with a set of keys
that didn't fit anything. On Friday, he had to drive to Minne-

apolis and pick up new radio gear the Council finally approved. Maybe he'd swing by Carroll Johnson's house and try the keys there, as his were the only locks Charlie hadn't stuck them into. Once he even tried them in his own locks. But he liked to think of Dutch fishing from an old dock somewhere along the Yucatan Peninsula. He'd never been to the Yucatan and wasn't sure he could find it on a map, but he enjoyed the sound of it. That's where a guy like Dutch would go—Yucatan. The word felt warm and pleasingly foreign.

He'd borrow an atlas one day and look it up. Damned if he wouldn't.

Epilogue

BANYAN BAY CLUB, ISLA DE ROATAN, HONDURAS

The late afternoon sun baked relentlessly on the thatched roof and the sandy-haired man sat alone at the bar smoking and drinking Salvavida. He'd been there long enough to become invisible, though the bartender kept an eye on him. He seldom spoke, unlike the North American tourists common to the place, but preferred his own company and was cautious with his money.

He sat opposite the ocean to catch the breeze. His gaze extended southwestward across the Gulf of Honduras toward La Ceiba some fifty statute miles distance. A crowded dive boat rounded the point, heading for its moorings behind Flat Cay.

"Not out this afternoon?" inquired the bartender, a handsome middle-aged Honduran with buck-brown skin and graying hair.

"Had enough this morning," he said, drawing a hand nervously across his face. "Trying to get used to the water again."

"Not been diving in some time?"

"That too. I had a bad experience."

"More beer?"

"Why not?"

It came without a glass. "Can you speak of it?"

"Put a snowmobile through the ice and nearly drowned." The man's eyes were hazel in the warm light reflecting from the sea. "Seems long ago but I dream about it sometimes."

308

"Ah," the bartender nodded. He didn't know the word snowmobile, and ice cooled a rum. "A strange country where you have been?"

"No stranger than here." He drank thirstily. "Different. Cold."

"I have been once to Miami," Javier said. "Many come here from the cold estados. But you can tell me what is this snowmobile, a snow machine? I have seen them on CNN I think. They blow snow in the air to clear a street."

"Those are snow blowers. A snowmobile is a vehicle for recreation, for fun, like a motorcycle with a track instead of wheels."

"And it goes on water?"

The man looked up from the rings he'd been connecting on the bar with his sweating bottle and laughed, wondering if maybe the bartender wasn't pulling his leg. "No," he said. "The lakes are frozen mostly in the winter so the ice can support even a car or truck, but I went on it too early and it broke."

Javier's face was blank a moment. "You rode this machine into the water?"

"Yes."

The bartender considered this for some time. "Verdad," he said, digging deep inside the cooler for two beers this time. "How is it you are alive then?"

"I was resuced by the nineteenth century," the man smiled at the memory. "The northland's last trapper." He saw the puzzlement on Javier's face. "A man who makes his living catching small animals in traps (he opened his palms to form a trap) and kills them for their pelts. Furs. Not many do this now, but a few still have licenses from the government. He was walking along the lake on snowshoes (he drew snowshoes with the bottle sweat) and saw me go in. I managed to swim to the surface and he helped me out onto the ice, then to shore where he built a fire and dried my clothes." He reflected on his story for a moment and added, "My life was spared for some reason."

"Si," Javier nodded. He remained thoughtful a while as if running through it all again. "This is a fine story," he said at last and rested his back against the credenza of liquor bottles and examined the man's face more closely. "I was thinking one day I remember you from before. From another time. You come from Texas?"

The sandy-haired man smiled. "I'm Canadian."

"Ah," said the Honduran. "But you were here before?"

"In another life." He smiled broadly. "With another woman."

The bartender was a man of the world and understood a man's hunger for the uncharted ways of another woman. "Fifty-two years old," he admitted. "I am still bueno with the womens." He removed his straw hat and wiped the sweat-band with a bar cloth. "What is your woman now?" he asked glancing about the empty bar.

"She'll be coming on the plane next week."

"No good to be alone. *Evelyn* and I take you to her plane. I think I remember her. Alto," he said, stretching his hand above his head. "A rubia with eyes like the sea."

The man shook his head. "That one is dead."

This did not please the bartender. "We will drink to her, my friend. Life is hard and it is the devil's garden."

They raised bottles. "After she died I retired. I live quietly."

"Less," he said. "Always less."

The hazel-eyed man said, "You are wise for a man still bueno with women."

The bartender laughed and replaced his hat. "Life is good," he contradicted himself. "We are in the shade."

Gazing awhile at the empty sea the man said, "I drink more than I should."

About the Author

Jimmy Olsen didn't start writing fiction until he was well past forty. In the tradition of American writers like Jack London and Louis L'Amour, Olsen spent much of his life seeking adventure. He began scuba diving in 1961 at age thirteen and continues today. A machinegunner in Vietnam, after two tours, he settled down a while, married, started a family and graduated college with a BS in English. Still at college, he published his first national story in a diving magazine. A year later he moved his family to Santo Domingo in the

Dominican Republic where he taught at a private American school and started the Republic's first professional diving school, Scuba Dominican C por A. Hearing rumors of shipwrecks and gold, Olsen and a small group of adventurers discovered the site of the French Man-O-War *Imperial* and several other vessels. After five years in the Caribbean, Olsen completed his MA at the University of Alabama and returned to writing, taking a job with a small daily newspaper in Athens, Alabama for a year before becoming an editor back home in Minnesota. This lasted four years before the thirst for adventure overtook him again and he was back in the diving business, traveling to dive destinations from the Caribbean to the South Pacific. The snorkeling scene in *Things In Ditches* comes directly from the author's own rich experiences. Jimmy Olsen has written two additional novels, *Scuba*, due to be released next year, and *YR-71*, a Vietnam seafaring adventure set near Da Nang. In addition, he's completed twenty short stories, some set in his native Minnesota and others from around the globe. Several of these have recently been sold and will soon be in print. Olsen continues to travel extensively, returning to the Dominican Republic in 1998 to dive his old haunts only hours before Hurricane Georges. Equally at home at the keyboard of a computer or his ancient Royal, Olsen spends his writing days in a northwoods setting without even the basic comforts such as running water or electricity and at his modern office in the city. He has three children, now grown, and lives with his wife in Minnesota.

Contact the author at:
jimmyo@cloudnet.com